An Inescapable Attraction

DEFIANT HEARTS BOOK 3

Sydney Jane Baily

cat whisker press
Massachusetts

Published by **cat whisker press**

Cover: Philip Ré
Book Design: **cat whisker studio**
Editor: Chloe Bearuski

ISBN-13: 978-1957421018

DEDICATION

To two wonderful ladies in my life
**my mom, Beryl Baily
and my aunt, Evelyn Reid**

With love and gratitude.

OTHER WORKS

The RAKES ON THE RUN Series

Last Dance in London
Pursued in Paris
Banished to Brighton
Gretna Green by Sunset

The RARE CONFECTIONERY Series

The Duchess of Chocolate
The Toffee Heiress
My Lady Marzipan

The DEFIANT HEARTS Series

An Improper Situation
An Irresistible Temptation
An Inescapable Attraction
An Inconceivable Deception
An Intriguing Proposition
An Impassioned Redemption

The BEASTLY LORDS Series

Lord Despair
Lord Anguish
Lord Vile
Lord Darkness
Lord Misery
Lord Wrath
Eleanor

PRESENTING LADY GUS

A Georgian-Era Novella

ACKNOWLEDGMENTS

I offer heartfelt gratitude to my diligent beta readers: Renee Sevelitte, Tammy Thompson, and Kathy Davie. Special thanks to award-winning romance novelist Marliss Melton for taking the time to read this book during the manuscript stage and to talk me through the sections where I was just plain stuck. Thanks to my cheering section. You know who you are. And my love to a couple of extremely faithful friends, Perry and Sabby, and as always, much love to my children.

CHAPTER ONE

1887, Wataga, Illinois

The drifter knew exactly how slowly the train would take the curve. It was the best place on this stretch of track to get aboard. Often, he had a boxcar to himself, which he liked. Not that he couldn't afford a ticket, but he didn't much care for traveling with loads of people. Or, at least, he didn't like their small talk. He was used to solitude, moving from place to place before anyone got to know him and before he had to bother about anyone else.

Stretching out in a boxcar with his head on his bag, he could sleep, think, plan. Usually, he would decide where to go and what to do next. This time, though, he had somewhere he had to get to on time, which irked the hell out of him. Other people's deadlines made him edgy.

He could tell which boxcars were empty by the way they swayed on the tracks. Also, sometimes, a thick rope or chain was threaded through a boxcar's two handles if it carried something particularly valuable. Those were darn near impossible to board, and there was no sense in trying.

With watchful green eyes, he chose one that obviously held no cargo. At the blind spot of the curve, when he was fairly certain neither the conductor nor the engineer could see him, he left his hiding place.

Tossing down the stub of his cigarette, he ran from his cover, sped up next to the train, and jumped, grabbing onto the thick metal handle with one hand and slamming the heavy door open with the other. He was in.

Instead of the utter darkness that sometimes greeted him, this car had a two-foot-by-two-foot hole punched in the far side. Maybe at one time, it had contained animals that needed air. In any case, he was glad for the sunlight streaming in, making a square of light in the middle of the floor. He planned to have a good long snooze in that sunny patch.

Before he'd had a chance to settle in and toss down his bag, he heard a noise and drew his gun, realizing instantly he wasn't alone. Not a rat, not by the moan. Narrowing his eyes, he surveyed the car. Not much to see except some old hay and a pile of rags in one corner. A moaning pile.

Placing his worn leather bag by the door for a swift getaway, he walked cautiously toward what he could now discern was a slender form lying in the shadows—with loose pants, a long duster, a pale face, and a hat that had fallen to the side.

"Hey," he said, touching the toe of his boot to the small man's side.

The stranger's eyes flew open, and astonishingly, the heart-shaped face broke out into a smile.

"Thaddeus," said a woman's voice, not just any woman's either. No, this was the voice that haunted his dreams and spurred his non-stop travels. "I thought you were here," she said, making no sense whatsoever, "but then I lost you again."

His heart galloped painfully as he shoved his gun back into its holster and dropped to his knees. This simply could not be!

"Ellie?" What in the hell was she doing there and talking so strangely, too? He hadn't seen her for over three years. Why would she assume—?

"Thaddeus," she said again. "I thought I was dreaming. We were dancing, weren't we?"

She said something else, which he couldn't hear. As he bent lower, she lifted her arms to him and draped them around his neck, trying to pull him close. Her lips parted as though she wanted him to kiss her.

Stunned, he held still. *Was he the one dreaming?* He'd kissed Eliza Prentice before and had wanted to do it again since he was eighteen. Maybe he'd hit his head or something. She was waiting, with her heavy-lidded eyes locked on him. He leaned closer, putting his cheek against hers.

She was hot, too hot, burning up with fever. *Christ!*

He started to pull back, and she moaned, briefly trying to hold him in place.

"You're merely a dream, aren't you? I'm so cold. Gonna die alone in a dirty boxcar." And she dropped her arms and turned her face away from him.

His heartbeat seemed to speed up, and he realized he was scared. Not much scared him either. He'd traveled across the country numerous times and met some downright mean and frightening people. However, nothing had ever made his blood run colder than the sight of Ellie lying limp and nearly lifeless. And him with no idea what to do. He couldn't jump off the train with her in this condition. In another half hour, however, it would stop to fill its water tanks.

"Ellie, listen to me. You're not gonna die on this damn train."

No response. He touched her shoulder. "Darlin'?"

She moaned at the gentle word.

"You're gonna be fine," he added, stroking her burning cheek, although he wasn't sure of that at all. She should've married that doctor she'd been engaged to. Riley would've known precisely what to do.

It seemed like an eternity, waiting for the train to stop. Luckily, he always carried a waterskin, but he dribbled water against her lips with little success. What she needed was a cold bath. At least, that's what he assumed. First, he had to get her off this blasted stuffy boxcar.

A few miles past Wataga, Illinois, even though there wasn't any station, the train stopped at a water tower, to replenish its tanks. Hearing the water crane being hoisted and the tanks filling, Thaddeus knew it wouldn't take long.

Slamming the door open, he tossed his bag down onto the ground below. It held just about everything important to him in this world, except his only sister, Charlotte, who was happily married with children and living in Boston. When he found Ellie's well-used carpetbag next to her, he sent it out after his. Lastly, he picked her up, sat down on the edge of the boxcar, and jumped down the few feet to the ground.

He heard a man shout, perhaps an angry conductor, but he ignored him. Holding Ellie against his side, he picked up both bags, securing them around his shoulders before lifting her into his arms again. Then he started walking.

The town was small, too small for a station or a fancy hotel, smaller even than his and Ellie's hometown of Spring City, Colorado. However, after asking a few questions, he found a rooming house run by an older couple. A bored couple. A couple who asked questions.

"Are you married?" came the first question from the old man, eyeing Thaddeus with an unconscious woman in his arms. "We're God-fearing, son. We don't hold with no loose morals."

Thaddeus took one glance at Ellie, with her red cheeks and sweat on her forehead.

"Yes, sir, we are. My wife took sick, and we had to get off the train." No need to tell them they weren't in the passenger car.

"You got money," asked the old lady.

"Yes, ma'am, enough for a room and a meal. But my wife needs ice and maybe a doctor, if there is one."

"No doctor in town. Got a barber," said her husband, making a sour face as though he wouldn't recommend the man. "You can have a room. Follow me." He picked up their two bags and led the way.

Thaddeus carried Ellie up the stairs to a bedroom off the first-floor landing and lay her gently on the bed, big enough for two.

"Do you know what's wrong with her?" asked the old lady, who'd followed them upstairs, holding Ellie's grimy duster, which had clearly seen better days. Thaddeus took the long coat from her and tossed it over the only chair in the room.

"No, ma'am, except she's burning up."

"If I were you, I'd strip her off. Henry'll bring you some ice from the icehouse. You can rub it on her skin. And I'll find you some rags. You can soak 'em in cold water and wrap 'em around her."

Thaddeus nodded with gratitude. This was far outside anything he had knowledge of, such as playing cards or pool, whether straight rail or fifteen-ball.

"Tell you what," the woman added, warming to the task of directing the healing, "I'll make some raisin tea, like my mama used to make. It'll bring down her fever for sure."

"Thank you again, ma'am," Thaddeus said, and in a flash, he and Ellie were left alone. He looked at his "wife" and shook his head. Eliza goddamn Prentice was in a room with him. And she'd welcomed him with open arms in the boxcar. By name! What in blue blazes had just happened to his life?

He reckoned he ought to do what the old lady said. After removing his own narrow-lapelled black coat and gun belt, he began gingerly taking off Ellie's layers, glad the couple hadn't balked at her strange garb. It wasn't every day you saw a lady in trousers, especially when her husband was dressed in a good suit, replete with embroidered vest, intent on looking like a man of business when he got off the train in Chicago.

He started by removing her boots that turned out to be miles too large. He'd left her hat behind on the floor of the boxcar. Now, he flicked off the close-fitting kerchief tied around her head, relishing the sight of her long blond hair, braided into one thick rope, oddly pleased it wasn't chopped off to enhance her disguise. Then he began unbuttoning her shirt.

He swallowed hard and kept going, all the while, she was feverishly moaning and muttering. After unbuckling her baggy pants, he slid them down her slim legs, finding she had on knee-high men's stockings underneath. He left them untouched for the time being, along with the short white shift she had under the shirt. No corset, nothing else, except her drawers. He definitely didn't touch those.

Jumping at the sound of a sharp rap at the door, he said, "Come in."

The old man stepped in, took a quickly peek, and then looked sharply away from the bed.

"Here's some ice, son." He put down a large tin pail. "There's more if you need it."

And he skedaddled away from the sight of the distraught man and the partially undressed woman.

Thaddeus set to rubbing the ice across her forehead, her feet, her wrists, and across her shivering shoulders. His own body seemed to be getting heated while stroking her skin, although he was trying not to think about that. Rolling her over, he lifted her shift and ran the last piece of ice up and down her spine.

Mesmerized by the delicate shape of Ellie's back and hips, he didn't realize there'd been a knock at the door until after the old lady came in and stood beside him. He tore his gaze away to see what she had in her hands.

"You're a natural at this, young man. Sit her up and we'll try to get this tea into her."

Thaddeus rolled Ellie back over, and she opened her eyes.

"Thaddeus," was all she said, then she frowned at the old woman holding out the mug of tea.

"You try," the woman told him. "Use the spoon and get some into your wife."

"My wife," he repeated, gazing into Ellie's crystalline blue eyes, the eyes that had haunted him for years. Now, they were unfocused and overly glassy. "Of course."

He took the spoon and the cup and proceeded to insert a little tea between her lovely blush pink lips. Then some more.

He spooned it in while she grimaced, until she closed her mouth firmly and wouldn't take anymore.

"Half the cup," remarked the woman. "Not bad. I gots to go fix dinner. Try to get the rest into her." She was at the door when she turned. "You hungry?"

Thaddeus realized he was. "Yes, ma'am."

"I'll call you when it's ready, then." And she disappeared.

He sighed. This was not how he'd planned his day. He had a buyer to get to in Chicago and some filched swag to sell that would set him up, he hoped, for years to come. After that, he'd intended to enjoy a fast poker game that was calling to him down south in New Orleans before he made a rendezvous with destiny in Montana territory.

But then, Eliza Prentice had screwed up more than this one day. In some ways, she was responsible for his whole damn life turning out the way it had. First, her come-hither smile when they were both in their teens, then her surprising engagement to his friend, Riley.

He'd taken one look at her excited face and the sparkling ring on her finger, and Thaddeus had high-tailed it out of Spring City. Very rarely, he'd gone back to see his sister before she'd moved away to Boston, but his visits were brief and designed for the least chance of contact with Ellie.

Was he jealous? *Hell, no!*

Then he'd heard she'd changed her mind and let Riley go free, right before the man became a full-fledged, licensed doctor, too.

And Thaddeus had never stopped wondering about Ellie, who'd left Spring City without telling anyone where she was heading and, as far as he knew, had never gone back. That had been about eleven months ago, not that he was keeping track.

She moaned, and he felt her forehead. Still hot. Jumping off the bed, he ran down the stairs, encountering the old man in a chair reading a newspaper.

"I think I could use a little more ice, sir, if you don't mind."

"Icehouse is in the back. You can help yourself."

Thaddeus grabbed the bucket and went outside. He was gone only a couple minutes, but when he returned to their room, he blanched.

"The devil!" he exclaimed.

Ellie had obviously tried to get up, delirious as she was. She'd slipped off the bed onto the floor and was half on her side with her cheek resting on the floor. Her shift in disarray exposed her legs as well as the underside of her right breast where the neckline gaped open.

He put the bucket down and hoisted her into his arms, feeling all the soft curves of her body, along with the heat of the fever, as he lowered her back onto the bed.

She flung her arms around his neck, holding him close. Her eyes were shut, but her uneasy breathing indicated she was not in a peaceful sleep. Ellie pressed her scantily clad body against him, and heat shot to his groin.

He mentally scolded himself. She was helpless, and he didn't take advantage of women. Ever.

And especially not the one who'd stomped on his heart.

Carefully, he unclasped her hands from behind his neck and released himself. She moaned again. Time for more ice.

Grabbing a chunk, he started at her white shoulders. She hissed when he pressed it against her, and he flinched at the sound. Still, he persisted in stroking it across her heated, shivering skin. Over her forehead, her cheeks, her throat, down her chest to . . . *sweet Jesus*, the valley between her breasts.

He gulped and ran a cold hand over his own forehead.

Skipping over her middle parts, he stared at her legs and, for a split second, wished to God he'd chosen a different boxcar. The next moment, he knew that was a bold lie. Glancing at her pretty face, surrounded by flaxen hair plastered with sweat and ice water, he knew he didn't regret helping Ellie for a second. He couldn't imagine the horror of her awakening alone on that train, disoriented with fever. Or worse, her not awakening at all.

He was all she had, and he would damn well do his best.

Her stockings had to go, but he hesitated a moment, his heart racing. Removing a lady's stockings was usually an erotic experience, followed by an enjoyably sensual dalliance. However, touching Ellie while she was unconscious and removing intimate articles of her clothing without her consent made his hands clammy and his mouth go dry.

He took a breath. Avoiding the stockings was not going to make them disappear. Feeling as though he was breaking all boundaries of decency, he peeled them down over her knees and past her trim calves, before whipping them off her feet and tossing them behind his back. He glanced at her nervously, but she hadn't stirred. He wasn't done yet, though. He had to apply the ice.

From the ankle of one lithe leg, up her smooth skin, he traced the ice, going as high as he dared up her thigh. Then he moved to the other, going in reverse from top to bottom. At last, when he reached her other ankle, he gasped in a ragged breath, only then realizing he'd forgotten to breathe.

Turning her over, Thaddeus reached for another piece of ice before sweeping his eyes over the backs of her calves and higher.

"Shit!" he swore when he saw the red wound, roughly two inches long, on her left leg, festering an inch below her knee. It looked about a week old, although it hadn't scabbed over. Instead, it was oozing and inflamed. She had other scrapes, too, but none nearly as bad.

"Shit," he said again, thinking of Doc Cuthins, who had been the doctor in Spring City for Thaddeus's whole life. Or even Riley, although he was now practicing in San Francisco. Ellie needed a doctor, not him, a man with no skills whatsoever except for winning at cards and shooting straight.

Not wanting to leave her alone again, he opened the door and called out until the old lady returned.

"Ellie . . . my wife . . . has a wound on her leg. I think it may be causing her fever."

He showed it to the old lady, who made sympathetic clucking noises.

"*Hm,* how'd she get it?"

Damn! He'd know that, wouldn't he, if they were married?

"She scraped her legs getting out of a wagon, back in—" he considered what town they might've been visiting on the rail line "—in Hannibal. Must've been something on the backboard."

"I've got some witch hazel tincture that we can put on it. Might help. Helped Henry when he cut his thumb, and it swelled up somethin' awful."

"I'd be obliged," he said, feeling a little relieved that he had an ally. She disappeared for a few minutes and came back with a brown glass bottle.

"Don't be shy now. Pour some on her leg and then more on this cloth. You can lay that on her leg or better yet, tie it on."

Thaddeus looked at the items in his hands and then at Ellie. Gingerly, he dribbled the witch hazel onto her red wound, watching the liquid penetrate the cut and the excess run over her skin. He swallowed, feeling sweat break out between his shoulders under the old lady's scrutiny. Did she want to push him aside and do it herself? Should he ask her to? Or was this a husband's natural job?

He glanced at her, and she smiled encouragingly.

Next, he soaked a patch of the clean cloth and wrapped it around Ellie's leg, tying the ends so it stayed in place.

"You done real well. Let her sleep and come have supper with us."

Thaddeus gauged Ellie's present state—eyes sealed shut, still on her stomach curled around a pillow, dead to the world. She seemed to be sleeping heavily, but the thought of returning and seeing her on the floor stopped him from leaving the room.

Glancing around, he spied the chair, a heavy, upholstered monstrosity, still draped in his and Ellie's coats. Dragging it beside the bed, he faced it away, hoping the large chairback, pressed against the mattress, would protect her from another fall.

Satisfied he'd done all he could, he went downstairs to eat.

Returning from a hearty meal of boiled mutton, stewed liver, and vegetables, Thaddeus heaved a sigh of relief to see Ellie still asleep, although she'd turned over.

Gaping at her bare legs with her shift only just skimming her shapely thighs, he hurried over to grab their one blanket and cover her. His own body reacted again, getting all worked up at the sight of her.

Good Lord! He was behaving as though he'd never had a woman!

Removing his boots, his vest, and his shirt, he stood by the window, looking out into the twilight. Where had the day gone? One minute had slipped into the next and then into hours while he'd stayed in the small room tending Ellie.

For the life of him, he couldn't shake the wonder of this, one of the strangest days of his life. Every past recollection of her crowded his mind—seeing her at a school desk primly ignoring everyone while turning the pages of a book, singing their morning songs, handling her recitation without making eye contact. He'd never minded going to school, if for no other reason than so he could admire her.

Glancing over at the bed, his breath hitched, merely looking at her. He'd never seen her hushed and subdued until today. She was always so vibrant back home, usually flying into a rage over something or other, but other moment, quieter ones, he'd catch her by herself and they'd share a smile and a laugh.

In her present state, she looked smaller, paler, and dimmer. Simply not herself. Her essence always shimmered like the sun, and her blue eyes used to look right inside of him. Or so he'd thought, until the day she'd agreed to be Mrs. Riley Dalcourt.

His stomach clenched as if he'd only then watched her run across the dusty street toward him, before she told him her news, dashing his dreams of them being together.

How he hated recalling that feeling, like it was the end of the world and he could do nothing to change it. He'd scarcely been able to breathe, and then something had given way in him. A river of hatred let loose, making him want to lash out at her for not loving him and at Riley for being the better man who'd gained her love. Instead, he'd done the only thing he could do. He'd left Spring City as fast as possible.

So how was it that being in the same room with her made his happiness blossom like a parched flower finally receiving the spring rains? He took a deep breath and eased the knot in his stomach. Perhaps he could stand here all night and look at her. Maybe he would. He scoffed at himself. What a sorry sap he was!

Shaking his head, he turned back to the window and tried to get his emotions in order. *Damnation!* He was not going to let Ellie worm her way under his skin ever again. For years, he'd done just fine not thinking of her, or at least, not much. He'd had his share of financial success, although often fleeting, and he'd had some sweet women to share his bed. He never wanted to feel that pain, that hatred, that self-loathing again. And she could do it to him, too, in an instant, as easily as blinking. He knew that.

Setting his jaw, Thaddeus leaned his head against the windowpane and watched the stars come out. Eventually, he yawned, acknowledging his own bone-deep tiredness.

Looking at the bed, he couldn't figure out how it could have shrunk so much. Could he really lie down on it and not touch her? His shoulder would be against hers and probably his hip and thigh, too. Perhaps he should sleep on the floor. But what if she needed him in the middle of the night and he didn't know it?

In another minute, Thaddeus climbed over the footboard and squeezed himself into the narrow space between Ellie and the wall. Staring at the low ceiling, he listened to her breathing. He could smell a faint floral fragrance in her hair, despite her sweat and her having been in a dirty boxcar. She was still a golden princess, as he'd always considered her.

Yep, he needed to keep his distance. All the same, he was going to do whatever it took to help her get well.

His body heavy with exhaustion, Thaddeus closed his eyes, wishing he could close down his thoughts as easily. He couldn't blame her for choosing Riley. But it hadn't simply stung. It had crushed him. He'd believed they had an understanding, one that grew stronger every time she shot him one of her dazzling smiles, every time she gave him a little wave from her front porch when he went by. Hell, every time he'd ever laid eyes on her or spoken with her!

But he'd had no prospects. His parents were long dead, his sister had been nearly a recluse despite being a successful writer, and him? He was a passing fair pupil in school. However, when learning was over, he was a bit of a scamp. More than a bit!

After all, Spring City was fairly tame, and a young man had to do what he could to liven it up. But a plan for the future always eluded him. Riley had been the smart one, always knowing he wanted to be a doctor, whereas Thaddeus had a vague idea he would, perhaps, work at the feedstore for his friend Dan or at the town's only stable.

In the end, though, he couldn't stay and watch the girl he . . . he fancied over all the other girls marry his friend.

He'd begun riding the rails, quickly discovering the card palaces and the gaming halls. He found out he was good at keeping numbers in his head and counting cards, which gave him the edge in some games. He even had good fortune with craps and twenty-one, sometimes winning big with the 10-to-1 blackjack bonus, though they weren't his preferred games. No, he chose poker over everything else, including faro, and when he won, he lived well. When he didn't, he didn't.

And once he'd even go so far in over his head a man had swindled him and tried to pin a murder on him. With coincidence, a great deal of luck, and help from her then-fiancé Reed Malloy, his older sister, Charlotte, had sorted out that heap of trouble.

That had been a couple years earlier, and Thaddeus didn't need any help from anyone, anymore.

Except suddenly, he did. He sorely wished he knew what to do for Ellie. She may have cut him to the quick, basically demonstrating how worthless he was in front of all of Spring City, but he still cared if she lived or died. And now her father was dead, she was alone in the world. At that moment, all she had was him.

She flung her hand out in her sleep, and the back of it slapped his chest before coming to rest on his arm. He reached down to move it, and as he did, she clasped his hand in hers, turning on her side to face him and resting her leg over his.

"Jesus!" he bit out. She was practically on top of him. She snuggled closer and lay her head on his bare chest, breathing deeply, seemingly comfortable for the first time since he'd found her.

He sighed. It was going to be a long night. The next thing he knew, however, sleep relaxed his tense body and claimed his troubled thoughts.

CHAPTER TWO

Two days later, after many cakes of ice, gallons of raisin tea, and the whole bottle of witch hazel, Ellie's fever broke for good.

Thaddeus was sitting in the chair in the corner of their bedroom, putting on his socks when she stirred as she had so many times previously. Her head turned, her eyes opened, and she looked directly at him. This time, however, her gaze struck him as clear and focused.

"Thaddeus," she said, as she had in the boxcar, her voice raspy with disuse. "Is that truly you?"

"Ellie!" He leaped from the chair to the bed in two strides and leaned over to place the back of his hand on her forehead. *Thank heaven, she was cool.*

He sat down beside her and picked up her limp hand while her watchful gaze roamed over him. Only then did he remember he had no shirt on. He'd become so used to her insensible presence in the room he'd taken to dressing and undressing as if she wasn't there.

"How can you be here?" she asked, sounding confused and achingly vulnerable. Then she narrowed her eyes at him and at their joined hands, and he thought he read wariness in her look.

15

Hearing her voice surprised him, like finding her all over again. Before he could answer, she swallowed and winced.

"I need water."

"I'll get you some," he said, standing quickly. Then he glanced back at her, adding unnecessarily, "Stay there."

She rolled her eyes, making him grin, and then she closed them, shutting him out.

He hurried to put on a shirt before charged out of the room and down the stairs, finding Mrs. Grindel, as he now knew was his hostess's name, scrubbing pots in the kitchen.

"She . . . uh, my wife is awake and thirsty."

"No wonder, after what she sweated out." She walked outside to the water pump and filled a bucket. Back in the kitchen, she handed him a cup of well water. "Tell her to take it slow."

Thaddeus nodded and hurried back to their room. Ellie's eyes were still closed, but they fluttered open when he sat down beside her on the edge of the bed.

"Water?" she asked.

"Right here." He helped her sit up and brushed from her face the stray locks of fair hair that had escaped her braid. Then he held the cup to her lips. She took a gulp and he pulled it away.

She glared at him.

"Don't drink too much," he advised.

She glanced longingly at the cup, then at his face.

"Why?" she asked.

He shrugged. Riley would have some scientific reason for it. "I don't know. Mrs. Grindel said so."

Ellie's eyes narrowed again. "Who's Mrs. Grindel?"

"We're staying in her and her husband's rooming house."

She nodded, reaching for the cup anyway and managing to hold it on her own although her hand shook a little. She took another sip.

"How did I get here? With you?"

He rubbed his hand through his unruly brown hair.

"You're not going to believe this," he told her, "but I boarded a boxcar on a train bound for Chicago, and you were in it."

Her eyes widened, and she put her free hand to her head before dropping her gaze to the bed covers and wrinkling her forehead as she visibly tried to recall what had happened.

"I was going to Chicago, too," she said, "but I didn't feel right. I decided I'd simply rest a bit on the train, and then I must have fallen asleep."

She looked at him and cocked her head. "I dreamed about you, and now, here you are."

"It wasn't a dream." But it seemed like one. How else could they be together in the same room after all this time?

"I guess not," she agreed, sipping the last of the water. "Strange though. Implausible, really, don't you think, that you'd get into *my* boxcar?"

"*Your* boxcar?" he asked, raising his eyebrows. "Why wasn't Eliza Prentice, richest gal in Spring City, Colorado, in the passenger car or even in a sleeper with her own compartment?"

She shrugged, looking down at the bed covers. "Just trying to keep my presence on that train a secret."

"Why?"

Her head snapped up. "You ask a lot of questions, Thaddeus Sanborn," she said in the imperious tone he remembered so well.

Most folk in Spring had considered her a conceited terror, though Thaddeus always found her confidence somewhat awe-inspiring. Sometimes, it was even downright arousing, especially when she had her hands on her shapely hips and she was giving someone a thorough tongue-lashing.

Then, he used to imagine snaking his arms around her, pulling her to him, and tasting on her lips the passion she exuded. But that was all before he went away.

"It's my turn," she continued. "What were *you* doing on that train, and why were *you* hitching a ride for free?"

He smiled at her, recognizing how she'd changed the focus from herself to him but letting her do it anyway.

"Free is always better, darlin'. I was heading to the next good poker game." No need to tell her what he wanted to pawn in Chicago.

"I see." She handed him the cup as if to a servant, without a thank you, before she started wriggling around to get more comfortable. When she moved her left leg, she caught her breath.

"Does it hurt?" he asked.

She shot him a quick glance.

"Does what hurt?" The wary expression returned to her face.

"Your leg," he said. "I couldn't help but see you're injured."

She bristled, lifting the bedclothes and peeking underneath to see herself in nothing except her shift. Her cheeks reddened.

"You couldn't help but see because you took off my clothes and my stockings, and rolled me onto my stomach."

"You were feverish," he protested.

"What the deuce!" She raised her voice. "I suppose that gave you the right to strip me and examine my person without a by-your-leave?"

A loud knock at the door heralded the entrance of Mrs. Grindel, who barged in before either of them could say "Enter."

"Good to see you awake, girly, but what's all this hollerin' for?"

Thaddeus looked between Ellie and the old lady, wondering how to finesse this and keep the peace at the same time.

"She's a bit confused is all," Thaddeus said.

"Confused?" Ellie spat out. "I am *not* confused."

"Well, don't be yelling like that, girly. Not at your husband what's taken such good care of you. You're a lucky young lady indeed!"

Thaddeus cringed as Ellie's pink lips rounded into a perfect "O" of astonishment.

"My husband?" she sputtered, slicing through him with her glacier blue eyes.

This was going to unravel real fast if the Grindels found out they weren't married.

"I told you she was confused," Thaddeus said, with a weak shrug, giving Ellie's leg a warning squeeze at the same time.

Before she could say anything else, ruining her reputation and getting them kicked out into the street by their properly pious hosts, Mrs. Grindel crossed her arms and became Thaddeus's champion.

"This young fellow carried you in here, right off the train, tending to you night and day, trying to get your fever down. He's hardly left your side except to eat."

Instead of looking grateful, Ellie scowled at Thaddeus.

"Why?" she demanded.

He clenched his jaw. *Jesus! Could she bend just a little?*

He patted her hand and sent her an imploring look, begging her to go along with his pretense.

"What kind of husband would I be if I let you travel any farther with a festering wound and a raging fever? I took you off the train to care for you. That's what a husband does for a wife, dear."

For a moment, Ellie's mulish expression indicated she wouldn't play along. Then she sighed, looking as unhappy as a horse on a boat.

"Of course," she muttered.

"That's better," said Mrs. Grindel. "Now, do you have an appetite, girly?"

Ellie stared hard at Thaddeus for another long moment, then glanced at Mrs. Grindel.

"Actually, I think I do."

"Best to start easy," the old lady cautioned. "Otherwise, your stomach won't appreciate it. I'll get you some broth and a little bread."

Ellie said nothing as the woman retreated from the room. Then she looked at Thaddeus again with no trace of kindness. Rather, she seemed to be stewing.

"Husband and wife?" she asked, crossing her arms over her chest, which only served to draw Thaddeus's gaze to her bosom. Then he wrenched it back to her sour-looking face.

"How else was I going to get us a room here? They're Methodists or Protestants, or some such." He scrubbed a hand through his hair again, not caring it was probably standing up on top of his head. Awake merely a few minutes and she was already beyond infuriating.

"Why?" She'd lowered her voice and stared at him with big questioning eyes.

He frowned. "Why what? Ellie, what are you asking?"

"Don't call me that."

"I always have."

"That was before," she said.

Before what? he wondered. *Before she'd crushed his dreams of them being together?* He shrugged.

"I don't care. You'll always be Ellie to me." He caught himself. His remark sounded as though they would know each other a long time. By the pout on her face, however, she'd be rid of him as soon as she felt well enough to travel. He would be damned if he'd let her discard him. Again. He'd leave first.

He watched her take a deep breath, while her glance skittered around the room before resting on his face once more.

"*Why* did you help me? That's what I'm asking."

Why indeed? He wasn't sure he knew. Some rash feelings from the past had made it impossible for him to turn his back on her.

"I brought you here and looked after you because we were friends once. That's why," he said.

She pursed her lips, still pinning him with her gaze. Then she shook her head. Was that disappointment he saw? Was she expecting some other answer? He couldn't imagine what.

"All right then," she said at last, leaning her head back against the headboard and letting her eyes sink shut. "I'm dog-tired, and I feel like I've been run over by a team of horses, I swear."

Looking at her pale face with the dark smudges of exhaustion under her eyes, he wanted to stroke her cheek, so he crossed his arms to stop himself. The worst was over. She'd be much better soon and heading off to wherever she was heading. He didn't care where. Yet he heard himself asking her that very question.

"Where were you going in Chicago? In *your* boxcar, I mean."

"It doesn't matter where," she answered, eyes still closed, a touch of defeat in her tone. "I don't care where I go. It's where I was leaving that matters."

"Running?" he asked, although it seemed inconceivable Eliza Prentice might have anything to run from.

Her lower lip trembled, and intrigued, he leaned closer.

"Yes," she admitted on the merest of whispers.

His pulse picked up, but he tamped down the immediate urge to help her.

"You want to tell me from what or from whom?"

"No, not particularly."

"How'd you get the scrapes on the back of your legs?"

"Escaping," she answered after a brief pause. "Rusty nails sticking out of the window sill I climbed out of. Hurt like the devil."

She opened her eyes and stared directly into his. The ghost of a frightening memory haunted her lovely eyes.

He shook his head. "It's hard to picture you of all people, with the nicest house in Spring and the finest clothing and—well, just about anything you wanted that your daddy's money could provide—climbing out of a window and fleeing."

"My father's dead," she said, her voice dropping on the last word. "You know that, and I don't live in Spring anymore."

"You must still have money," he insisted.

She lifted one shoulder in a negligent shrug.

"Some," she agreed, her eyes darting toward her carpetbag.

He blew out a breath of exasperation. "Look, I've got to get going soon," he admitted with rising impatience. "I have a pressing engagement."

Interest flared in her eyes, followed quickly by a spark of indignation.

"You can't dump me on these people and abandon me," she protested. "You owe me more than that."

"Owe you?" he asked, his eyebrows shooting to his hairline before settling into a frown. The memory of her saucy smile when she announced her engagement to Riley had him pushing to his feet in sudden anger.

"How in the hell can I possibly owe you anything? I just saved your damn life for no reason that I know."

A lovely pink color suffused her cheeks. "I think we both know you owe me," she said, her tone subdued, even as her eyes practically shot sparks at him. "However, I suppose my life is an even exchange at that."

Before he could ask her what in tarnation she was talking about—*an even exchange for what?*—Mrs. Grindel returned with a tray of food.

"For you, girly. Your man here will have to eat at the table."

"Oh, he can go." Eliza dismissed him indifferently with a wave of her hand, not even looking at him.

Simmering with resentment and more than a hint of confusion, Thaddeus followed the bemused old lady out of the room. He ate his supper without tasting a morsel of it. Ellie was talking in riddles while, at the same time, managing to get under his skin like a painful chigger. And why was she recklessly riding boxcars and running from God knows what?

Setting down his fork, he thanked Mr. and Mrs. Grindel for the meal, excused himself from the table, and headed upstairs, ready to demand some clear answers, only to find her sound asleep again. He stared at Ellie, looking his fill at her sweetly bowed lips and long lashes fanning her pale cheeks.

What an angel . . . when she was sleeping!

Eventually, Thaddeus climbed into bed beside her, hoping for peaceful slumber, only to find the night became a challenging battlefield. Aware of a soft female form against him, he caught himself reaching for her time and again, pulling back when he realized it was Ellie. That fact didn't make him want her any less. Rather, it increased his desire tenfold. But she'd always been off limits to the likes of him, and nothing had changed in that regard.

Staring at the ceiling, drifting in and out of sleep, he tossed and turned for hours, trying to focus on his gratitude she was no longer feverish, rather than on the warmth of her enticing body.

As soon as the sun's rays fingered the wall by his shoulder, he clambered out of bed, trying to ignore the physical frustration he couldn't deny, not to mention the growing irritation at having been delayed four days on his journey to Chicago.

Shoving his legs into his pants and doing up his belt, he was determined to say goodbye to Ellie and continue on his way.

His movements must have awakened her, for she sat up slowly and swung her feet to the floor. Lifting her slim arms overhead, she arched her back.

He swallowed, his mouth feeling dry, as he watched her long braid sway, brushing across her bottom while she stretched. He squeezed his hands shut, realizing he wanted to undo her braid and run his hands through her hair more than he wanted to breathe.

"I think I should have a bath this morning," she said, seemingly to herself. Then turning her head and blinking her blue eyes at him, she asked, "Can you arrange that for me, Thaddeus?"

The question drove home her unfamiliar helplessness and dependency, too vulnerable for him to turn his back on. Yet. Despite hankering to far get away from her, the woman who with a few words could make him feel like he was less than cow dung, he decided to stay a little while longer.

Wordlessly, he nodded and left the room to find Mrs. Grindel, for he certainly couldn't be the one to help Ellie bathe. Just the idea made him sweat. He only hoped she would behave and not speak to the old woman as though she were her servant.

After securing Mrs. Grindel's help, Thaddeus waited downstairs, sitting at the dining table drinking coffee, feeling nervous. He couldn't put his finger on the reason for his edginess, but he remained taciturn while Mr. Grindel tried to engage him in the news of the day.

At last, after what seemed an excessive amount of time for one female to get herself scrubbed and dressed, he heard footsteps on the stairs.

The old lady came first, with Ellie descending unhurriedly behind her. She stopped at the foot of the stairs, taking in her surroundings for the first time.

Thaddeus stared. It twisted his gut to see her standing upright, a little shaky, all five-foot-two of her, tiny and blond and perfect, if too thin for his liking. With reluctance, his eyes roamed over her, in a dark blue traveling gown that accentuated her curves far better than the baggy trousers and man's shirt he'd found her in. Her freshly washed hair was pulled back from her face and somehow secured in a large twist high at the back of her head.

With annoyance, he felt his pulse speed up, especially at the sight of her long neck and delicate collarbone. He dragged his gaze away.

"Well, would you look at what the cat dragged in?" Mr. Grindel remarked, putting down his coffee cup. "I'm only teasing, girl. You look a picture!"

Thaddeus winced inwardly when, in classic Eliza style, she ignored the man's comments and fixed her eyes expectantly on Thaddeus. He jumped up and pulled out a chair for her.

"Your wife has made quite the recovery," Mrs. Grindel said kindly. "And no wonder. She's a hardy little thing."

Thaddeus expected the woman had been treated to Eliza's imperial attitude with which she approached everyone, tough as pig hide.

"I'll go get her some strong tea and eggs," the old lady added.

Ellie gave a faint nod, but said nothing, not a word of thanks, which didn't surprise him. Her manners were considered poor to none in Spring City. Oh, she had them all right. She simply chose rarely to use them on lesser beings. He ignored her behavior and studied her face. Despite the shadowy circles under her eyes, she looked worlds better than when he'd found her.

"I'm glad you're feeling better," he said and started to put his hand over hers.

She shot him a glare that would freeze water.

Lord! She was a difficult woman. He remembered her as spirited and often ornery, but just as often smiling and fun and laughing, at least around him. True, she was often amused at someone else's expense, although to hear the sound of her laughter was worth it. At least to him.

They ate in nearly complete silence except for the banter of the Grindels. When they'd finished eating, Thaddeus escorted Ellie back upstairs, enjoying the view of her rear end as she climbed the stairs in front of him.

Get a grip, man, he told himself. He had to get to the broker in Chicago and then all the way back to Montana before his deed expired.

Back in their room, she practically tossed herself back onto the bed.

"You all right?" he asked, closing the door behind him and leaning against it.

"Feeling weak as a kitten," she said, eyes closed.

"Just lie there then, but we have to talk." He had an inkling she wouldn't like his words, especially as he'd made up his mind to leave that very day.

Smiling at her unladylike grunt as she grabbed for a pillow and wedged it under her head, he reached into his pocket for his packet of Old Golds, before remembering, for the umpteenth time that day, that he was out of cigarettes. Not even any tobacco and rolling papers, never mind the ready-mades. He put that situation high on his list to rectify as soon as possible.

Better to get this over with, he thought, crossing his arms over his chest. Still, he said nothing for a moment while he watched her breathing, her chest rising and falling steadily.

What was that tightness in his own chest and why was he delaying telling her he was leaving? She was so peaceful, even fragile, and he hated to poke a peaceful snake. He decided to start with a different subject.

"Tell me why you're running."

She said nothing at first, and he wondered if she'd drifted off to sleep. After a slight pause, however, she simply said, "No."

"I guess I can't help you then."

He barely managed to mask his relief. If she'd told him something he could do for her, he would probably feel bound to do it.

Silence was her sole response.

Doubt troubled him. It wasn't like Ellie to keep her woes to herself. He'd heard her express every grievance, small and large, in a loud voice to any and all who would listen. He recalled distinctly when she got stung by a bee and shrieked as though the whole town was burning. Or the time Jessie brought her lemon cake in place of apple pie at Fuller's restaurant. Ellie had been outraged Jessie didn't remember how much she despised lemons.

He shook his head. *But what if it was something serious?*

"Well, can I?" he heard himself ask.

"Did I ask for your help?" she retorted, her voice low and soft, like a sigh.

His curiosity expanded, near to bursting.

"No, you didn't," he admitted, "but now you're dressed in that pretty dress and not in your grand disguise. So, what are you going to do?"

Another grunt.

Frustration got the better of him, and he raised his voice. "Jesus, Ellie! What in Sam Hill happened to you?"

Finally, she opened her eyes and shot him a glance. "What do you mean?"

"You seem so . . . so distant and rigid."

She laughed, but it wasn't a happy sound. "I think you're forgetting something."

"What's that?" he asked.

"Everyone in Spring considers me a holy terror," she said, her voice choked with resentment. "And they always have. I'm mean and selfish, don't you know!" She shrugged as though "distant and rigid" meant nothing in comparison.

He felt unexpectedly sorry for her. Pushing away from the door, he dragged the heavy chair out from the corner and sat down on top of their coats and clothing, which he hadn't bothered to put away. Sprawling his booted feet out in front of him, he reminded her of one plain fact.

"*I* never did."

She looked at him levelly, then blinked. "No, that's true. Why is that?"

He grinned. "They didn't know how to handle you, is all."

She sat up abruptly, scooting back so she could lean against the headboard. Chin tilted, she cocked her head.

"Oh, and how is that exactly?"

Thaddeus felt his smile fade. The urge tugged at him to cross the small room, take her in his arms, and kiss her. He'd always wanted her. *But how to handle her?* Gently, tenderly, passionately, firmly, and with everything he had.

But it was too late for that.

"You ought to be handled with a switch or a paddle. Back home, you were spoiled and sassy and took what you wanted and said things you shouldn't." All of which he'd liked about her. Nevertheless, it hadn't made her any friends in Spring City, including his own sister, who couldn't stand her.

Ellie made a face at him. "If I'm rigid, as you say, it comes from deflecting everyone's anger and jealousy and insults for so darn long."

Everyone's except Riley's, who'd liked her just fine, enough to want to marry her. Thaddeus didn't want to think about Riley, Ellie's fiancé of nearly three years until she'd released him from their engagement.

Apparently, the breakup hadn't worried the man much since Riley had up and married less than two months later. He'd dutifully attended the wedding in San Francisco since Riley had married into the same family as Thaddeus's own sister, Charlotte. It was almost like he and Riley were related now, at least as in-laws.

But Ellie and Riley had three years together. Three years. It was hard to believe they hadn't shared a lot of intimacy and embraces, and maybe more. He shook his head.

Hadn't he told himself not to think of Riley?

"Is that why you won't go home? Because of what people think of you?" Now that he'd spent time helping her beat the fever, he wanted her tucked safely away in Spring City, the way she was in his memories.

"What about your nice house?"

"That's all I've got." Her lips twisted with bitterness. "No family, no friends, only a house. I might as well be on the road, don't you agree?"

Agree? Of course he didn't agree! He liked to think of her sitting on her wraparound porch, the same one he'd looked at every day of his life until he'd left, always hopeful of catching a glimpse of the enticing Eliza Prentice.

"Besides," she added, bringing him back to her present situation, "I can't go back home. I have to disappear."

Slivers of fear shot through him at the thought of her vanishing forever.

"Who in the hell are you running from?" Determined to drag an answer from her, he leaned forward, elbows on his knees, and waited.

Crossing her arms obstinately, she glared at him.

He glared back. "Tell me, or I'll . . ."

She narrowed her eyes to slits. "You'll what?"

Blast it! He had no leverage. Nothing she wanted, nothing she needed. The one thing he knew she cared about, except herself, was her father, and he was dead. After that, she valued her reputation in Spring City.

Did she still? he wondered.

"I'll tell my sister where I found you and how you were dressed. Charlotte will no doubt write all about it to her good friend Sarah Cuthins. And once Sarah knows . . ." He let his words hang in the air, like a fat pigeon.

Ellie blanched, and he knew she still prized her place in Spring City's society, which was squarely at the top of the heap.

She puffed out her cheeks and then sighed. "It's a long story."

"I'll listen until I have to leave," he said, wondering why the words made him all sorts of prickly.

She stilled, eyes widening for a split second, then repeated, "Leave?"

"You've recovered now, or nearly," he pointed out. "We both have places to go." Though, *damn it all*, he felt as though he was letting her down.

She nodded, biting her lower lip and sucking on it while he watched, captivated beyond belief. *What would it be like to suck on her lip?*

Distracted, Thaddeus almost missed the slight trembling of her fingers as she plucked at a thread on her gown. Almost. But he was good at cards precisely because he didn't miss the details, like when a man twitched or sweated, gloated or reddened. He could see the difference between someone holding a bum hand or a full house just by reading a face. Still, he didn't know what he should attribute Ellie's quivering to. Was it weakness from the fever or fear or even sadness?

"Then why bother telling you anything?" she asked, her voice grown softer again.

He didn't know the answer, but curiosity had him by the throat. And he knew she was finally going to open up to him by the way her body relaxed against the headboard.

"Tell me what's going on?" he urged again.

"Fine," she sighed. "I've got nothing else to do except sit here and—"

Loud voices downstairs interrupted her, along with heavy boots on the floorboards, and more men's voices floating up from outside.

Ellie sat bolt upright, eyes wide with alarm. Only then did Thaddeus recall he'd heard horses thundering by earlier, perhaps with riders searching door-to-door.

Alarm feathered his spine. Considering what he'd taken from one powerful man, he was fairly certain they were looking for him.

CHAPTER THREE

Slipping out the back door would probably save his hide, not to mention the illicit belongings in his bag, which he could not afford to lose. On the other hand, Thaddeus couldn't leave Ellie alone and defenseless with armed men stirring up trouble. Every instinct in him screamed to protect this woman who had no one else in the world. He had no choice but to stand his ground.

"Shit!" Reaching for his gun in its holster by the door, he then retrieved another one from inside his bag, making sure they were both loaded before going to the window and nudging the curtain aside.

Three men were milling about in the street. One looked up at him, his face set and emotionless. Thaddeus was sure he'd seen him before, one of Jack Stoddard's goons. He'd been right—they were there for him, armed and ready to shoot. People could get hurt in the process, Ellie included.

"Shit!" he said again.

"Stop saying that," she scolded, getting off the bed and coming toward the window.

Thaddeus spun around. "Now'd be a good time to shut pan altogether. I want you to get in that corner and crouch down."

He indicated the corner farthest from both the window and the door.

"And hold this." He held out his spare revolver, offering her the handle.

He must have made his point because she took the gun and did what he said, wordlessly and fast. He peered out the window once more. All three of the men were looking up at him now, having caught sight of movement in the room, although they hadn't drawn their weapons. Then he heard footsteps on the stairs.

"Mr. Sanborn?" It was Mr. Grindel. "Some men are here to see your wife."

He heard Ellie gasp behind him at the same time as he tried to wrap his brain around the fact they were there for her and not him.

What in blue blazes had she done?

"She's not up for visitors yet. You know that, Mr. Grindel," Thaddeus said, stalling for as long as he could.

If they were looking for Ellie, then they weren't looking for a married lady. They doubtless wanted merely to see her, to determine either way if she was the woman they sought. And from personal experience, Thaddeus knew no one could ever forget Ellie's angelic face once they'd seen it.

With no time to disguise her, he had to keep her out of sight.

His gaze darted around the room as if an escape were possible. What had he been thinking, taking a room on the upper floor with no second door and no back window? He'd broken every one of his failsafe rules because of his distraction over Ellie's health.

A fist pounded unexpectedly on the door, perhaps someone's version of a knock, and his pulse kicked. Undoubtedly, the hand didn't belong to Mr. or Mrs. Grindel. He glanced at Ellie, who stared at him, her face chalk white.

What the devil had she gotten herself into?

Adjusting his grip on his gun, Thaddeus considered shooting through the door, except the chance he'd hit his host was too great. Instead, he took a fortifying breath, aimed his revolver chest high, and yanked the door open, hoping to catch off guard whomever was on the other side.

It worked. Both Mr. Grindel and the large man he was with took a hurried step back.

Mr. Grindel spoke first. "Now, Mr. Sanborn, there's no need for—"

"You!" blurted the man who unfortunately was no stranger.

"Bart," Thaddeus said, more puzzled than ever. How did Ellie know Blackheart Bart or his cohorts down in the street? And of course, now they had his real name, not the alias he'd been using when last he was gambling in Hamilton on Bart's employer's riverboat. This was getting worse and worse.

Bart's face registered his surprise, which Thaddeus instantly decided to use to his advantage.

"What do you want with me?" he demanded.

"Nothing," Bart said. "We're looking for a woman."

"Not *my* wife." He scowled as though this was merely a nuisance.

Bart paused, then tried to peer past Thaddeus and into the room. "I didn't know you had one."

Thaddeus bristled, drew himself up taller, and set his feet apart to fill the doorway. "That's my business, not yours."

"You gonna lower that weapon?" Bart asked, not backing away.

"You gonna keep pounding on my door?" Thaddeus asked, pointing the revolver at the man's broad chest.

Bart looked at him a long time, and then he shrugged.

"Nah, I'm not here for you, *Mr. Sanborn.*"

He turned and walked down the hallway to the top of the stairs, before looking back.

"Not yet anyways." His smile was a sneer of contempt. But all Thaddeus could think was how Bart's boss obviously didn't yet know what Thaddeus had in his well-worn leather bag, or Jack Stoddard's men would have come at him with guns raised, no questions asked.

Thaddeus looked at Mr. Grindel, still standing in the hall, staring as he lowered his weapon.

"Sorry for the disturbance," he said to the older man, expecting him to say they had to get out at once. But Mr. Grindel merely nodded, giving him another long look before turning away.

When Thaddeus closed the door and turned around, Ellie stood up slowly. Their gazes locked, and suddenly, she hurtled herself into his arms, laying her head on his chest and holding on tightly. Grasping his shirt with her left hand, unknowingly she pressed the gun she still held into his other side.

Nervously, he eased the weapon out of her grasp and laid it gently on the chair along with his own. It took him another moment to close his arms around her, so stunned was he by having her pressed against him.

He patted her back, feeling awkward. If she was crying, he would make soothing noises, but she wasn't. She was dead silent, still as a statue. Then he felt a little tremor that began in her fingers where she clutched him. It spread throughout her body until he could feel it under his hands where they rested on her back.

Heat shot through him, and he felt himself growing hard. He hoped to hell she couldn't feel him through her skirts, but he angled his hips away, all the same.

Over his thudding heart and hers, he heard the men talking and then their horses' hooves as they rode away. Only then did he relax. Ellie must have heard them leave, too. Lifting her head, she glanced toward the window and then up at Thaddeus.

Having her so close, her arms around his waist, he couldn't think clearly. He'd been sleeping beside this woman, trying desperately not to touch her, night after night. Now, she'd gone and thrown herself at him. He was no saint.

He moved his hands up to cup her face and lowered his head, seeing her crystalline eyes close and her eyelashes fan her cheeks at the last moment before he touched his lips to hers.

They'd kissed before, when they were teens, and for a moment, it was as if no time had passed. They could be standing behind Drake's barn in Spring City with the blazing sun on their heads and all around him, the smell of grass and wildflowers and Ellie's hair.

Her soft lips felt like warm satin under his, and he kissed them lightly at first. However, as the ache in his groin persisted and as she opened to him, he deepened the kiss, nibbling on her lower lip before slanting his mouth and fitting it tightly against hers.

He heard her moan, a throaty purring sound, and felt her fingers move from his waist to his chest where she clasped his shirt. It was his undoing. Next thing he knew, he'd slipped his tongue into her mouth to dance with hers. Her tongue flicked against his in response.

A groan slipped out of him, and he lowered his hands to her hips, pulling her against him so she could feel what she was doing to him. What she'd always done to him.

Effortlessly, he backed her up until they fell headlong onto the bed. Still locked in an embrace, he slid his leg between hers, trapping her skirts, and pressed his thigh against the warm mound between her legs.

From her lips, he kissed along her jawline and down her neck, as she arched back to expose herself, smooth and porcelain-white. Nipping at the skin at the hollowed base of her throat, he ran out of bare skin at the neckline of her gown. All his lust-filled brain could think of was undressing her, fervently, rapidly, so at last he could look his fill of her naked body.

As he reached down for her skirts, she spoke.

"Thaddeus," she breathed out his name, and her soft voice stopped him cold, frozen from head to toe. She was not one of his whorehouse harlots. She was Ellie, his childhood dream, whom he'd just tumbled onto her back.

Damn it! He was not going to take her for a quick roll then get up and leave.

Scrambling off her, he leaped from the bed as if he'd been hit by a bucket of cold water. He wanted to punch someone, mostly himself. He wanted his throbbing erection to go down, though probably he needed actual cold water for that to happen anytime soon.

She sat up, breathing hard, and immediately looked away from him. He had no idea what she was thinking.

"I'm sorry, Ellie. I got carried away."

She shrugged. "I guess we both did. It was easy to do."

She sounded sad. *What the hell?* He'd expected her to be angry at him.

With his heart still racing and a rush of heat surging through his body, Thaddeus knew he had to get out of the room or he was going to do something he shouldn't, something he'd regret as soon as he jumped the next train, maybe never to see her again.

"I've got to get going. Those men were after you, but next time, it could as easily be me."

Her head snapped around and her eyes fixed on him. "Why?"

Trying to ignore the reddish swell to her lips from being kissed, he dodged her question with a statement he hoped was untrue.

"You know Stoddard, apparently, if Blackheart Bart is after you."

She nodded. "I do." Her voice was scarcely above a whisper.

He shook his head. *Foolish woman!* Jack Stoddard was not someone she ought to know. He wished he'd never laid eyes on the man some days, but you couldn't make a living in gambling, particularly faro and poker, and not encounter him.

In Thaddeus's case, he had done a little more than encounter him. He'd beaten the man fair and square, and then—well, he'd collected his debt somewhat surreptitiously when Stoddard hadn't been forthcoming with what he owed.

"I know him, too," he admitted, "and he may not be thinking too kindly of me at the moment, and it's only going to get worse. Blackheart Bart was on his best behavior today, but he'd as soon skin a man as look at him, if he's been paid to do it."

"I don't know much about this Blackheart fellow," she said. "But I know Jack Stoddard. He's a persistent man, a ruthless man, and a cheat, although he'd undoubtedly go to his grave denying it. I guess that makes him a godless man, too, and a flannel-mouthed liar. You know, my father was ruthless in his day, but he was as honest as the day is long."

Thaddeus didn't think it was time for a stroll down memory lane about Elijah Prentice.

"How do you know so much about Stoddard?" he pressed her.

She sighed. "Regrettably, I've gotten myself entangled with him."

Her delicate confession unleashed all kinds of unpleasant mental images.

"Entangled?"

"*Mm,*" she murmured, more interested all of a sudden in smoothing her rumpled skirt under her fingers than in talking to him.

"Ellie, what are you trying to tell me without telling me?" he asked through his teeth.

She hesitated, patting at her hair that was in utter disarray after their roll on the bed. Then she sighed again.

"I'm . . . married."

Her words knocked him back a step. It wasn't at all the response he was expecting. An image of his tall, handsome friend Riley shot into his brain, and then he dismissed it. He narrowed his eyes and waited.

She glanced at him and then hurriedly away.

Softly, she spoke, seemingly to the faded, flowered wallpaper. "I don't think it's Blackheart Bart you should concern yourself with. It's my husband."

Her husband! *What husband?* He had a bad feeling.

"Just tell me you're not married to—"

"Stoddard."

The blood drained from his head. It was an odd sensation.

"Jack Stoddard? You married Stoddard? You are Mrs. Jack goddamn Stoddard?"

She nodded, looking even more miserable than he felt, if that were possible.

"I see." He ought to grab his bag and hightail it out of there right then.

"You love him?" *Why had he asked her that? How could that conceivably matter now?*

Her face collapsed in disgust.

"Of course not."

That was a relief, he supposed. If Ellie had switched her affections from upstanding Riley to shifty Stoddard, who was twenty years older than either of them, shrewd and dishonest, and round as a huckleberry to boot, then he'd be disappointed as all get out.

"I have a bag of foreign coins in this room that some may say don't belong to me," he told her, "and a deed to land with someone else's name on it, and now I find out I'm pretending to be the husband of the wife of another man, a man who happens to be a cold-blooded killer. Can this get any worse?"

"I ran away from him."

It could.

"He's going to think I helped you," he realized, his voice growing hoarse.

She nodded again. "You told Bart I'm your wife. When they find out the woman in this room was me, then, yes, you'll look rather culpable, I'd imagine."

Her eyes filled with tears, and she appeared so unlike the image of the ever-spunky Ellie he kept in his mind's eye—the sassy girl who was always in control of any situation—that his anger and jealousy dissipated.

"I'm gonna get myself killed," he muttered aloud.

She paled, shaking her head.

"No, he won't kill you in a jealous rage," she said reassuringly. "He doesn't want me that way."

"What are you saying?" Thaddeus couldn't imagine any man not wanting her *that way*, as she so delicately put it.

"I mean, he might offhandedly be attracted to me, but that's not why we married."

Thaddeus collapsed into the chair he'd previously occupied and ran a hand over his forehead.

"Why *did* you?"

She stood up and then abruptly sat down again. The room was too small for pacing. "I lost a bet."

"A bet?"

She nodded. "I was on the North Missouri Railroad, between Hudson and St. Louis. Jack had a whole Pullman to himself. Can you imagine? Naturally, I had to see who he was."

She flashed him a rueful smile. "You know me, I marched straight in. Next thing I knew, we were playing a friendly game of cards."

"A friendly game of cards?" Thaddeus couldn't believe anyone would sit down willingly with Stoddard, especially when trapped on a train.

"I may have been a bit too arrogant concerning my gaming abilities."

"You, arrogant?" He didn't smile at his little joke. Neither did she. She pursed her lips.

"Do you want to hear the rest of this or not?" she asked.

He leaned his head against the high back of the chair and closed his eyes.

"Go on. Tell me why Eliza Prentice, a good girl from a small town in Colorado, believed she could take on Jack Stoddard."

She narrowed her eyes at his words. "For your information, I've had more than a little luck at cards. And I've been tutored by Kelly Morgan."

"I know Kelly," he said, thinking it another strange coincidence.

"I know you do."

When she didn't say more, he opened his eyes and looked at her.

"Why would Kelly help you?" he asked, remembering the older man as a little standoffish.

"I told him I knew you. That seemed to be enough."

She blushed a little, and he had to wonder what she'd actually told Kelly, who was the smartest, most ill-fortuned gambler on the West Coast. No one could be more likely to succeed and yet always lose. What a fine teacher she'd chosen!

"So, on the strength of your extensive learning from Kelly," he couldn't help rolling his eyes, "you challenged Jack Stoddard?"

"You make it sound like it was a duel."

"Darlin', if you're married to him, I'd say it was a helluva lot more like a duel than a friendly card game. The stakes were damn high, don't you think?"

"Well, yes." She arranged her dress. "Anyway, he cheated."

Stoddard had been accused of it before, although no one had ever caught him at it.

"How do you know he cheated? Maybe he was simply better than you, or luckier."

She bristled. "I know for sure because I had the fourth ace up *my* sleeve, but he had one, too. I'd palmed mine from the deck, so where'd he get his?"

Thaddeus's mouth hung open at her words, but she continued.

"I couldn't produce my ace after he showed me his hand because then he *would* have shot me, so I had to marry him. But only because I didn't have the money to cover the pot. He let me play on credit, you see."

Ellie crossed her arms, plainly annoyed at having been out-foxed.

When he remained seated, stock still, apparently flabbergasted, she prompted, "Say something, for goodness sake."

"How much money do you owe him?" His own voice, strangled by disbelief, sounded like a stranger's.

"The good news is he agreed to divorce me if I pay him back."

"How much?" Thaddeus repeated.

"With interest, of course. That's the catch," she added, blowing her hair up off her brow with a twist of her lips and a hard puff. "But the other good news is, as I said, that we haven't consummated our marriage. He was far more interested in my family than in my person. When he checked into my background, he realized my father owned just about the whole town of Spring."

She was babbling and stalling.

"How much?" He felt his temperature rising along with his temper.

"Five thousand dollars," she admitted.

Shit! Good thing he was sitting down. Thaddeus was sure he'd have fallen if he hadn't been. Where in the hell was he going to get five thousand dollars?

Wait, why was he thinking he had to get it in the first place?

He sprang from the chair. "I'll be seeing you around. Let me know if you're ever in . . . anywhere except here. We'll catch up then."

"You're leaving me here?"

"Yup."

"Are you serious, Thaddeus?" It was her turn to look flummoxed.

"Yup." *Deadly serious, at that.* He had no desire to be swinging at the end of a rope or catching a bullet between his eyes for any number of infractions that had already occurred or were going to occur before this was over. The least of which was how it appeared he'd absconded with Jack Stoddard's wife and was holed up in a motel, pretending to be her husband. He had to get out of there and fast.

"I see," she said.

Was it his imagination or did she collect herself before his eyes, as though she were the shattered pieces of a broken vase somehow gluing themselves back together? For certainly, she seemed to straighten her spine and grow an inch taller. Her eyes shone more brightly, her chin tilted at an angle, and her lips even reddened, unless his eyes were deceiving him.

Regal was the word that came to mind, as though she were some monarch on a European throne.

"You ought to get going then, before Bart comes back for either one of us. You'd best leave anyway, for I can't stand to have you in my sight one second longer."

Yes, she was sounding more imperial by the moment, as though the Queen of England had arrived in upstate Illinois.

"Oh, I'm going, darlin'."

He reached for his gun belt and strapped it on while she watched him. Then he gathered his bag and stuffed the other gun inside.

"You have a heap of trouble here, Ellie. But knowing you, you have a plan to get out of it. Your fever's abated, you're strong enough to travel or will be by morning with more food in you. You can get back on another train and head northeast the way you were when I got in your boxcar. Go far enough and Stoddard will never find you. You can disappear."

That was the best thing, to have her simply disappear. So why did he feel like howling?

Jamming his hat on his head and picking up his coat and bag, he was out the door fast, slamming it shut so he didn't have to think about her or her circumstances or what would happen next. However, he only got a few steps along the narrow, slanted hallway when he stopped.

Closing his eyes, he saw her face, serene and resigned. When he opened them, he took a deep breath before he crashed his fist into the wall beside him.

Man, that hurt, but he felt better.

Eliza Prentice, the female he'd wanted all his life was merely yards away. And she didn't need Riley, the doctor. She needed *him*, someone who knew the world of Jack Stoddard and card parlors and cheating and guns. He stared at his throbbing hand, glad it was his left one. He counted to ten, then twenty. Then he turned around.

Thaddeus stopped outside the door to the room that held a grown woman, no longer the girl he'd always been infatuated with. *He didn't know this woman at all, did he?* He didn't know this Eliza Prentice, who could palm an ace and marry a stranger. Then he heard her. Crying.

Damn! Just a quiet sniffle, then a snuffling sound that clutched at his heart and squeezed it so hard he couldn't breathe.

This was not his battle, was it? *Hell, no!* He listened a moment longer.

The devil take him! He was going to help her.

Shoving the door open, he was surprised to see instead of being curled up on the bed weeping, she was still sitting as he'd left her, ramrod straight, with tears rolling down her cheeks. She wasn't trying to stop them. She wasn't even dabbing at her lovely face.

He dropped to her side, laying his possessions on the floor, and wiped at her tears with his thumbs. *That wasn't right.* He fumbled for a handkerchief he knew he didn't have and, in the end, grabbed for the edge of the blanket on which she sat, using it to dry her face.

Riley would have had a clean white handkerchief. Thaddeus sighed. He was no hero, that was for sure, but he was all she had.

Her eyes were big as all-day suckers when she looked at him.

"I hate you," she murmured.

That was the first sensible thing she'd said all day.

By dinnertime, Ellie had slept several more hours, and Thaddeus was determined to get her as far away from Wataga and the Mississippi River and especially from Jack Stoddard as possible. What she really needed was another good night's sleep and another full day of rest because "weak as a kitten" wasn't going to get her far. But he couldn't risk waiting around any longer.

Bart must have made it almost all the way back to Stoddard's riverboat in Hamilton by then, and sure as God made little green apples, Thaddeus knew Stoddard would send him out hunting right quick.

And not for Ellie, alone. The items from Stoddard's safe were burning a hole in Thaddeus's bag, and he could almost hear Stoddard screaming for their return. He would be suspect number one.

Over a last meal with the Grindels, he formed a plan to get Ellie to Boston. His sister, Charlotte, was a problem-solver, and this was a problem if ever there was one. And luckily, Charlotte had married a top-notch lawyer. If anyone could help Ellie get out of her sham of a marriage, it was his sister's husband, Reed.

He argued with himself whether to tell her what he had in mind or keep it to himself until they were approaching the steps of the Malloy house on India Wharf and could smell Reed's French chef's cooking.

"What are you thinking about so hard? Your forehead's all wrinkled."

Ah, she was awake at last. He supposed he had to tell her the only plan he could think of. He couldn't see her cooperating otherwise.

"Sit up, darlin'. You missed supper, so I brought you up a bowl of Mrs. Grindel's fine stew." He put the tray on her lap and waited until she began eating.

"I think we need the help of a trusted lawyer," he said, watching while she swallowed the first spoonful. "And I know exactly the man for us, someone you know."

"Someone *I* know?" she repeated. "The only lawyer we ever had in Spring was that Dunphy fellow, and I think he was as crooked as a grasshopper's hind legs."

Thaddeus remembered him, too. "No, not him." He took a deep breath. "You remember Reed Malloy?"

She paused, with the spoon halfway to her lips. Oh, he could see she remembered him all right. Thaddeus had heard from Charlotte how, despite being engaged, Ellie had done her fair share of flirting with the handsome attorney. Of course, Reed had eyes solely for Charlotte.

Thaddeus smiled. He couldn't be happier for his sister having found such a faithful and fervent love, especially given the years of loneliness she'd endured after their parents passed away.

"Why are you grinning?" Ellie demanded. "What did *she* say regarding me?"

Yup, no love lost between 'em. "*She* didn't say anything, except you were surprised she'd caught Reed's interest."

Ellie rolled her eyes. "Your sister was always welcome to him. I was merely looking for a dance partner when Riley was away. Nothing more than that. Charlotte has a penchant for stories."

Ellie started eating again.

Thaddeus narrowed his eyes. "Charlotte tells the truth, not stories. That's why she's such a good journalist. Besides, we're not asking *her* for help. We're asking *him*. Reed can get you a divorce."

She finished her supper in silence, then asked, "What makes you so sure?"

Thaddeus sighed. "Reed is a crack attorney and drawn to hard luck cases. You're about as hard luck at the moment as I can imagine. Marrying Jack Stoddard!"

He couldn't help twisting his mouth into a grimace of disgust. "Honestly, I can't get over the stupidity! At least I understood your wanting to marry Riley."

"I didn't want to marry either one of them," she protested, shaking her head so her golden tresses flounced.

Distracted by the movement, he reached out to touch a lock of her hair. Then he realized what she'd said and stopped himself.

"What do you mean you didn't want to marry Riley?"

She picked up the tray and put it on the other side of the bed so she could get up.

"Thaddeus, I am not going to sit here discussing Riley Dalcourt with you. If you think Reed Malloy can help me, and *will* help me, then let's get moving. I never felt more like a fear-frozen possum than I do right now."

She was right about that. They'd better move along. He was already packed. She seemed to have very little to her name, although he supposed she'd left belongings behind when she'd fled Stoddard's riverboat.

"Get your things together, and I'll pay the Grindels the rest of what we owe. We'll leave as soon as you're ready." He started out the door.

"Thaddeus," she said, stopping him. "Thank you for not abandoning me."

He nodded, keeping his face shuttered although something inside him lurched and gave a brief *hurrah*. It was the first time he could remember hearing words of gratitude from Ellie to anyone, and wonder of wonders, she'd said them to him.

However, his still-aching hand was a reminder this was not a hog-killin' good time, and more importantly, he hadn't stayed to help her because of the lightness in his heart when he was around her. That was in the past, before she'd made him feel like the least worthy piece of dung in Spring City.

CHAPTER FOUR

Thaddeus was going to spend the next two days or so riding with her soft body pressed against him. And by his own doing. *What a dim-wit!* After settling with the Grindels for their lodging, he'd bought a horse from the local blacksmith, who'd received a nag as payment the week before and didn't need her.

Not exactly a mustang, Thaddeus mused. Still, he appreciated the horse's well-defined withers, long, broad back, and balanced gait. It would suit them fine for the next fifty miles until they reached the big station at Peoria, and even fifty or sixty more after that, if they went on to Panola.

Ellie stood on the front step of the Grindels' rooming house, in the deepening twilight, hands on her hips, and laughed when she saw him leading the swaybacked horse.

"It certainly lives up to its name," she remarked when Thaddeus told her their new ride was called *Fortuna* by the Mexican who'd given it to the blacksmith. "I'd say it has *bad* fortune written all over it."

Indeed, the horse had scars on her hind legs and over her reddish-hued rump where she'd nearly been felled by some wild animal. But to Thaddeus, the "nearly" made all the difference between life and death. The seemingly docile pinto had to have some spirit to fight back and escape.

He patted the horse on the neck and she turned her head, either to get a good look at him or to bite him.

"She's not crow bait, yet. She'll do us fine."

Thus, a few moments later, Thaddeus found himself on the back of Lucky, as he decided to call their horse, with Ellie nestled between his thighs.

Immediately, she leaned comfortably back against his chest as if she didn't have a care in the world. He caught himself sniffing her hair before he told her sharply, "Can you sit up a little? I can barely breathe."

She did as he asked for a few minutes, although she soon relaxed against him again, and he let her. *Damn*, but it felt good to have his arms around her, even just rocking in the saddle. If he closed his eyes, he could be eighteen again.

They rode that way for an hour, with her humming occasionally, which made him smile, and him scanning the horizon although it was almost too dark to see anything at all.

Suddenly, the blast of a gunshot cracked loudly through the air, followed by a second one, close enough to startle Lucky. Thaddeus began counting as he always did. Two bullets spent. Without hesitation, he urged the horse into a hard gallop, directing her right then abruptly left, even though he wasn't certain if someone was aiming at them or not.

"Keep your head down and hold on," he advised Ellie, and they crouched low, his body hunched over hers, both of them as close to the horse's neck as possible. Two more shots reverberated through the night air, and Thaddeus saw dust kick up where they would have been if he hadn't jerked Lucky viciously to one side.

"Shit!" He knew now they were definitely the target. While the light from the half moon was enough for him to see how closely the bullets missed, he hoped it wasn't enough for their pursuer to take better aim. He counted off two more rounds, praying whoever it was had only one six-shooter, needing his other hand for the reins.

After the sixth shot, Thaddeus kicked Lucky into a bat-out-of-hell straight line for another twenty yards before he jerked her into a zigzagging path once again.

Tiny pricks of light shone through the darkness up ahead, given off by candles in the windows of what looked to be a small town. Probably too small for a train station, yet perhaps it had a sheriff or someone who passed for the law. And no one but a fool would head into a town of any size, guns blazing, even at night.

Sure enough, no more shots were fired although Thaddeus kept pushing Lucky to maintain a steady gallop, thundering onto the main street. Then he slowed her to a cantor and straightened up, his back aching from the bent position.

"You all right?" he asked Ellie.

She didn't answer, as she sat up, but she grimaced before peering behind them.

"You think that was one of Stoddard's men?"

"I'd bet on it," he told her. "And not betting like Kelly Morgan does. More of a sure thing, I'd say."

She slumped against him again, not in a relaxed way but with an air of defeat.

"Darlin', you didn't think this was gonna be easy, did you?"

She shrugged and said nothing.

"This is only the beginning," he told her. "Every step of the way Stoddard's gonna be on our heels. Or worse—ahead of us."

She mumbled something.

"What'd you say?"

She turned her face, and they were so close, he could read the resignation in her eyes.

"He's not a man who likes to lose, and he's not going to ever give up. Divorce or no," she said, sounding subdued.

Thaddeus had entertained that very thought, but he intended to try every means within the law before he took matters into his own hands, if it came down to it. No way in hell was he going to let Stoddard get Ellie back.

A few minutes later, she spoke again, "Are we stopping here?"

They were already on the outskirts of town, having traveled right through from one end to the other, and Thaddeus was weighing his options.

"No," he said. "We keep moving while it's dark. I'd rather take my chances on the move than find we're surrounded come daybreak." For all they knew, three or four men were out after them.

Hours later when the sun was coming up over the horizon, they found a place to hide and to sleep, a near-empty hayloft in a rickety barn on a destitute farm. Perfect, except for the fear that the whole structure would collapse around them.

"Not as nice as the Grindels', but not the worst place in the world either."

Thaddeus tried to sound cheerful, knowing every muscle must be aching in Ellie's body since she wasn't used to traveling by horseback. Her absolute silence for the last hour confirmed she was exhausted.

He tethered Lucky to a tree about a furlong away. If the horse was discovered, their hiding place wouldn't necessarily follow.

At the bottom of the loft's ladder, Thaddeus helped her reach the lower rungs before pushing her up from behind, his hands squeezing her rear while stopping her from falling back. Together, they collapsed onto the creaky wooden platform, sparsely littered with remnants of hay bales. Ellie slumped down, looking utterly miserable, her eyes already closed.

"At least it's not a boxcar," he said, easing down beside her.

He had his waterskin and a pack of sandwiches from Mrs. Grindel, which he hadn't mentioned to Ellie, not wanting her to eat while on horseback. However, when he unpacked the provisions, her eyes snapped open.

"You have food? Why didn't you tell me? I'm starving." She didn't speak again until she'd demolished two sandwiches and drank half the water.

"I'd love a cup of tea," she said, after giving a small burp.

He was still eating his second sandwich, savoring it, not sure when they would eat again.

"Personally, I'd like a beer and a cigarette."

She wrinkled up her nose. "I despise cigarettes."

He shrugged. He didn't have any anyway, so there was no use in talking about them.

"Now what?" she asked.

He wiped his mouth on the shoulder of his coat. "What do you mean?"

"Well, what are we doing?"

"We're getting a few hours of shut-eye, then we'll continue. I think Peoria's too obvious in the direction we're heading. If I were Stoddard's men, that's where I'd be waiting for us. But after the junction, they won't know whether we headed north, south, east, or west."

He leaned back against the splintered wall, stretching his long legs out in front of him and crossing them at the ankles, boot over boot.

"Let's aim for Panola, after all. We have at least another day's travel to get there, and then we'll get on a train to Fort Wayne, and on through to Pittsburgh and Philadelphia. From there, it's a straightforward trip to Boston."

She nodded and looked around her with a sigh. He figured she wasn't thrilled with her accommodations. Plus the journey ahead sounded exhausting, even to him.

"How did you survive on the road?" he asked with a wry smile. "You don't seem like the roughing-it type, despite the getup you were in when I found you."

She blinked at him. "Oh, the gentleman's pants," she said, then laughed. "I'd forgotten about those. I stole them from one of Stoddard's dealers. Don't ask me how," she added when he opened his mouth to ask precisely that. "I left some lovely dresses behind, too," she said with a touch of regret. "My disguise got me away from the riverboat and all the way to Galesburg before I started feeling ill."

"Before that," he prodded, "after you left Spring City, what did you do?"

She looked thoughtful. "What did you do in the years after you left?"

He laughed. "I doubt we did the same things." He'd taken a walk on the wild side, which nearly culminated in his death, and he was glad those years were behind him. Mostly. He wasn't exactly settled down on a rocking chair smoking a pipe. He was, as usual, on the run, but this time with the prettiest woman he knew.

She pursed her lips and looked even prettier.

"No," she agreed, "probably not. I rode a lot of trains because that seemed like fun. I was a waitress at a restaurant in Denver, and I was terrible at it. All those people were giving me orders."

He guffawed, laughing so hard he had to wipe tears from his eyes while trying to picture a waitress who didn't want to hear what her customers wanted.

"It wasn't funny," she protested. "I was propositioned by every male who walked in, or so it seemed."

Thaddeus stiffened, his laughter stopping immediately, yet she didn't appear to notice.

"They fired me because I dropped so many plates and couldn't keep the orders straight." She smiled wistfully. "Then I went to San Francisco because I'd been there once with Riley, and I found it quite fascinating."

Thaddeus told himself to uncurl his fists despite her face lighting up at a memory, maybe one of her and his childhood friend.

"I took a boat ride around the harbor," she continued. "I began playing cards on that boat, and then I met a man who said he could show me some easy games on the Barbary Coast." She laughed. "Even I could see that wasn't the place for a lady."

"Thank the Lord," Thaddeus muttered, thinking of how dangerous that area of San Francisco could be. The only place worse was The Bird Cage in Tombstone, where he'd had the time of his life with a painted lady, scarcely escaping with his life. A few bullet holes were added to the ceiling that night.

"I was on the Central Pacific for days. Lovely journey," she added. "I ended up in Reno. That's where I met your old friend, Kelly Morgan."

"How'd you know to bring my name into it?"

"Actually, he mentioned you first, much to my surprise, when he found out I was from Spring City. He said you were a quick study at cards."

Thaddeus shrugged. There were better things one could do with one's time, but poker had come easy to him.

"Yes," she added, "he said you were *almost* as good as me."

He rolled his eyes, not believing her.

She shrugged. "Anyway, he showed me a thing or two, and we even worked a couple games together."

"You mean you helped him cheat?" Thaddeus could easily imagine gamblers so distracted by her loveliness, they didn't even notice Kelly fleecing them.

"I don't know about that. I wasn't infamous or anything." She shot him a grin. "I'm not Canada Bill or Umbrella Jim," she said, referring to the notorious three-card monte swindler and the shell-game con man. He was amazed she knew so much about his world.

"It was more like, with Kelly's bad luck, I was helping him to even the odds," Ellie continued. "Why, I could beat that man nine times out of ten, yet he knew oodles more than I ever will about faro. He can keep track of *all* the cards that are played, and I nearly can."

"Really?" That was an impressive skill if she could do it.

"Riley always said I had a good memory."

Riley could go to hell, but she'd brought him up yet again, so he might as well ask.

"Why'd you leave him?"

"Kelly?"

"No."

"Oh." She was quiet a moment. "It's a long story I'll tell you sometime."

"Did you sleep with him?" *Good God, how had that slipped out?* Thaddeus decided he must be more tired than he thought. It was the last thing he wanted to know. Her answer had the potential to eat him up inside for the rest of his life.

She gave him that long, contemplative stare of hers. "Yes. I had my head on his bare chest one night, and I fell asleep. That was right after my father died."

"You know that's not what I meant," Thaddeus said. "And you don't have to answer anyway. My question was completely beyond the pale. I don't know why I asked, and I don't care to know the answer."

Another one of her long stares. Then she spoke again. "I couldn't have relations with him, even if I'd wanted to."

Thaddeus noticed she didn't say she didn't *want* to, only that she couldn't. *Wait, why couldn't she?*

"Why not?" He'd gone this far down an inappropriate path.

She gave an exasperated sigh and then looked away from him. "He would've known I wasn't a virgin. He's a doctor, remember? I couldn't have him thinking so poorly of me."

His mouth fell open before he realized, and when he did, he closed it with a tooth-cracking force. He didn't know what to say to her astonishing admission. But his stomach twisted uncomfortably like he'd been sucker punched. Disappointment he had no right to feel surged through him.

He had to say something into the vast quietude.

"Riley probably wouldn't have minded," he offered, wondering who the lucky bastard had been. "That is, I don't believe he would've thought badly of you."

He looked down and saw his hands were fisted again. If he didn't change the course of this conversation, he was going to get angry as a hornet, and he needed his other hand in good working order for firing his gun and punching people. Slowly, he unclenched his fists and tried to give her a reassuring smile that he feared was closer to a grimace.

"We need to get some rest," he said. "Sleep gives me the upper hand when I need it."

He was babbling, but he couldn't stop, especially with her staring at him with those guileless blue eyes.

"If I'm too tired, I won't be of any use to you. We better stop talking and settle down."

He desperately wanted her to shut up concerning her sexual escapades, and he needed to stop trying to understand her.

"Fine," she said, sounding angry.

What had he done now? Setting his bag down for a pillow, he watched her use her old stolen duster for the same. Then she relaxed into what little hay remained and turned her back on him. He took another look around before lying down beside her, careful to face away, staring at the weathered wall.

They'd been sleeping in the same bed now for almost a week, but suddenly, he couldn't stand the notion of touching her. He knew he was being a sore loser and childishly possessive. After all, he'd lost count of how many women he'd bedded, but they'd meant nothing to him, not a one. None had compared to the girl he'd left behind. And now to hear her tell, and rather cavalierly, that she'd been intimate with another man, well, it just beat all!

It would be better if it *had* been Riley. At least he liked Riley again, now the man was married to someone other than Ellie. Instead, Thaddeus was haunted by some faceless scoundrel pawing his Ellie, stripping her clothes away at her behest, and settling between her thighs. He'd imagined it himself so many damn times, it was almost a memory rather than a fantasy.

"Sleep," he mumbled to himself. *You stupid bastard, just sleep.*

It didn't seem very long before he felt an elbow in his back, awakening him, followed by her warm body pressing against his. He realized, against all odds and despite his tortured thoughts, he'd managed to follow Ellie's lead and fall asleep in the loft. He must have sorely needed the rest. After all, he couldn't protect her if he nodded off while on horseback.

The rider who'd shot at them might have kept on riding, too, and could be looking for them as soon as they broke cover, a fact he hadn't mentioned to Ellie. She seemed to think they'd lost their pursuer.

Peering through the broken slats in the roof, he took stock of the time of day. Late afternoon. They couldn't possibly ride out in the open now. He closed his eyes again. The close, scorched air in the loft and the sound of bees buzzing nearby were like an opiate. He drifted back into a shallow doze, still feeling her snuggling behind him. He had no idea how long he lay there, enjoying the sensation of her body next to his.

"Thaddeus," he heard her murmur against his ear, jolting him awake again. He sat bolt upright, his gun in his hand before he was fully alert. It was sunset.

He looked down at her, reclining, unperturbed, blinking up at him.

"Damn it, woman, what is it?" His pulse was racing.

"Nothing, I . . ." She quirked her mouth in a shy smile. "Nothing."

His heart still ricocheted around in his chest, but he took a deep breath to settle his nerves and truly looked at her. She had something to say, perhaps, or . . . *hm, what was that look on her face?*

Her cheeks were infused with a pale blush, and she raised an eyebrow, her lovely mouth crooking up on one side in a secret smile.

If he didn't know better, he'd say this lovely lady lounging in the hay was giving him a come-hither look of invitation.

He swallowed. He had to be reading her wrong.

"Ellie?"

"Thaddeus," she said again, her voice like a cat's purr. Then she stretched out her arms to him, and he had no doubt.

Blazes! He was being tempted by an angel. How could he resist? The yearning washed over him and through him, and he put his gun aside. He leaned down until she could reach him, and to his delight, her arms slid around his neck, while he rested his forearms on either side of her.

Looking down into her face, he saw only openness and longing. Naked longing. For him!

Bending lower, he kissed her. The rush of warmth and longing when he claimed her lips was even stronger than at the Grindels'.

She opened her mouth to him, and he took what she offered. It had been so many years of wanting her. Of course, he bumped his nose against her in his hurry to meld his lips to hers, and naturally, he bit her lower lip too hard when he found he couldn't get enough of her, causing her to hiss.

All the years of being intimate with women whose names he now couldn't recall—and yet here he was, feeling clumsy and green with Ellie.

He trailed kisses down her pale neck and encountered the eyelet lace of her shift at her neckline and over that her dark blue blouse with a daunting row of buttons down the front, disappearing into her skirt.

With slightly shaking hands, he unbuttoned her, pulling the shirt out of her waistband. Underneath was the white shift he'd seen before at the rooming house. No corset. She certainly had no need of one, so slender was she. But the blasted shift had more buttons! He tackled these with earnest at least as far down as her waistband, and all the while, her hands were in his hair, ruffling it, then stroking across his shoulders and down his chest.

At last, he parted the cotton undergarment and feasted his eyes on her breasts. The last rays of the sun slid across her skin, turning it golden. His manly parts appreciated the view as much as his eyes. Her twin peaks of pert womanhood topped by perfect rosy nipples caused his shaft to swell and press painfully against his fly. Had anything or anyone ever looked more delicious or inviting? He didn't think so.

Bending lower, he rubbed his cheek, stubble and all, against first one breast, then the other. So soft, yet firm.

She muttered something incomprehensible but clearly encouraging him to continue.

With hot open-mouthed kissed, he devoured one breast, while alternately stroking and kneading the other, until he took hold of her nipple between this thumb and trigger finger, rolling it gently. When he latched onto her other nipple with hungry lips, she arched against him. At her movements, his erection pulsed harder.

Calm down, he told himself. But he couldn't stop from using his teeth against one of her hardened buds. At the same time, he felt her hand stray down his torso to the front of his pants. He stilled, her nipple in his mouth, as she ran her palm over the length of him through the fabric of his pants.

He groaned against her skin, letting her breast slip out of his mouth.

"Keep touching me," he urged, his voice low. And he switched breasts, paying equal attention to the other pearled bud that thrust up at him for some sensual consideration.

Leaning on one elbow, he raised her skirt, not a fancy one like she used to wear back in Spring City when she was the princess of the town. It was a plain blue cotton skirt, and he couldn't wait to remove it or at least hike it up high enough so he could gain access to her smooth thighs and treasured woman's core.

He stroked his hand across bare skin in no time, and he pushed her skirt and shift higher. A second later, he felt her undoing his belt and his button fly. Soon, she was tugging at his pants to pull them down, even as he was slipping his hand into her drawers.

She gasped at his first touch and spread her legs under him, but he didn't settle between them so far that she couldn't gain access to him. In fact, as he brushed his fingers across her damp curls, she slipped her hand inside his open pants and was doing the same to him.

God Almighty, it felt good to have her fingers wriggling near his shaft, but he longed for . . . His breath hitched as she caught hold of him in a firm grasp. At the same time, she lifted her hips, pressing against his hand, and he remembered what he was doing. Sliding a finger between her petal-soft folds, he felt her slick with desire.

She rewarded him with a faint moan. It was the sexiest sound he'd ever heard. He wanted to taste her next note of pleasure, so he kissed her again while gently easing his finger into her passage. He caught her next moaning sigh in his mouth. She moved her hips higher, and he slipped a second finger into her opening. *So tight.* She gasped again.

Without warning, she began to stroke him.

"Sweet Jesus," he exclaimed, feeling his climax building faster than a bobcat chasing a rabbit. In turn, while he pressed the heel of his palm onto her woman's mound and flicked his thumb across her swollen nub, she bucked against his hand.

He practically came from the feel of her alone, so hot under his touch.

She broke free from his mouth, arching her head back, and he felt her body start to contract around his fingers. Crying out, she rode his hand, no longer pumping him with her encircling fingers but merely holding on.

In seconds, she climaxed, shuddering against him, tightly squeezing his manhood. But as soon as her body relaxed, she began to stroke him again. Rolling onto his back, he let her finish him. It didn't take long. Soon, he was seeing stars and spurting into the hay beside them before he closed his eyes, feeling thoroughly spent.

He hadn't had sex like that, without penetration, for years. Some would call it tame and yet, it had been a most satisfying experience, having Ellie's hand on him, better than he could remember having in a long while. *Where the devil had she learned to do that?*

The smile died on his face. Where indeed and with whom? He went from sated to blindly jealous in the time it took him to do up his pants and consider the man who'd deflowered her and taught her about these types of things. If he knew him, Thaddeus would have no trouble shooting the man, although killing him with his bare hands would be preferable.

Sitting up, she lowered her skirts and began buttoning her shift, and he felt his temper flare.

"What the hell was that?" he asked, glaring at her.

She recoiled at his tone.

He was even angrier at seeing the pink spots blossom on her cheeks, flushed from what they'd done, and the bits of hay in her hair. He wanted to lash out at her, to punish her somehow for not being the virginal girl he'd remembered. He'd set her above all others, and in the past day, he'd found out she wasn't the innocent he'd believed, and then—*goddamnit!*—she'd let him grope her. She had, in fact, enticed him to it.

What next? Would he find out that his only sister was a harlot?

"Are you angry?" she asked, clearly bewildered.

"I don't like being surprised and ambushed is all."

She stiffened at the implication that what happened between them was all her doing.

"You seemed to like it fine a moment ago." Her voice was clipped and even.

She had him there, but he wasn't going to let her best him.

"You know something," he said, not hiding the sneer in his tone, "if someone shoves a piece of sweet cake in a man's face, he's probably going to take a bite, just to see how it tastes. It doesn't mean he wants to wolf down the whole thing or even that he likes the cake, for that matter."

She flinched as if he'd struck her, and that made him even madder. He wished he could feel reasonable about her having had sex with someone else. However, he could see nothing but red. And to think a man would do that with her and then let her go. *By God!* She'd wasted herself on some lowlife who hadn't even stuck around to cherish her!

He was as angry at her for that as he was at the lowlife. Standing abruptly, he almost conked his head on the rafters. He had to move away from her immediately, or he was going to say something even worse that would make it impossible for him to continue helping her.

Snatching up his belongings, Thaddeus was in such high dudgeon, he nearly fell out of the loft. Regaining his balance, he started down the ladder. At the bottom, he strapped on his holster and slipped on his jacket. He noted she'd remained sitting perfectly still after his little fit.

"Ellie," he called up to her, trying to bring a note of reason to his voice. "I'm going to go feed and water Lucky. When I get back, we'll head out."

He almost groaned at the thought of sharing the saddle with her again, after what they'd done. *Sweet Lord, why was he being tested?*

She didn't stir or answer him, and he didn't blame her. So he left, going stealthily out into the dusk, noisy with crickets and whip-poor-wills, among other critters.

He stayed away half an hour. Plenty of time, he figured, for her to get over being annoyed at him. It had been more than enough time for him to realize they'd shared something incredible and what an unfair muttonhead he'd been. More than unfair, he'd been downright cruel.

"Ellie," he called up to her. Nothing. Boy, she could stay silent longer than any female he'd ever met. Maybe she'd fallen back to sleep.

Climbing the ladder, he let his gaze dart around the small space. Even in the dimming light, he could see she was gone. Woman and bag, coat and boots, gone!

Shit!

CHAPTER FIVE

She couldn't have made it far on foot. She might even be
hiding close by, thinking he would leave and then she could
make her escape. He had no one to blame but himself as his
heart raced like a wild horse. *You're an idiot, Thaddeus!*

He hated to break the stillness of the burgeoning twilight, the
perfect cover for their journey, but he did.

"Ellie," he called out, then listened. Again, more loudly, he
yelled, "Ellie." Nothing. "Damn it! I'm sorry. I said some
thoughtless things because . . ."

He couldn't tell her why. It scarcely made sense to him.

"Where *are* you?" More nothing.

For hours, he rode slowly in circles, ever larger circles, away
from the dilapidated barn, and then he headed in the direction
he was going to go anyway, hoping she was walking the right
way. His mood grew darker, more desperate, with every step the
horse took without her. If anything happened to Ellie now, it
would be entirely his fault.

Eventually, he came to Minonk, right where he expected it
to be. He'd been through the town before, so close to the
junction that would take him east. But he was minus his most
important cargo.

What in blue blazes was he supposed to do now? He could abandon this foolish stunt of trying to be a hero and get back to doing what he did best, looking out for himself. He needed to pawn the illicit wares in his bag, which would make it a helluva lot lighter, and then he would hightail it to Montana. He had a mine to open.

Where the hell was she?

He checked in at the Webber's House hotel, paying in advance for a room. Making use of their safe, he paid the young clerk extra to secure his bag so he could find a saloon and try to relax without fear of robbery. In the first drinking hole, he bought cigarettes and a glass of whiskey and then decided he ought to eat something since he couldn't remember his last real meal.

The aroma of a savory chicken dinner reminded him of Ada's food at the sole saloon back in Spring City, tempting him although he could hardly eat a bite, not while agonizing over Ellie's whereabouts. He took a moment to watch a card game, but seeing the trifling pot and the tame players, he moved on.

On the next block, The Silver Dollar, a large, red-brick building, seemed more promising with a noisy crowd spilling right out onto the sidewalk, perhaps providing the diversion he needed.

Thaddeus pushed his way inside the well-lit establishment and took stock of the situation. Full tables, scantily clad waitresses, even a man strumming a guitar. Yup, he liked it. Heading first to the bar, he decided to order another drink. After that, he would circle the room, asking if anyone had seen a blond angel in the flesh.

On the other side of the saloon and gaming hall, where the largest crowd was gathered, somebody was winning big. Groans and hurrahs rent the air, then a hush, then more shouts. He smiled. He'd had games like that, when everyone was with him or against him but interested all the same, hanging on every card that was played.

He knocked back his drink and slid off the stool. Making his way over, he was within yards of the table when someone bumped into him.

"Careful, friend," he said to a mustached man who'd stepped back without looking.

"I ain't yer friend," the man said, slurring every word.

Thaddeus sighed. Why did men drink to excess? How could you play cards if you were inebriated, and how could anyone choose drink over cards?

"All right, then, but be careful, just the same."

"Be careful, my ass!" The man threw a punch, which Thaddeus easily ducked. He only wanted to see the blasted card game. The drunk swung again, practically falling over when his follow-through corkscrewed him around in a complete circle.

"I won!" Thaddeus heard *her* voice in the momentary hush after the last hand was turned over. *Ellie!* He glanced toward the table, still blocked two men deep all around.

Everyone erupted in noise at her victory, at the same instant the drunk sent his fist into Thaddeus's jaw. Luckily, the man was barely on his feet by that point and the glancing blow merely turned Thaddeus's head without causing any damage. The drunk's efforts must have sapped the last bit of strength out of him, for he slithered to the ground, unconscious.

"Fight, fight," someone yelled. *A bit late*, Thaddeus thought. The fight, if one could call it that, was over.

"Get the sheriff," someone else said, which evoked gales of laughter. Apparently, no one was going to call the law, if any even existed in the town. However, the effect was immediate: the crowd parted to get a better look at the two pugilists, and as they did, Thaddeus finally caught sight of his quarry.

There she was, looking right at home—eyes sparkling, shuffling cards in her hands, cash in front of her. She even had a drink by her side. Good God, he wouldn't be surprised if she pulled out a cigar and began puffing away. And he'd never been so relieved in his life. He'd found her!

"Ellie," he said and she looked up. Rather than a welcoming smile, she frowned.

"Yes?" she prompted as though not quite recognizing him.

Uh-oh, she wasn't going to come easy, and the prickling on the back of his neck told him it was time to go. They'd been out in the open too long.

"Come on, darlin'. We have to get going."

"Don't 'darling' me." Her expression turned mulish.

At that point, he realized their section of the room had grown still. Everyone seated at Ellie's table and those surrounding it fell silent. Heads snapped in his direction, then swung back toward her, and he knew she was enjoying a typical Eliza Prentice scene, all eyes on her.

"We have to leave," he said firmly, trying to make her understand he would tolerate no argument. She was too easy a target sitting in a saloon, making a spectacle of herself. And then, he got that prickly feeling again. *Shit!*

"I'm not going anywhere with you."

All eyes returned to him to gauge his reply.

"You remember *where* we're going, right?"

Every face swiveled back to her.

"Yup," she said, as their audience's attention swung back again. "I'm simply not going there with you."

Someone snickered. And one man at the table glowered, a sharp-eyed, mean-mouthed man who was as unhappy as a man could get playing cards.

"Are we goin' to play or not? She's got a lot of our money and I, for one, am ready to win it back."

Thaddeus looked at him. "She's all done." Then back at Ellie, he said, "You're coming with me. Now."

A short, wizened man standing nearby saw fit to get involved. "I don't think she wants to, son."

Thaddeus ignored him.

"No," she said plainly. "I'm not. I'm making a little travel money, right here, aren't I, boys?"

Some laughed, except those who were losing badly to her.

"Ellie," he said through gritted teeth.

"You are *not* my husband," she pointed out. The men's heads all swiveled again, looking more appreciatively at her as a free woman, before swinging back to Thaddeus with pity. "And you are not even someone I fancy," she added for good measure.

"Whoa!" the men chorused in unison at her bold words.

"And I don't have to go with you," she finished.

"That's right," said the player to her left, a carefully groomed man in a threadbare suit. "She can stay right here with us. Let Willy win his money back, sweetheart."

She made a sound of disgust. "As if I'm going to suddenly drop down a notch."

Thaddeus rolled his eyes. He'd had enough.

"If you don't get up in the next three seconds—"

She slammed her cards down. "What? You'll do what exactly? Shoot the place up?"

Some of the bystanders took a healthy step backward and away from him. Good.

"I will pick you up and carry you out of here."

She picked up her glass and drained the clear liquid in one swallow. Then she slammed it down, making Willy jump.

"You wouldn't dare." She eyed him with one perfectly arched eyebrow raised high.

Thaddeus sighed. *Why did people say things like that?*

"I'm at three, Ellie."

In two strides, he was upon her. He pulled back her chair, hefted her up by her forearms until she was on her feet, then he grabbed her at the waist and tossed her over his left shoulder, clutching her around her thighs to brace her.

"Put me down," she hollered.

"You shouldn't have dared me, darlin'." And he started for the entrance.

"Wait," she shrieked. "My money."

Thaddeus stopped. A win was a win. Turning, he bent backward, dipping her to the table so she could grab up her money. Then he headed toward the swinging front doors again.

Good thing he was tall. He noticed the exact moment when the Indian entered the saloon. The man wore a filthy gray hat, and trail dust covered his face. He scanned the room, like a hawk seeking its prey. Obviously, he had no interest in gaming, and just as obvious, he was a tracker.

Goddamn! Thaddeus whirled in the other direction, and Ellie shrieked again.

"Shut it," he muttered, giving her a swat on her soft behind that was perched near his cheek. He knew there'd be a back door, probably more than one. If he could just get them out unnoticed.

Too late. He heard a commotion behind him. No doubt Stoddard's man was thrusting people aside to get a good look at the screeching woman. Thaddeus sped up, although he doubted anyone would shoot them in front of a saloon full of people.

Reaching the back door at an off-balanced run, he kicked it open and stepped out into the dark alley, littered with bottles and other refuse, but otherwise deserted.

Instinctively, he turned right, thinking to come around the building and return to the more populated street. Looking back only once as he rounded the corner, Thaddeus stared into the face of Stoddard's half-Cherokee hired gun.

Stoddard had boasted of him as the best damn tracker he'd ever hired, and Stoddard was a man who needed to find people more often than other folks. Thaddeus's heart sank. He doubted they'd ever manage to lose him.

Putting Ellie down as he reached the sidewalk, Thaddeus grabbed her hand in a grip she could never break and ran, moving around and in between people until he reached his hotel. He knew they weren't safe, but for now, it was the best he could think of.

With a nod to the younger man at the front desk, he charged right up the stairs with Ellie in tow, to his back-corner room, with windows on two sides.

Shoving her inside, he slammed the door and locked it before pushing the small wooden desk chair up under the handle. They could've run right to the hotel's livery yard, retrieved Lucky, and been on their way, except his bag was in the hotel safe. And no way in hell was he leaving that behind.

He turned to find her standing, glaring at him, arms crossed with a fistful of dollars hanging from one hand, and an expression of outrage still on her lovely face.

"Where are your things?" he asked her, going to the window and drawing the curtains while staying out of sight. Only then did he light a lamp.

"My bag and coat are behind the bar at the saloon you kidnapped me from." She made a sound of pure exasperation. "There was still plenty of money to be had from those men, and I'm not joking."

"I guess you didn't see Stoddard's man."

She paled. "No."

"Did you ever meet the Indian?"

She shook her head.

"He's good at what he does. He probably knows I won't head out during the day." Thaddeus started pacing. "Which means he's already figured we'll be on the move now while it's dark. He'll be looking for us as soon as he hears a horse. Why, he's no doubt camped at the stable right now, just waiting for us to get Lucky. Or we could wait and leave at first light when he's not expecting us, but maybe he knows I'd think that, and he's catching some sleep until morning."

"I have no idea what you just said," Ellie admitted, and she sat down on the bed.

He considered his words. "Neither do I. But I think I'll take my chances with darkness. I can see as well as most men in the dark and shoot better than any of them." Hopefully.

He ceased walking back and forth. "I suppose you want your bag?"

"I'm not leaving town without it," she declared.

He sat down on the bed next to her, and she scooted away from him. How were they going to share a horse if she couldn't even bear to sit beside him?

"Did you eat?" he asked.

"Of course, I did. I'm not stupid."

"Really? You don't think it was downright asinine to put yourself on display in the middle of a busy saloon?"

She shrugged. "I needed money. Not only for travel, but I owe Stoddard five thousand dollars, don't forget."

"How could I?"

She looked at the money still clutched in her hand and sighed. It certainly wasn't close to what she owed, but it looked to be a fair amount.

"They let me into the game even though I had no ante for the pot 'cause they figured I was going to lose anyway. In the first pot, someone put in a scrap of paper saying I'd owe him a 'good bed creaking' upstairs when I lost. I took everything he had." She smiled remembering.

He had to smile, too, since a sleazy card player couldn't raise his ire. Much. There were too many of them to be bothered with. In fact, he nearly admitted his admiration for her skills, but she'd put herself in a heap of danger unnecessarily.

Watching her fold up her wad of bills, his eyes followed her movements. It *was* a goodly sum.

"Were you cheating back there?" He had to ask.

"No," she scoffed. "I didn't need to. They're not even in my league."

That was Eliza Prentice all over, as confident as she was tough. Or so it had always seemed. However, he'd hurt her with his words, and he'd better own up to it.

"I'm sorry 'bout what I said in the barn." He was staring at her shell of an ear because she wouldn't look at him.

She shrugged again, but this time, she sat primly on the edge of the bed, continuing to stare straight ahead.

"No, honestly, Ellie. I was angry, but I had no right whatsoever to take it out on you."

She bit her lower lip, and that was the only way he knew she was even listening. Then she spoke.

"You didn't do anything different than most people, at least in my experience. Folk often seem nice, but they can turn like snakes. Used to happen all the time to me in Spring. Everyone would be sweet as sugar cookies if they wanted something from me, such as asking a favor from my father to lower their rent or get them a job or what have you. If I didn't do it, then they'd be livid. Just like that." She snapped her fingers. "The way you did in the barn."

He imagined she was right, and that plenty of people tried to use her. He'd never intended to be one of them.

She faced him, and her eyes looked especially luminous in the flickering lamplight.

"But you never treated me like that before, Thaddeus." Her voice had dipped to a whisper.

He felt lower than those snakes she'd mentioned. Without even knowing he was going to do it, he reached out and stroked the side of her lovely face, tucking her blond hair behind one ear.

"I'm very sorry," he told her. "I behaved badly."

She nodded slightly as if it had come clear to her. "You didn't get what you really wanted, and that made you mad. Is that right?"

"No, no," he said. *How could she think what they'd done hadn't been wonderful?* What she'd shared with him had been more than he'd expected, much more than he deserved. "I swear, that's not it at all."

He didn't want to explain to her about his jealousy, as inappropriate and useless to him as tits on a boar. Not only useless, but unwarranted and unfair, too. Yet real to him, all the same.

If they'd been *thoroughly* intimate, if he'd taken her right there in the loft, he had a feeling his possessiveness would have been even worse the moment after they'd done the deed.

However, right then, despite everything, he wanted to kiss her again and feel the heat spread through him, but that was what had got him in trouble in the first place. Instead, he made sure she was looking him in the eye when he spoke.

"Please don't run away like that again. You scared me half to death."

"Only half?" She asked, still looking solemn, but then she gave him a small smile when he said nothing more. "I need my bag back," she added, batting his hand away from her face.

She'd forgiven him, apparently.

"I guess I could slip out and get it, but I hate to leave you here alone."

She rolled her eyes. "I made it miles through the countryside by myself. I think I can rest on this bed without anything happening to me." She fanned herself with her winnings and he grinned.

"OK, I'll be right back. But don't go anywhere." He checked his gun as he always did, then returned it to its holster. "Promise?"

"Promise," she said, as he slipped out the window into the darkness.

However, seven minutes later, with her bag and duster in hand, Thaddeus returned to find the door open and the room glaringly empty. He stamped his feet like a child and tossed her things down on the floor.

Damn it! They were taking baby steps to Boston. Every time they got a mile closer, something got in their way. This time it was plain old abduction. Evidently, Ellie hadn't gone willingly. The room was torn up as though she'd fought like a Kilkenny cat.

The Indian tracker! Had to be. Who else? And he was ahead of him by mere minutes, no doubt heading right back to Stoddard's riverboat. Scooping up Ellie's possessions, Thaddeus thundered down the front stairs and charged into the street. No sign of them, of course, but he hadn't expected any.

Before he could take a step toward the livery yard and Lucky, he heard his name.

"Mr. Sanborn," called the young desk clerk, running out of the hotel behind him. "Are you leaving?"

With his temper short, he practically growled at the man, "And that's your business why?"

The desk clerk took a step back. "Your bag, sir. It's in the safe."

Thaddeus looked down at what he held in his hands, Ellie's carpetbag and coat. He broke out in a cold sweat. He'd been so caught up in rescuing her, he'd nearly left without his bag.

He marched back into the hotel, the young man in tow.

"I'm in a hurry," Thaddeus prompted.

The clerk scurried into the back room, and Thaddeus cooled his heels, wondering what was happening to Ellie at that very moment. In truth, he was glad he'd had time to cool down. Something was unsettling him, and his gut warned him this wasn't the work of the half-Cherokee tracker, after all.

If the Indian were responsible, Ellie wouldn't have had a chance to fight him. The tracker would have entered noiselessly through the window, pointing a gun at her head, and she would have gone quietly with no other choice.

The clerk was back in under a minute with Thaddeus's bag. "Here you are, sir."

"I thank you," Thaddeus said, meaning it.

Looking the young man in the eye, he reached into his bag and pulled out a gold coin, plunking it down on the counter and sliding it toward him. The clerk's eyes widened at his good fortune.

Tipping his hat, Thaddeus gathered his and Ellie's things and turned away.

"You and that pretty lady have a fight?" the clerk asked, undoubtedly thinking they were now on friendly terms.

Thaddeus froze. *The pretty lady!* The clerk had seen Ellie.

He glanced back. "Why do you ask?"

"Because she came in with you, but left with Willy Young."

Who the hell? "Willy Young?" Thaddeus prompted.

"Yes, sir."

Thaddeus reached into his bag for another coin. "Tell me everything you know and how I find this Willy Young."

CHAPTER SIX

Riding east to the other end of town, Thaddeus felt relieved Ellie had been taken by no one more dangerous than a sore loser. For the love of God, though, it was amazing to him that she'd lasted this long without getting herself killed. A single woman, unaccompanied, traveling around the country. What's more, she plain rubbed people the wrong way. Especially gambling men who didn't like losing to a woman. Especially to a woman with a lovely face whom they expected should be naked in their bed, not beating their asses at cards.

As the horizon shifted, he spied a ranch looming over the town on a plateau about half a mile distant, lit by moonlight and by lamps in the lower windows. According to the hotel clerk, that's where he would find Willy Young.

Looking at its location on high ground, with no trees around, Thaddeus swore. No doubt Willy had men working for him who'd been told it was their job to keep anyone from getting close.

On the other hand, one man could slip by a whole posse if he was determined. And Thaddeus was quite determined. He couldn't afford to hesitate, let alone think of a clever plan. He figured the half-Cherokee was lined up ready to scalp him at daybreak, surprised the man hadn't jumped out to do that already since he and Ellie were making such a damn spectacle.

Why, Thaddeus wouldn't be surprised if the Indian helped him get her away from Willy Young just so this latest adventure wouldn't interfere with getting her back into Jack Stoddard's clutches.

He sighed. *One adversary at a time, Sanborn!*

Since he couldn't think of anything better, he kept riding closer. There came that point—and he hated to do it—where he walked next to Lucky, using his horse as a shield. Most men, particularly ranchers, wouldn't waste good horseflesh to shoot a man. Looking at Lucky's long swayback, Thaddeus sure hoped she still qualified as good horseflesh.

He reached the outer gate that proudly proclaimed the ranch as "Big Willy's."

Leaving Lucky tied to a post, he went through the gate and along the fence, crouched low and noiseless. Senses on high alert, he was almost disappointed by the lack of defense. No gunshots, not even a knife came his way. In fact, no movement of any kind, he realized, surveying the empty paddocks on either side of him, only long lines of fencing holding nothing. It was the bleakest ranch he'd ever seen.

Once past the outer corrals, Thaddeus stood within spitting distance of the modest house when he heard the first warning, "Get off my land."

My land? This was Willy, himself, and still no ranch hands in sight. Curious. Ducking behind a water barrel, Thaddeus decided to be direct: "Give me back . . . uh . . . my wife!"

Silence. Then Willy spoke again, "Your wife?"

Thaddeus didn't know what else to say. "Yes, my wife." She'd neglected to mention their little pretense, it seemed. "I want her back. Unharmed."

More silence. Presumably Willy was discussing the matter with Ellie.

"Well, hell," said Willy. "You better come in. I'm backing away from the window."

Nothing in the man's frustrated voice made it sound like a trap, and Thaddeus didn't feel that all-overish sensation he got when he was walking into danger. Nevertheless, as he opened the front door and ducked inside, he kept his gun out and his finger on the trigger.

It took him a moment to comprehend the scene in front of him. Willy Young, whom Thaddeus recognized from the gaming table at The Silver Dollar, stood with his gun drawn and pointed at Ellie. She sat, arms crossed, pig-headed expression in place, at a table strewn with cards.

Feeling the same rush of relief after he found her the last time, Thaddeus gave her a long look, checking for injury. Except for a scratch on her neck and her hair being mussed, she seemed none the worse.

"Lower your weapon," Willy said.

She clucked her tongue. "He's not going to shoot me, Thaddeus. Don't even listen to him."

Willy cocked his gun. "I've had enough of your snippiness."

"You know what, darlin'," Thaddeus said, putting his gun in its holster. "I think we better listen to him. His gun could go off by mistake because his hand seems to be trembling with rage. What have you been doing to Mr. Young?"

The chair tipped over backward, as she shot to a standing position.

"What have *I* been doing?" She stalked toward him. "What have *I* been doing?"

"I'll tell you," Willy interrupted, also lowering his gun. "She's been giving me the runaround. I simply want her to show me how she won. Every. Damn. Hand."

Thaddeus raised his eyebrows and looked at her with even more respect.

"Really? Every hand?" He whistled.

She smiled and ducked her head, blushing slightly.

"If you two are finished with the admiration, get back over to this table, missy." He raised his gun again.

She sighed. "Honestly, Mr. Young, there is no trick. I have a knack is all."

"A knack for bilking people," Willy conjectured.

Thaddeus didn't like where this was going. "You can't kidnap a woman and accuse her of cheating. Where's your proof?"

"Let's play, then," Willy said. "Right here, right now. She can't cheat if she never handles the cards. She can pull her sleeves up high, too. If she wins, I'll let her go. If she loses, then heaven help her."

"Fine," Ellie said at the same time as Thaddeus said, "No."

"There are no guarantees you'll win," he warned her. *Nothing worse than a cocky gambler.*

"Against him?" She jerked her thumb at Willy. "I'm not worried." And there was the cockiness Thaddeus had feared.

"You can tell me how you did it, and then we don't have to play," Willy offered.

"Let's play," Ellie said, letting Willy right her chair for her. "Thaddeus, you sit in, too. And while we're playing, Mr. Young, I'll show you everything I'm doing and how I win. Then you'll let us go. If we have a deal, then you can deal." She laughed a little. "Deal?"

"What about my money?" Willy whined, laying his pistol down and taking a seat as Thaddeus did the same.

"It's *my* money now. I won it fair and square at The Silver Dollar. But I'll give you a chance to win some of it back," she promised. "We'll play three hands, seven-card stud, like at the saloon."

She put some of her winnings in the center of the table. "Everyone, ante up."

"Wait," Willy said. "Push up your sleeves."

She rolled her eyes but did as he asked, and then both men put money on the table.

For the next, twenty minutes, Eliza narrated what she was doing at every moment, without giving her own cards away. She was watching what was played and keeping track.

Thaddeus narrowed his eyes. Whether dumb luck or real skill, she won the first hand with trips, while he had merely a pair, but it was higher than Willy's pair.

Reclaiming a little of his masculinity, Thaddeus beat Ellie's hand on the second round, but just barely, his queen over her jack. On the last hand, however, she trounced them both soundly with a full house.

Thaddeus whistled. "Well, there you have it, Mr. Young. She's a natural, and she counts the cards is all. It's not cheating. It's as much skill as you can bring to a game that depends so much on luck of the draw."

Willy rubbed his jaw. "I guess so. Perhaps I ought to keep her around, though. I could pay her to play for me. I can make it worth your while, missy."

Looking at his worn suit and thinking of his empty ranch, Thaddeus couldn't imagine how. Clearly, Willy Young had no cattle and no money, no men working for him and, apparently, no luck at cards either.

"We had a deal, Mr. Young," Ellie said, getting up. "I'm going with my . . . husband."

Willy looked as though he might pick up his gun again. But he didn't. He hung his head, then cradled it on his arms on the table.

They regarded the dejected creature, then shared a commiserating look. Gesturing for her to move toward the door, Thaddeus went right behind her on quick and quiet feet.

Swinging it open, he pushed her ahead of him and stepped out into the night, at the same time as he realized Willy Young was sobbing.

"Gonna lose everything," Thaddeus heard him moan.

Dreading the sound of a single desperate gunshot, he hurried them away from the house toward Lucky.

"That poor man," Ellie said.

Thaddeus turned astonished eyes on her. "He nabbed you from our room."

"I know, but I see now he was at the end of his tether."

Helping her onto their horse, he swung up behind her, not bothering to fight off the relieved feeling that he was right back where he should be, close to Ellie.

"I think Willy Young should've quit gambling a long time ago," he said, flicking the reins. "But that's the bad side of it, I guess. Everyone can't win, and some lose more than others."

"I wish I could help him somehow."

He almost slipped off the back of the horse in disbelief. Then he laughed.

"What?" she asked.

"You continue to surprise me, darlin'."

She shrugged. "That's because you don't know me very well."

Maybe he didn't know the grown-up Ellie as much as he knew the girl.

"I guess I don't."

"You should've stayed friends with Riley. Do you truly think he would have agreed to marry me if I was the terrible person folks were always trying to make me out to be?"

"I never thought you were terrible," Thaddeus said, tamping down the familiar vexing feeling of useless jealousy, as ugly as the muddy mottled skin on a toad's back. That she would believe Riley'd seen more in her than he had gave him a bellyache.

Ellie was on her pulpit now and continued, "Some people do some good in the world and don't feel the need to shout about it on the rooftops."

"And you're one of those people?" He couldn't hide the smile in his voice. She might not be on a rooftop, but she was boasting all the same.

"Never mind," she said, falling silent. "I'll let my actions speak for themselves."

"I noticed you didn't leave him his money," Thaddeus said.

She shook her head and tried to turn an earnest look his way, even though it meant twisting around and practically falling off Lucky.

He held onto her. "Stay still, damn it." But he liked having his arms around her.

"I was only going to say Mr. Long wouldn't have wanted that type of charity. No man would. He lost to me fair and square.

Besides, the piddling amount of money I won isn't going to save the man his ranch. It would hardly buy him a couple horses."

Thaddeus hated to argue with her, but his gut told him Willy Young would've taken every red cent of charity anyone gave him. He seemed *that* desperate.

"Where are we going?" she asked, abruptly changing the subject as she noticed they were not going in the direction of the hotel.

"I'm not rightly sure," he said truthfully, although he knew by the moon's locale they were headed in the direction of Panola. "Do you have any other friends here besides out-of-luck gamblers? Some town drunks perhaps?"

She laughed. It was a delightful sound, and with her still in his arms, he felt it through his whole body. *Sweet mercy*, how he l . . . liked her. A lot. Too much. He had to focus on getting her to Boston and safety, and then he needed to get on with his business before he was as down and out as Willy Young.

"If we don't get shot at, we'll keep riding. If we do, then we'll ride faster, but I'm thinking eventually, we'll need another place to hide."

She stiffened, probably remembering how it turned out the last time, with him behaving abominably and her running away.

"But we'll keep riding for now," he added hurriedly. "We haven't seen the Indian even though we've been out in the open."

"Maybe he gave up?" she asked.

"More likely he got the telegraph operator out of bed and sent a telegram back to Stoddard telling him he'd found us. Now, he's waiting for Bart and his men to join him."

"Oh." She used her small voice that evoked all his protective instincts and made him want to lock her away where he alone could find her.

"Maybe we should have stayed at Mr. Young's then," she said.

"Nope, too easy a target. Too many windows and doors for me to guard. And staying in Minonk was asking to be caught."

He felt her sigh, but she said nothing more. In fact, they didn't speak for at least an hour until they came to a small rocky stream. Lucky didn't like it, especially in the dark, so Thaddeus got off and led him.

"It's perfect," he said to Ellie. Despite hating wet boots, he appreciated the coolness of the water and the sweet, moist air by the stream, a welcome break from the heat that hadn't abated much even at night. "Nothing better for losing a tracker than water."

Instead of crossing, he picked his way cautiously along the stream bed for a few minutes. Hopefully, their exit point wouldn't be obvious.

When at last he chose a spot that had no soft mud to show hoof prints, it was precariously rocky and getting Lucky out without Ellie sliding off would be difficult.

"Come on down, darlin'." He held up his arms to her.

"What? Thaddeus, no!" She gripped the saddle horn even tighter.

"What's the matter? I'm not asking you to swim. I just need to get the horse out of the water safely without her breaking a leg or you falling in."

She hesitated, looking all around. "I can't see the bottom. Besides, there might be snakes."

Chuckling, he lifted up his feet, wet only to his knees. "I can feel the bottom. It's not deep at all. As for snakes," he glanced around, "they're all sleeping."

He didn't know what else to say. It hadn't occurred to him she might be fearful. After all, his sister used to kill rattlers with the shovel head.

"Sleeping?" she repeated. "Really?"

Even this tiny lie made him uncomfortable, but he needed to get her off Lucky's back.

"Sure they are. Anyway, you can step on this rock," he said, gesturing to a flat grey stone that rose up out of the water like a table. "It'll keep your feet dry."

Leading Lucky to one side of it, he held out his arms to Ellie again, and she let him help her down. He didn't mind the way her body slid down his, not one bit. She couldn't step away as Lucky was pressed behind her. Thaddeus knew he ought to back up and give her room, but for a moment, he held onto her.

With her hands resting on his chest, she kept her head down, regarding the moonlit water that trickled around her small stone island. If she tilted her head, Thaddeus could kiss her easily and would have. He waited another heartbeat, but when she didn't look up, he stepped aside.

Grabbing Lucky's reins, he pulled the resisting horse carefully over the slippery rocks and up the bank before tying her to a tree. When he turned, Ellie was on her knees.

"What in the Sam Hill are you doing?"

Raising her head, she said, "I thought I'd take a drink and maybe wash my face. It seems like forever since I had fresh water."

She was right about that.

"Good idea. I'll fill the canteen." Untying it from the saddle, when he glanced at her again, his breath caught in his throat. Perched at the edge of the rock, Ellie's hair captured the pale moonlight and transformed into an unearthly glowing mane.

"You look like a fairy," he blurted out. "Or a water sprite."

"Silly goose," she said, but her smile grew broader. She dipped a hand in and brought it to her lips. "It's chilly, but delicious." Inching closer to the edge, she used two hands to bring more water up to her lips, then she patted the back of her neck with wet hands.

Leaning farther over the water, she splashed her face and dribbled more cool relief onto her neck. Thaddeus watched as, almost in slow motion, the smooth, flat rock began to tilt.

"Oh," Ellie wailed, as she felt her world tipping. And when the rock slanted farther, she had nowhere to put her hands to stop herself from sliding face-first into the stream. Which she did.

"Ah," she screamed as soon as she lifted her head out of the water.

"Ellie!" Thaddeus was at her side in an instant, helping her up and trying very hard not to laugh.

She flailed around angrily, managing to soak herself even more, until finally, she was on her feet, standing knee deep in the middle of the stream with her skirt swirling around her legs, and even her old duster and bodice were soaking.

He held her elbow until she wrenched it free, nearly falling again before he grabbed her arm again and steadied her. She took a look at the offending rock, and they both noted it was flat as a flapjack once more.

"Must be another rock under it," he said, keeping all trace of humor out of his voice. "It's acting like a fulcrum. You disturbed the balance."

Ellie had a habit of doing that, it seemed, to more or less everything and everyone.

"Oh, do you think so?" she asked tartly, glaring at him, before gingerly picking her way out of the stream.

"At least you got your face washed," he said, following her and wishing he could bring back her stunning smile. "And your hair."

She made an exclamatory sound and sat down on the rocks next to Lucky to remove her shoes. Next, she peeled off her drenched stockings while he watched, unable to look away. Then she stood up and shimmied out of her skirt, at which point, he tore his gaze from her and stared in the other direction.

"How much are you going to take off?" he asked, looking at the stars that were going to wink out in an hour or so as dawn approached.

"All of it, down to my shift. I can't ride around soaking wet."

He swallowed and joined her on the bank. What else could he do? He started to strip.

"What on earth?" she asked him, pausing as she unbuttoned the waistband of her sodden skirt.

"I'm getting in that stream. You made it look so inviting," he said, shooting her a grin, "and my feet are wet already. I might as well have a cold swim."

He put his boots down next to her shoes. "Besides, with you undressing, I don't think we're going anywhere for a while." Laying the rest of his clothes in a pile, he stood before her in only his black pants. "You better turn away now," he challenged with another grin. "Last chance."

To his amusement, she did as he said, standing up and disappearing a few yards past Lucky where the rocks gave way to brush and trees. Unfastening his fly, he removed his pants and waded into the water. Finding the deepest spot, he sank down in the middle of the stream and splashed. Then he got down to business, soaking his head long enough he hoped so his dust-covered hair was back to its normal brown color with what his sister liked to call "highlights of russet."

He laughed, scrubbing at his face with his hands and thinking how great it would be to see Charlotte again. Finally, he sat still, letting the water soothe his muscles.

From dressed, armed, and riding a horse to the two of them naked and soaking wet—how vulnerable he and Ellie now were! But the water felt good, he couldn't deny. All week, even though it was only May, it'd been unseasonably hot as a whorehouse on nickel night, and the cool stream was pure bliss. He glanced over to where she'd disappeared from view, he frowned.

"Ellie?" he called out, uneasy at having her out of his sight. "Come on back. I'm decently hidden."

"No," she said. "I'm not properly dressed. Do you think I'm going to stand in the middle of the great wide open?"

He glanced around the secluded copse of trees surrounding the streambed.

"Hardly wide open," he muttered, shaking the water from his wild wet hair.

Suddenly piercing the tranquility, Ellie screamed, bloodcurdlingly loud and long.

CHAPTER SEVEN

Thaddeus surged out of the water and slipped, going down hard on his knee before he stood again and hopped from rock to rock. Racing past Lucky, all the while shouting her name, he found her standing stock still.

"Ellie—" Her name died on his lips at seeing the expression on her ashen face. "What?" he whispered, dreading her next words.

She pointed at the tree next to her.

"Snake," she croaked, almost unable to speak. He could scarcely hear her anyway over the pounding of his heart. "Snake," she repeated.

Swinging his gaze to the tree, he expected to see a rattler of epic proportions or a cottonmouth. But it wasn't either, and it wasn't even a snake.

"It's a blasted salamander." Taking two steps forward, he grabbed the lizard by its sizable tail and hurled it across the clearing. *Good Lord!* The woman was going to be his death. He could still feel his heart racing.

"Of all the addle-headed, ridiculous, loopy, half-witted" He trailed off when she said nothing to defend herself. In fact, she'd gone very quiet. He thought she was looking down in disgrace, but no, she was looking down at . . . him.

And—*damnation!*—there wasn't very much of him to look at.

"Shit!" He turned away quickly and stomped back to his clothing. How could he explain to her about the cold water and his male parts? *Ah hell!* He brushed any remaining water from his legs with the edge of his hat before he snatched up his trousers.

Letting out another curse as he tugged and jumped, struggling to get his pants on over his damp legs, he turned and damn it all if she wasn't right close, nearer than he'd expected, and staring at him with big eyes. She didn't say a word.

Was she smiling? She had better not be smiling, so help her God!

No, she must have been looking at his backside, he concluded, for even in the pale light, he could see her face burned red. He hoped that looking at the rest of him had made up for the earlier view.

"Well?" he asked, glaring at her for scaring the life out of him and then humiliating him to boot.

"Did you throw away my man pants?" she asked. Her glance took in his own pants from crotch to toe and back again.

"I left them with Mr. Grindel." Thaddeus said, his tone rough, still feeling completely exposed, picturing the image of him that was probably stuck in her craw.

"I guess I'll have to put on my other shift while everything dries." She went over to Lucky and began digging around in her bag tied to the back of his saddle. "It's all I have. When I escaped from Stoddard in his dealer's clothes, I grabbed my bag and stuffed in just the one outfit."

She chatted while she clutched her dry shift, which only served to draw his attention to the sodden chemise clinging to her like a second skin. Yes, she'd better change, or heaven help him, for his manhood was rapidly overcoming the effects of the chilled water. Even then, with her hair wet and hanging about her like river weeds, she was as lovely as any woman he'd ever known.

She turned her back on him giving him a view of her gently rounded buttocks where the white cotton stuck to her skin, and his heart thumped like a trapped rabbit.

He waited. Was she going to strip off her thin wet shift and send him to paradise with his first glance of her entirely unclothed body? She edged around Lucky and then even farther around the tree he was tied to. Thaddeus could see nothing and went back to dressing.

"That turned out to be more of an adventure than I'd imagined," he said, as he pulled on his damp boots and she reappeared. Knowing she would be riding while pressed against him in nothing but her shift had cheered him up. He slipped on his shirt.

"I guess we're fortunate the Indian didn't show up and take his clothes off, too," he added with a chuckle, but it died out fast. They were still deep in trouble, and recalling that fact was crucial.

She hooked her bag on Lucky's saddle again, and let Thaddeus tie her wet clothes on top of her bag to dry out.

"It looks like the darn horse is wearing my skirt," Ellie said, but she couldn't help giggling. "For pity's sake, don't give her my shoes, too."

Thank God she'd regained her good humor. Helping her onto Lucky, he climbed on behind her and groaned.

"What is it?" she asked.

He couldn't tell her his entire body had gone as taut as a banjo string. Images of her sweetly curvaceous figure with her wet garment plastered to it filled his head, and those same curves now leaned against him. *Why had he ever thought this torture would be pleasurable?*

"It's nearly daybreak. We'll be at Panola by midday, but right now, we have to find a place to hide and sleep. I'm dying."

They rode on, and Thaddeus wasn't sure if it was his imagination, but it seemed as though the more he tried to distance himself, the more she pushed back against his chest and his crotch, tormenting him.

"Ellie," he ground out, feeling himself grow tumescent for the umpteenth time. Unthinkingly, he took the reins in one hand and a moment later found he was cupping her breast through her thin cotton shift with the other.

She gasped.

"Sorry," he muttered, pulling his hand away as if he'd been burnt, but she shook her head and didn't reprimand him. Hearing her sigh, he wondered if maybe these rides on Lucky were no easier for her than they were for him. His other hand, still clutching the reins, lay lightly on her lap, feeling the warmth between her legs.

Heaven help him, but he had nowhere to put his hands that didn't touch her.

They needed a place to take a break from all this bodily togetherness and to catch up on sleep, at least for an hour or two.

Another mile and his gaze lit upon a tin-roofed farmhouse, sitting in the middle of a poorly tilled field. Thaddeus leaped nimbly off Lucky before helping Ellie down. He knocked on the door. A bedraggled woman who could be any age from twenty to forty pulled it open, a shotgun in her hand.

"My husband's in the field," she told him when he explained what he wanted. But likely desperate for money and having made her point with her firearm, the farmer's wife allowed them access to the barn for approximately the same amount as a good hotel room would cost.

"Why, that's robbery!" Ellie protested, coming up behind Thaddeus as he handed the woman two crumpled dollar bills.

"Then you can get off my land," the wife suggested, eyes narrowing at seeing Ellie in her shift.

"No, no," Thaddeus said. "It's very good of you to let us stay. My wife's clothes are drying. She fell in a stream," he added with a shrug, hoping to lighten the mood, but the farmer's wife merely raised an eyebrow, snatched the money out of his hand, and slammed the door.

"At least we can stay here and not get shot as trespassers."

Ellie shook her head. "You should have offered her half that amount."

He could tell she was fuming. Nevertheless, she strode ahead of him to the barn and climbed the ladder like it was the most natural thing in the world.

He sighed, and the sight of her figure climbing to the hayloft gave him pause. This was his chance to redeem himself. All he had to do was be a gentleman and keep his hands to himself.

"Don't forget my bag," she called down to him.

"Yes, darlin'. I'll be right up."

He took care of Lucky, with hay and water. Then he climbed the ladder with both bags under one arm. Half of him hoped she was already asleep while the other half . . . would wait and see.

Her watchful blue gaze struck him like a bolt of lightning as he crested the ladder and heaved the bags and himself into the loft. What did she want from him now?

"Everything all right?" she asked.

"Yup." He put the bags down. "We should get some sleep," he said, despite how his body was clamoring to hold her. Removing his still-damp boots and his hat, he lay down beside her, flat on his back, crossing his legs and closing his eyes.

She rustled around, perhaps turning on her side. With a whisper that sounded practically in his ear, she said, "I never got a good look at a man's parts before."

He wanted to die right then and there, to sink beneath the hay and fall to the floor below and keep on going. Her first good look and it was at the wrong time in the wrong place.

Then he frowned, opened his eyes, and stared at her. He stared so hard she looked away from him, a pale blush on her cheeks.

"Just a doggone minute," he said, "I thought you . . . I mean, are you *sure* you're not a virgin?"

Perhaps she didn't know what the actual act was. He knew she hadn't seen much when they'd pleasured each other with their hands, but if she'd done the deed before as she'd confessed, then surely she'd seen something.

Her head snapped up, and they locked gazes again.

"'Course I'm sure," she said, eyeing him levelly.

Why would she be so direct with him? So casually familiar. The way she spoke, as if he should already know, made him feel strange. He sat up again, just as she gasped.

"Oh, my God," she exclaimed, her eyes growing round as plates. Then the color of her cheeks deepened. "Are you telling me the one memory of us together that I've carried all these years, you don't even remember?"

His head spun with her words.

"Are you saying that we," he paused, swallowing, "that *I* deflowered you?"

She shook her head in disbelief. "You were sozzled, I think from whiskey, but I was sure you'd remember. And it was more that I *gave myself* to you than you deflowered me," she added with a toss of her head before she lay on her back and covered her face with her hands. "In your barn."

He wanted to cry. *His dream girl!* He'd had her and hadn't known it, all this time! *He* was the scoundrel he wanted to kill with his own bare hands!

"It was in July, after that so-called 'firefly' dance when I was eighteen. You'd been so attentive all evening." Her words trailed off.

He recalled that night, part of it anyway. After the dance, after drinking mightily with his friend Dan, he'd gone looking for her. He'd found her on her back porch.

"I knew we'd kissed," he said, rubbing his hand around the back of his neck, willing more memories to come forth.

"We kissed quite a bit," she reminded him, "and did a whole lot more than that."

He'd always vaguely thought they'd somehow ended up in the barn back at his own house—touching, kissing—but he'd woken up alone. And then he hadn't been certain what had been real.

He gaped at her with the burgeoning horror of having no memory of the moment they were intimate. If he'd taken her virginity, it must have been a piss-poor performance, and maybe he hadn't even completed the act. One thing he knew for sure, he would like another chance for a more memorable demonstration. No wonder she'd turned to Riley so fast that fall. She had probably hated him.

"I am so sorry I did that to you."

Ellie lifted a hand off her face and peered at him with one eye.

"Just hold on a minute, Thaddeus Sanborn. You didn't *do* anything to me. You snuck up on my back porch, and you kissed like a dream. I could have gone inside safely upstairs to my bed, and that would have been the end of it. But when you looked at me that way and smiled at me like that," she said, flashing him a shy smile, "I decided to take a chance on something exciting."

She'd taken a chance on him, and he'd let her down.

"I knew what I was doing when I went with you to your barn, though I could have wished you'd been—" she paused, searching for the words.

What? he wanted to scream, feeling worse with every passing second. Had she wished him gentler, kinder? *Dear God, had he hurt her?*

"I wished you'd lasted longer and not gone to sleep so quickly," she finally finished.

He would have laughed if he hadn't felt so low. Seriously, if he could beat himself up, he would. Perhaps he could tie himself to Lucky and let the horse drag him around a while. What a cad! What a jackass! All these years, he'd prided himself on never taking advantage of a woman, despite having his share of willing ones and few others he'd paid, but that was their job. And he'd always paid well, at that!

But to have taken Ellie's innocence right in his own barn and then passed out? If she didn't need him now to get her securely to Boston, he would shoot himself.

Into the silence, her voice came, sounding nervous, worried even.

"For pity's sake, Thaddeus, say something."

He stared at her, wishing he could see her more clearly. She didn't sound angry, she sounded anxious. Why would she be anxious? As if she had reason to be embarrassed when it was entirely his fault?

"Honestly, I don't know what to say, except you deserved a helluva lot better than what I did. It should never have happened, and I'm truly sorry."

Ellie blanched and removed her other hand from her face, so both her eyes were staring right up into his.

"You're sorry you ever kissed me and made love to me, aren't you?" She looked away. "I figured that was the case when we kissed at the Grindels. You said sorry then, too. And we didn't quite 'do the deed' in the last barn, did we? It was plain, then, you were mad at me for even doing what we did. I shoved my 'cake' in your face, as you said."

He cringed. *Christ! Did she think he didn't want her?* Well, that wouldn't stand.

"Darlin'," he said, touching her chin to make her look at him. "I have wanted you since I was fourteen years old. You were fifteen and way out of my league. But you were my angel, and I watched you grow up. And I never stopped wanting you." He owed it to her to tell her everything.

"But what we did in my barn was not making love. That was the drunken groping of an overheated teenage boy, and you were sweet to tolerate it. Maybe I didn't believe you were really there, not after all the whiskey I'd had. I'd already spent many nights pleasuring myself while thinking of—"

He broke off. Maybe she didn't need to know that much. "Anyway, I do remember finding you on your porch that night. But I didn't just happen to find you, did I? I sought you out like a bee to nectar, sneaking into your back garden. I thought you were the prettiest thing to ever walk the earth. I always have. Now you've reminded me, I vaguely remember us running in the dark to my house. You smelled so good. But when I woke up in the straw, for all I knew, you'd been only a dream."

He touched the side of her face. "I wish I remembered every last second of whatever we did together. I swear it. Do you believe me?"

She nodded, opened her mouth to speak but, instead, yawned broadly.

It was time to end this dreadful conversation. Later, he could tell her, or better yet show her, how much he wanted her still.

"You sleep. I'll keep watch," he said.

She closed her eyes but snapped them open again, and he was riveted as always by her clear blue scrutiny.

"Keep watch for what? No one knows we're here. You need to sleep as much as I do. More even, for that matter, so you can shoot straight." She raised an eyebrow. "You *can* shoot straight, can't you?"

He nodded, amazed at the warmth flowing through him simply looking at her, all drowsy in the hay.

"Good," she said, closing her eyes again. "Then maybe you can teach me. I'd like to learn to shoot. A woman needs to be able to protect herself."

"Especially you," he uttered softly.

"Especially me," she agreed, a small smile on her lips, as she drifted off to sleep.

Thaddeus fell asleep, about as quickly as she did. When he awakened, it was late morning and he'd slept for hours. Lying still, he wrestled with the urge to turn toward Ellie and kiss her. He could imagine starting to make love to her while she remained sleepy and yielding. It would be so easy to slip off her thin shift, sweep his hands over her satiny skin, and pleasure her as she deserved.

But after their last barn experience—make that two, now that he knew—she didn't need him pawing at her. Just because she'd invited him once, that didn't give him free rein to take her whenever he wanted. They had no understanding between them at all, and he couldn't see past the end of the week when they'd be at his sister's house. That was if they finally had a stretch of good fortune.

In the end, he woke her with a quick shake to her shoulder before hastening down the ladder to tack up Lucky, avoiding temptation while Ellie put on her now-dry clothes.

Not wanting to encounter the farmer's wife again, even to ask for food, they left quietly, walking beside Lucky for a good twenty minutes to loosen their stiff, sore muscles.

When he told her it was time to ride and get some miles under them, she didn't complain. Apparently, good rest and dry clothes perked her up. Surprising him, she quite contentedly climbed aboard Lucky, who moved along at a good trot after her hours of respite.

Thaddeus had every confidence they'd make it to the train by midday. Though fervently wishing they weren't riding the last part of their journey in broad daylight, he'd learned a thing or two about staying out of sight over the years, and he kept to the tree line.

Ellie didn't have much to say, not that he did, either. Holding her was enough. He let her lean back against him, not caring she left him perpetually aroused. He deserved the torture, still hardly able to believe what she'd told him. They'd been intimate! And her words kept returning to him, how she'd carried the memory of him and her together. It sounded as though she meant with fondness, not with bitterness or regret. But how could that be?

Trying to get his mind back to the business at hand, getting on a train as soon as possible, he tightened his arms around her in a gentle squeeze.

"What were you planning on doing when you got in that boxcar?"

She didn't answer right away, perhaps taking a moment to follow his thoughts.

"I planned on getting far away from Stoddard and the Missouri-Illinois state line and then . . ." She shrugged in his arms, and he fought the desire to nuzzle her ear and kiss her neck.

He settled for resting his chin gently on the top of her head, waiting for her to finish.

"To tell you the truth, I didn't have much of a plan," she confessed. "I couldn't go back to Spring City, because Stoddard knows my home is there. At least, my house is. I'm not sure where home is at the moment."

Home, for him, was on this horse holding Ellie, but he wouldn't tell her that. She had a heap of trouble, a huge debt, an unwanted husband, and the last thing she needed was him latching onto her like a lovesick puppy.

For God's sake, man, get a grip! He spurred their horse, and Lucky jumped before breaking into a faster trot.

"What's wrong?" Ellie asked, jolted by the change in cadence.

"Nothing," he ground out, wishing he could make things right for her and hoping Reed could help. "This is taking too long, is all."

She stiffened at his harsh words, so he hugged her again.

"Sorry, darlin'. I just want to get you safe and sound to Boston."

She relaxed and didn't speak again until they came upon the rail line at Panola. Surveying it as they approached, Thaddeus swore under his breath and then loudly over it.

His heart had started to pound at the first sight of what should be Panola station, and as Ellie exclaimed in dismay, his stomach clamped uncomfortably. Rather than a busy station greeting them, a husk of collapsed beams and bricks and melted glass gave evidence of a devastating fire.

From astride Lucky, they stared at the remains, as if looking at it long enough would fix things.

Well, damn! What next? A Biblical wave of locusts in their path? Or maybe a tornado to wipe out the tracks?

Wordlessly, Thaddeus helped Ellie down off the horse, and they both stretched.

"Now what?" she asked, walking around in circles to get the cramps out of her legs. "How far to the next station?"

He peered up and down the track. "About eight miles in either direction, but we're not budging. We'll wait. The train'll blow its whistle as it gets to that bend," he pointed into the distance, "and then we'll be ready to jump on."

Disappointment lanced through him. He'd been looking forward to buying two tickets and getting on the train with Ellie like respectable people. Or at least, he hadn't anticipated having to toss in their bags before doing a fast run and grab, while scooping her up and hauling her onto the train at the same time. When he thought about it, he wasn't even sure it was possible, not with her wearing a skirt. It was beyond dangerous.

They barely spoke while they waited, both feeling antsy. In less than an hour, the whistle of a train heralded its approach. In another few minutes, they could feel low rumbling underfoot and a cloud of steam billowed in the distance. *Thank the Lord Almighty!* He wanted to get this over with.

Patting Lucky on her neck, Thaddeus acknowledged a pang of regret, hating like hell to lose this horse. But that was the price of train travel. Hoping when set free, Lucky would plod across the tracks and wander into the town to be claimed, Thaddeus had a hand on the saddle buckle when another rumble thundered in the distance.

With a sickening feeling, he knew exactly what the sound was. Horse's hooves. Sure enough, on the southern horizon, four men approached. Not Biblical locusts, but equally dangerous. The half-Cherokee had brought more of Stoddard's men, sure as a coyote forms a pack to hunt.

In a split second, Thaddeus realized what he had to do.

"Ellie, listen to me."

She might be listening, but she wasn't looking. Frozen in place, she stared at the approaching riders. At least, they weren't shooting. Yet. They wanted her alive, and maybe him, too.

"Ellie," he said again, giving her a little shake. "You're gonna do what I say." At last, her crystal blue eyes locked on his, and she nodded.

He could feel the shaking of the ground as the train got closer.

"I'm going to help you get on this train, and then I'm going to draw those men away from it. Me and Lucky, OK?"

"You're leaving me?" Her big blue eyes seemed to get even larger, and his heart ached. He would do anything to erase the fear he saw.

"I'm going to divert those men, and I'll meet you in Boston. I promise. You can get there easily once you get on this train. You're smart, you can do it."

Time had oozed like molasses for days. Now, it advanced at a fast canter. He mounted Lucky, simultaneous thoughts firing in his brain of what they had to do in the next few seconds.

"Get your bag. Toss it to me."

She did as he told her, and he caught it, nestling it between his legs. "Now, use my stirrup and get on up behind me. Come on, darlin'," he urged her as she stepped into the stirrup with her dainty foot and let him haul her onto the horse. In the unfamiliar position, she slipped her arms around his waist and pressed against his back.

"Hold on," he said.

The train steamed toward them, and like an answer to his prayers, one of the boxcar doors stood wide open, offering sanctuary within its shadowed recesses. The locomotive slowed to go under the empty coal loader and past the abandoned station. Digging his boot heels into Lucky's flanks, he urged her into a smooth gallop. As they rode alongside the train, Thaddeus leaned the horse in as closely as he could.

"Grab the handle," he shouted to Ellie. "We'll keep steady. You can swing right on in."

She didn't let go of him. "No, I don't want—"

He cut her off by pulling her hands apart at his waist and extending her left hand toward the boxcar. She had no choice but to grab hold of the iron handle. Her left foot followed, stretching toward the boxcar's runner. In the next instant, she lifted off the saddle behind him and stepped aboard the train, diving to safety inside.

"Good girl," he called out, keeping Lucky even with the boxcar. He tossed in Ellie's bag, at the same time hearing their pursuers start to yell. Someone shot off a round, perhaps in frustration.

"Empty?" Thaddeus yelled to her.

She looked around the car, then stuck her head out again. "Yes," she yelled back, her voice thin.

The train began gaining speed as the track straightened, and he and Lucky, unable to maintain the pace, fell behind. With a lump in his throat, Thaddeus pulled the horse to a skidding stop and held up his hand in farewell, watching as she did the same.

The compulsion to comfort her, to tell her something, anything, burned in his gut, but he didn't know what. He wished he'd had time to give her a proper goodbye kiss to let her know how he felt. That would be the first thing he'd do when he saw her in Boston, kiss her until she couldn't stand.

He watched her a moment longer before turning his attention to the problem at hand.

Stoddard's men were still about two hundred yards away— the Indian, Bart, and two others. If they rode hard, they could catch the train the next time it reduced speed on a curve. It would be easy for two of them to jump in the boxcar, right from their horses, and abduct her, or even stop the train by placing their horses on the track. He had to make sure they focused on him and not her.

"Sorry, ol' gal," he muttered to Lucky, as he spurred her once more into a hard gallop, while shooting off a couple rounds in the riders' direction, not bothering to aim but desperate to distract them.

Seconds later, a barrage of bullets whizzed past his ears as Stoddard's men returned fire. *Goal achieved!*

Riding west, in the opposite direction to Ellie's train, he found himself sorely missing the Colorado terrain as he scanned the flat land around him for some place to take a stand and pick off the pursuers, one by one. He saw no good vantage point, no rocky overhang, no mountain pass, no nothing except a cluster of shrubby trees.

He followed the land as it rose ever so slightly toward those trees. Reining in Lucky behind the buckeyes, Thaddeus climbed right from his saddle into the lower branches. He kept ascending until he found a stable spot from which to watch the rapidly approaching men.

Although not nearly as good a shot with his left hand, he drew both weapons and prepared to open fire. Thaddeus took no pleasure in killing, but he'd do whatever it took to keep Ellie safe.

Aiming at one of the men, charging on horseback, Thaddeus was distracted by movement just past the rider's shoulder. That's when he saw her—his pretend wife, his longtime obsession, the bane of his goddamned existence—jump off the train in a flurry of skirts and flailing limbs as it decelerated at the next curve.

"No!" he yelled involuntarily. *What in the hell was that woman doing?*

He watched her roll a few feet, her bag and all, then get up and brush herself off. Thankfully, she didn't seem hurt. His heart moved back down out of his mouth and into his chest where it belonged. But four ruthless men on horseback now stood between him and her.

At least, for the moment, they didn't know that.

"Thaddeus," she screamed.

And now they did! *Shit!*

Turning as one at the sound of her voice, Stoddard's men spied their vulnerable prey, unarmed and on foot. Apparently, she was a more valuable captive than he was, even with what he carried in his bag, for they yanked their horses around and surged toward her, like floodwaters over a dry creek bed.

He gripped the handles of his guns so tightly his knuckles hurt. He wanted to close his eyes against the frightening scene unfolding before him, managing to get only a single shot off that clipped one rider's arm. Then they were out of range, and he was stuck in a tree.

Ellie shrieked again, not his name this time, just a yelp of fear, before she was silenced by Blackheart Bart, who slid from his horse and clamped a hand over her mouth.

Feeling sick with helplessness and dread for her, Thaddeus watched her kicking and struggling, but in a moment, she was hogtied and tossed over Bart's saddle, where he rested his hand on her buttocks, letting her head hang down one side and her feet the other.

"I swear to God," Thaddeus murmured, focusing on Bart's ugly black hat, "I will kill you."

A moment later, after one of the other men retrieved her bag, and the Indian offered him the briefest of backward glances, they rode away.

He wanted to scream, loud and long. He didn't. All he could do was drop out of the tree onto Lucky's back and start trailing along behind at a respectable distance, stewing on the mass of emotions roiling in his gut—cold fear for Ellie and what Stoddard would do to her, mixed with white hot fury at the infernal woman for jumping off the train and wrecking his sound plan.

Jack Stoddard had her, but Thaddeus aimed to get her back. And he realized with certain clarity, Stoddard's men had known if they took Ellie, Thaddeus would follow, and Stoddard would surely get them both.

CHAPTER EIGHT

The trail before Thaddeus stretched endlessly, all the way across the state, clear to the Mississippi River, and he could scarcely believe he was heading once more in the opposite damn direction to any of his goals, Boston or Chicago. And all the while he was riding Lucky, his body clamored for Ellie's proximity, missing her more than he could have believed possible, considering the brevity of their time traveling together.

Thaddeus spent most of the long days swearing or praying, and hoped Stoddard's men were treating her well. They wouldn't hurt her on purpose, he was sure of that, because, after all, she could still claim status as Jack Stoddard's wife. But that didn't mean she wouldn't suffer.

He knew he couldn't hope to rescue her, not while they were still on the move. Whereas Stoddard's men could take turns keeping watch during the few night hours they rested, he hardly closed his eyes for fear one of them would double-back and kill him while he slept.

By the time the Mississippi River popped up on the horizon like a glinting black snake in the distance, Thaddeus felt wrung out to dry. He skirted the bustling port town of Hamilton with its many buildings, both brick and wood. Heading south a mile, he was familiar, too familiar, with the way to the cleared riverbank and private dock at which was moored Stoddard's gambling business and also his home—a bright white riverboat with black and gold trim.

He heaved a sigh of relief when he saw it. At last, this nightmare chase was coming to an end. All he had to do now was wait for Stoddard's goons to turn their backs, sneak aboard the riverboat, and nab Ellie. *Easy as pie.* Sure, it was.

This was no desolate, unobtrusive boat either. People came and went in a constant flow, eager for the gaming that was enlivened by music and dancing girls, as well. Not too many of these riverboats remained, not after the war with the South. Gambling had come to a halt as the army commandeered the boats to carry soldiers and supplies, rather than hard-luck gamblers. After the war, the boats were sold off or left to rot.

Everyone knew Jack Stoddard had taken full advantage of a certain scarcity in the area and refitted an old boat to be the belle of the river, despite never moving from its mooring. With only two enclosed decks above the waterline and an open deck on top of those where right then a number of men strolled with pretty women in Stoddard's employ, it wasn't the largest riverboat that had ever been made, by any means. However, right there in Hamilton, even with its bright-red paddlewheel dead in the water, it remained the liveliest.

Stoddard would expect Thaddeus to come in alone. And generally, that would make it easier for him to maneuver. He'd realized that fact when traveling with Ellie. But for this occasion, he needed a partner to divert attention from himself, and he knew exactly the person to help him.

Doubling back, he crossed the river via the bridge, grumbling at the exorbitant cost of fifteen cents, and passed the hospitals that had been set up for the Union soldiers, which were now mostly empty. Heading to the northern-most street in the town of Keokuk, Thaddeus dismounted, tied Lucky to a post, and climbed the outer steps to a second-floor balcony next to a sign that read "The Pork and Swallow."

The door was locked, so he climbed through the open window of his favorite local saloon, right into Miss Josephine Holland's bedroom.

The dark-haired beauty with the birthmark on her cheek shrieked, then laughed when she recognized him.

"Teddy, you about near killed me with fright."

"Don't call me that," he said, by way of greeting. He allowed no one to call him that except his sister, but Josephine had found it amusing to say it in the throes of amorous congress, and now she did it to tease him.

"Jo, I need a favor."

She rolled to her feet from her reclining position, wearing something black, lacey, and sheer, and approached him.

"No favors, sweetie. You have to pay like everyone else." Parting her barely-there robe, hands on her hips, she displayed all her generously proportioned wares. Then she laughed in that same husky timbre.

"I'm jesting, Teddy. You've been so generous in the past. For you, a complimentary roll in the sack."

He kept his hands firmly at his sides and tried to look anywhere else but at her luscious body. She had the looks to drive any man wild, any man but him at present. He had a taste for only a certain petite blond woman, and Jo was the opposite. Raven-haired, busty, curvy, and tall, she was someone a man could grab onto and ride. And he had done so a number of times, but not tonight. Especially not tonight.

"Cover up, Jo. It's not that type of favor."

She arched a dark shapely eyebrow and sat down on the bed, defiantly leaving her robe open and her body uncovered.

"All right, then, what is it?"

"First, for the love of God, give me a cigarette."

She reached over to her bedside table, delicately choosing a cigarette from a pink glass bowl, handing it to him along with her shiny silver Dangerfield match case.

He slid the case's button forward and a match emerged, flaring into flame as it popped out past the striking mechanism. Lighting the cigarette, he took a long drag and sighed.

"I need you to come with me, no questions asked."

"Where?"

"That's a question," he reminded her. "But fair enough. A friend of mine is in trouble right across the river."

"What kind of trouble?" She crossed her legs and settled back as if she intended to have a long conversation.

"That's another question, Jo." He ran a hand through his hair, feeling frustrated. "Can you agree first, come outside, get on my horse, and we can talk on the way?"

She eyed him without answering.

"I'll make it worth your while," he added, puffing on the cigarette.

She smiled wickedly, palming each of her own breasts before sending him a pouty smile.

He swallowed hard. The woman oozed sensual appeal.

"I meant with money, darlin'."

She shook her head. "I've got money." Then she cocked her head. "Is it dangerous?"

"Maybe. Probably. Yes." *Would she say no?*

"I'm in." She jumped up excitedly, and he chuckled despite the seriousness of the situation. "I'm bored as sin, Teddy, so I'll do it."

However, when Jo sauntered close again, he stopped laughing.

"Are you sure we don't have time for a little fun first?" She rubbed herself against him and looked up into his unsmiling face.

He frowned at his body's lukewarm reaction. It was coming to life, not wholeheartedly, but definitely showing some attention. Some of the best sex of his life had taken place right there in that very room with this passionately uninhibited woman. Now, it didn't seem worth getting undressed.

Right then, he wanted solely one woman, not only for her body but for the way she made him feel whenever he got near her. Something inside of him sort of melted, like candle wax, whenever he was in Ellie's presence, and that warmth sparked into flames when she smiled. God, how he wanted to see her smile again.

"Sorry, Jo. I've gotta keep moving. But you'll like this adventure. Not only is it dangerous, but I need you to dress in your best bib and tucker. Only real stimulating, if you know what I mean, not exactly your Sunday best. Something that'll keep all eyes on you."

She narrowed her gaze at him, perhaps still stinging from his rejection of her erotic offer. But then she managed a smile.

"All eyes but yours, right?" She disappeared behind the screen where she kept her vast wardrobe.

A few minutes later, during which he paced the room and imagined every scenario, good and bad, which could play out that night, Jo emerged.

The cigarette almost fell out of his mouth. He grinned. He'd definitely come to the right woman. Josephine's crimson red satin gown hugged every one of her generous curves. It plunged low to show her ample cleavage, and the slit over her right thigh came up to her red satin garter straps. It would more than do the trick.

She pinned a matching crimson hat onto her silky dark hair, checking herself in the mirror to make sure the long, black feather rode seductively on its brim. Pulling on black satin gloves up to her elbows and matching black shoes, lastly, she grabbed a red beaded purse and posed for him.

"You are an amazing woman," he said. "But can you ride a horse in that getup?"

Her catlike smile appeared. "Absolutely not. How about we use my quick little buggy instead? We can tie your horse to it if you like."

And just like that, they were speeding back to Hamilton in Jo's gaudy red and purple trimmed buggy, with her lightning-fast gelding cantering along the distance. Lucky was being dragged behind but gamely kept up. Thaddeus would need her later for the getaway. At least, he hoped so.

"That's highway robbery," he exclaimed as the price of crossing the bridge went up to twenty-five cents for the one-horse buggy and the second horse in tow. "If I lived here, I'd get a small boat," he added sourly.

Briefing Jo on what he hoped to accomplish with her help, he sent her across the gangplank while he remained in hiding behind empty beer barrels. Thaddeus could see she'd immediately caught the attention of anyone hanging around near the railing. Men's eyes popped out of their heads, jaws dropped, and conversations ground to a momentary halt. Then, as if the riverboat's inhabitants gave a collective swallow, everything came back to life, except all eyes remained on Jo.

She sashayed from the gangplank to the main entrance, stepping onto the plushly carpeted floor, making eye contact, waving as if she knew people. In a moment, she had a drink in one hand and at least three ardent admirers on the other and disappeared from Thaddeus's view.

Yes, Jo was the perfect choice.

Suddenly feeling invisible, he left his hiding place, boarded the boat, and slipped aft along the outer deck, until he came to the stairs at the stern, next to the motionless paddlewheel. He knew Jack Stoddard well enough to guess his stateroom would be upstairs in the bow with the best view. And if he were Ellie's husband, that's where he'd take her.

With his finger on the trigger of his gun, he stole up the stairs on nimble feet. Creeping silently along beside the railing, he made his way forward, pausing to peer in the open windows of the second-floor public gaming room.

Naturally, it was the height of opulence, which a man like Stoddard could easily afford. Three crystal-and-brass chandeliers swayed gently with the river's current and underfoot lay a colorful Persian carpet. At a huge honeyed-oak bar, men imbibed every kind of liquor. The gaming tables that Thaddeus was too familiar with teamed with hopeful gamblers.

Of course, plenty of skimpily clad women on Stoddard's payroll milled around both to distract winners and to placate losers. Not one of them could hold a candle to Jo. *Where was she?*

A murmur of voices heralded her ascent to the second floor. Sure enough, the crowd in the room turned, as if of one mind, toward the main interior oak staircase, and he knew Jo was making her way upstairs, as he'd asked her to do.

At once, every man's gaze fixed directly on her. Some admirers even moved in her direction, seemingly helpless against her mesmerizing draw. When he saw her black feather swaying seductively from the top of her hat, he made his move.

Slipping inside the gaming room via the farthest door along the deck, he skirted the back of the tables and ventured down the hallway where three closed doors confronted him. Ignoring the ones to the right and left, he approached the one straight in front of him.

Locked! Of course it was. He pulled out the pick hidden in the band of his hat and in mere seconds, undid the lock. Cracking the door open cautiously, Thaddeus found it contained a bedroom set—two small side tables with green-glass lamps, and a velvet covered bed that gave him pause. The bed clothing stood in utter disarray.

Where was Ellie? And why would Stoddard lock an empty room with nothing more interesting in it than pretty lamps? Thaddeus was well aware the gambler kept his valuables in a safe in his office on the first floor, and not simply locked but guarded. If Stoddard had imprisoned Ellie in his office, the rescue was going to get a whole lot trickier.

Turning to leave, it struck him as odd that only one of the velvet ceiling-to-floor drapes hung closed. If he had the layout of the boat correctly in his mind, it had no window behind it. The other drapes in the front of the cabin were open, revealing the evening view upriver and the fully lit city of Hamilton.

Curious, he crossed the room to investigate. Drawing back the curtain, he found a door. His pulse quickened at the sight.

Noiselessly, he tested the knob. It was unlocked. Taking his time, in case someone had a gun trained on him from the other side, he turned the handle. Well-oiled, the door made no sound as he pushed it inward, staying crouched low on his knees so his head wouldn't get blown off.

What met his astonished eyes was a massive clawfoot tub, within which he could hear water splashing at the sides. More water sloshed over the edges, dripping onto the polished wood floor. A dainty foot and slender calf covered in bubbles lifted out of the tub. And he heard humming—soothing, slightly off-key humming.

Ellie's golden hair, freshly washed and still wet, hung down her naked shoulders and over the side of the tub, nearly to the floor as her head reclined against the white, enamel-covered cast iron. She faced the far wall that had a window with a view of the other side of the river. From the bathtub, she could see both Iowa and Missouri, if it weren't dark out.

After a brief scan confirmed they were alone, he stood up, shutting the door behind him at the same time with a firm click.

She jumped, startled, sinking into the water and sloshing it over the sides of the tub, while turning to see who'd entered.

Irritation flashed through him. "What in the hell are you doing?"

He'd never been so relieved to see someone. On the other hand, she didn't look like a suffering prisoner, nor was she ready to take flight with him. More like she was preparing for an evening with her husband.

"Thaddeus!" She stood up, bubbly water running in rivulets down her lithe body. For a brief moment, he saw her in all her glory.

"Oh," she exclaimed, realizing she was giving him an eyeful. Her hands flew up to cover herself, one over the darker-haired triangle between her legs and the other, unsuccessfully trying to conceal both her breasts as best she could.

He had trouble forming a thought or making a sound. In any case, he couldn't remember what he wanted to say. All the blood that he figured was normally circling through his body and maybe making his brain function was now rushing pell-mell to his manly parts.

Instead of sinking back down into the water, Ellie spun around, almost slipping in the tub, and giving him a prime view of her pleasantly rounded backside. It did nothing to help his cognitive ability one bit. He wanted to squeeze those perfect pale cheeks. He took a step.

"Please, hand me my towel," she said, keeping her back to him and reaching out her dripping arm.

Towel? Towel? *Oh, towel.* Reaching for the white plush one that lay draped over a brass rack, Thaddeus held it out to her, knowing decency demanded he look away but finding it impossible to do so.

Snatching it, she glanced over her shoulder at him.

"You came," she said wonderingly, as if she'd doubted it, which bothered him, but then she flashed him a brilliant smile, making his intelligence slip down another notch.

He nodded in agreement, watching her dry off and then shake out her damp hair. When she finally tucked the towel firmly in place around her body and stepped out of the tub, he began to think clearly once more, and his anger returned.

"If you truly were my wife, I'd tan your hide for that stupid stunt you pulled back in Panola. You wouldn't sit down for a week."

Why was she still smiling? She was supposed to be fearful of his fury or mightily contrite. Or at the very least, ashamed of getting herself captured.

"You rode all the way back to get me." She beamed at him again.

Just as he was about to speak a rational sentence, Ellie closed the distance between them and flung herself at him. His arms went around her automatically. When she lifted her lovely face to his, suddenly they were kissing and he forgot everything else.

As her arms snaked around his neck and he held her tightly, he contemplated laying her down on the bed in the next room, whether Stoddard's or not. Or perhaps, here in the bathing room, he could press her up against the wall, pull that towel off of her, and . . .

He was momentarily overtaken by the idea of uniting with her much more closely and deeply than a mere kiss. Sliding his tongue into her sweet mouth, he felt captured by the clean scent of her, her soft warmth, the essence of her that always snared him when she was close. *Ellie.*

But he'd never been caught with his pants down, and he didn't intend to start that day.

Basking in her taste and her scent and the feel of her body against his for one second longer, he ended the kiss regretfully and thrust her from him.

"Get dressed," he croaked, and then cleared his throat. "We have to get out of here now."

No doubt Jo was running out of ways to distract. And so far, he'd seen no sign of Stoddard.

Ellie hesitated. He hated it when she did that.

"Do you have an actual plan?" she asked.

"Does it matter? We're wasting time."

He still wanted to berate her for jumping off the train in the first place. He couldn't fathom why she'd done it, but he would discuss it with her after they were safe.

Right then, relief at finding her unharmed battled with annoyance at having discovered her lounging in the lap of luxury, bathing rather than being ready to go. *Had she no faith he would come for her?*

"Where are your clothes?" he demanded.

She sighed, and he found out the reason for her hesitation in getting dressed.

"Jack took them. He made me strip them off because they were so dirty, and so was I."

Thaddeus knew what she meant. After a couple days on the road, riding and sleeping on the ground, a person tended to get a little ripe, and dirt got into crevices one didn't even realize one had.

Then Thaddeus considered the untidy bed and looked once more at the bath. Had she been bathing because Stoddard had raped her?

"Did he hurt you?"

She shook her head vehemently. "No, God, no. He . . . well, he watched while I undressed." She frowned. "He threatened me and said I'd regret running away, but then he took my dirty clothes and my bag and left. Of course, he locked me in."

Thaddeus swore. Stoddard probably could've left the door unlocked. Without any clothes, Ellie was as firmly imprisoned as if she'd been in chains.

"Did he mention our association?"

"Not when I first got thrown in here, but then he had a talk with those men, Blackheart Bart and the others. Then Jack came back and questioned me concerning you, how I knew you and all. He seemed to be quite amused by the coincidence that you and I were traveling together."

"You had this talk while you were undressed in his bedroom?" He was having trouble picturing how that had occurred without it going badly for Ellie.

She blushed furiously. "I wrapped myself in the bed clothes."

"Are you willing to travel wrapped in a sheet? Because I don't know how I'm going to get you a set of clothes right now."

As if on cue, a rap on the bedroom door startled them both into silence.

CHAPTER NINE

They shared a glance. Jack Stoddard certainly wouldn't knock, but Thaddeus pulled his gun out all the same. He moved quickly to stand behind the door. With a finger to his lips, he gestured for Ellie to let the person in.

To his great relief, a young woman entered, one of the dancing girls who entertained the men if they seemed tired of losing and in danger of leaving. She held a tray of food.

"Mr. Stoddard thought you might—"

Thaddeus kicked the door shut and pointed his gun at her.

"Don't scream or I'll shoot."

He'd never shot a female and had no intention of ever doing so, but he found the threat usually made people do what he asked. This time was no different. She kept her ruby-red painted lips firmly closed.

"Set the tray down on the bed and take off your clothes," he ordered her.

With shaking hands, the woman placed the tray on the end of the bed and proceeded to strip down. Apparently, she was used to doing that in her line of work, for she boldly stared right at him as she did so, seemingly unperturbed.

"Stop," he told her when she got to her corset and skimpy drawers. His command met with a startled look. Perhaps no man had ever told her to leave her drawers on before. "That won't be necessary. Ellie, take her clothes and get dressed."

Wordlessly, she grabbed up the discarded gown and, more modest than the dancing girl, went back into the bathroom to dress. In no time at all, she emerged, looking like one of Stoddard's employees, except the dress dragged on the ground and her wet hair hung tangled down her back. Between the mishap at the stream and the bathwater, he was beginning to get used to that look on her, but it would draw too much attention.

"Excuse me, miss," Thaddeus said, stepping toward her and removing the pins from the young woman's hair, as he'd done to many a lady. He handed them to Ellie. "Can you do something with these?"

She tried, piling her hair onto the top of her head and pinning it in a sloppy bun that left nearly as much hanging down as was held up.

"Here, take this, too," he said, plucking the feather from the girl's hair and sticking it into Ellie's, right behind her ear.

"Now, the shoes."

At this, the woman appeared truly peeved, but she removed her feet from her pliant leather slippers. Ellie put them on.

"A bit big," she said. "I'll probably trip out of them."

"You'll need them," Thaddeus insisted, and then he used the curtain tiebacks to tie the woman's hands together. Marching her into the bathroom, he stuffed a washcloth in her mouth and tied up her feet, too.

"Sorry about this, miss," he added before closing the bathroom door on her annoyed glare.

"That should gain us a little time, if we're lucky," he added, drawing Ellie behind him as he slowly opened the bedroom door again and saw the back of one of Stoddard's men at the end of the hallway.

So much for luck. First, he didn't like the idea of shooting a man in the back. Secondly, if he fired off a shot, the entire boat would be alerted.

He backed into the bedroom.

"I went out the window last time when I had a room at the back of the boat," she reminded him. "That's how I cut my leg."

He stared at her, thinking how resourceful she was and awfully glad she wasn't the panicky type.

"I guess we're going out the window," he agreed.

Her grip on his arm tightened.

"It'll be fine, darlin'," he assured her, praying it was, and chose one of the windows over the bed so she could better reach it. He undid the latch and slid up the window sash. Not the largest opening in the world, but they would fit.

"I'm going first, then stick your arms out and I'll pull you through."

She nodded, her big eyes scared but trusting.

Standing on the bed, he climbed through the window headfirst, held immobile for a moment as his shoulders got wedged in the small space. However, the leverage of the bed allowed him to push out. He twisted so he was facing up to the night sky and ended up sitting backward on the sill before working one leg out and sitting astride. Pulling his other leg out without falling off the sill was a little tougher, but soon, he lowered himself to the deck.

They'd had a stroke of luck after all. Stoddard could have chosen a boat with no upper level fore deck. Without it, they quite possibly would have broken their necks on the long drop to the main deck below. Instead, it was a mere few feet before his boots touched the planks.

Ellie's hands appeared through the window opening, followed by her head and arms. As he started to help her out, she stiffened and swiveled her head around to look behind her. Her expression changed to panic, and she scrambled out the window into his arms.

Thaddeus tucked her behind him as the face of Blackheart Bart loomed in the opening where she'd been only a second before. With a furious expression, Bart scowled down at them.

"Sanborn," he spat. "You are so dead."

Probably true, Thaddeus thought. Without replying or giving Bart time to draw his gun, he grabbed Ellie's hand and took off around the side of the boat, not even pausing as he issued an earsplitting whistle to signal Jo. He hoped she could hear it over the noise of the people enjoying Stoddard's riverboat hospitality.

Speeding past the upstairs gaming room with Ellie in tow, they ran aft and headed down the outside stairs. Before Thaddeus could do more than whistle again in case Jo was in the lower gaming room, the first shot rang out, hitting the brass railing next to his hand.

Sheltering Ellie with his body, he flattened them both against the hull, while firing randomly at the deck above him through the stair risers. He hoped the gamblers had the sense to stay inside the boat. Another bullet shot through the walkway above them and tore up the deck next to his boot.

Shit! He and Ellie were sitting ducks. He hadn't bargained on Stoddard allowing his men to open fire while the gaming was going on. It seemed to Thaddeus a gunfight would be bad for business. In fact, people had already halted in their approach to the gangplank. However, Stoddard evidently didn't care.

"You might hit *Mrs.* Stoddard," Thaddeus called out when the shooting stopped. She glared at him for using her married name, but he continued, "Where is ol' Jack anyway?"

He hoped for an answer so he could determine where Bart was. He heard a chuckle from directly above.

"He's occupied at the moment, maybe with the soon-to-be new Mrs. Stoddard."

Thaddeus and Ellie looked at one another as Bart continued.

"Not much 'tween wife and widower, just a heartbeat."

"How poetic," Ellie muttered.

Thaddeus shot straight up through the deck and heard the satisfying sound of a cry of pain. To his disappointment however, the man who fell over the upper railing and onto the dock two stories below was not Bart. At least he wasn't an innocent gambler, though. If the gun clutched in his hand was any indication, he worked for Stoddard.

Ellie gaped through the railing at the man's body, lying twisted and still. Seeing her face grow paler, Thaddeus grabbed her hand and dragged her to the other side of the stern, passing the giant paddlewheel again.

He'd evened their odds a little by shooting one man. They might still escape with their lives, but the alternative remained—that Bart, or even Stoddard, himself, would have the pleasure of tossing their bodies into the Mississippi. Then, he had an idea.

"You can swim, right?"

"Yes," she answered distractedly, still looking at the deck above for Bart.

He remembered spying on her in the lake that fed the spring from which their hometown got its name. It didn't seem like the time to tell her that, however, as he looked over the side into the dark water.

She realized why he was asking and took a step back.

"Oh no, Thaddeus."

He ignored her.

"Swim a hundred yards or so, or let the current carry you, and we'll get to shore when we're out of range."

"Range?" she asked, looking at the swirling eddies below.

"Of the gun shots," he clarified.

"Thaddeus, I don't think this is a good—"

"Hold your breath, darlin', and please don't scream," he said as he picked her up, lifted her over the rail, and without warning, let her go. She plunged into the water with a light splash.

Bart and his men were still on the other side of the boat, expecting them to try to escape down the gangplank. Thaddeus sure hoped Jo could handle things inside. He took a deep breath and jumped in after Ellie.

Tepid, muddy water closed over Thaddeus's head, filling his nose and ears. Letting the current carry him some distance from the boat, he breached the surface as soon as he guessed it was safe, scanning the swirling water for any sign of Ellie. He spotted her, bobbing along, a short span ahead of him.

"Ellie," he sputtered, striking out toward her with a fast crawl to close the gap between them. She was paddling, not making much effort but not drowning either.

When he reached her side, he glanced back at the well-lit boat, hoping it was dark enough no one would see them until they were so far away it wouldn't matter.

"I can't believe you threw me off a boat," she said between gulps of water and air.

"Stop talking and you can thank me later." He caught hold of her arm and, treading water, rode the current a few moments longer, but he was growing weary and figured she was, too. He headed toward the bank mere yards away, but they seemed to be going nowhere fast.

"Can you swim to shore?" he asked, hoping they wouldn't stay in the water until they hit New Orleans. The idea of Ellie amongst the plethora of loud and ruthless gambling houses down south sent shards of alarm racing through him.

"Yes, I can, if you'd only let go of me." She yanked at her arm, and he released it.

Together, they reached the shore, crawling up the bank, glad of the darkness but not the thick mud.

"Sort of makes your bath back there rather pointless," he remarked, lying on his back, breathing hard. She panted breathlessly next to him. And then, against all odds, she laughed.

"I suppose it does, but it was nice to be clean while it lasted."

He thought it was damn *nice* no one had shot at them in the past few minutes. Perhaps his plan had worked.

Thinking of plans, he couldn't restrain himself for one more second from asking her the question that had haunted him for days and miles.

"Why did you jump off the train? Everything was going according to plan."

"Plan!" she scoffed.

"What? You don't trust me?"

She laughed again with less humor. "No, surely not. You just flung me off a boat. And you shoved me on that train and then what? You were most likely going to get yourself killed, and doubtless I'd would've been captured again, anyway. And if I made it to Boston without you, then what? Do you really think your family would have helped me?"

"Yes, I do," he said. "Charlotte never understood why you didn't like her in the first place."

Silence.

"Ellie?"

"I'm getting cold. And now I've lost my bag and my coat," she said with bitterness. "What's the rest of your rescue plan?"

Was that sarcasm in her voice, after he'd gone to all this trouble to get her off that infernal boat? And alive, at that?

"We can walk back toward the dock and see if Lucky is still where I left her. Then we head to Keokuk?"

"Why?" she asked.

"My bag is in a saloon there."

"Why?"

"Stop asking that," he said, annoyed she was so damn critical. "Let's go."

He got up and hauled her with him. They squelched through more mud until they hit drier dirt, and then they fought their way through the thick greenery before reaching the road.

Out of the blue, she said, "You know, if I weren't a strong swimmer and if this dress weren't so thin, it might've dragged me down to the river bottom. Did you think of that?"

He hadn't, so he simply shook his head. They were both alive, and that was all that mattered. In a few minutes, despite the darkness, they found Lucky along with Jo's buggy, both untouched, right where he'd left them, concealed half a mile from the gangplank to the riverboat.

He didn't know if it was a good sign or a bad one that Jo hadn't yet left, but in his gut, he knew she could take care of herself as she'd been doing all her life. And if he had to, he'd ride back and rescue her, too, if she hadn't returned to The Pork and Swallow by morning.

Ellie said nothing regarding the gaudy vehicle to which their horse was tethered. She let Thaddeus help her onto Lucky's back like so many times before. As she slumped against him, shivering in the night air, he held her firmly, telling himself it was only to keep her warm. Truth was, it felt better than great to have her back in his arms, even though they were both soaked through and covered with slippery, pungent mud.

By the time they got back to the saloon, Ellie had nodded off to sleep. Thaddeus felt irritable and frustrated. Uncomfortable as a cow past milking time, he woke her rudely as he dismounted. Reaching up, he grabbed her by her waist and dragged her down the side of the horse.

She fell awkwardly against his body. Before he could stop himself, he kissed her soundly with more punishment than pleasure, expressing all the relief and pent-up anger he'd felt during the long days of trailing after her and her infernal captors. She came fully awake in seconds and, surprisingly, kissed him back, turning his ire into full-blown passion.

When he pulled away, thinking only of taking Ellie upstairs and using Jo's bed, she looked up at him with her large blue eyes.

"Thank you for the rescue."

Turning away, she headed for the brightly lit entrance, then glanced back at him. "But don't try to send me off again like that," she scolded, shooting him a smug smile before regally entering the saloon as if she wasn't wearing a gaudy harlot's gown and plastered in mud from head to toe.

Good God, what a crazy woman!

Thaddeus paid to have Lucky stabled and then went looking for Ellie.

Holding court while sitting on a stool in the middle of the dimly lit bar, she had five men paying homage. She held a drink in one of her delicate hands and a handkerchief in the other, with which she'd apparently wiped her dirt-smeared face. Even when she was a mud-splattered, sopping mess, Ellie radiated something that enchanted a man.

Despite her outrageous appearance, every man-jack no doubt hoped she was a new girl for sale. Given her stolen dress, Thaddeus supposed she looked the part, although the feather and hairpins were long gone. He couldn't blame the men for lusting after her. Perhaps they'd all be less captivated if they were on the receiving end of one of her infamous tongue-lashings, although that had never dimmed his interest in the slightest.

"Thaddeus." Someone called out his name.

He swiveled his gaze to Pete, one of the bartenders who was also Jo's business partner. Nodding his head in greeting, he made his way over to the long, polished bar, all the while keeping an eye on Ellie.

They shook hands. Everyone at The Pork and Swallow knew him, which was somewhat unsettling and could be dangerous, but it allowed him access to the upstairs rooms, off limits to anyone not personally invited by Jo or one of her other girls.

"Someone said you were here earlier, with Miss Josephine."

Thaddeus nodded, not about to get into a discussion of his private business.

"This lady," he gestured with his head toward Ellie, "is with me. Can we get a bath and wait for Jo . . . I mean, Miss Josephine in her room?"

Pete shrugged. "'S all right with me." And with raised eyebrows, he held up an empty glass.

Thaddeus nodded, appreciating the bartender as a man of few words and no questions. In one gulp, he drank down the whiskey Pete poured for him. Now to extricate Ellie from her admirers.

"Excuse me, gents," Thaddeus said, insinuating himself between the men and Ellie's stool. "This lady is going upstairs with me."

A murmur raced around the room, along with a few protests and a wolf whistle or two.

"Now, see here, son," began an older man sitting closest, "we hadn't rightly decided with whom this gentle creature was sharing her favors."

"Sharing my favors?" Ellie repeated, then she blushed, realizing she'd got herself into the middle of a sticky situation.

"That's right, little lady," said another man, kicking out his chair and standing tall and broad. "Maybe she's going upstairs with me." He looked at Ellie with a wolfish smile that curdled

Thaddeus's insides. "I can handle a woman like you and be back down for the next round of drinks."

Thaddeus wasn't sure that was something the man should be boasting about, but since the fellow had fists like hams, he could say anything he damn well pleased.

Sighing mightily, Thaddeus didn't intend to get involved in a ridiculous bar fight, not at the end of the long day he'd had. At least, not with his fists. Hoping Pete would forgive him for any damage, he pushed his coat aside to reveal his double-action six shooter.

Ellie's voice cut through the mutterings. "My husband is quite correct, gentlemen. I *am* going with him."

Thaddeus thought his ears must have stopped working right. It was the first time she'd willingly brought up the ruse of him being her husband. And it sounded damn good.

Instantly, the mood in the saloon changed. Even these men who paid for sex as easily as they paid for a beer respected the sanctimony of marriage. They looked at Thaddeus with newfound respect and relaxed their postures. The ham-fisted man sat back down, but he wore a sour, defeated look on his ruddy face.

Then she ruined the calm moment: "Besides, I wouldn't share a bed or anything else with any one of you, not simply because you bought me a drink," she said, scowling at one man, "or because you loaned me a rough handkerchief."

She tossed the aforementioned item at the older man, and it settled over his balding head.

"Why, I've never seen such a group of desperate delinquents in my—"

As every chair in the place scraped back and the men stood as one, Thaddeus clamped a hand over her mouth. How else could he stop the rant that could get them both beaten up? He could shoot her, he supposed.

CHAPTER TEN

"Sorry, gents. My wife is feebleminded. Why else would she have gone swimming in the river and made me dive in to rescue her?"

Thaddeus half dragged, half carried her away from the men's mostly pitying gazes. A couple of them, such as Ham-fists, glared angrily, so Thaddeus kept her constrained until they reached the stairs. Then he lifted his hand from her mouth.

"How dare you?" she shrieked.

"How dare *I*?" *God give him patience.* "How dare *you*? You almost caused a fight, for no good reason."

She stamped her foot right on his booted one, then headed up the stairs ahead of him, even though she had no idea where she was going. Over her shoulder, she questioned him.

"Shouldn't you have been willing to fight for my honor?"

"Your honor?" He rolled his eyes behind her back. "Darlin', the fight wouldn't have been about that. It would've been because you sauntered into a saloon, dressed like a soggy Jezebel, and toyed with a roomful of men until any one of them would've paid you good money for a few minutes of your time. Then you threw their honest appreciation right back in their teeth."

He passed her in the hallway and went straight to Jo's room. He hadn't told Ellie of his willing accomplice. Yet.

Lighting one lamp, then another, he turned as she entered the room after him. Despite everything, he couldn't help grinning at her appearance.

In the light, she was a disaster and he must be, too, for, after scanning him from head to toe, she smiled back.

"If I look as bad as you do, how could those men have wanted me?" She shook her head wonderingly.

He almost told her how. Those men had seen past the grime to the shapely woman beneath, and after her gown was off, they wouldn't be looking at the Mississippi mud anyway.

Instead he said, "I ordered a bath. Let me see if they've got it ready for us."

He left her standing in the middle of the room, and when he came back, she hadn't moved.

"Why don't you sit down?" he asked.

She eyed him, then looked around pointedly. He wasn't sure if she thought herself too good to sit in a saloon girl's bedroom or if she considered herself too dirty.

"How did your bag get here?" she asked, spying it in the corner.

"I dropped it off earlier. I needed Josephine's help to rescue you. She provided a distraction on the riverboat."

Ellie nodded slowly. "That was *kind* of her."

Before he could say more, a rap on the open door announced two of the young boys who kept the saloon swept and who carried in their alcohol deliveries. Between them, they dragged a long narrow tin bathtub into the middle of the room. They left quickly and came back a few minutes later, each carrying two steaming pails, which they emptied into the tub. They dropped off two more for rinsing and some towels before leaving them in peace.

"Not quite as fancy as Stoddard's bath," Thaddeus remarked.

"It's fine," she murmured, although she still hadn't moved. "They're very accommodating here, for a saloon, I mean," she added, avoiding his gaze as he studied her through the steam rising from the partially filled tub.

Thaddeus nodded. It had cost him a few coins to secure hot water, but right then, all he could think about was how he was going to get through the next few minutes without begging. With Ellie unclothed . . .

"Why don't you go first?" he offered. "I'll go downstairs and get a drink."

"No," she said sharply. "I mean, don't go. I'd feel more at ease if you stayed. I keep thinking the Indian or that Blackheart man is going to pop up out of nowhere."

He nodded. She wasn't going to make this easy on him. But she'd been through a lot in a short time, and he must have seemed like the closest thing to security she had left.

"I'll just turn my back," he offered. And he did, swiveling around and taking a seat on the edge of Jo's black trunk to keep the bedding clean.

She laughed. "You've seen it all before, Thaddeus, but I appreciate the gesture."

He smiled to himself as he stared at the wallpaper, consisting of stripes of red poppies he'd never noticed before. But his senses remained on high alert, and his mind imagined everything she was doing behind him.

He heard her undress, the dancing girl's gown rustling against her before falling with a moist thud to the floor. He imagined Ellie's toes testing the water before she climbed into the tub. Listening to her splashing a moment, he could easily picture the water sliding over her smooth skin, and he gritted his teeth to stop himself from turning to look.

In a few minutes, he heard her stand up, imagining her rising like a goddess whom he'd seen in an illustrated book, water dripping off her firm, round breasts. He swallowed. *Don't turn around,* he repeated to himself.

"I'm just going to use one more pail-full to rinse my hair again." She sighed. "You don't want to pour it over my head for me, do you?"

His breath caught in his chest. "No," he croaked. "Not a good idea."

"Very well. I'll manage it myself."

After another couple of minutes, he heard her get out of the tub.

"I'm finished," she said from the other side of the room. "Sorry. The water is not very clear anymore."

"Are you covered?" His voice didn't sound like his own.

"Yes."

Gingerly, he turned, trying to keeps his eyes on her face, but practically against his will, his gaze swept over her. She'd used her towel to wrap up her hair and was clutching a medium-sized satin pillow from Jo's bed in front of her, but he could still see the flare of her hips.

"Christ Almighty, Ellie! I'm only human."

She shrugged, perhaps enjoying the power she held over him. She had to have felt him hard as a rock every time they were on that damned horse. She was playing with fire whether she meant to or not.

And he had a suspicious notion she meant to, torturing him simply because she could.

"There must be a robe behind the screen," he said, knowing his voice sounded rough. "Put something on. Anything!"

She hesitated. He knew how much Miss Eliza Prentice hated taking orders from anyone. But as soon as she moved behind the screen, he sighed and stripped off hurriedly. Then he looked at the brown water. At least it was still warm. It would do. Most of the mud was on his clothes anyway.

He eased into the bath, thinking it oddly intimate that her naked body had been submerged in the same water moments earlier.

"Get a grip," he muttered.

"What was that?" she asked, coming out wrapped in a clinging silk turquoise robe that was miles too long and which clearly outlined the shape of her body beneath. It was not much better than the pillow.

Despite being in water that was rapidly cooling, his shaft sprung to attention. If he could have sunk all the way under and hidden himself, he would have.

"Your turn to look away," he said, trying to sound casual.

She paused, and he thought she scanned the water, but it was too murky for her gaze to penetrate even if she had.

"I'm going to lie down and close my eyes," she said. "It's been a hellish long day."

She climbed onto Jo's bed and settled her head delicately on one of the pillows, after giving it a curious sniff. Thaddeus stared at Ellie lying in Jo's bed.

Man alive, but these were strange circumstances.

He finished up quickly, using the last pail of water she'd left him for a final rinse, making sure he'd removed all the mud from behind his ears, his neck, and his hair. Then he stepped out, grabbing for the second towel as he did. It was hardly big enough to wrap around his hips, but a glance over his shoulder told him Ellie's eyelids were already shut.

Opening the door, he whistled loudly, and in mere moments, the boys came scrambling up the stairs. He gave them each a penny, and while he pushed, they heaved, dragging the bath out into the hall. Jo would not have appreciated seeing that dirty water in the middle of her elegant, frilly room.

Pete could come help them from there, Thaddeus decided, yawning widely as he closed the door on the scene of silly boys and sloshing water. Looking at Ellie, sprawled peacefully asleep, her lips upturned in a small smile, he thanked God he'd wrested her from Stoddard. But as he gently climbed in beside her, still wearing the towel around his hips and trying to keep his distance without falling off the bed, he wondered who would protect her from him.

When his head sank into the pillow, utterly knackered, he realized he could safely sleep for the first time in days without the worry someone was going to put a bullet into him. Then he was out as swiftly as a candle flame in a strong wind.

Thaddeus awoke to a hand on his thigh. As he stirred, he imagined he was in his family's barn again, but then he felt the plushness of the bed under him and took in his surroundings by the light of midmorning. It was later than he'd intended to stay, but his body and brain still wanted to sleep. Then, gentle fingers grazed his thigh again, and the jolt of energy instigated by the soft touch, plus the instant surge of desire, made further sleep out of the question.

He turned his head to see Ellie's pale blue eyes blinking at him. She smiled sleepily and ran her palm up and down his leg. His towel had come off while he slept and was bunched up beside him. The robe she wore had fallen open, barely held on by a loose belt. He noticed his own hand already rested on her hip. It took little effort to raise it and run his fingertips over the flat of her stomach, then higher to the curve of each breast, one then the other.

He watched, fascinated, as her nipples hardened into rosy buds.

Rolling toward her, he captured her body under his before lowering his mouth for a tender kiss that deepened as his tongue slipped between her welcoming lips. Her tongue touched his, and he captured it, sucking on it, then backed off so he could nip gently at her lower lip. How he loved her bowed lower lip!

Ellie moaned softly and curled her arm up above her head, grabbing at the brass headboard, wrapping her hand around one of the rails. He glanced at it and froze, even as her lower body arched into his.

Jo's headboard! In a flash of memory, Thaddeus knew he'd seen Jo's hand, with her many silver rings, draped around that same headboard while they'd done the deed. *Hell, no!*

Jerking away from Ellie, disentangling himself as quickly as he could, he jumped off the bed as if he was on fire.

She sat up, frowning at his sudden exodus, especially as she was taking in the fully erect site of him.

He was practically hopping around the room, looking for his pants. Then he remembered he had a nearly dirt-free pair in his bag and hunched down to retrieve them.

"What's wrong?" she demanded, clutching the robe closed around her.

He didn't risk a glance at her again, not with her near nakedness and the image of her perfect breasts fresh in his brain.

"Not here," he ground out. "Not in that bed."

She got up, not as quickly as he had, but not slowly either. She looked back at the bed as if she would see something to explain his bizarre actions. Then she cinched the belt snugly at her waist as he continued dressing. He didn't know if she understood he'd slept there before while not doing much sleeping.

At that moment, the door sprang open, and seeing a vision in red and black, he felt even gladder he wasn't in the middle of intimate relations with Ellie.

"Teddy," Jo said by way of greeting, then she stopped mid-sentence, eyeing the blond woman in her room. In *her* robe.

Ellie eyed her right back.

"Who's this?" both women said at once.

Before Thaddeus could speak, Ellie demanded, "Why do you have my bag?"

It was clutched in Jo's gloved hand.

"*Your* bag? Well, dang!" Jo dropped it on the ground as if it might bite her. "Take it. I was given it, but it's empty anyway." Hand on her hips, she faced Ellie and demanded, "Why are you wearing *my* robe?"

Thaddeus spoke to Jo first. "She had to have something to wear," he explained. "This is an old friend of mine from Spring City. Eliza Prentice, the lady you helped me rescue last night."

Before he could say more, he saw Jo's eyes widen as her expression became a smirk.

"Eliza Prentice? Eliza Prentice *Stoddard*, you mean." She started to laugh.

Ellie's voice was frosty as she asked, "What is so funny?"

"Why, honey, I just spent the night with your husband."

Ellie opened her mouth, but nothing came out. Thaddeus's eyebrows disappeared practically into his hairline, and a wave of concern washed right over him.

"Jo, are you all right? You didn't do anything you didn't want to, did you?"

"Don't be ridiculous." She walked across the room and gave her bed a cursory glance, noting its rumpled state with pursed lips and an eyebrow raised at Thaddeus.

Sitting down, she removed her shoes. "I have to admit I was running out of ways to distract an entire boatload of people. Then Jack Stoddard took a liking to me. I sang for him. I even danced for him, and after that, we decided to get cozy in his cabin." Jo glanced at Ellie.

"He said he wanted to make me his riverboat queen, except he already had a wife. If only she'd stop escaping. And here she is."

Ellie remained speechless.

"Eliza Prentice, this is Josephine Holland." Thaddeus acknowledged a certain awkwardness now that both women were in the same room. "She provided distraction last night so I could sneak onto the boat undetected."

He looked at Jo again. "You did great, by the way."

She smiled. "Teddy, you know I can take care of myself. And Jack Stoddard, despite all the rumors of his ruthlessness, was quite the gentleman. And very generous."

Eliza snorted and rolled her eyes.

"What?" Jo asked, bristling.

"That man is a four-flushing cheat and a brute."

"Maybe you simply don't know how to handle a man," Jo said, peeling off her gloves and tossing them down beside her.

Eliza blushed, and a storm cloud of emotions crossed her face.

"Obviously, I'm not as experienced as you."

This was going to get ugly, Thaddeus thought.

"Ladies, please. Let's not argue. Everything worked out fine. I got Ellie out, and I didn't have to go back and rescue Jo, as I was fixing to. So, it was good all the way around."

Jo shrugged. "Nice to hear you care, Teddy."

"Stop calling me that," he said, but he was grateful when Jo leaned over and grabbed a cigarette out of her dish for herself and handed him one, too. She lit hers and his, and they both took a long drag before Jo offered one to Eliza. She shook her head sharply, looking away.

Jo shrugged again. "So, you enjoyed yourselves in my room last night?"

Thaddeus, discomfited by her remark, felt his skin warming with a blush of his own, and Eliza made a coughing sound of protest.

"We needed a place to *sleep*, Jo," he clarified, "and we're grateful. I'd like to compensate you, and then we'll be on our way."

"I told you, I went along for the amusement. I don't need your money. Besides, after last night," she reached up under her dress and pulled out a small purse she had tucked away, "I need it even less."

Eliza curled her lip in obvious distaste, and Thaddeus knew he'd better get her out of there before a fight ensued. It would be just like Ellie to become all high and mighty over Jo getting paid for sex.

Personally, he didn't see it as a problem. The woman was good at what she did and ought to be paid for her talents. But if a man didn't need her services, so be it. It seemed silly to be judgmental, but it wasn't the right time to argue the point or confess to Ellie he found her so desirable, he'd pay her a king's ransom if she asked him.

"Ellie needs something to wear," Thaddeus said, stating the obvious. "She had one dress, which Stoddard took from her, and I borrowed one off a dancing girl, but it's covered in mud."

"Indeed." She gave Eliza an appraising eye. "Let me see if I can find something I don't need anymore."

She disappeared for a few moments behind the screen while Eliza glared at him just for the sake of doing so. And then Jo returned looking satisfied.

"I left you a gown on the chair. With my blessing." She offered an extra-large smile.

"I appreciate it," Eliza said woodenly, visibly unhappy at being beholden to the woman who'd already aided in her rescue, and Thaddeus noted she didn't exactly thank her.

"Say nothing of it," Jo responded, waving her hand and giving all her attention to Thaddeus when Eliza went to change.

"Where are you off to?" Jo asked, getting closer and dropping her hand on his arm. "More importantly, how long before your next visit?"

Thaddeus didn't like where this was going. He certainly didn't want Ellie to know how often he'd visited Jo in the past.

"We're going to Boston," he said, dodging Jo's second question.

She hadn't missed the fact he wasn't traveling alone. But she wiped the frown off her face.

"You mean, I won't see you next month?"

That implied she saw him every month, which was a gross exaggeration. Wasn't it? He pondered a moment, hoping Ellie wasn't listening, but then he heard her exclaim aloud.

"Honestly!"

"What's the matter, honey?" Jo asked, settling even closer into Thaddeus's arms. With her leaning against him that way, he had no choice but to encircle her or get knocked back a step.

"You *know* what the matter is," Eliza called out from behind the screen. "I can't wear this."

"It's the only thing that will fit. We're not exactly built the same, you and I," Jo responded, her dark eyes gazing into Thaddeus's, while she squeezed her ample bosom against him so her breasts nearly burst from the top of her red dress.

"You did this on purpose," he heard Ellie say, right before his attention was captured by Jo, who abruptly kissed him full on the lips.

Stunned, he wondered at her sudden ardor. Even when they were being intimate, they never kissed, at least, not on the lips. In his peripheral vision, he saw Ellie emerge from behind the screen, and it dawned on him Jo was using him to hurt her.

Trying to pull away, knowing it made him look even guiltier, Thaddeus put his hands on Jo's waist to push her away. In turn, Jo laid a hand to his cheek, as if sharing a loving caress.

"What the hell, Jo?" he exclaimed.

She arched an eyebrow, no doubt enjoying herself.

"I was merely saying goodbye to an old friend," she said innocently. "After all, you never know when exactly you'll be back next time."

Thaddeus rolled his eyes and only then fixed his gaze on Ellie. His jaw dropped. If Jo's red dress was designed to tempt and distract, what Ellie wore now was intended to incite pure, unadulterated lust.

A skirt of gaudy violet, trimmed in cheap black lace, angled up from the back to expose most of her legs at the front. Cinching Ellie's waist was a bodice so sheer he could see the shadows under her breasts and cut so low, he could glimpse the very tops of her nipples.

"God Almighty!" he swore, realizing Jo's intention to humiliate Ellie with this overly suggestive getup. Jealousy, no doubt. Perhaps he'd miscalculated after all, by asking his occasional bed partner to help him rescue another woman.

Jo finally stepped away from Thaddeus and faced Ellie straight on, looking her up and down with an amused grin.

"But it's truly all I can spare. We working girls don't have clothes given to us by husbands. I have to earn every dress."

"On your back," Ellie spat out.

"And what of it? You've probably been on your back for free!" Jo said, giving it right back to her.

Ellie glanced at Thaddeus, and her cheeks reddened.

"That's what I thought," Jo said. "Now, everybody out. I need some sleep after my adventuresome night. Unless you want to join me, Teddy, for old time's sake." She shot him a smoldering glance.

Sassy to the end—that was Jo. But what was he going to do with Ellie dressed like that?

"Here," he said to her, "take my coat and—"

"Nonsense," Ellie said, drawing herself up and shooting Jo a look of haughty righteousness before addressing him again. "The dress fits me perfectly, and I can see how your friend here might have trouble getting into it, what with her rather corpulent figure."

She grabbed up her bag and started for the door.

"Are you calling me fat?" Jo demanded, but Ellie kept on walking.

Wordlessly, Thaddeus was urging her to do exactly that, keep going before a catfight broke out.

Jo turned to him. "Is she calling me fat?"

"No, darlin', don't be crazy." He stuck what was left of his cigarette between his lips, grabbed up his gun belt and his coat, and hoisted his bag onto his shoulder.

"I'll be seeing you, Jo. Thanks again."

He headed out after Ellie, expecting to feel something hit him in the back of the head.

CHAPTER ELEVEN

"Of all the impolite, uncouth, rude, bad-mannered, offensive, vulgar, rude—"

"You said rude twice," Thaddeus interrupted her tirade as they went through the saloon, catching the attention of every man there, most already fortifying themselves with drink before noon. Whistles and catcalls abounded, but Ellie didn't even break her stride.

"And I'll say it again. Rude! Your taste in women is downright dreadful." She stopped outside, tossing down her empty bag. "Now, where's our damn horse?"

"Ellie, please." He sighed. Arguing over Jo was not productive. "And don't swear. You sound crude." He puffed on his cigarette, and she glared at him.

"What?" he asked, ready for the next fight.

"You shouldn't smoke," she bit out between clenched teeth.

He sighed, purposefully taking a long drag before letting it out through his nose.

"And why is that?" he asked, unable to take her seriously in her present state of dress.

With her hands on her hips, her breasts thrust against the fabric and, hell, if she wasn't almost completely exposed standing in the streets of Keokuk.

Without asking her this time, he dropped his coat around her shoulders.

"Riley said smoking isn't good for you," she replied, slipping her arms into the long sleeves and beginning to roll them into cuffs to free her hands.

He scowled. "What did he mean by that?"

"He dissected a human lung, and he said the smoke had blackened it and filled it with gunk."

Gunk! Thaddeus swallowed before taking a deep breath, making sure he still could.

"Shit," he said at last. "Everyone does it. How bad can it be? I've heard some doctors use tobacco smoke to cure everything from headaches to stomach cramps."

Riley and his blasted medical opinions.

She shrugged. "Besides, I don't like the way it smells."

He stared at her, long and hard. *Women!*

Nonetheless, he tossed the cigarette to the ground, putting it out with the toe of his boot. *Didn't like the smell.* He didn't smoke for the goddamned smell but for the taste. Still, if Ellie didn't like it . . .

Blast! He was becoming like a tame dog.

"Stay here, I'll get Lucky." He began to walk away, then turned back. "Take this." He handed her his gun. "Just in case. I'll be back in a minute."

He could still hear her muttering as he walked away, and for the second time, he imagined something might hit him from behind. Women were dangerous creatures.

And torturous. As they started the next phase of their journey, seated close once more on their horse, Thaddeus's brain kept picturing what she was wearing under his coat. Even worse, his body was reliving how she'd responded to him, so warm and willing, in Jo's bed.

Looking heavenward, he attempted to get his mind off her body. Here he was, in broad daylight, once again heading for a train, this time with a scantily clad woman, and they were both wanted by one of the most dangerous men in the Midwest, who happened to be her husband.

And all he could think about was settling down somewhere and taking Ellie up on the honey-sweet invitation she'd offered when they'd awakened.

"I can't believe we've even made it this far," she said out of the blue, voicing what he was thinking.

They should have stayed put, if not at Jo's saloon, then somewhere else through the day and then traveled that night. Perhaps they still should, but the longer they stayed in the area, the tighter Stoddard's hold would become. If Jo hadn't kept Stoddard busy all night, they probably would have been captured already.

"I imagine every sane man thinks we're staying put, and that's why no one's after us. But we're on the wrong side of the river now, and we're gonna stay on the wrong side until we get up to Burlington. That'll take us a day. From there, we'll catch a train to Fort Wayne. If the Indian's following, he won't know if we've gone northeast to Toledo or southeast to Lima or even Columbus."

He shifted in the saddle, trying to get comfortable. "As far as they're concerned, we could be going anywhere. Except seeing how they found us last time, all the way in Panola, I guess Stoddard knows we're heading east."

He hated to admit it, but he felt mighty discouraged by how far they still had to go. And on top of that, they were on the west side of the Mississippi heading north.

"Why in God's name did my sister have to end up in Boston? It's the bloody edge of the world!"

He stayed quiet for a few minutes, then he added, "It's striking scenery up there, though, and Boston is an amazing city. You'll probably like it."

"If we stay free that long," Ellie said doubtfully. "Jack may have had some fun with your friend Jo, but he's madder than ever at me. And you, too, I'm sure."

"I don't get something," he said, trying to ease back a bit away from her, wishing, not for the first time, he'd paid for two horses. "If Stoddard took you as his wife to get your money and your property in Spring, which he basically can lay claim to with or without your presence, why is he trying to get you back so desperately?"

"He hurt me," she said, not answering his question, her voice small and angry.

His chest constricted at the thought, but before he could speak, she continued.

"My father told me never to stand for being treated badly, and I never have, except once."

She was silent for a moment, and he had the terrible realization that his taking her innocence in his barn when he was a drunken fool was the one time she'd been treated badly. She didn't bring the point home, so he wrapped his arms around her, damn the consequences of how antsy and frustrated it made him feel.

She hesitated. "After Jack locked me up the first time, before I escaped and cut my leg, he didn't treat me well. He seemed to be, as Jo said, a gentleman when we were on the train and playing poker, but when I couldn't pay, he showed a mean streak."

"I asked you before if he'd done anything to you."

"He didn't assault me," she said defiantly, "but he imprisoned me and withheld food and water at one point until I signed papers giving him my inheritance. He always threatened worse, but apparently, I'm not his type. Jo is."

"Good God, woman, don't tell me you're feeling sorry Stoddard prefers rounded brunettes to slim blondes. You're lucky he didn't force you."

"No, it's not that." She paused. "Anyway, do you?"

"Do I what?" he asked.

"Prefer rounded—oh, never mind, I don't know what I'm asking."

But he knew what she was asking, and it didn't help Jo had deliberately left Ellie with the image of him and her kissing while locked in an embrace. Or that Ellie probably knew Thaddeus had lain with Jo in the very bed they'd slept in. What a mess!

Eliza Prentice was his angel, cantankerous and willful, but still his angel, and different from any woman he'd ever met. He hated that she believed she didn't measure up. She did, and then some.

Should he blurt it out, how very much he admired her? He opened his mouth.

"Anyway, I took something of Jack's because I was so mad at him, and he's still looking for it."

Whoa! What were they discussing again? He focused on her words. *Took something of Jack's?* What would make him send out his men in force?

"What did you take?"

She seemed to be digging around in her cleavage. Thaddeus swallowed, peering over her shoulder to get a better look until she elbowed him. Still, he was burning with curiosity to see what she retrieved. She slipped something onto her thumb and then held her hand up for him to see.

At first, all he could see was the shimmer of sunlight and a brilliant flash on her hand, blinding him. Then, as she changed the angle, he saw it.

His pulse sped up. "Shit! You *are* insane."

She wore Stoddard's prized diamond ring. Everyone who'd ever met the man had seen it. When he played cards, he twisted it around and around his finger. And everyone knew Stoddard loved it, especially for having won it off some visiting German prince.

Ellie snatched her hand back. "He can have it back after he gives me my divorce. In fact, I don't want a divorce anymore."

"What?" Thaddeus jerked the reins, and Lucky whinnied.

"No, I want an annulment. Complete and utter. Like we were never married."

That made sense to him. But the ring. *Lordy, that ring!*

"He will hunt you down and skin you alive," Thaddeus said.

Ellie crossed her arms across her chest mutinously. "He's already hunting me down."

True. "How come I never saw it before?"

"I move it around. Sometimes I keep it in my bodice, sometimes in my hair, if my bun is tight enough, sometimes in my drawers. I'm sure that's why he had me strip on that infernal boat. He was looking for it."

"What did he say when he didn't find it? Wait. Where was it?" Thaddeus had a disturbing image of where she might have hidden it, even when naked.

"As luck would have it, it was in *your* bag at the time you tossed me on the train. So, you had it all along. And Jack wasn't too pleased he couldn't find it, but if he killed me, he knew he'd never retrieve his precious jewel." She looked down at the ring again.

"He was coming back to give me a thorough search after his gaming tables closed, but luckily for me, you arrived first, and Jo ended up having the particular pleasure of his company."

Capturing Ellie's hand, Thaddeus took a long, hard look at the ring. It was a beauty, but it wasn't worth dying for. Perhaps if he returned it to Stoddard, all other debts would be forgiven. Any reasonable man would be grateful.

There was his answer. Stoddard wasn't reasonable. He was crazy half the time and insane the rest.

He let her hand drop. At least he knew the real reason why she'd jumped off the train. Not because she didn't want to go to Charlotte's house without him, but because she'd put her security in his bag without telling him.

"Don't put that damn thing in my bag again. Understand?"

She nodded, slipped it off her finger, and tucked it back into her dress. He didn't think with the lack of material, it was the safest place, but that wasn't his problem. His problem was getting them to Boston without losing *her* again and then making sure Reed agreed to help get her legally un-married.

Riding all day, they stopped once for food, which they ate sitting in the tall grass outside of a town. He couldn't take her into a decent restaurant dressed like that. As it was, in the heat of the day, she'd needed to discard his coat, and Thaddeus had to look elsewhere than at her nearly see-through gown while they talked. Elsewise, his brain went entirely blank. In doing so, he learned about everything she'd been through in the previous year, and he told her a slightly whitewashed version of his own adventures.

If they hadn't been on the run for their lives, it would have been quite a pleasant picnic.

"I know we're doing things all backward, riding during the day, but maybe that's why this is working," she offered. "Jack wouldn't expect us out in daylight."

"You may be right." It was precisely what he'd been thinking. "Or we are just unbelievably lucky. But we will need to sleep eventually, and this horse can't go on forever."

He figured it was a calculated risk if they slept in a real hotel. After all, they were hours from Stoddard's boat, and they could have ridden in any direction. When the first chance came around dinnertime, he took it.

"Let's get a room. And I need a cigarette and a drink."

She wrinkled up her nose, but he ignored whatever she was taking offense to and secured a room for him and his "wife."

With the way she was dressed, though, Thaddeus was fairly certain the desk clerk, who couldn't keep his eyes off her, took her for a harlot. Not that he'd tell Ellie any such thing. She would fry his griddlecake to a crisp if she thought people were mistaking her for someone like Jo.

He led the way up two flights. "Sure glad I'm not carrying you. Not that you aren't light and all," he added, pushing open the door and letting her sashay past him.

While he lit the lamps against the deepening dusk, she glanced at the tidy bed and the cheerful curtains, the polished furniture and the clean braided rug.

"This is nice. It reminds me of Fuller's."

He laughed. "Why did you ever need to go into a hotel room in Spring City? You had a perfectly good house of your own."

She blushed. "I own it."

"Own what?"

"The hotel."

"Excuse me for being dense," he said, drawing the drapes before lying down on the bed and putting his hands behind his head, "but I thought Mr. Fuller owned Fuller's."

"Take off your boots if you're going to lie on that quilt, Thaddeus."

He started to lower his feet, then stopped himself.

"Darlin', a man in my position does not remove his boots unless he absolutely has to. I've had to make too many quick exits, and if I lost my boots every time, why, I'd be the sorest-footed man in America."

"*Hmph*," she said, acquiescing to his logic and continuing her examination of the room, picking up a lace doily from the dressing table, then replacing it.

He relaxed again. "So, how do you come to own Fuller's?"

"The same way I own nearly all of Spring."

She sighed and sat in the rocker in the corner, folding her hands in her lap.

He didn't like her being by the window, but since he'd already pulled the curtains, it was probably all right.

"Daddy helped the Fullers out when they couldn't pay the bank. Same story with the mercantile, Drake's barn, and with Riley's family."

"Riley?"

She nodded. "In that case, I had a bit of a personal interest, as you can imagine."

Thaddeus's whole body tensed at her personal interest in Riley.

"I stepped in to make my father buy out their mortgage and give the Dalcourts a break from the bank's threats."

"I suppose you couldn't let your fiancé lose his family home."

"You're right, even if I never had any intention of living there."

He raised an eyebrow at her questioningly.

"They don't have indoor plumbing, except a cold tap at the kitchen sink," she reminded him. "Can you imagine?" She shook her head in amazement.

"I mean, bathing in the middle of that . . . of Josephine's bedroom is one thing, on a single solitary basis which I hope never to repeat in all my livelong days. But a life of bathing in the kitchen in a tin tub?" She shuddered. "That would not be for me. No, sirree."

"So, you were betting on Riley making a lot of money as a doctor and building you a big modern house?"

She frowned. "No, silly, I have a lovely house, as you said. I didn't need another one."

"But you had your cap set for Riley, nonetheless."

"I had to. He made Papa feel as though I'd be all right. Riley was focused, knew what he would do with his life, and he was stable as a rock. Besides, you didn't offer me anything better."

"Me?" He almost sat up but willed himself to lie still. "I didn't even know I was being considered." He tried to make light of it.

She blushed. "You couldn't be, not really. Daddy didn't like the idea of you. I mean, not *you* exactly, but your lack of . . ."

"Prospects?" Thaddeus supplied.

"Something like that. He could only put his mind at rest after I got engaged to Riley."

"I see." It was starting to sound less as though Riley had been a choice of her heart, after all. He smiled. If only she knew how well he'd done financially, despite his lack of "prospects."

And despite how his fortunes had been up and down, he was about to come into something steady. Or he would, if he could get to his appointed meeting sometime before the turn of the goddamned century!

Breathe, he told himself. Tonight, he was going to let old grudges go. He was in a comfy hotel room with Ellie, who was dressed indecently underneath his coat. And that very morning, she'd offered herself to him.

Swinging his legs onto the floor, he stood up. Stretching his sore muscles, he considered what he wanted to tell her. Slowly, he got to his knees in front of her chair, leaning back on his heels and resting his hands on his thighs.

"Darlin', I didn't have much to recommend me to your father when I was eighteen. But now—"

She leaned forward, the coat gaping open, giving him an astounding view inside the front of her dress, right down to her navel, and she kissed him. Easy as pie.

He pushed her back into the chair and held her arms firmly on the armrests.

"Damnation, Ellie! Every time I go in for the first move, you beat me to it. Let a man take control once in a while."

She didn't smile. "Let a man take control!" she scoffed. "I'll never do that again."

He figured she was referring to her father. Before his illness, Elijah Prentice was considered the type of man who would manage ants at a picnic. Thaddeus could imagine the restrictive rein he kept on his only daughter.

Yet Thaddeus was not Elijah. He didn't want to control her every move. In fact, he was quite interested to find out what she was like when she wasn't on the run and in fear for her life. However, by the look on her face, he'd gone and said precisely the wrong thing.

"If you don't like my kiss, just say so. In fact, why don't you see if they have another room?" she said, tossing her tangled hair over her shoulder. "I'm sure between the two of us, we can afford it. Or you can find some whore to bunk with for less money than a hotel room, I'll warrant."

He sighed and returned her glare with a level gaze of his own. *Why was she going all uppity on him now?* Instinctively, he knew she was scared of something.

"I'm not going to go find another woman, and I liked your kiss just fine. But I swear you are the most difficult, orneriest woman I've ever met." *And desired,* he wanted to add. "Why are you so ill-tempered?"

She flounced as well as any female ever did while trapped in a chair.

"What have I got to be so darned happy about? My mother died when I was three—"

"Lots of people lose their parents. I did," he interrupted.

"You were a heck of a lot older when that happened. And you had Charlotte. I had no siblings and an elderly father who scared everyone in town. Folks would look at me and say, 'There's that Eliza Prentice, so stuck-up,' even when I wasn't doing anything but walking down Main Street. People only tolerated me for my father's money, and frankly, that can wear on a person."

She struggled against his hold. "Difficult and ornery, indeed! I had nothing else but my temper and my snappish reputation."

"You had *me*." That slipped out without him thinking it through, but it didn't win him back her lovely smile. Quite the opposite.

"You had sexual relations with me and forgot!" Her tone resonated with scorn, but she stopped fighting him.

He puffed out his cheeks and then expelled his breath. This was not going well. How could he start over? He couldn't.

CHAPTER TWELVE

Thaddeus released his grip on her arms. "Ah, hell, Ellie. I was drunk."

"I thought I loved you." The words were out of her mouth in a rush, and her eyes widened as if she wished she could retrieve them. Then she crossed her arms and glowered at him again.

What could he say? She thought she'd *loved* him? Unlikely, though he could believe she felt something for him, they'd had so much fun together, flirting and laughing. *But love?* She was looking at it now through the misremembered haze of years gone by and ruffled emotions.

Still, it felt good to know all the time he was fantasizing over this beautiful girl, she'd had feelings for him, too.

He had to ask: "And now?"

She shook her head, managing to look disdainful and delectable at the same time. "And now I don't."

Hm! He wasn't so sure her feelings for him were all gone.

"So, if I kiss you, you wouldn't enjoy it?"

She paused, as if considering, but then the smallest of smiles played across her lips.

"I didn't say that. I'm a woman, after all."

"And if I took you in my arms and pulled you close."

She laughed at him. "I'd slap you."

He leaned in closer.

"And if I tossed you on that bed, undressed you, and made love to you?"

She stopped laughing. "Thaddeus, I have no doubt you could do what you say. I also know many folks think you capable of doing so. After all, your reputation is that of a rascal, at least a bit of one. But I know you'd never do anything against my will. I trust you with my life and my virtue. I always have."

He sighed. He'd already dallied with her "virtue" and apparently made an absolute hash of it. And he supposed he was worse than a cad to attempt anything again.

"Sweet Jesus, Ellie! You take all the fun out of it."

She cocked her head. "Oh, not all the fun, surely?"

She was teasing him after all. Her eyes danced like pale blue flames, inviting, flirting with him. Perhaps his advances wouldn't be unwelcome.

He moved closer until he could feel her breath on his mouth. Slowly, keeping his eyes on hers in case she got angry and hauled off to slap him as she'd threatened, he kissed her. Not too hard, not too soft, merely to tell her that he meant business.

After a moment, she returned the kiss, increasing the pressure against his mouth, then voicing a sensual sound that fired his blood.

He lifted his head and leaned his brow against hers. All the air seemed sucked out of the room. At least, he was having trouble drawing any into his lungs, and by the look on her face, she felt it, too. After a moment, however, he felt her tense as if she were putting on armor, like she'd done the day he nearly walked out on her at the Grindels' boarding house.

She sat up taller, which caused him to draw back.

"Unlike yourself, Thaddeus, I've been lonely a long time."

He assumed she was referencing him having had relations with Jo, and naturally, she presumed there were other ladies with whom he'd fornicated. And of course, she was excusing herself from reacting to his kiss. She turned her head away.

"Even before Riley fell in love with Sophie Malloy," Ellie said, not looking at him, but at some distant memory playing out over his right shoulder, "I knew I was not what he wanted. It's like being second best before there was a first best."

Her voice held not a trace of self-pity. "He and I had an understanding about getting married, but we didn't share any passion. Not like what sparked between him and Sophie. As soon as my father died, I let Riley go. And there's been no one since."

He was elated she hadn't had feelings for anyone since Riley. However, there was so much wrong with everything else she was saying, he didn't know where to start. He began by taking her hand and telling her the truth.

"I never thought you were second best." He could have added, "I've loved you since forever," but he wasn't about to make a fool of himself in front of her, not while she was being so volatile.

She looked at her hand in his, then up at his face. "I believed you were my friend at the very least, but then you stopped speaking to me."

"When you got engaged to Riley, I lost two friends," he confessed, his voice gruff, remembering again the anguish of his youthful heart. "I couldn't stand being in Spring City or laying eyes on either of you. My sister wondered for years why I never went home, or almost never."

He'd been a coward when it came to the raw, painful feelings that came up at the sight of Ellie and Riley.

"Because of me?" she asked.

He nodded. *So much for not making a fool out of himself.*

"I had no idea you cared for me like that, especially when you said nothing after we . . . you know, in your barn."

He groaned. How much had that damned whiskey cost him? But she had to know she was absolutely in a class by herself. And if she didn't, he would make sure she understood.

He lifted her hand to his lips and turned it over, searing her palm with a kiss. He heard her gasp.

"I think I behaved even worse after that night," she said, "and the funny thing is people let me get away with behaving terribly. The more they accepted from me, temper-wise, the more I knew they didn't care a dang about me, and the worse I got."

She reached out and touched his hair, which seemed to Thaddeus a most intimate act.

"Except for you," she added, "and then, after you were gone, Riley. It didn't matter what I did or said, he always saw through it. He was so patient. That infuriated me, actually. The man was like a saint."

Thaddeus didn't want to hear any more about Saint Riley. Leaning closer, he caught her gaze.

"I'm not such a patient man, darlin'."

Standing up, he drew her to her feet before kissing her again. He could feel his blood pulsing erratically through his body. Pulling away, he hoped he could see understanding in her crystalline blue eyes.

"I wish I hadn't been such an absolute imbecile the night of the dance. If I could take it back and do it over, I would."

She nodded, but he wasn't sure if she was agreeing or simply being kind. Maybe, given the opportunity, she wouldn't do it over, not with him, not at such a young age, even if he had been sober.

Breaking away, she went to the washstand and poured some water in a bowl. She used the clean towel hanging on the stand to dab at her face. It took a moment for him to see she was crying faintly and trying to hide it. Then she dried her face and turned to him.

"So much of my life, wasted," she said bitterly.

At first, he didn't know how to respond, except to comfort her. Closing the space between them, his eyes never leaving hers, he ran his thumb along her smooth cheek and then over her full lower lip, which he could feel trembling. He ended by holding her chin in his hand and making her look at him.

"Any life that brought us to this point, right here, can't have been wasted. And right now, there's no place I'd rather be than in this hotel room with you. I'd like to make up to you any squandered time. If you'll let me?"

He left it as a question. *Would she let him?* Holding his breath, he counted the seconds with each hopeful beat of his heart.

For an answer, Ellie turned her face into his palm and kissed it, as he had done hers. The sensation of her lips on his skin made him catch his breath. Then she released him.

He slipped both of his hands beneath his coat, which she still wore, and circled his fingers at her waist, pulling her against him, then lifting her high against his body until he had to look up at her.

She stared down at him with bright, expectant eyes and a small smile on her perfect lips.

Deliberately, slowly, he slid her down his front, letting her feel his hard physique against her pliant, soft one. She rested her hands on his shoulders as he brought her face even with his, then he claimed her mouth again.

When at last, he set her down so her feet touched the ground, he deepened the kiss and felt her hands slide from his shoulders to his chest, her fingers curling into the fabric of his shirt.

Intoxicated by her, he groaned, pulling back enough so he could look down into her eyes.

"Yes," Ellie whispered, in case he was still in any doubt.

And just like that, a weight lifted from his shoulders. Riley was long out of the picture and although she legally had a husband, she didn't want Stoddard any more than she wanted a wart on her chin. In that moment, they had only each other to worry about or to please. And he intended to please her. He started by slipping his coat off her shoulders and sending it flying across the room.

Before he could pull Ellie close again, however, she danced out of his reach, grasping her purple skirt between her fingers and looking down at herself. His gaze followed.

"Let me get out of this dress," she said. "I've felt like a strumpet all day."

"You look like a princess in whatever you wear," he avowed, "but later, I'll find you something else to travel in."

He trailed off as she untied the silken sash at her waist and slipped the scandalously transparent gown off her shoulders. It hung a moment on her hips and then fell to the floor, along with the diamond ring, which made a clinking sound as it dropped, rolled, and came to rest by his feet.

He expelled his breath in a rush and couldn't seem to draw in another. She was naked. Stark naked in front of him. Then perhaps out of shyness, perhaps out of eagerness, she stepped from the pile of clothing and moved right up against him, circling her arms around his neck. It was the most sinfully arousing experience he'd ever had—Ellie, absolutely bare, and him, fully clothed.

He ran his hands over her shoulders, down her arms, across her back, and then came to a halt by cupping her buttocks and pulling her snugly against his rigid shaft.

For long minutes, they did nothing but kiss. Then he set her back and looked down at her.

"You are so perfect," he whispered, rubbing his thumbs across her nipples, which pearled in response.

"I always thought you were, too," she said matter-of-factly, giving him the cutest of bowed smiles, and her hands went to his shirt, unbuttoning and sliding it open. He pulled it from his waistband and shrugged out of it, then reached for her warm, silky skin.

"I love your calloused hands," she said visibly shivering as he skimmed his palms over her hips and up her body once more.

"I love your soft ones," he countered, and she ran them across his chest while he thought of other places he'd like her to touch.

As if reading his mind, she slipped her fingers down over his taut stomach to his gun belt and unbuckled it. He caught it before it hit the floor, lowering it down and nudging it out of the way with the toe of his boot. Then he wished he'd done as she'd asked earlier and removed his boots, for now he had to stop and do so, hopping around as he pulled them off before tossing them aside.

As soon as he stood before her again, she began unfastening his fly. Her unpracticed hands trembled, but he was helpless to do anything more than watch. Fascinated at seeing her slender fingers stripping him, he had dreamed of this a hundred times.

In moments, his arousal sprang free, proudly standing out like a single-barreled shotgun, and she hesitated. At that point, he tugged his pants the rest of the way down and stepped out of them. Pressing the length of his body against hers again, he dropped his head to the satin skin of her neck and nuzzled it.

"I want to feel you inside of me again," she said, "like in the barn."

He lifted his head at her and raised an eyebrow.

"No, I mean the first time. In *your* barn. Not in the last barn, when we only touched."

"Maybe we should give up on barns and vow to make love in beds from now on."

Was there going to be a "from now on"? For his part, he assumed there would be and welcomed the assumption.

She turned pink and smiled sweetly. "I don't know. Let's see if I like it first."

Growling at her playful words, Thaddeus swept her off her feet and laid her gently in the middle of the bed. Straddling her hips, he looked down at her body and grinned.

"What?" she asked.

"Better than looking down at Lucky."

She started to struggle in outrage.

"I'm only jesting, Ellie. Lie still. We're making up for lost time, remember?"

She quietened, eyes big, staring, watching, waiting.

At last, the woman of his dreams lay completely exposed beneath him. He almost didn't know where to start. Almost. Fortunately, his instincts took over.

After allowing himself the indulgence of gazing uninterrupted on her upturned breasts and dusky pink nipples, which had been playing peekaboo all day at the top of Jo's shocking gown, he reached out to touch her with his fingertips.

From the hollow at her throat, down between her breasts, he traced feathery touches over her silken skin.

She arched off the bed as he slid his hands lower, across the flat of her stomach to her small navel that begged to be kissed. Why not? Right then, she was his.

Moving down her heated body, he slipped his arm under her back, splaying his fingers across her spine to hold her in position. Then wickedly, he flicked his tongue into her navel, feeling his groin tighten as she murmured some indiscernible sounds.

Licking a trail from her navel, down to her silken thatch, he halted when suddenly her hands fisted in his hair, tugging him upward, at the same time as her body stiffened.

Hm. She wasn't yet ready for such a pleasurable intimacy. He'd give in this time, but eventually, she would let him feast on her. He just had to take it more slowly.

Still, he needed to have his mouth on her skin. Working his way upward, he kissed her flat stomach and the underswell of each breast, before nuzzling the valley between them.

She fairly purred and stretched her arms up over her head.

He took advantage of her breasts thrusting up at him. Her nipples, already puckered from his regard alone, now turned to pebbles as he lowered his mouth. He circled one pink bud, flicking it with his tongue, making her breath catch before he teased her with his teeth.

Feeling her pelvis arch under him, he suckled in earnest at the stiffening peak.

"Thaddeus," she murmured his name. "Don't stop."

He had no intention of doing anything so idiotic. He simply moved his sensual ministrations to her other nipple, relishing her throaty sounds of appreciation. When she wrapped her fingers in his hair again, this time she anchored him there, making him chuckle against her skin.

"I've wanted to kiss your breasts like this forever," he said, nuzzling her shoulder.

She giggled, giving him the invitation he needed to lower his head once more and lick the shadowed valley between her peaks.

Unhurriedly, he dropped his hand to the smooth skin of her stomach, trailing his fingers down between their bodies before resting his palm over her womanly core. Instantly, she pressed back. Feeling her desire and dampness, he couldn't refrain from stroking her.

Are you sure you want to do this? he nearly asked, but managed to stop himself from uttering such a stupid question.

Her breath came in hard draws, and the lightest sheen of moisture graced her upper lip. Her pupils looked bigger and darker to him than they ever had, and she bit her lower lip. If ever a woman looked like she wanted him, Ellie did.

Easing himself between her parted thighs, he felt her soft curls against his lower belly as he placed open-mouthed kisses down her throat. He wanted to take it slowly and do it right—especially since she'd carried a memory, as she said, for years of some terribly quick grappling that probably in no way came close to satisfying her. It was a wonder she wanted to do it again at all. Ever.

He intended to do much better this time.

She moaned as his finger dipped into the slickness at the juncture of her thighs and his lips grazed the sensitive skin of her neck. Her head bowed gracefully back, her eyes closed.

He smiled. Definitely doing better. And he was burning every moment of this seduction into his brain so he'd never forget a second of it.

He stroked her again, one finger delving lightly between her soft petals, until she began to shudder. So sensual, so ardent, she was close to climaxing, as she'd done in the hayloft. This time, he intended to be deep inside her when she did. Raising himself up, he seated the head of his shaft at her opening.

"Open your eyes," he commanded.

She did so, her blue gaze locking with his green one.

"Just while I enter you, darlin'."

It wasn't that he thought she would forget who was making love to her, but he wanted to see inside her at the precise moment when they joined, the same moment he'd squandered so carelessly years earlier. He intended to imprint this memory more forcefully than whatever he'd done with her before.

Pressing his hips forward, he eased into her snug passage, still unsure he could have been there before, so tight was she.

"Are you sure we did this?" he managed to grind out, scarcely making any progress, as above all, he didn't want to hurt her.

"Thaddeus," she said, "Shut. Up."

He didn't smile, although he wanted to. He continued to enter her gradually, despite her grasp on his arms urging him to move faster. At last, he was seated in her so deeply, their hips were pressed together.

Trying hard not to put all his weight on her, he rolled slightly onto his left shoulder so he could get his hands under her rear end and tilt her, adjusting the angle so they were even more closely melded. As he did so, she sighed.

"That's good," she murmured.

"We're not done yet," he said into the crook of her neck, beginning to pull slowly out of her.

"Thaddeus?"

Oh, God, was she going to start giving him orders?

"*Hm,*" he said, against her neck.

She ruffled his hair. "We can't look into each other's eyes unless you lift your head up."

She *was* still directing him. He grinned. That was Eliza Prentice!

Licking the skin at her throat, he made her gasp again. Then he raised himself up to rest on his forearms.

"All right, woman," he said, ducking to kiss her lips before lifting his head and looking her squarely in the eye. "You can look right at my face while I make love to you."

He pulled out unhurriedly, watching the spark flare in her eyes. She was so snug, it seemed her female passage was tugging him back. It was exquisite. When he was nearly crowning, he reversed direction and slid back along her sensitive tunnel.

She bit her lip and spoke no more. But she panted and then she moaned, and when he used one hand to stroke her swollen nubbin between their bodies, she cried out with pleasure. He was thrusting steadily by this time, feeling a sheen of sweat on his back.

All the years slipped away, and he and Ellie were right where he'd always wanted them to be. He quickened his pace, gliding in and out of her, feeling her body respond, watching her breasts dance tantalizingly with each of his thrusts.

Her body tensed and her eyes darkened, or so it seemed, and she parted her lips, sucking her lower one into her mouth, biting it.

He was captivated by each tiny movement and every sound she made, by everything her body was doing. Compelled to kiss her again, he realized he'd never made love to a woman while kissing her, never felt her climax around him while his lips were sealed to hers.

All at once, her eyes fluttered closed and he felt her stiffen, then her body clenched around his shaft, squeezing and rippling, until he saw glorious stars. He wanted her to be totally gratified before he let himself go, although it was getting harder by the second to maintain control.

At last, when her trembling peaked and began to subside, he surged into her again, sheathing himself in Ellie's heat for a few seconds longer. Then he pulled out of her warmth and spilled his seed in an arc beside them on the bed.

His body entirely spent, he slumped beside her and gathered her in his arms.

For a moment, he could pretend they weren't in some strange hotel room. They could be in his barn in Spring City, and this could be their first time. It had been as damn near perfect as he'd ever had.

"You OK?" he asked.

She had a satisfied honeyed smile on her face, and her fair hair spread around her. Angel and vixen.

"You were right," she murmured against his chest. "This was nothing like the first time."

He smiled against her hair. He would take that as a yes.

CHAPTER THIRTEEN

Thaddeus desperately wanted to stretch his arm, which was pinned under Ellie, but he waited another excruciating ten minutes before he pulled free and sat up. Their bed enveloped him in coziness, but he was getting too comfortable, practically drugged by the heady sensation of sleeping next to her naked body.

He needed to remember they were in danger, and she was in reality another man's wife—an angry, powerful man, at that.

He also needed a breath of air and a bracing drink!

As quietly as possible, he slipped on his clothing, but when he placed his hand on the doorknob, she spoke.

"Where're you going?"

He sighed. "Go back to sleep, Ellie. I'm just going for a walk."

"Wait, I'll get dressed and come with you."

No, he needed to be alone. *Didn't he?* A part of him, maybe too big a part, wanted to slip back into the bed, hold her warm, pliant body against his, and never let go. But that wasn't realistic. He had to think and have a drink and maybe a smoke.

"I should stretch my legs before we get on Lucky again," she said, sounding perfectly reasonable.

He was completely responsible for her safety, for getting her to Boston, for ensuring she stayed alive, for returning Stoddard's ring to him. He'd never been responsible for anyone or anything before in his life—and he felt downright terrified.

Turning around, he sounded harsher than he meant to when he spoke.

"Good God, woman, let a man have some freedom."

Her eyes widened, but she didn't meekly settle back into the bed, chastised.

"Freedom is it?" She sat up, gathering the sheets and clutching them around herself. "Why doesn't that surprise me? You've taken my virginity. Twice!" she added with a hiss. "And now you need some *freedom*! Where was that freedom a few hours ago when you were all over me like a snake's skin?"

"You can't lose your virginity twice!" he corrected. As soon as he did, seeing her start to seethe, he knew it was a stupid mistake.

Sighing, he wondered why he hadn't simply pretended not to have heard her and walked out?

"Oh!" She tossed a pillow at him with as much force as she could muster.

He laughed. That was wrong, too. She looked so beautiful with her hair mussed and her eyes blazing angry at him. But no way was he going to wait while she dressed and fixed her hair and asked him a million questions.

And he didn't really want to take a walk. He wanted a drink.

"Darlin', I am going out this door. Alone."

"Good. Why don't you just stay out! Don't bother coming back."

He rolled his eyes. "I'll be back. Don't you worry."

Closing the door on her still furiously muttering to herself, he felt uneasy. Women were delicate creatures and he'd handled that badly, but he had no idea how he could've made it any better and still got out by myself. He'd noticed The Wagon Wheel saloon on the next block when they'd entered town, so now he made a beeline for it. So much for fresh air.

Rejuvenated by his first sip of whiskey, Thaddeus wondered at his need to escape the hotel room. If he'd stayed even another instant, with her fizzing at him like an angry bumblebee, he'd have leaped back in bed and rolled her under him—she looked so unbelievably appealing. *Why did that scare him, too?*

He took another sip. He had to fight the hold she had on him. But why fight? Because the alternative was surrender, giving in to her power to control him and to hurt him.

Yup, that was a lot scarier than taking a bullet.

Two stools down, hunched over the bar, sat a man in a stained hat, an old cowboy maybe, who looked like he'd been bending his elbow at the bar for hours. Thaddeus had never been that way, except for the first time he'd gone for a drink after leaving Spring City and Ellie and Riley behind. Then he'd sat in a saloon in Denver, getting all roostered up with whiskey and trying to forget his dreams.

When he'd awakened in an alley with no recollection of having got there and with all his money gone, he knew it wasn't the right path for him. Since then, he drank in moderation, never in excess, and usually in good company while playing cards.

Tonight, however, he enjoyed being by himself, and he didn't feel like gambling. He knew he'd be no good at poker, not with his head full of one ornery woman and a host of distractions.

Ellie was everything he'd always believed her to be: smart, witty, sometimes crabby, mostly good company, and as appealing and passionate as any woman he'd ever had the privilege of knowing. Only more so. He almost groaned out loud thinking how it had been to finally take her as his own.

Except she wasn't his. The constant companionship and the pretense of being married had made him think of her that way, but she wasn't. More to the point, he didn't want her to be his, did he? *His* worry, *his* responsibility, *his* to look after.

If she became his woman, did that mean spending every waking hour stuck together?

True, being on Lucky was abnormally close quarters, and under normal circumstances, it wouldn't be like that. He didn't think so, anyway. But he didn't know for sure, never having had anything other than brief encounters with women who were not the type you married.

He realized he'd drained his drink without noticing, and he signaled for another, tamping down the notion Ellie wouldn't approve. Tamping it down, but feeling guilty all the same.

See, that was exactly the type of thing he didn't want to get used to, someone telling him what to do. *Blasted woman!*

"What'd you say, son?"

Thaddeus realized he must have spoken out loud. He looked over at the old cowboy who was now directing his watery gaze at him.

"Sorry, I'm talking to myself."

"Don't apologize. Sometimes yourself is the only one worth talking to."

He was slurring, but Thaddeus nodded, acknowledging the man's words, and turned away.

"Woman problems?" the cowboy asked after a moment of silence.

"What?"

"I say, you got problems account of some woman?" The man turned toward him, his whole body saying he was ready for a good ol' heart-to-heart.

"Not really." Thaddeus didn't want to talk to this stranger about Ellie. She'd given him the gift of herself, and any complaining he did was beyond disloyal. He ought to be on his knees thanking her for the best sexual experience of his life.

He set down his empty glass and started to get up.

"Bring my friend here another," said the cowboy.

He couldn't refuse a man who bought him a drink. That was the code of the saloon whether in California or Nebraska or . . . Where the hell was he anyway? Iowa or Illinois?

"I thank you kindly," Thaddeus said, getting comfortable again on his stool.

"No need. I was young and some say handsome once. I had my share of the ladies. And they made sure to get a piece of me." He chuckled for half a second and then grew somber. "But I married one by mistake. What a piece of work! You married?"

"No, sir."

"Good. Stay that way. You hear me?" The cowboy fixed him with a hard stare.

"Yes, sir."

"Well, were you planning to marry before you ran into me and my words o' wisdom?" He looked dead serious. "Were you?"

Thaddeus took a swallow to let the liquid burn a trail down his throat, except it had stopped burning. He knew that meant he'd had enough. But the cowboy was only being sociable. No one was beating each other at cards or trying to get the upper hand. This was just good, friendly talk, and the older man was helping him sort out his thoughts and giving him some good advice.

He pondered Ellie and how she'd tried to keep him in the room so he couldn't go meet the cowboy. Or at least, that's how it seemed now. Why wouldn't she want him to talk to the cowboy? The man was his friend. She was so damned controlling. Thaddeus shook his head.

"No, sir. The last thing on God's green earth I'd ever want is to tie myself down to the likes of the hellcat I got waiting for me in my hotel room."

He slapped his hand on the polished bar for emphasis, but then he paused. *Was that true?* He frowned. He loved her, didn't he? He'd always loved her. But he remembered hardly being able to take a breath and how his heart felt squeezed in his chest when she'd chosen Riley over him.

She'd hurt him so badly, right when he was going to confess his love to her at the tender age of eighteen.

Ellie had considered him a worthless piece of shit, cow crap, not good enough. Never good enough. The sole reason she was with him now was only because he could help her. Everyone knew Riley wasn't anywhere near as good with a gun, and as far as Thaddeus recalled, Riley had never jumped on a boxcar in his life.

"Is that so?" said the cowboy, interrupting his wildly ranging thoughts. "I know a thing or two about hellcats. You gotta tame 'em, if possible. Show 'em who's boss. And if you can't, you gotta let 'em go. If'n you don't, a woman'll eat you up, your land and your house and everything. And don't forget your heart. If you got one, she'll want it. And she'll eat that, too."

The man was mumbling more now, facing his drink again, talking more to himself than to Thaddeus.

Thaddeus stared. He didn't intend to end up broken and bitter like the cowboy. He couldn't let Ellie get under his skin.

"I've *always* been free," Thaddeus proclaimed, "like the *mestengo*, you know?"

The cowboy nodded at his words but didn't look at him.

Thaddeus continued, "You've seen them running, the wild horses. They're so beautiful."

Why did the notion of a mustang bring Ellie to mind, with her hair flowing and her velvety soft skin? He shook his head. *He* was the free-roaming horse, not her.

"I like my life the way it is, and I want to stay a mestengo until the end of my days."

"Unless something better comes along," said the cowboy, looking into his glass.

"Unless something better comes along," agreed Thaddeus, like, for instance, Eliza Prentice, the finest woman he'd even known.

Damn it! She'd just told him not to bother going back. After all he'd done for her! Got shot at and everything.

"But not that shrew in my room," he finished.

The cowboy put his head down beside his glass and closed his eyes, maybe lost in his own private misery. Thaddeus finished his drink. He wanted to put his head down, too, and sleep, but not there, not on a bar top. He'd get that fresh air after all, and then he'd go apologize to Ellie. He owed her one, but he couldn't think why right then. He couldn't think of anything much at all.

Thaddeus could hardly believe it when, without mishap, they purchased tickets and boarded an eastern-bound train the next day. He even ignored the long, perusing stare the ticket-seller gave both him and Ellie, chalking it up to him not having shaved and to her being so surefire beautiful. Perhaps the man thought them an unlikely pair, although she now wore a plain-spun cotton skirt and a white lady's shirt he'd bought at a mercantile near the hotel. At least she was dressed decently and had shoes that fit.

Together, they sat in their seats, each lost in thought.

"Better than a boxcar," he said, just to say something into the silence that had reigned all morning. Although in truth, he'd always found it perfectly acceptable to stretch out in one, take a rest, and ride for free.

Ellie didn't even acknowledge his words. She leaned away from him, her head resting against the cushioned seat back, not looking at him, not touching him.

When he'd returned to the room the previous night, with his head spinning and his mouth dry, he'd made sure she was still in the bed and hadn't run off in a fit of anger. Then he'd undressed and lay down beside her, sleeping fitfully if at all. Next thing he'd known, it was morning, a morning with an obviously peeved woman.

She remained silent now as had been the case since he'd awakened and found her already sitting in the chair, wrapped in his coat, waiting for him to go buy her some clothes. He'd also had to sell Lucky, which had made Ellie's lower lip quiver despite how she'd only shrugged when he'd told her.

He was determined to enjoy the train ride, chiefly because Ellie sat beside him, even if she didn't speak a word to him. He watched her watching the countryside go by, and after an hour, he relaxed, stretching his legs out in front of him and closing his eyes.

When he opened them, she was gone.

He jumped up. There was no way someone had come and abducted her, no way she'd been kidnapped again. Impossible!

He would have heard any kind of struggle. That meant she'd gotten up quietly and gone away on her own accord.

He looked across the aisle at a man reading a newspaper.

"Excuse me. Did you see my wife?" He was so used to saying it now, it came off his tongue and didn't even feel like a lie. "I fell asleep and—"

"Pretty lady," the man said. "She went that way." He pointed along the train toward the rear. That way was the dining car and the toilet stalls.

Sitting down again, he willed himself to relax. She wasn't his prisoner. She could go where she wanted, but he sure didn't like the antsy feeling of worrying about someone else. Not one bit. He stroked his three-day growth of beard and waited. He would give her five minutes, not knowing how long she'd been gone already.

He counted the time down in his head, since he'd long ago gambled away his only pocket watch and never saw the need to replace it. Two minutes. He kept counting and realized he was jiggling his leg anxiously and stopped himself, looking over at the man who was reading.

Thaddeus couldn't count and read the headlines, so he kept counting. Three and a half minutes. At four minutes, he stood up involuntarily, staring along the aisle toward the train's caboose. He had to fight the urge to start running.

And then, at four and a half minutes, the door to the compartment opened and in she walked—regal, smiling at people on both sides of the aisle, bending to talk to a little boy who was traveling with his family. As she straightened, she looked up and saw him. He caught his breath and felt he might melt like candlewax, right onto the train floor. She was that beautiful and that important to him. He slumped into his seat.

Ellie took her seat beside him. "Were you going somewhere?"

"Nope. Just stretching my legs," he lied.

"I didn't want to disturb you," she said and, once again, leaned away from him to look out the window.

He nodded and then added, "Next time, I'd appreciate you telling me where you're going." Was his tone gruff? He cleared his throat.

"All right," she agreed in clipped tones.

"We're still not in the clear, you know."

"I said all right, already. I won't even blink without telling you." She crossed her arms over her chest.

"You do that," he said, looking straight ahead at nothing, until he could stand it no longer. Something had changed drastically in her temperament between the night before when she'd been the teasing, laughing woman who'd let him make love to her and that morning, when she'd been distant, reserved, and cool.

"Is something wrong?" he asked finally.

She didn't answer immediately. In fact, it seemed as if she hadn't even heard him. Eventually, she turned from the scene she was viewing outside and glanced at him.

"What could be wrong?" she asked tightly.

"I don't know. That's why I'm asking." He crossed one booted foot over his knee and waited.

"Let's see. I'm married to a killer and traveling with a thief. I've been kidnapped and shot at, and I may have brought danger to my whole town, and I'm speeding directly toward the home of a woman who disdains me," she paused and frowned.

"Oh, and I have scarcely any money. I've lost all my clothes except for the one dress I'm wearing and a whore's gown. What could possibly be wrong?"

He opened his mouth, then shut it. She'd summed him up with the word "thief." Really? Simply because he had some things in his bag from Stoddard? He hadn't expected that.

They sat in silence again for a long while. Then at last, she broke it.

"I'm hungry."

He sighed, but in truth, he welcomed the excuse to get up. "Let's go to the dining car."

Train travel the legal way proved to be long, tiresome, and boring. Except for Ellie's occasional burst of chatter, which then subsided into the same cold stillness, particularly if their discussion turned to Boston and what they would encounter when they reached Charlotte's house. It seemed to make Ellie more and more uneasy.

"I know my sister will help you," he reassured her after they'd pulled out of Chatsworth station. "I'd like to say she'll do it without asking questions, but that's not her way. She'll ask a hundred questions and then some."

"More likely, she'll spit in my face and slam the door."

He was shocked by her vitriolic notion. "Why would you say that?"

"I know she hates me. She was smarter than me at school, she had a mother, she was statuesque where I was a runt. She had everything. Including you for a brother."

He would have laughed if she hadn't looked so serious.

"If you believed she was so much better than you, then why did you torment her mercilessly, as if you were miles above her?"

Ellie looked out the train window. "Because I could."

He did not understand women. "You know, Charlotte didn't have it easy. We lost both our parents at the same time. She was lonely and a bit awkward, and she had to look after me. Imagine having me for a brother. You wouldn't actually want that, you know."

"It was lonely at my house," she said.

She was feeling sorry for herself again, and he hated that. She had no cause to, at least not for who she was. Why, she was as smart and lovely as anyone he'd ever met. But he wouldn't argue that she'd certainly brought herself into a very sorry situation now, entirely through her own doing.

"Charlotte thought *you* didn't like her, and she wasn't going to go out of her way to make friends. In fact, most people believed you didn't like them, but that never stopped me," he added. "Despite your temper. No one knew what was going to set you off."

She folded her arms again. "Riley had no problem with my temper."

For the first time when she mentioned his old friend, he smiled, and Thaddeus realized, rather childishly, it was because he'd been intimate with Ellie whereas Riley never had. He also realized she was throwing her ex-fiancé's name out to goad him, and today, he felt no compunction to take the bait.

"I bet he ignored your temper."

She frowned. "He did. He never let it bother him one bit."

He pried her arms free and took one of her hands in his. He wanted more than anything to have the Ellie from the night before back with him.

"Could you put your frown away and give me one of your smiles, darlin'? I've been sorely missing them all day."

He thought she was going to snatch her hand back. Then she looked him in the eye and gave him the briefest of smiles.

"In case you hadn't noticed, I've been trying ever so hard over the past few days to be sweet."

"You're nearly succeeding." He lifted her hand and placed a kiss on her knuckles. "I think Charlotte will be surprised."

Just then, shots rang out. Such a familiar, unwelcome sound. Dropping his hold on her, Thaddeus leaped to his feet, his gun drawn, before the last reverberations died out. Despite the echoes, he could tell the gunfire came from the front of the train. Two carriages stood between their carriage and the coal car, and in front of that was the engine.

"Get down on the floor," he ordered Ellie, who was peering out the window, as he felt the train start to slow. "Everyone," Thaddeus called out, his eyes honing in on the boy to whom Ellie had spoken earlier, "get down. You'll be safer on the floor."

They all moved at once. Then another shot rang out, sounding like rifle fire, and this time from the back of the train. Thaddeus swore under his breath. He would bet all he had men were on the track at the front, and as soon as the train stopped moving completely, more men would circle around behind them. You could halt a train this size with three or four men easily.

"Do you think they're here for me?" Ellie asked from where she crouched beside the seat.

Noting how her words came between shaky, panicky breaths, he didn't answer. That was exactly what he thought, but if she said it any louder, some of their fellow passengers would likely as not turn her over to the men outside just to get the shooting to stop. These weren't the wild days of the pioneers when gunfire was a regular occurrence. In fact, since the end of the war between the states, people were used to a measure of decorum.

He heard another shot, and it seemed to emit from inside the train. There was often a spotter on these long-distance stretches, housed in the caboose. Apparently, this one was doing his job and returning fire.

Thaddeus took out his second gun and held it out to Ellie, who stared at it but didn't reach for it.

"We didn't get to any lessons, but you can point and press the trigger. Just don't put it up to your face to aim, or the kickback could give you a black eye, or worse."

"Don't leave me," she pleaded, even as she took the gun from him.

He hesitated, hearing the fear in her voice, but he couldn't delay, not when he could be moving through the train, perhaps getting the upper hand. Anything was preferable to waiting for trouble to come to him.

"I've got to go take a look. Don't move from this spot."

She blinked at him.

"Darlin', promise me you won't do anything rash. Don't follow me. And, for God's sake, absolutely no jumping off the train."

She pursed her lips, looking anything but obedient.

"Ellie," he warned.

"All right. I'll stay put," she promised.

"I'll be right back." He opened the door in the front of their car and stepped onto the platform attached to the connecting car. Taking a cautious peek through the glass, he saw nothing but frightened passengers. Grabbing hold of the iron ladder, he climbed up top.

Everything looked clear, so he eased himself onto the carriage roof. It was easy with the train stopped. He'd once run the whole length of a train with it going full speed, and that was something he didn't ever want to repeat.

Thaddeus crawled forward along the top of the first carriage and then the next, until he could see in front of the train without standing. Two men sat on horseback. He could tell by their size neither one was Bart. Perhaps this had nothing to do with either him or Ellie.

He figured there were at least two more shooters in the back. The train had passed some outcroppings, and the men had probably hunkered down behind the rocks. If whoever was wielding the rifle had good aim, the train's spotter could end up dead.

And if Thaddeus stuck his own head up too high and was seen, perched like a rabbit in the noonday sun, these men would be on him like hawks. Hawks with nasty lead bullets.

Could they be Jack Stoddard's men? Or was it just an old-fashioned holdup? He sure hoped it was the latter. He hated to think Stoddard had this kind of power to find them. It meant the gambler had bribed people at the various eastern-bound stations to keep an eye out for them. Maybe the ticket-seller at the last station had recognized them from a description. A quick telegram and Stoddard would have discovered where they were.

Below him, he heard the conductor going through the carriage calling loudly, "Is there an Eliza Prentice on board?"

CHAPTER FOURTEEN

hit! The lily-livered conductor would undoubtedly give her up to save his own skin. And the man was heading into their car next. Thaddeus had to act fast. Getting on his knees, he fired unswervingly at the closest man on horseback, who was pacing back and forth across the track. His target spun sideways and fell off his horse.

Only a shoulder wound, *damn it!* Thaddeus had been aiming for the man's head. If he'd taken another moment to aim properly . . . but now, he had to get back to Ellie.

In any case, all movement halted for a split second. The other horse stilled then shied sideways, no shots were fired, even the conductor had fallen silent. Then gunfire erupted in earnest both from the back of the train and from the remaining man at the front.

Deciding the odds were in his favor, Thaddeus crawled forward on his belly a little farther. Though four men could stop a train, three men couldn't hold it, not if even a few people on board were armed.

The injured man had managed to take hold of his horse's reins, swing himself onto its back, and ride away. The other man, realizing the precariousness of his position was jerking his horse right to left across the tracks, keeping the train from proceeding. Taking aim at him, Thaddeus steadied his gun when he heard Ellie scream. At least, he assumed it was her.

Raising his head, a bullet whizzed past him. He'd been spotted, robbed of his advantage.

Focus, he told himself. Taking aim once more, he shot the other man off his horse and knew with grim satisfaction that particular gunman wouldn't be getting up again.

The engineer blew the whistle, signaling the train was going to move again, and the gunfire exploded once more from the rear. This time, he heard Ellie scream his name.

Blast! Scrambling on all fours along the carriage roof, Thaddeus ignored the ladder's rungs, using its rails to slide down to the platform. Thrusting open the door, he came up short. Ellie stood cornered, gun raised in her shaking hand, facing the conductor and three passengers.

"What in the hell?" Thaddeus exclaimed.

"She has to get off this train, and they'll let us go," the conductor said, never taking his eyes off the revolver Ellie held. "That's what one of those bandits up front told me."

"As a passenger of this line, I have rights," Ellie stated in her haughtiest voice. "You can't throw me off the train."

"I have to do what's best for *all* the passengers," the conductor insisted as shots sounded once more, both from the front and the rear. The train lurched to a stop again, and the passengers in the carriage sent up a collective cry.

"While you were cowardly trying to sacrifice this woman," Thaddeus said, "one of the men from the back has circled around to the front."

"There are already two at the front," the conductor said, keeping his gaze trained carefully on Ellie.

"I took care of them."

The conductor swiveled his eyes to Thaddeus for the first time. "And you are?"

"This isn't the time for introductions. Can't your spotter get one shot off at the gunmen in the back of this train?"

"He's been hit already. You can see the blood running down his window."

Ellie gasped and exchanged a look with Thaddeus.

He could tell by her expression she was feeling responsible for everything that had gone on, and she started to lower her weapon.

"Ellie, darlin', you keep that gun pointed just like you're doin'. What did I tell you?"

"To stay here."

"Right. Good girl." He turned to the conductor. "Do you have any more weapons?"

"The engineer has a rifle."

"Then for heaven's sake, decide, man. This is *your* train. Are you going up front to take care of that shooter, or are you going to handle the gunmen in the back?"

"Unarmed?" the conductor spluttered.

"Take my gun if you're going to the back, and I'll go up front and use the engineer's rifle."

The conductor hesitated a moment.

"I'll go to the back." He held out his hand. Thaddeus stared at him hard. He swallowed and gave him his gun.

Winking at Ellie, Thaddeus turned to go. Clear as a church bell, he heard a hammer cock. *Son of a bitch!* Putting his hands up, he spun slowly to face the situation.

Sure enough, the conductor pointed Thaddeus's own weapon at him.

"I've been up front doing *your* job," Thaddeus ground out, wondering if he could kick his revolver out of the man's hand before he pulled the trigger.

The conductor's hand shook, nearly as much as Ellie's.

"My job is to keep the passengers and this train safe. The greater good of all is the important thing, over the good of you and your troublesome lady. Now get your things and . . ."

A second later, an explosion rent the air. Thaddeus flinched, but it was the conductor who dropped. It took Thaddeus another moment to realize Ellie had pulled the trigger. She stayed on her feet but had been forced back against the window and was staring, eyes wide, at what she'd done.

First things first. "Ellie, get the hell away from that window."

He didn't have to say it twice. She dropped to the floor in front of her seat.

Turning his gaze to the compartment of shocked passengers, he asked, "Can anyone here handle a gun?"

The man with the newspaper got up from his crouching position between the seats.

"I can, young man. I was in the war in the sixties and fought with the Army of the Potomac under McClellan."

"Will you take my gun, sir?" Thaddeus picked it up from where it had fallen out of the conductor's hand and stepped over his wounded body.

When the aged Union soldier nodded, Thaddeus handed it to him without qualms.

"I'll see what damage I can do to that ruffian in the back," the man said.

"Thank you, sir," Thaddeus told him before turning his gaze to Ellie once more and giving her what he hoped was a stern look she would obey. "You—"

"I know, I know," she said, on her knees between the seats. "I'll stay put."

He nodded and disappeared back through the carriage door, this time, unarmed.

Threading his way through the alarmed passengers in the next two carriages, Thaddeus instructed people to keep calm and keep low. When he reached the coal car, he had to scuttle over the top like a beetle over rocks. Twice he was shot at before he dropped into the cab of the locomotive, crouching low.

"Friend, not foe," he said at once to the startled engineer.

The fireman, responsible for feeding coal into the boiler, was dead, as he'd had less cover at the open end of the coal car. The engineer had been shot in the arm. It didn't look mortal, although the man was in rough shape and couldn't hold his rifle.

Thaddeus stripped off the fireman's shirt knowing the man would never need it again, and looping it high on the engineer's arm, he tied it tightly to make his bleeding stop. Then picking up the rifle that had fallen to the floor, he grabbed the engineer's hat and lifted it toward the window. A bullet went right through it. Evidently, Stoddard had hired a better shot than most of his usual goons, who were more apt with their fists than their accuracy.

But Thaddeus was certain he was even better. He had to be, and the engineer's rifle was a quality Winchester. The question was simply how to fire a shot without getting his head blown off?

"Peephole," the engineer said abruptly. "Made it myself." He gestured to a metal disk fastened with a bolt.

Thaddeus raised it and peered outside. Sure enough, he could see a rider going back and forth twenty feet away, either waiting for a signal or for the chance to get off another shot. Buckskin pants and shirt, gray hat, long black braid—it was the half-Cherokee tracker. Sure enough, he'd led Stoddard's men to them yet again.

Thaddeus put the rifle's barrel to the hole, but the Indian went out of view, probably circling to the other side of the engine. He swore in frustration.

"Made only the one," the engineer said with a shrug as Thaddeus glanced at the other side of the locomotive.

"If I were you, when this is over," he advised, "I'd make a hole on the other side, too."

The engineer smiled wryly. "Reckon you're right, at that."

Thaddeus waited. Meanwhile, he heard his own gun report from the back of the train and prayed to God the Union soldier was a sure shot.

A horse's hoofbeats signaled the return of Stoddard's Indian tracker to Thaddeus's side of the train, and he wasn't about to waste another opportunity to take out this irksome thorn in his side. Taking careful aim, and despite the man and horse moving swiftly, he fired.

The Indian went down hard, face in the dirt, and his horse ran off a few steps and then stopped to graze. For an instant, Thaddeus felt regret at the waste of such a capable and skilled tracker. Then it passed. The half-Cherokee had chosen the wrong employer, plain and simple.

Rising to his feet, Thaddeus glanced at the engineer. "I don't suppose you'll be able to get this train going."

The engineer grinned. "With a little help. Only thing stopping us is the dead man pedal. And I'm mighty glad it don't apply here."

Thaddeus helped the engineer back into his position, wedging his foot on the pedal that acted as a brake if it wasn't depressed. Before long, they began to inch forward, then rumbled up to speed. For a few minutes, Thaddeus took over the fireman's role, shoveling coal into the boiler, until it was fully stocked.

"I've got to go back and see how everyone's doing."

"You do that. Tell the conductor—"

Thaddeus cut him off with a shake of his head, not bothering to explain how the conductor got injured.

The engineer, his expression grim, glanced at the dead fireman behind him and then back at Thaddeus, no doubt thankful to be still standing.

"Well then, son, you go tell everyone we're not stopping nowheres till we get to Gilman. They got a good doctor there, so that's where I'm getting off. We're going straight through. It'll take half hour or so. I bet a whole bunch of other folk'll want to get off, too. We'll send the sheriff back to see about the mess on the tracks."

Thaddeus made his way back to his carriage, reassuring passengers as he passed through the cars. Damn if he didn't feel like the law.

Reaching his own car, he opened the door, and his gaze landed squarely on Ellie, still crouched, gun in her hand. And next to her, standing guard, was the Union soldier.

"Thaddeus," she cried out, dropping the gun to the floor and launching herself into his arms.

The soldier sent him a timid smile. "Got him with one shot," he said, referring with a jerk of his thumb to the gunman he'd apparently killed at the back of the train. Then he bent to pick up the gun Ellie had let fall, holding it out along with Thaddeus's own revolver.

"My name's James Ellis, by the way."

Thaddeus released Ellie and took both guns back. In truth, he felt undressed without the solid weight of one in his holster. Then he slipped the other one into the back of his waistband.

"Thaddeus Sanborn," he offered, and shook the man's hand.

The conductor groaned, and Thaddeus was glad Ellie hadn't killed him, for her sake. Still, the man was gravely injured.

"He's probably more comfortable on the floor than in a seat, but let's move him out of the way."

"I think I hit his thigh," Ellie offered, sounding shaky.

Thaddeus figured, at such close range, she'd shattered his large leg bone at the very least and shredded his muscles. In all likelihood, the man would never walk again. But he wasn't going to tell her that.

"I'm happy to have you watching my back any time, darlin'," Thaddeus told her. And he meant it. He'd been alone so long, it was strange reaching out to Ellie and the soldier for help.

After they got the conductor settled, Thaddeus straightened. "I'll go check on the spotter."

"No," James Ellis said. "You've done enough. Stay here with your pretty missus, and I'll see if anything can be done for him."

Thaddeus collapsed into the nearest seat and grabbed Ellie onto his lap, unmindful of what the other passengers thought.

"You were stupendous," he told her.

"All I did was shoot the conductor."

"I look at it more as you saved my life." He brushed a kiss across her lips.

She blushed. "You saved the whole train." She put her hand up to his face, her palm on his cheek. "I love you."

His breath caught, and he went still as a statue. A hundred thoughts and emotions flooded his mind and heart at hearing Ellie say those words while looking deeply into her sparkling blue eyes, dancing like rainwater. He recalled how exquisite it had been the night before to kiss her, to stroke deep inside her, and to have her come undone beneath him. He also remembered the desperate urge to leave behind his hometown and everything he knew, feeling worthless because of her. And he dredged up the terror in his gut at seeing Stoddard's men take her away.

If he admitted his love and took what she was offering, he wondered how he could live with the constant worry of what could happen to her next. In any case, he didn't believe she loved him, not for a second.

Capturing her hand, he removed it from his cheek.

"Don't confuse gratitude with love," he cautioned, and watched the expression on her face change from one of obvious devotion to one devoid of any sentiment whatsoever.

"Why, you're right, of course." And stiffly, she climbed off his lap and into the seat beside him.

Damn it! She had to understand the likes of her was not meant to go willy-nilly falling in love with the likes of him. When she was out of this mess with Stoddard, she could have her pick of fine gentlemen, maybe even a Bostonian, a man like Charlotte's Reed Malloy.

Thaddeus didn't want her thinking she had to declare her love and tie herself to him, merely because he seemed heroic one day out of his sorry life. Although, when this was all over, if they found themselves still in close company . . .

"Look, Ellie, I didn't mean—"

"No, no, you're right." She turned a sweet smile his way looking completely composed again, and he thought, perhaps, he'd merely embarrassed her, not offended her.

She shook her head. "You're right. My emotions are running high. It's not every day that I'm in a gunfight. Well, it has become more common lately, but still, it left me feeling all-overish."

Turning away, she looked out the window, and his stomach twisted as if he'd just lost something precious, had let it slip right through his fingers. For the briefest of moments, he'd been the recipient of her admiration, if not truly her love.

"How long until we're at the next station?" she asked, her voice resolute and unperturbed.

When he didn't answer right away, she turned. "Thaddeus, are *you* all right?"

He shook it off, whatever *it* was that had momentarily come over him. What he was or wasn't, he was not what Ellie needed, or wanted, despite having spent a lot of years wishing he could be.

"The engineer said half an hour, and that was about ten minutes ago."

She nodded and looked away again.

They didn't have long to wait for the next train, and this time, they had a sleeper car. Or Ellie did. Thaddeus decided she could use a rest, and he needed time to think. Alone. What was he hoping to accomplish besides helping her out of a terrible situation? Did he want her beholden to him or to start depending on him? Was he ready to settle down in one place, maybe Spring City, and carve out a life for them both?

Try as he did, he couldn't come up with the answer. She was so easy for him to love, in spite of what others had said about her all his life, but he didn't know what he could do to satisfy her. He went over and over it in his head.

If she still wanted to travel, he could do that with her, he supposed, although this lifestyle was wearing thin. But if she wanted to live in her house in Spring City, how would he occupy himself? Was he any better a choice for husband now than he'd been at eighteen?

He had some money squirreled away, and some was even in an honest-to-goodness bank account. But he couldn't simply put his feet up and sit on her porch for the rest of his life. He was not like Dan, who had never minded following his father's footsteps to work at the feedstore.

Thaddeus had toyed with the idea of becoming a bounty hunter, but that seemed a tad dirty, in his mind. Often, the bounty was based on some poor sap's bad luck. Why, any given year, there could be a bounty on his own head for some rash decision or other. He'd ruled out sheriff and deputy. Who in their right mind would put him in charge of a town?

No, first, he had to make his fortune with the ill-gotten gain in his bag. Then, he would figure out the rest of his life. And if that included Ellie, he'd be a happy man, but he just couldn't see it happening.

Pulling his hat down over his eyes, he drifted off to sleep, his questions still unanswered.

CHAPTER FIFTEEN

Misgiving roiled in Eliza's stomach like butter in a churn as the train neared Boston. She thought of Tennyson's *Lady of Shalott*, who was "half sick of shadows." Far beyond half sick of trains as she passed through Indiana, Ohio, and Pennsylvania, Eliza decided if she never got on one again as long as she lived, it would be too soon.

That was childish! She knew she'd have to get on a train again eventually to get back home. But as much as she wearied of the feel of the tracks, she felt equally nervous at getting off the train and facing Thaddeus's sister.

She'd once told Sophie Dalcourt, who was then still Sophie Malloy, Charlotte's sister-in-law, that she'd never read Charlotte's work. That was one of the few lies she'd ever told, that and pretending to be in love with Riley Dalcourt.

Eliza had, indeed, read Charlotte's articles whenever she came across one and knew her to be a talented writer. But she had trouble thinking of Charlotte as anything other than Thaddeus's too-clever sister, the one she'd loved to torment because she envied Charlotte her family.

That was before the cholera took half of the Sanborn family, and they'd stood more as equals when the devastation was over.

Except Charlotte had a brother who meant everything to Eliza, while she had only her father, domineering, controlling, loving, and powerful. Until he wasn't anymore, until he was dying.

And as she'd dreaded would happen, Eliza ended up alone in the world, whereas Charlotte somehow, against all odds, stood surrounded by family—husband, children, brother, and in-laws.

In preparation for living by herself, Eliza knew early on during her father's illness she had to present the strongest appearance to the world. Otherwise, every man-jack would walk all over her as soon as she became an orphan. No matter what property or businesses she owned, if anyone believed she didn't have a spine of pure steel and a hot temper to go with it, she'd be bear bait or worse. So, she got engaged to Riley and maintained her independence at the same time.

And then she lost it to Stoddard. That had been a blow. She'd been careless and arrogant, not to mention reckless because a part of her didn't care about her past, her holdings, or even her future. A part of her grieved for her lost hopes and dreams.

Now, she headed into the dragon's den, as she'd come to think of Charlotte's home, protected by Reed and his family, too. All people who dearly loved Charlotte, according to Thaddeus. And here she was with a reluctant knight, who would no more defend her against his sister than wear a lady's corset and pigtails.

Trying to rest, Eliza tossed and wriggled, unable to get comfortable on the narrow bed in the sleeper car, certain she'd never fall asleep. However, when she opened her eyes, her cabin was light with early morning sun and Thaddeus was bending over her.

She clenched her hands into fists to stop herself from reaching up and pulling him down to her for a kiss. Thaddeus Sanborn had been the man of her dreams since before he was really a man, and the man, himself, was so much better even than her fondest dreams.

However, she wouldn't make the same mistake she'd made days earlier. He'd dismissed her declaration of love as if she were a confused child, even after he'd been intimate with her in the hotel room. Apparently, he remained the unreliable gadabout her father had warned her of, although she'd always believed he was so much more.

He was never going to fall for her or commit himself, not when he had women like that flamboyant Josephine no doubt waiting in towns all over the country. They represented excitement and variety. She couldn't possibly hope to tie him down to a life with only her.

How could she blame him? She'd tried to be as interesting as he was, traveling, gambling, finding adventure, but she would never be truly comfortable as a drifter. As much as she'd wanted to get out of Spring City, mostly because Thaddeus, the man she loved, was somewhere out in the world, she now wanted to go home.

Regrettably, that was the one thing she couldn't do, not with Stoddard coming after her, ready to claim her holdings as his own. He could so easily ruin the lives of the people she'd grown up with, and no matter what they thought of her, she couldn't let a crooked killer take over Spring.

"We're almost there, darlin'."

Thaddeus kept his verdant gaze on her eyes until she stretched, and she saw it dart to her breasts, then to her lips. A frisson of longing streaked through her.

"How did you get in here? I locked the door. I know I did." She'd heard the satisfying click when she secured her compartment for the night.

He offered her a wry smile and shrugged, implying the train's security was no match for him.

Struggling to sit up, she yawned and put her feet over the edge.

"Did you sleep well?" she asked him.

"Not as well as you, it seems. I have a crick in my neck only a hot bath will fix."

"I told you that you could share my sleeper car," she reminded him, then wished she hadn't mentioned it.

He'd turned her down on this train as he had on the previous one to Philadelphia. For some reason, he'd decided to play the perfect gentleman, and she guessed it had to do with her rash declaration of love.

She blushed. "I mean, we could have taken turns lying here."

He shrugged again and pulled open the curtains. They were already rumbling into Boston.

"I'll be fine as soon as we get to Charlotte's," he said. "They live in an old sea captain's home, but it has all the modern comforts and then some."

Ellie nodded and tried to produce a little enthusiasm.

"Hey," he grinned at her. "You look as though you're paying a visit to the dentist for an aching tooth."

She almost wished she was.

He touched her chin. "It'll be fine. You'll see."

But it wasn't fine. They got out of a cabriolet in front of the Malloys' house on India Wharf, and a middle-aged Frenchwoman whom Thaddeus called Jeanine ushered them in. Moments later, Charlotte appeared and stared, wide-eyed, from her brother to Eliza, visibly flabbergasted.

After she got over her initial shock, Charlotte closed in on Thaddeus and hugged him hard. Then, still holding his hand, she beheld Eliza with a frank gaze. Twice, Charlotte opened her mouth, then closed it again as though she had no words.

Eliza was struck by how much Charlotte looked like her brother, with the same rich chestnut-colored hair and green eyes, eyes that clearly expressed how puzzled she was by Eliza's presence. Perhaps more than puzzled. Was she vexed?

Thaddeus spoke into the awkward silence. "Charlie, I brought Ellie here because she's in some trouble, and I think Reed can help."

"Ellie?" Charlotte repeated, as if he were speaking another language, while she continued to gape at Eliza, clearly stunned to have her in her front hall. "Reed should be home any moment."

They stood in silence again.

Eliza didn't know what to say. She hadn't expected a warm welcome, but she'd hoped to be invited to sit down and not left standing in the entryway. On the other hand, even though Charlotte wasn't overflowing with affection, at least she hadn't shown her the door. Yet.

"You have a lovely home," Eliza managed.

Just then, a toddler rushed in on unsteady feet and grabbed for his mother's skirts. Charlotte's face was transformed from one of cool restraint to unrestrained worship. She beamed.

"Here's my little man." Before she could bend down to pick him up, however, Thaddeus scooped him into his arms and swung him high, making the boy squeal with laughter.

"Ellie," he said, turning toward her with the boy she guessed to be about two, "this is my only nephew, Emory."

"Maybe not your *only* nephew for long," came Reed's voice. He'd come unheralded and unheard through the front door and was already setting down a stuffed leather satchel. Shrugging out of his overcoat, he hung it on a wooden rack by the door and came forward, appearing unperturbed by the gathering in his foyer.

Eliza's gaze flickered over the supremely handsome man, with his raven black hair and dark blue eyes, whom she'd encountered a few years earlier in Spring City. She'd thought she'd been successfully flirting with him back then—merely for the sport, of course, as she'd been engaged to Riley.

However, Reed had been completely captivated by Charlotte, who now blushed profusely at her husband's brazen remark, although her winsome smile matched his.

As if drawn by a string, Reed approached his wife and snaked an arm around her waist, tugging her close.

Eliza felt even more of an intruder in their home, especially when they were discussing such a personal family event.

"Another baby?" Thaddeus asked, boldly staring at his sister's figure. "But you don't look it."

Charlotte laughed. "I'll show soon enough, dear brother. Maybe you'll get a niece this time. Girls are such fun, too."

"Speaking of which, where are my little cousins?"

"Not so little anymore," Charlotte said of her and Reed's adopted children, Lily and Thomas, second cousins to Thaddeus and Charlotte. "They are at their grandmother's. You can see them tomorrow, either here or at Alicia's."

Thaddeus grinned and turned to Eliza. "Wait till you meet my Grandmother Alicia."

She felt the blood drain from her head. Wasn't this enough, facing Charlotte and Reed, without having to be paraded in front of his extended family?

"Dada," Emory piped up, holding out his arms. Reed took him from Thaddeus.

"Why are we all standing in the front hall?" he wondered aloud. "Come in, let's get comfortable."

Eliza glanced at Charlotte who hesitated, most likely reluctant to let Eliza any farther into her home than absolutely necessary. However, with cautious politeness, Charlotte gestured for them to follow Reed into the sitting room at the back of the house.

"Dearest," Charlotte addressed her husband, "Teddy and Miss Prentice have a problem to discuss with you. I'll go ask Jeanine for some refreshments and tell Pierre we have two more for dinner."

"If it's no trouble," Eliza said, finding her voice.

Charlotte frowned at her. "Family is no trouble." And she turned and walked away.

Eliza caught a glance between Thaddeus and Reed. She ought to follow Charlotte for a moment alone with her and apologize for some of her past behavior, but Thaddeus called her to his side.

"Let's get right to business," he said, gesturing for her to sit beside him on the sofa in a gracious but unassuming room overlooking the sea. "Reed, we need your expertise."

At that moment, Reed didn't look like an expert on anything other than his son. Emory stood on his father's lap and jumped, up and down, up and down.

"Just give him a moment, Thaddeus," Eliza said. "The boy wants his father."

"No, no," Reed contradicted, "if we wait for little man here to stop bouncing, we'll never get to talk. But he's quiet, so let's begin. And Miss Prentice," Reed focused his cobalt-blue gaze on her, "I didn't say it before, but it's a pleasant surprise to see you again and so unexpectedly far away from your home. I hope we can find a solution to your problem."

She felt startled by his words of kindness. His tone seemed genuine. Didn't he know her history with his wife? She gave him her polished smile.

"I truly hope so, too," she said and let Thaddeus describe the mess she'd gotten herself into.

However, by the time Charlotte returned with Jeanine and a tray of refreshments in tow, Reed looked grim.

"Fill me in," she said, and Eliza had to sit through the mortification of hearing her story a second time, this time from Reed. By the end of it though, she thought the lawyer seemed more optimistic.

"I'm fairly certain we can obtain a divorce and perhaps even a civil annulment, but by the sound of this Stoddard fellow, he's not going to take the loss of a fortune lying down, nor will he simply accept a judge's decision."

"I'll make him accept it," Thaddeus said, surprising not only Eliza but Charlotte, too, or so it seemed by the stricken expression on her face. "If you get the legal work done," he added to his brother-in-law, "then one way or another, Stoddard's going to let her go free."

Eliza blushed to hear Thaddeus championing her. If he thought her worthy of his assistance, that had to count for something in Reed and Charlotte's eyes.

"Very well, then. Come down to my office tomorrow," Reed said. "I'll take down all the details and get started on your case, but I can't meet with you until two in the afternoon." He fixed his piercing gaze on Eliza, who'd kept silent for most of the discussion of her sad situation.

"Miss Prentice, we don't know each other, but obviously, you're a friend of Thaddeus and my wife—" Eliza felt her cheeks heat up at that mischaracterization of her relationship with Charlotte, never mind having no idea what to call her connection to Thaddeus "—and I will be glad to take your case. However, you'll have to trust me with the truth about everything that happened."

She wished she came off looking better in the whole affair, but instinctively, she trusted this man, with his fierce blue eyes, radiating intelligence and understanding.

She nodded her agreement. "I'll tell you everything."

"Good." He gave her an encouraging smile. Then he turned to Thaddeus. "Why don't you catch up with your sister? I'm going to take Emory upstairs for a little while before dinner."

Eliza watched Reed hoist his son to his hip with one arm and reach out his other arm to take his wife's hand in his. He brought it tenderly to his lips, his eyes locked on Charlotte's. She blushed under his gaze and smiled at him. He winked at her before disappearing up the stairs.

It was so sweet, a shot of envy raced through Eliza.

"It's his nap time," Charlotte said, taking a sip of tea.

Thaddeus laughed. "Emory's a good lad."

"No, I meant Reed. He'll take a nap, but only for a few minutes."

Eliza couldn't help the unexpected giggle that escaped her.

Charlotte continued, "Emory will lie down with him and, hopefully, close his eyes, too. They'll both come down for dinner much refreshed."

"Emory seems like a sweet and cooperative little boy," Eliza remarked, hoping her words would be well-received.

"Thank you," Charlotte said, her tone barely warmer than before. "But after the jumping would have come the singing at the top of his lungs. Reed could tell Em was about to blow."

Thaddeus stretched and yawned, snagging Charlotte's attention.

"You look tired, Teddy. Maybe you'd like to take a nap yourself before dinner." Then she looked at Eliza again. "Have you booked a hotel room, Miss Prentice?"

"Charlie," Thaddeus cut in, as Eliza opened her mouth to speak. "I hoped we could both stay here."

But she had no intention of begging for a room. While Charlotte seemed to consider her brother's request, Eliza stood.

"I'm sure there are plenty of lovely hotels here in Boston. Perhaps you can direct me to one near to your husband's office."

"Charlie," Thaddeus warned, and Charlotte narrowed her eyes at him for a second. Then she took a deep breath and rose to her feet, facing Eliza.

"If you don't have a hotel room already reserved, then you're welcome to stay here for as long as you like."

Eliza didn't feel welcome, not in the least. "No, that won't be necessary."

"Thanks, Charlie. We both appreciate it," Thaddeus spoke over her.

Eliza glared at him. Charlotte crossed her arms, apparently enjoying Eliza's discomfort.

Thaddeus stretched again. "I don't know about you, but I'm tired of hotels. I want a good meal and good night's sleep. We can get both of those here. Right, Charlie?"

"Yes, of course, you can." Charlotte uncrossed her arms, relenting when asked by her only brother. "It might be a little cramped, but with the children away at their grandmother's across town, you can have two rooms." The she paused, her cheeks blushing pink. "That is, unless you only want one room . . . for both of you or . . . Blazes!" she exclaimed, her green eyes flashing from one to the other. "Are you together?"

"Yes," said Thaddeus.

"No," said Eliza at the same time.

They glanced at one another. Eliza knew her cheeks must be redder than Charlotte's. Thaddeus, himself, looked flushed. Why had he said they were a couple?

"Shall we try that again?" asked Charlotte, sounding more than a little amused. "One bed or two?"

"One," ground out Thaddeus.

"Two," whispered Eliza at the same time.

They stared at each other again. Did he really want her back in his bed? She wanted that, too, but he'd embarrassed her on the train and then rebuffed her offer of the sleeper car. And now . . .

"Oh, for goodness sake!" Charlotte exclaimed. "Teddy, take Eliza upstairs. You know your usual room? I want you to give that one to Eliza, and you can take Thomas's bed in the nursery, or not. It's up to the two of you. I'll make sure Jeanine changes all the sheets before bedtime."

With a chuckle floating back to Eliza's embarrassed ears, Charlotte disappeared down the hallway.

"Jesus, woman, what was that all about?" Thaddeus demanded, rounding on her.

"I don't want your sister and her husband thinking that I, that we . . . you know."

"But we did 'you know.' And as far as my sister's concerned, we can continue to 'you know' here in her house."

"I will not be humiliated any further in front of them. The way you described my so-called marriage and husband was bad enough."

"And you think sharing your bed with me is humiliating?"

She stared at him, chin raised, trying to look every bit like her formidable self despite the fact he'd seen her at her worst. But her attempt at putting on airs had never worked on Thaddeus Sanborn before and had no effect on him now, except to spur his annoyance apparently.

"Well, darlin', far be it for me to demean you any more today. Let me show you to your room, and then I'm going to grab some shut-eye before dinner. If you can stand eating with me, that is."

He started up the stairs. She rolled her eyes at the back of his head.

"That's not what I meant," she began, not wanting to alienate her only friend on the East Coast.

He raised a hand to silence her without looking back. Shrugging, she followed him up to a pleasant room, in which he dumped her nearly empty carpetbag on the bed. Almost out the door, he turned to her.

"You'd better ask Charlotte if she's got something you can wear tomorrow when we go to Reed's office. Or you can always wear your *other* gown." He strolled out, not even bothering to shut the door.

Rat! He knew the only other dress she had with her was the outrageously unsuitable one from his whore. The sole reason Eliza hadn't thrown it away was because she'd been left with nothing too many times lately to take a chance. But the idea of ever putting it on again made her shudder.

Josephine's voluptuous body had been clad in the sheer violet gown at some point—maybe when she was about ten pounds lighter—and perhaps Thaddeus had even been treated to the well-rounded, raven-haired beauty wearing it. Why wouldn't he have liked it? Then that witch had forced Eliza, petite and slender, to put it on, probably knowing he would compare their bodies.

However, she let her mind wander to the entirely agreeable memory of how Thaddeus had looked at her that night just before she'd removed the dress and to what they'd done afterward. Maybe she would keep the gown after all.

Humming to herself, she picked up her bag and, after dumping out its contents, inspected the interior of it. She could feel the wad of cash sewn inside. Luckily, Stoddard hadn't discovered it before he'd carelessly given her bag to Josephine.

After dinner, Eliza intended to unpick the lining and extricate what money she had. It wasn't nearly enough to pay back Stoddard, not even close, just the winnings from a few other games before Thaddeus had found her. Combined with the pot she'd won from The Silver Dollar, however, her wealth was enough to buy a few dresses.

After all, she was in Boston, and if it was anything like Denver or San Francisco, she knew she'd have no trouble spending all of it on clothing, probably by lunchtime.

CHAPTER SIXTEEN

To that end, Eliza rose early, or so she believed, but when she pushed open the kitchen door, she encountered not only the staff and the heavenly smell of sausages, but also Charlotte and Reed, who looked to have just finished his breakfast.

"I'll see you and Thaddeus at my office later, Miss Prentice," he said, before giving Charlotte a thorough kiss on the lips and heading out the side door.

"You're very lucky," Eliza said before she considered her words.

Charlotte fixed her with a curious stare and then said, "I generally take my breakfast in here." She gestured to the table in the center of the copper and oak kitchen. It was already laden with platters of poached eggs and sausages. There was a bowl of stewed tomatoes and mushrooms, and another bowl of fried potatoes. Eliza's mouth watered.

Charlotte scooped up the remains of Reed's meal and set his plates in the sink where Jeanine was already washing up.

"If you prefer, we can bring eat in the dining room."

"Oh, no," Eliza said, having had no plans to take a morning meal at all but now feeling as though she must or appear rude. "Breakfast right here will be fine."

Charlotte resumed her seat. Without asking, the Frenchwoman placed a clean plate in front of Eliza.

"Do you take the tea or the coffee?" she asked, in her heavy accent.

"Tea," Eliza said, gazing distractedly at the mountain of food before her.

Charlotte coughed in precisely the way Eliza's father's housekeeper, Mrs. Longwood, used to do to remind her to use her manners.

"Please," Eliza added hurriedly, and as Jeanine placed a cup of steaming tea down beside the plate, she said, "Thank you."

How did Charlotte not expand like a ripe blueberry if she ate like this each morning? Eliza and Thaddeus had eaten such sporadic meals over the past weeks, this was practically an assault to her senses. It smelled divine, however, and even though unused to so much food, she helped herself and tucked in.

"You're right, by the way," Charlotte said, picking up on Eliza's earlier remark. "It was incredibly good fortune a man such as Reed would come into my life when he did. I shudder to think of myself still stuck in Spring City, sitting behind my desk with life passing me by."

It was a long confession for Charlotte to make, and since Eliza's mouth was full, she only nodded in agreement.

Charlotte sipped her tea and then added, "It was fortunate for him, too. He was going through his life with his heart all locked up because of something that had happened to him years ago."

Eliza drew in a big breath and choked on her toast. She coughed, tears springing to her eyes as Jeanine rushed forward to wallop her on her back. After a few moments of the woman's firm palm smacking her between her shoulder blades, Eliza managed to hold up her hand and wave her away. She sipped her tea to rinse down the rest of the crumbs, all the while thinking Charlotte could so easily be describing her.

When Thaddeus seemed to use her so callously that night in his barn, never even making mention of it, Eliza, too, had locked up her heart. She'd turned easily to Riley, who, as far as she was concerned, was no threat to her heart whatsoever.

Indeed, if Thaddeus had made any kind of promise or even the smallest of declarations, Eliza would have fought her father in order to marry him. To her, his reputation for lacking ambition, for drinking, and for generally being a ne'er do well had mattered not a whit.

"I'm truly glad it worked out for both of you," Eliza added, when she could breathe and talk again.

Charlotte shook her head, looking bemused, as if surprised to find Eliza in her kitchen.

"Frankly, I didn't expect ever to see you again, at least not this side of the Mississippi."

"Nor wanted to, I should think," Eliza said, seeing by Charlotte's expression she'd hit the mark.

"We weren't exactly friends," said Charlotte with tactful understatement, taking a bite of toast.

"No," Eliza agreed, "nor even neutral acquaintances. I went out of my way to pick at you whenever our paths crossed."

This time it was Charlotte who coughed, perhaps startled at Eliza's blunt confession. Jeanine slapped her on the back until her eyes watered, and Charlotte held up her hand.

"I'm fine," she croaked out, and the Frenchwoman sailed out of the room with a load of kitchen towels. "Very helpful woman, our Jeanine," Charlotte remarked.

"I can see that," Eliza said, but she wasn't going to change topics now she'd made her confession. "But it's true what I said."

"Do you want to tell me why?" Charlotte asked, grabbing a napkin and wiping her mouth.

Eliza shrugged. "I suppose 'because I could' is not enough of an answer for tormenting you."

She was relieved to see Charlotte smile at that remark, despite their years of antagonism.

Eliza continued, "I resented you for having your family when we were younger. I wanted everything you had, until you didn't have it anymore."

"You mean my mother."

"Most specifically, yes. And of course, you had a sibling and I didn't."

"But you don't feel in the least bit sisterly toward Thaddeus, do you?" Charlotte remarked, getting right to the point.

Eliza felt her cheeks heat.

"That's all right," Charlotte said. "I can see where my brother would turn a woman's head. He's always been somewhat larger than life. If the boys started drinking, he'd get drunk. If they played in the mines, he'd have to camp out down under. If they learned to shoot, he'd have to develop perfect aim. And of course, there's the gambling. He either wins big or loses bigger."

"And there are the women," Eliza said, her voice scarcely above a whisper.

Charlotte faltered, then spoke. "On the rare occasions when Thaddeus came back to visit, he'd end up out drinking with Dan. You know that."

Eliza nodded. "Dan," she repeated, "who can share stories the way wildfire spreads through sagebrush." With Dan in town, everyone in Spring City knew Thaddeus had put his devilish good looks to use to gain a bit of female company, from coast to coast apparently.

Charlotte put her hand over Eliza's, and Eliza jumped at the touch. Then they locked gazes.

"I don't wish you any ill," Charlotte said, sounding utterly truthful. "What's past is past, and growing up together in Spring City seems a lifetime ago." She paused, apparently searching for the right words.

"I don't want you to get hurt by one of my kin. I don't know if my little brother is ready to grow up, so I can't advise you to hitch your wagon to him. Do you understand me?"

Eliza nodded, grateful she hadn't had to grovel out an apology after all. Instead, they'd moved on to unfamiliar territory.

"I'm trying to be cautious where your brother is concerned. Thaddeus can be rather confusing at times. For whatever reason, right now, he's decided to focus his attention on solving my problems," she paused, "although it seems to me, he has a few of his own. Maybe you can help him. Someone needs to talk to him about what he carries in that bag of his."

Charlotte frowned, a light of interest flaring in her eyes. "I will. You can be sure of that."

The moment passed, and Eliza drew her hand away.

"I need to go shopping," she admitted. "Along the way, between escaping from Jack Stoddard and then fleeing with Thaddeus and being abducted once or twice, I've lost all my clothes."

"Blazes!" Charlotte exclaimed. "But you had the prettiest gowns in Spring."

Eliza shot her a quick grin. "Still do, probably. I left most of them behind. But they don't do me much good packed up in my house."

Charlotte eyed her thoughtfully. "The shops are magnificent. I'll take you myself. Nothing opens for another hour anyway, so eat and then we'll go." She stood up. "If you'll excuse me, I have to check on Emory."

Eliza was startled by how quickly Charlotte had taken over.

"You don't have to accompany me. I'm very capable of managing my life, despite the pickle Thaddeus described last night."

"I'm sure you are, but it's pleasant to have a friend in the city. When I first arrived, my Aunt Alicia took me around the shops. Frankly, it's not nearly as fun to shop alone, don't you agree?"

And with that, she was gone. How strange! She and Charlotte were going shopping. Why, Eliza had never had a woman friend in her entire life, and to think, her first one would be Thaddeus's sister. Anyone else and she would be filled with mistrust, but Charlotte was inherently honest and true and, at the end of the excursion, Eliza was certain she wouldn't be wearing a garment like the one Josephine had thrown her way.

Eliza could eat only a few more bites. Pushing the plate to the center of the table, she tapped her fingers and waited.

When Charlotte did not readily reappear, Eliza hoped Thaddeus would come down to breakfast in the meantime. She hadn't seen him since dinner the previous evening, after which he'd headed out for a walk without a word to anyone.

While he'd seemed perfectly placid, Eliza could tell by the sharp glance he'd sent her way he still simmered with annoyance—clearly frustrated with her for not wanting to carry on amorous congress in his sister's house.

Knowing what she knew of Thaddeus, he had likely as not ended up in a bar. Her stomach compressed, threatening to return the delectable breakfast. What if he hadn't come home but instead had visited some woman he knew in Boston?

After draining her tea cup, she pushed uncertainly to her feet. Humming quietly to herself, she climbed the stairs, passing her own bedroom door and continuing along the hallway toward Thaddeus's room. She slowed her steps as she approached the nursery where he'd slept, if he'd come home at all.

Pausing with her hand on the doorknob, she wondered if he might have brought a woman home with him. Her heart pounded, as she tried to banish the thought. Surely, he wouldn't do that, not in his sister's home. Would he?

Burning with curiosity and a little dread, she turned the doorknob and crept inside. The curtains were closed against the early morning light, but she could see him, alone, tangled in the sheets of his young cousin's too-small bed. His unclothed body stretched diagonally, one foot hanging off the side, almost reaching the floor where the blanket had already fallen.

Closing the door behind her, she felt drawn involuntarily closer so she could gaze at him. Recalling all they'd been through, she couldn't help but smile.

Without a sound, not realizing she was still moving, she approached him. He sprawled on his back, one of his arms thrown over his eyes, the other hanging off the side of the bed. His exposed chest rose and fell in easy slumber, and she looked her fill of his sculpted muscles.

Fascinated, staring at the darker hair showing just above the sheet that twisted low over his hips, she took another step. They'd been sleeping in the same room since he'd found her, except for on the trains, but she'd never had time to stare leisurely at him, unclothed as he was now. Wickedly, she wished the sheet had fallen off him along with the blanket.

He was splendid, and her heart felt full as it always did in a calm moment when faced with Thaddeus Sanborn, or even a memory of him. He was so perfect in form, as far as she was concerned. She loved the timbre of his voice, the familiar scent of his skin, the way his green eyes darkened to show his moods, the salty sound of his laughter, not that lately they'd had much to laugh over.

Unwittingly, she reached her hand out—perhaps to lightly touch his skin, maybe to move the lock of hair off his forehead, she hadn't decided—when with lightning speed, his arm snaked out and grabbed her, his other arm lifting from his eyes. She squealed in surprise. She was captured.

"Ellie," he said, pulling her down and across his body without waiting for an explanation.

He tilted his head to look at her, a profound desire stirring in his eyes. Blinking at what she saw in that green gaze, a sensation of heat pooled low in her belly while passion flared throughout the rest of her. She licked her lips, feeling breathless.

With a rough groan, he dragged her up his torso, then she could feel what was under that thin sheet. He was rock hard and ready. Both his hands were on her buttocks now, grinding her against him. At the same time, he claimed her lips, tasting her like a starving man.

She relaxed onto his warm body, feeling tingly where their hips touched and where her breasts lay heavy on his chest. His hands released her to begin pulling her gown up, and the cool air caressed the back of her legs above her stockings. She didn't struggle, and when he had both her dress and shift up around her hips, with nothing but the thin sheet between them, he stilled his movements.

"You're not wearing drawers." His voice was raspy as he replaced his hands on her bare buttocks, caressing her skin. He kneaded her soft flesh, and she sighed. Their faces were mere inches apart.

Undergarments were something else she needed to buy that morning.

"Neither are you," she teased.

He grinned, and it did funny things to her insides, which were already performing tumbles of excitement. He managed to pull the sheet out from underneath her hips and the scorching heat of his skin against hers was her undoing.

"Don't you know better than to sneak up on an armed man?"

"You're not armed," she countered and was rewarded with a thrusting of his hips, causing his rigid shaft to stroke against her exquisitely sensitized private area.

Her breath caught in her throat. She'd missed him in her bed, not only the previous night but those nights on the train, too. Indeed, she hadn't slept as soundly without his presence.

But sleep was the last thing on her mind right then. She let her legs fall on either side of his hips, and the tip of him slid just inside her opening. Closing her eyes, she laid her head on his chest and listened to the thundering beat of his heart that belied his languid attitude.

With his hands at her waist guiding her, he eased her body onto his erection, sheathing himself inch-by-inch, until she was fully seated.

God help her, he felt so good. She was captive, absolutely wanton, sprawled across his naked body. She didn't even know if the door was locked or if someone might enter at any moment to witness them in this sordid position. She didn't care. She couldn't stop him now if she wanted to. And she absolutely did not want to.

Lifting her hips with his strong hands, he began a deliberately gradual gliding retreat, although she could feel her body trying to cling to him.

She moaned, maybe too loudly, for he claimed her lips again, moving one of his hands to the back of her head to hold her close. Each noise she made, he took into his mouth.

With his other hand, he made lazy circles over her exposed buttocks, all the while continuing his unhurried strokes.

When she pulled back against his hold on her head, he released her.

"Where . . . where were you?" She was panting, lost in him already but fighting to think clearly. "Last night."

At first, he didn't seem to hear her, continuing to slide deliberately and leisurely in and out of her woman's passage. She arched her head back and closed her eyes. But then he spoke.

"Went for a walk and a drink." Then he groaned, his mouth against her neck.

"Is that all?" she persisted, needing to know. *Please say yes.*

He kissed her neck before letting his head drop back onto the pillow.

"Yes, Ellie." He gave an energized thrust into her, and she gasped again. "I looked in on you," he added, "all alone in that big, comfy bed."

While she was sleeping, he'd been watching her. She shivered.

"Almost joined you."

He thrust again, and she moaned with satisfaction.

She would have let him.

"Didn't want to humiliate you," he added, surging into her.

"Thaddeus, I didn't mean—"

But he pulled her head back down to his and planted his lips on hers.

Her body grew taut as the physical pleasure built. In her core, everything heated and liquefied and melted. She kept her eyes closed and let his hands work their magic over her body, only wishing he had removed her dress entirely, so he could cup her breasts.

In another moment, she could think no more. Her sheath compressed around him, seeming to milk the length of him. She heard him murmur her name as she lost herself in exquisite sensations, reaching an explosive pinnacle before every muscle in her body stiffened and then, at last, relaxed.

Thaddeus rolled her beneath him, holding her hips still, as he surged into her again before taking his own release and collapsing beside her.

They lay in silence for long moments, his hands lightly stroking her hip. Her racing heart finally slowed, and she realized they were both hanging off the side of the small bed.

"Eliza, are you ready to go?"

They froze at the sound of Charlotte's voice.

CHAPTER SEVENTEEN

Eliza knew her face had gone beet red upon hearing Charlotte. Thaddeus put his fingers to her lips, quietly pulling her to a sitting position and then onto her feet.

"She'll be right out, Charlie," he said, sounding nearly normal. He took a moment to smooth her hair and help her arrange her clothes.

"We were discussing our meeting with Reed," he added loudly, and Eliza rolled her eyes.

He had to hang back out of sight, since he was stark naked, but touched her cheek and whispered in her ear, "Go on, you're dressed. She'll never know."

Eliza breathed deeply, hoping the flame in her face had died down to a dull pink. Under her shift, she was sticky and realized with a start Thaddeus hadn't pulled out of her fast enough as he had before. But what could she do?

She grabbed the small towel from the washstand, and turning her back to him, she lifted her skirt and wiped the residue. Tossing the cloth into the bowl, she opened the door and stepped into the hall without looking back.

"I'm ready," she said brightly, wishing she'd had time to clean up properly, but she would have settled for putting on drawers if she'd owned a pair. She had a feeling Charlotte Sanborn Malloy had never ventured out without her undergarments on.

But Charlotte scarcely glanced at her or, at least, had decided not to comment on her disheveled appearance. "Let's get you outfitted for Boston."

Charlotte delivered Eliza to Reed's office after lunch, newly clothed, including drawers, a shift, and a functional but pretty corset under a new ensemble. Eliza was still smiling at the morning she'd had. Besides the intimate adventure in bed with Thaddeus, her shopping trip had been one of the most fun things she could ever remember doing.

She'd marveled at how Charlotte had changed from the introverted girl she'd known in Spring City to a society maven who could navigate the shops, steering clear of tasteless items on sale while still finding the best prices, and who knew the shopkeepers and, more importantly, their fitting room assistants.

Soon, Eliza felt more like her old self, clad in a two-piece dress of dark-blue and ivory corded silk, with a fashionably narrow front and pleatings and ruchings trimmed with white lace over the bustle. Her money hadn't gone as far as she'd hoped, and she pictured the diamond ring in the bottom of her bag in her room on India Wharf. If she sold it, she could shop until there wasn't much left for anyone else in Boston. However, without that ring as security, Stoddard would undoubtedly kill her.

"Come on in." Charlotte led her into the waiting room of her husband's business on Scollay Square. Eliza took in the elegant robin's egg blue walls with white chair rails.

A gentleman with a close-cropped moustache sat at a polished reception desk with two speaking tubes attached. At seeing Mrs. Reed Malloy, he picked one tube out of its bracket, whistled sharply, and then spoke into the end of it.

"Mr. Malloy, sir. Mrs. Malloy is here."

"Thank you, Mr. Barley," Charlotte said to him, then turned to Eliza. "You'll be in good hands today."

Coincidentally, Eliza's glance fell on Thaddeus, sitting in a high-backed chair, idly spinning his hat on one hand while he waited. He jumped up from his seat when he saw her.

Good hands, indeed, thought Eliza, recalling how he'd caressed her that morning. She blushed as he walked toward her.

Before she could think of what to say to him, Reed came downstairs and, spotting his wife, outrageously took her into his arms and kissed her in front of everyone without even seeming to notice anyone else in the room. Only after Charlotte gave him a lingering farewell glance and closed the door behind her did he seem to remember where he was.

Reed took in the sight of Eliza and Thaddeus quietly standing in the middle of the waiting room, and with a sheepish smile, he gestured for them to follow him up to his office.

An hour into it, Reed had all the details—dates, names, circumstances—and a case for coercion to marry, which he said should result in an annulment.

"Miss Prentice, I have to ask you something quite personal, and please don't take offense at my question. Would you like Thaddeus to leave?" Reed asked before continuing.

Eliza couldn't think of anything he might ask that Thaddeus didn't already know. She shook her head.

"Did you have any physical relations with Mr. Stoddard after—?"

"Reed," Thaddeus interrupted the offending question.

But Eliza held up her hand to stop him. "It's fine to ask me, Mr. Malloy. I know it would alter my case. I'm quite pleased to be able to tell you the answer is unequivocally no. At no time, either before or after I married Jack Stoddard, did I have any relations with him, physical or otherwise."

Reed nodded. "That's good news. It makes this case easier all around. An annulment is going to take a little while, though, months even. A divorce might be quicker."

"No," she said firmly. Both men stared at her.

"Why, Miss Prentice?" Reed asked.

"I thought you wanted to be free of him," Thaddeus said.

"I don't care if it takes longer. An annulment means the marriage never happened," Eliza said. "Otherwise, I'll be seen as having a failed marriage." They had to understand how undesirable that was.

"There are worse things, darlin', than being divorced," Thaddeus interjected.

"Stoddard could refuse to divorce me anyway, or say I'm at fault."

Reed steepled his fingers. "True. Either way, he can fight, but if you want a clean slate, then we should go for the annulment. Meanwhile, the two of you need to behave," he added, out of the blue, surprising her.

"Excuse me?" Thaddeus asked before Eliza could react.

Reed leveled them both with a stare, eyes narrowed. "It's obvious to anyone that you have feelings for one another."

Eliza glanced at Thaddeus, who gazed back at her a long moment, then uncrossed and re-crossed his legs, fidgeting.

"If Stoddard were so inclined as to accuse you of adultery, Miss Prentice, then this case might go another way."

"But I know for a fact he's already committed adultery," Eliza said, thinking of Josephine's night with Jack on his riverboat.

"That doesn't matter. We're not trying to prove what *he* did or didn't do after the marriage. In point of fact, we're trying to prove that you are practically a saint whom Stoddard coerced into this union with the sole object of stealing your fortune." He tapped his pencil on his desk. "And no offense to my brother-in-law here, but he's not the kind of person with whom a saint socializes."

Thaddeus chuckled, but Eliza didn't think it was funny at all.

"What are you saying exactly, Mr. Malloy? How do we proceed from here?"

"Thaddeus moves on to wherever he's going next."

She felt a rush of fear, and her heartbeat galloped. The plan was for him to abandon her?

"Wait a minute." Thaddeus leaned forward in his seat. "I'm not just going to leave her unprotected."

Releasing her breath, Eliza's pulse slowed again. He didn't *want* to go.

"We'll keep her safe," Reed assured him.

Thaddeus stood and paced. "I'm not concerned with whether she can cross the road without getting run over, damn it! I'm thinking about men coming after her with guns, like this." He opened his coat to show his weapon. "Are you carrying one?"

Reed shook his head. "That's not done here, and you know it. But I'll hire a marshal to protect her. That'll be his only job. He won't get distracted by Miss Prentice's charms or my wife's chatter."

"And I'm supposed to do what exactly?" Thaddeus asked.

"As I said, move on. You have your own delicate issues with Stoddard, correct?"

Thaddeus glanced at Eliza, then back at Reed. "Yes."

"Unfortunately, I can't help you, not like I can help Miss Prentice. But your being in close contact with her, especially when you have property belonging to Stoddard, if I understand the situation rightly," Reed continued, "that only damages her case. Especially seeing how you've posed as her husband on more than one occasion."

Thaddeus ran a hand through his hair. "I can see that, I suppose."

"Charlotte will have my hide for this," Reed continued, "but I'm going to advise you anyway. If I were you, I would dispose of whatever it is you shouldn't have, or let me do it."

Thaddeus shook his head. "I can't let you get involved, Reed."

"That hot, eh?" Was that a glint of curiosity in the rich-blue eyes of Thaddeus's brother-in-law? Eliza supposed it was. After all, she wanted to know what he'd been carrying in that bag of his, too.

Thaddeus half-grinned. "Let's just say my future is resting on it, and I don't intend to jeopardize my future."

"Even if it means your life?" Reed asked.

Eliza couldn't help gasping, especially at the way they bantered around talk of life and death.

"I won't let it get to that," Thaddeus insisted. "Actually, could you steer me in the direction of a reputable pawnbroker? I had one picked out in Chicago, but my life has taken a detour of late."

He glanced at Eliza, and she wondered if all she was to him was one big nuisance. Then he winked and sent her a rakish smile.

However, Reed wasn't finished cross-examining Thaddeus. "Your future is resting on something you can pawn?"

"Only for seed money," Thaddeus said. "For the capital I need to get everything else going."

Reed raised an eyebrow, but then he grabbed a piece of stationery from inside his desk drawer and wrote on it. Folding it, he handed it to Thaddeus.

"Tell Randall I sent you. Now, I'm going to hire a marshal, and you're going to get ready to leave."

Reed stood up, and Eliza looked from man to man, both gazing back at her and both satisfied by what they'd discussed. It would appear their meeting was over. She got to her feet with the unsettling impression everything in her life was going to change and she had no control over that change, whatsoever.

Still, she held out her hand to Charlotte's very capable husband, who clasped it.

"Thank you, Mr. Malloy, for all you're doing."

"You're welcome." Reed walked them to the door. "Don't forget, Thaddeus, you can't linger in Miss Prentice's company any longer than necessary. I'll start the proceedings tomorrow."

Thaddeus stared hard at her. Perhaps his thoughts had been similar to hers and he'd been hoping to join her in her bigger bed that night.

"And the ring you mentioned," Reed added, looking once more at Eliza. "Would you please turn it over to me to keep in a strongbox here at my office? It will be safer for you, and I would prefer not to have it in my home."

"Yes, of course." *How thoughtless of her!* The presence of Stoddard's ring could bring danger to the Malloys. "I'll give it to you tonight."

Thaddeus shook Reed's hand, and they left.

Outside, enjoying the salty Boston air and the fragrant yellow flowers hanging from the linden trees, they walked along in companionable silence for many minutes. Out of the corner of her eye, however, she noticed Thaddeus glancing at her every few steps.

"What is it?" she asked him when she couldn't stand his quiet scrutiny a moment longer.

"You," he said. "You seem worried. Don't be. Reed will get your annulment."

"Mr. Malloy knows what he's doing. That's obvious," she agreed. However, despite believing Reed could free her from her marriage, she didn't think he could get rid of Stoddard for good. She knew Thaddeus was a better bet for accomplishing such a feat.

"What's bugging you, then, Ellie?"

"You know Jack Stoddard."

Thaddeus sighed. "I know. And I meant what I said. I'll make sure he lets you go, even if he doesn't agree with the legality of it."

They walked on without speaking until they were nearly back at the wharf.

She had to tell him what was really bothering her before they got back to Charlotte's.

"I don't want you to leave your sister's house." She sounded desperate, which she despised. Was that a smug smile forming on his face? "What I mean is *I* should be the one to leave. I'm sure there are many fine hotels in Boston." Although how she would pay for one, she had no idea.

"Forget it, darlin'. My sister loves me to pieces, but she'll never let you go to a hotel now that she's opened her home to you. You're here for the long haul."

"And what about you?" She needed to hear his answer, because she had a horrible inkling he was going away, far away.

"If Reed thinks I should stay away from you, then I guess I'll stay at my Aunt Alicia's."

Eliza breathed a sigh of relief, but then he added, "Though I'm only staying in Boston for another night. I have something I need to take care of out West."

At her shocked expression, he added, "I'm behind schedule. Remember?"

Her stomach knotted. She didn't want him to slip out of her life again, but she wouldn't beg, not even after what they'd shared that morning. She knew it hadn't meant to him what it had to her. Men were just different that way, and Thaddeus was more detached than most men. If he could walk away from her, then she would let him. Her pride left her no other option.

Realizing she'd said nothing in response when he took her by the arm and stopped her before they entered Charlotte's house.

"Reed's hiring a marshal. I wouldn't leave you if I didn't think you were safe. You know that?"

She nodded. Then a thought flittered through her brain. "Why?"

"Why what?" he asked, a small frown creasing his forehead.

"Why do you care if I'm safe?" She lifted her chin. She'd asked the question as plainly as she could, but she wasn't sure she wanted to hear his answer.

His eyebrows rose. "Lordy, Ellie, you know why."

A little hope blossomed in her heart. "Why?"

He removed his hat, then replaced it, all the while, looking at their feet. "We grew up together. We're old friends."

That was all? Friends? The same answer he'd given when she'd asked him why he'd helped her out of the boxcar weeks ago. As if he'd do the same for anyone from Spring City whom he encountered with a vicious fever lying unconscious. Their unbridled passion that morning turned sordid in her mind. She'd been merely another one of his willing females, like Jo.

"I know we're *friends*," she said, pushing the words past the lump in her throat. "And I appreciate all you've done for me and how you put your plans on hold." But she wanted so much more. She wanted him to love her wholeheartedly and to put her first above anything else in his life.

During the hours and days of traveling, she'd dreamed he would grow so attached to her he wouldn't be able to move on with the plans he refused to share. At that moment, however, her dream was dashed.

She couldn't take a deep breath, not while looking at his handsome, beloved face. Why couldn't he, the one man who'd always held her heart, fall in love with her?

She'd allowed him all sorts of liberties, even though he'd never even hinted at a long-term relationship with her. She had no one to blame but herself for being left behind with a broken heart and nothing to show for it. After all, she'd known Thaddeus's reputation all her life.

The front door opened and Charlotte stepped out.

"There you are," she said, dividing an astute gaze between them. "I'm heading to Alicia's to pick up Lily and Thomas. Would you like to join me?"

Silence hung thick for a moment.

Eliza spoke up first. "If you don't mind, I'll stay here."

Then she considered the big empty house, with only the two of them. That could be irresistible trouble because her brain seemed to give complete dominion to the long-held desires of her body as soon as Thaddeus got too near.

"However, I'm certain Thaddeus wants to say hello to his aunt."

He flicked Eliza a quizzical look. Then he turned to his sister.

"Actually, Charlie, I'm going to spend the night at Alicia's, and then I have to leave town tomorrow. I'll get my bag and go with you."

"Was it because of the small bed?" Charlotte asked as he scooted past her.

Again, his gaze locked on Eliza, although he answered his sister.

"No, I found the bed to be quite satisfactory."

Eliza averted her eyes and tried not to blush at his loaded remark.

He disappeared inside, leaving the women in silence, glancing at each other uncertainly.

Charlotte rocked back and forth on her heels a moment before speaking.

"Did you have a fruitful meeting with Reed?"

"We did. Your husband seems certain he can help me."

"I'm glad." Charlotte sounded sincere.

"You've both been very nice to me," Eliza blurted out, and to her horror, she felt herself choking up. "I'll go in, now, if you'll excuse me," she said, her throat thick with unshed tears. She had to get to her room and have a good cry.

She fled through the front door. How could she live in the Malloys' home for however long it took Reed to get her annulment—*without* Thaddeus? The peculiar torment of receiving kindness from someone like Charlotte, whom Eliza had wronged most of her life, was probably what she deserved, an apt punishment.

In addition, Charlotte would be a constant reminder of Thaddeus. Eliza imagined it would pain her every time she saw the similarity in their features.

His footsteps on the stairs halted her train of miserable thoughts. He stopped in front of her.

"I'll be seeing you, darlin'."

Standing in the hall, his bag in his hand, he spoke as if they'd meet again the next day. He was unmistakably excited to get going and that hurt even more.

"Be good," he added.

"Of course I'll be good." She tried not to snap at him, but without him to tempt her into trouble, how could she be otherwise?

He took her chin in his hand and made her look at him.

"Be *nice*, too."

"I'm trying," she muttered.

"I know. I've seen it."

Was he going to kiss her goodbye? She blinked. She would not cry.

He gave her a wry smile. "Don't go getting engaged again or marrying anyone else."

Why? Was that an indication he wanted her for himself?

"I won't." The lump in her throat thickened. *What if she never saw him again?*

As if answering her unspoken question, he said, "I'll come back, Ellie, when Reed gives me the all clear, if not sooner."

Did he mean it? Or was he just saying that to prevent a sentimental situation in his sister's front hall? Perhaps he gave every woman, including that awful Josephine, the promise he would return. After all, he'd offered her no declaration of his feelings or his intent.

She lowered her eyes to hide her feelings. Despite how he'd dismissed her words before, she would find it so easy to tell him she loved him. Again. But how terrible if in response, he returned only awkward silence.

"What did I tell you on the train?" he asked, taking her chin in his hand and making her look at him.

She frowned. "I don't know. What?"

He bent low and brushed his lips quickly across hers, as if he had the right.

"You stay here. Don't go anywhere." He kissed her again more firmly, but before she could sink against him, he lifted his head. "And don't do anything rash."

Then he slipped past her and was gone.

A month later, she realized she was pregnant.

CHAPTER EIGHTEEN

With a sense of satisfaction, Thaddeus left the pawnbroker Reed had referred him to. The meeting had surpassed his expectations, resulting in his unloading all but four gold coins, which he'd decided to keep—one each for his young cousins, Thomas and Lily, one for Emory, and one for Charlotte's new baby, who was still seven months away from coming into the world.

His heart felt lighter, not to mention his bag. It had been risky to steal the coins in payment for a debt Stoddard hadn't wanted to pay. But the man was the worst kind of sore loser. *Hell*, the man was even a sore winner! And when the coins had fallen into Thaddeus's lap, so to speak, by way of his charming a certain dancing girl into giving him access to Stoddard's office so he could crack the safe, well, he'd had to take them, hadn't he?

And she'd wanted only a kiss or two, and a few coins she'd deposited down her exposed cleavage.

However, the deed to the land he'd also grabbed, that was another matter. He didn't want to sell it. No, Thaddeus wanted that land with its potential for a metal mine, probably not gold but hopefully copper, and the new life it represented.

While he liked Spring City well enough, he'd never imagined himself going back to his parents' home. He wanted something of his own, and the land was a place to start. It was a sweet parcel in southwestern Montana territory, right in the heart of where the last gold rush happened. Land and maybe a fortune in the ground. Not a bad deal!

So why did a reluctance to start west again slow his footsteps to the train station? As he found a seat on the express, he felt hesitant to travel in any direction carrying him away from Ellie and her ability to take the edge off the endless loneliness. However, by traveling with her, not to mention the many detours she'd caused, he'd almost run out of time. He had to get to the surveyor's office in Butte's town hall before the deed expired.

He supposed he could have discussed the matter with Reed, although land law was not his specialty. Besides that, Thaddeus didn't want Reed or Charlotte trying to dissuade him from his latest venture.

As it was, Charlotte had had words with him the day before on their way to their aunt's house, right after he'd kissed Ellie goodbye.

"Tell me what's in the bag, little brother," she'd started, with a firm tone.

"Look, dear sister," he'd replied in his most patient voice, "I'm old enough to keep my business as just that, mine."

"Even when you bring *your* business to my doorstep," she'd fired back.

"Ellie can stay elsewhere if that's a problem."

"You know that's not what I mean." Charlotte seemed to grow contemplative. "What did you *do* to her, anyway? She actually thanked Jeanine for a cup of tea. I nearly fell off my chair."

He'd laughed at that. "Maybe I did tame her a little. But most of it is her simply growing up, I think, getting away from Spring and out from under her father's rule. Underneath all the pomposity and defensiveness, she's sorta sweet. You'll see."

And with that, he'd thrown Charlotte off her nosey questions. He'd seen no point in discussing what he had in his bag since he was selling the coins anyway, and the deed represented a dream that might not manifest, so why make it seem as if it were already chiseled in stone.

The land taxes needed to be paid, and if he didn't get to Montana before the deed's expiration, there was a real possibility squatters could take possession. All of it was making him nervous as a cat sitting by a rocking chair.

Without the security of owning that piece of land, Thaddeus didn't know what he was going to do next. How else could he make a steady income? And why did it matter now more than ever?

Oh, he knew why, if he was honest with himself. Light, sparkling blue eyes, golden hair, and a sweet bowed mouth were why.

He lit up a cigarette, which he'd stopped doing around Ellie, and tried to enjoy it. But all he could think of was gunk in his lungs. *Shit!* She'd gone and ruined it for him. He put it out in the ashtray in the train seat's arm rest.

After he left Boston far behind, he suspected he would feel better. When he got to Chicago—and he intended not to get off the train until then—he planned to stretch his legs and rest for a single night. He knew he'd find a first-class saloon, a hot bath, and a good barber with a sharp blade. Most likely in that order, too. What he wasn't looking for was any female company.

When he did encounter a couple of beauties in Chicago, eager to please for the price of one of his famed smiles and some good coin, he hastily declined. It might be the first time he'd ever spent the whole night alone in the famed city on the banks of Lake Michigan.

Was he simply being persnickety? Because not a single woman stirred his blood or caught his fancy. Instead, he enjoyed the bath and the shave, he played a winning game of poker, and the next morning, he kept moving westward.

He just wished he could shake the feeling he was missing something. Travelling with Ellie had been a pain in the neck, but nice, too. Except for getting shot at more than usual. He ought to be relieved to be unburdened again, but he couldn't summon up the excitement for his old life.

By the following week, Thaddeus looked out the window of the train pulling in to Butte, Montana territory, by way of Salt Lake City. At a livery yard, he bought a sprightly gray horse, thinking fondly of Lucky, who was somewhere in Burlington, on the Iowa side of the Mississippi.

Feeling unsettlingly light on his new mount without Ellie sharing the saddle, he rode west toward Cable, ending up on a toll road to Granite. Cresting a steep hill, he pulled his horse up short.

"Would you look at that?" he murmured, regarding the astonishing beauty of the area spread before him. His horse whinnied, and Thaddeus felt foolish for speaking aloud, but he sorely wished Ellie could see the huge pine forests spread out everywhere he looked, along with crystal clear lakes and enormous mountains.

After a few seconds longer of sheer appreciation, he rode down into a broad valley, covered in rich green grass. At any moment, a herd of bighorn sheep or whitetail deer was likely to spring across his path, and did! And he kept his new rifle at the ready for mountain lions or bears.

After a bobcat spooked his horse before turning tail and disappearing into the grasses, he thought of Ellie again. She wouldn't have liked the big cat. No, not one bit, but then, why was he always wondering what Ellie would think of this or that?

Here, a man could breathe. Well, he could breathe in Spring City, Colorado, too, or in Boston, for that matter, with the crisp Atlantic air rustling the blond locks of a certain lovely lady.

Damn it! He spurred his horse faster, trying to outrun his own thoughts.

She would go insane. Eliza was certain of it! She had to tell someone, but she couldn't. Who could she tell? Reed and

Charlotte would no doubt force Thaddeus to marry her. Or would, if she weren't still married and if he could be located. She couldn't stomach the notion of a so-called shotgun wedding, but in her case, as an already reluctant wife, she didn't even have the luxury of that ignominious fate.

On the one hand, as an unwed mother, her reputation, such as it was, would be shredded. On the other hand, as the wife of Jack Stoddard, the notorious gambler who was not the father of her child, she had no hope for any reputation at all except the absolute blackest.

And no one knew where Thaddeus was, anyway. He'd disappeared as quickly as the morning mist.

When she'd missed her monthly flow, she had dismissed it as being due to the stressfulness of her current situation. Then she'd begun to feel a little queasy. Granted, she was living on a wharf, but the house didn't move at all, and she'd never suffered from an unsettled stomach before, not even on Stoddard's gambling boat.

Charlotte had recently gone through similar symptoms, carrying her own baby, yet now she'd eased into a time of looking healthy and feeling good. No, Eliza could deny it no longer: She was carrying Thaddeus's child.

It gave her a little thrill, to be sure, along with a tremendous amount of terror and even shame. Jeanine looked knowingly at her one morning, and Eliza was sure the Frenchwoman knew. Of course, with no menstrual rags in the wash, it would become apparent.

Heaven help her! At least her father wasn't alive to see it. He would be most disappointed. She had no idea what her long-dead mother would've thought.

Her annulment was more important to her than ever, and mercifully, everything was moving along well in that regard. In a safe in his office, Reed kept the diamond ring, the size of which had made his dark eyebrows sweep toward his hairline.

Surely, Jack would be happy to trade his signature on a piece of paper granting her freedom for that blasted ring. Reed had a meeting with a judge that very day, and if everything went smoothly, then he would send paperwork to Stoddard at his riverboat, persuading him to go along with the decision.

Thaddeus sent no word as to his whereabouts. She'd hoped for a letter but not expected one. She didn't care. She didn't need him. She could raise her baby all by herself. And if she moved to some godforsaken backwater where no one knew her, she could pretend to be a widow.

Yes, the idea had some merit. There was something noble, not to mention sympathetic, in being a young widow. She couldn't go back to Spring City, unless she lied to the whole town. And that lie could easily be discovered if Charlotte happened to visit or, more probably, write to her friend Sarah Cuthins.

All of a sudden, however, Eliza desperately wanted to go home more than anything. She wanted to see her lovely house and sit on her own porch, front or back. True, her father had died in that house, but she had many happy memories of living in it, too. And from her house, she could look toward the Sanborn homestead and think of all her adventures with Thaddeus.

Yes, the more she considered, the more she longed for home, and sooner rather than later. She didn't want anyone telling her she couldn't travel after her condition started to show. She was already ever so slightly rounded at her waist and had to leave her fitted jackets unbuttoned. But soon, she knew, her skirt wouldn't do up unless she pushed it lower than normal.

A few evenings later, she borrowed Jeanine's sewing kit and moved her buttons over on her waistbands so she could still fasten them.

"I'm not hurrying you," Eliza said to Reed one night when they were all taking coffee in the parlor after dinner. "I just wondered how my case is going. Is there any progress?"

"The judge agreed you were coerced into the marriage. He wants to see you in his chambers. I think that will happen by the end of the week. I've also sent a notarized letter off to Mr. Stoddard, apprising him of the proceedings. Naturally, I mentioned a certain item you have of his that you would return to him when you were no longer Mrs. Stoddard."

Eliza clapped her hands. "I'm so relieved. I can go home soon, then."

"At least a few weeks, still," Reed said.

She felt her smile die.

"Come, Miss Prentice," he added. "Our hospitality can't be so bad."

"No," Eliza said, shaking her head. She looked at Charlotte, who'd entered the room after putting Emory, Thomas, and Lily to bed. "You two have been most gracious. I don't know how I can ever repay you. But I miss Spring City. Can you believe it?"

Charlotte nodded. "I can. Even though I was happy when I left. I still recall the little things, like Jessie's turkey pie and Dan's jokes. Mostly, I miss Sarah and Doc, and having people around me who've known me all my life."

Reed was staring at her. He reached his hand over and took Charlotte's.

"No, dear heart," she said with a smile. "I'm not sad. This part of my life is the best part, right now, having you and our children and more on the way."

She blushed prettily, patting her stomach, and Eliza felt a rush of happiness for her childhood nemesis. How incredible to experience such joy for someone else! Where was that feeling coming from?

"You have never looked prettier," Eliza said. "You used to have a fairly severe look on your face."

She gasped at her own words and, utterly mortified, covered her mouth with her hand.

However, Charlotte grinned and Reed laughed outright.

"I remember that look. She tried to frighten me away with it," he joked.

Eliza was glad Charlotte took no offense. "What I meant to say is that the life you have now obviously makes you happy, and I'm glad for you. For my part, I know I will feel quite content being home, even by myself."

Charlotte seemed to stiffen. "Have either of you heard from my little brother?"

Reed shook his head, but Eliza was puzzled. "Why would *I* have heard from him if you haven't?"

Charlotte glanced at Reed, then coughed. "I apologize," she said. "I thought you two, that is, Thaddeus seemed to . . . I mean, you and he. Oh dear. It's none of my business."

"What my fumbling wife is trying to say, Miss Prentice, is it seemed when you first arrived in Thaddeus's company, you and he had some kind of understanding. Given the way in which he was so concerned with your situation, it appeared he had feelings for you, and vice versa."

Eliza was sure her face was scarlet. Feelings for each other! If only they knew she was *enceinte* with Charlotte's niece or nephew.

Charlotte jumped up from her place next to Reed and sat down beside Eliza on the other sofa, clasping her hand.

"I'm so sorry, Eliza. I didn't mean to embarrass you. We'll say no more on the subject."

Eliza nodded. "It's fine. I can see how it looked."

Taking a deep breath, she chose her next words carefully. "In truth, I very much admire your brother. I know it seems he has no purpose other than his own wants, but he helped me when he had no reason to, risking his life in the process. He's brave and he's smart."

And so handsome and strong, he made her entire body tingle when he gave her the sweetest of kisses.

She sighed then sat up straighter because they were looking at her curiously.

"There's nothing between us. Nothing binding, I mean. No declaration of anything more than friendship."

How she wished there was! Thaddeus had made it clear, however, by rejecting her spontaneous words of love on the train and then leaving her in Boston, he was not interested in pursuing anything permanent with her.

"He's not the type of person to settle down, I think."

Reed smiled wryly. "He may, in time, be that person. He seemed changed already from a year ago. Don't you think, Charlotte?"

"*Mm.*" She was still focusing on Eliza's face.

Eliza, for her part, felt the less scrutiny of her emotions and her person, the better. She yawned behind her hand.

"I'm going to turn in."

In her room, she paced. Could she really stay a few more weeks and have her condition go undiscovered? She would hate to lose the small amount of respect she'd garnered from Charlotte and Reed. She didn't even know why, but it mattered.

CHAPTER NINETEEN

Four months into his venture, Thaddeus handed the deed to the land, as well as ownership of his mine, to his foreman, Tom Higgins. Behind Tom sat his wife, Alice, on a stool, peeling potatoes in the great wide open while keeping an eye on their two small children, who played in the grass. And Thaddeus knew he'd done the right thing.

He'd spent weeks scoping out the land for which he'd paid a princely sum in back taxes, and then he'd hired men to build him a frontier house—all wood, with a stone fireplace and real glass windows.

Opening a mine in the side of the mountain on the advice of a surveyor had yielded riches in the form of copper. He already had ten men employed and could foresee hiring more. Everything had happened so fast and gone as easily as a snake slithered into a hole in the ground. And all the while, Thaddeus kept getting more and more antsy, like he was in the wrong place at the wrong time and needed to get home. Home!

Where the hell was that?

Then Tom showed up with his gently efficient wife and young kids. They were dressed in well-worn clothes that some might call rags, and Tom had asked for a job. He'd take any small amount of wages to help him keep his family in food and shelter. And Thaddeus realized when he woke up one morning that without what this man had, life there would be meaningless, absolute crap.

No matter what Tom did—pounding a nail, working in the mine, felling trees to make a decent road—the man appeared satisfied at the end of each day to get back to the canvas tent he'd set up for his family in a sunny part of the valley.

Meanwhile, Thaddeus's spacious lodging was complete, yet he felt less compulsion to settle into it than to continue on the nearby toll road and head somewhere else.

What a screw-up he was! He was the proud owner of a copper mine, which was practically as good as a gold mine, and all he could think of was moving on. Or rather, heading back to Ellie.

But he didn't. He stuck it out and he watched. He watched his men to determine who got on with whom. He fired one at the first sign of dishonesty, and he fired another for fighting. But Tom was steadfast, committed, and honest. He could read and do math, and he understood when Thaddeus needed to run ideas past him.

"Tom, I've got something for you," Thaddeus said, walking over to the man he'd made his foreman. It only took a few minutes of looking over the papers for Tom to see what Thaddeus was proposing.

"You can't be serious," Tom said, taking a step backward as if he'd been hit.

"I am. It's yours, every damn bit. You can move your family into the house today because a Montana winter in that tent of yours would not be pleasant. I hope Alice approves of the house. It has room for all of you, but I didn't design it with a woman in mind, so I bet you'll be remodeling it before the month's out. Maybe build a bigger kitchen."

He'd grown fond of Tom's level-headed wife and even more so of her incredible cooking. Alice cooked for all the men who worked the mine, and Thaddeus paid her handsomely for that.

Tom shook his head, still disbelieving the good fortune that had fallen into his lap. He raised puzzled eyes to Thaddeus. "And what the tarnation are you going to do?"

Thaddeus grinned. It was the first time he'd heard Tom swear. "I'm leaving."

"Just like that? Come on, Thaddeus. I like to think we've become friends, as much as partners." He waggled the papers he was holding. "Tell me what you're up to?"

Not one to talk to anyone about his affairs, either in business or in love, Thaddeus nearly brushed off the question. However, thinking of Tom's devotion to Alice, he had a feeling the man would understand.

"This may sound plumb crazy, but I left behind someone, a lady, I mean, who I want to spend the rest of my life with."

"That don't sound crazy at all. Man can't live by copper alone."

"I've learned that," Thaddeus agreed, "although some would say this female is nothing but trouble. 'Course many people say that about me, too. But when we're together, me and her, everything feels right somehow, even though I've spent a long time believing I was the wrong man for her."

He realized he'd started to talk to himself, maybe convincing himself what he was about to do was a good choice. Tom looked at him with sharp eyes and a friendly smile, so Thaddeus added, "I don't think I'm gonna be happy without her, no matter where I live."

He left on the horse he'd ridden in on with his one bag, his hat, and some smokes just in case he decided to risk having one. Easy as pie, which was how he'd always liked his life. But now he wanted more. A lot more. He wanted connections and complications. He wanted something to live for besides his own needs. He wanted Ellie.

What had he been thinking, trying to put down roots with nothing to hold him to the land but profit? He could profit perfectly fine without living in Montana. He'd been struck by a bout of generosity where Tom and his family were concerned, but not by a fit of foolhardiness. In their agreement, he would receive thirty-five percent of the quarterly profits. With everyone wanting copper for wiring, he had a feeling he and Tom were going to be rich men.

So why was it, after he sold his horse in Butte and bought his first-class ticket through to Boston, instead of contemplating his imminent wealth, he was thinking of an adorably difficult blue-eyed blonde?

He couldn't wait to set eyes on her again. The train couldn't go fast enough, even though he knew Ellie would be hopping mad at how hastily he'd left and how long he'd stayed away. Yup, he was going to get an earful of her temper, so fierce his hair would blow back, and he couldn't wait.

When he'd told her he would return, he had meant it, despite having no timeframe in mind. He'd never worried much about the passage of time until that moment. Unexpectedly, it occurred to him he'd stayed away too long. And of course, he'd plain forgotten to send Reed notice of his whereabouts. No one had ever needed to reach him before.

He hoped Reed had been successful because he was starting to have unfamiliar but exciting thoughts. Perhaps it was seeing Tom and his devoted wife, perhaps it was all the other families around him on the train, perhaps it was his own sister's happiness, or perhaps Thaddeus was just growing up.

He couldn't say what sparked his desire to make an honest man out of himself, but if Ellie would have him, he knew he would try his damnedest to be a good husband to her.

With the best of intentions still circulating through his mind, Thaddeus smiled broadly when his sister opened her front door.

"Hi, Charlie," he said, waiting for her to hug him as she always did. She, however, greeted him with a full-blown scowl and her mouth grimly set, gesturing him inside without a welcoming embrace.

He'd had only a moment to take in her burgeoning stomach and rounded cheeks when Reed appeared.

"In good conscience, I have to do this," he said, and his brother-in-law punched him in the mouth.

Charlotte cried out, voicing the stunned surprise Thaddeus felt as his hat went flying.

With difficulty, he barely stopped himself from retaliating. Barely. For a man who'd been alone for so many years, Thaddeus had never had the option of not defending himself. But this was his sister's husband.

"What the hell?" he said, touching his cheek to see if it was bleeding. It wasn't, and he hadn't lost any teeth. Reed had pulled his punch . . . a little. But Thaddeus wasn't going to take another hit. He tossed his bag down and with fists held in front of him and his legs apart, he waited for an explanation.

For a moment, Reed's clenched jaw and Charlotte's grim expression were the only answers.

"I don't suppose you two want to give me a clue what in blue blazes that was for. It seems like I've returned to a mad-house."

Charlotte eyed her husband. "No more fisticuffs, please."

Reed shrugged as his expression turned a shade sheepish before he visibly relaxed his stance.

"It was my duty," he insisted.

Thaddeus wondered if, somehow, Reed had found out he and Ellie had been intimate in the bed upstairs and felt honor-bound to defend her.

As if confirming his suspicions, Charlotte said, "It's Eliza," and her look of worry sucked all the fight right out of him. He lowered his fists.

"What about her? Where is she?"

His sister glanced at her husband, who nodded for her to continue.

"She's gone," Charlotte said.

Thaddeus felt the same surge of fear that had rushed through him when seeing Stoddard's men haul her away.

"Gone? Gone where? When?"

"It's been three days," Reed said. "She slipped by the marshal, but he was looking for men coming after her, not expecting her to sneak past him. I don't suppose you have any idea where she would go?"

Thaddeus ran a hand through his hair, feeling utterly helpless. "For Christ's sake, I wouldn't be asking you if I knew. Back to Spring City, maybe."

He rubbed the back of his neck and saw them exchange a quick glance, the meaning of which he couldn't fathom.

Three days. He'd missed her by so little. But in that amount of time, she could be damn near anywhere.

"Did she get her annulment?"

"She did," Reed said, sending Charlotte another quick glance. "Darling, you should sit down."

He held out his hand and she acquiesced, letting him lead her to the parlor in the back of the house overlooking the sea. Thaddeus had no choice but to follow.

"Then why on God's green earth would she run away?" he demanded, after Reed stopped fussing over his pregnant wife.

Reed leveled him with a stare. "Unfortunately, Miss Prentice doesn't know her marriage is annulled. She ran out of patience, it seems. I informed you both early on that annulments take more time than divorces, especially when we're dealing with a hostile, uncooperative husband."

Thaddeus found himself making fists again. The word *husband* didn't sit particularly well, not when it applied to Stoddard.

"And Miss Prentice's former husband has been particularly uncooperative," Reed continued, crossing his arms. "The judge, on the other hand, saw the merits of our case. Proceedings went well until we tried to get Mr. Stoddard's signature. I sent one letter after another, then I sent messengers, all to no avail. My partner, John Trelaine, is on his way back now, however. I had a telegram from him a couple days ago. He was successful."

"So Stoddard signed, and Ellie is a free woman," Thaddeus said, "except she doesn't know it."

"Correct," Reed said.

"Why would she up and leave when she was so close to getting what she wanted?" *Infernal woman!* It was almost as if she begged for trouble. And he just knew, somehow, he was going to have to extricate her. He looked at their grim faces.

"Ellie hasn't changed a bit, has she? I bet she up and left and never even thanked you." When he saw her again, he was going to tan her backside, after he'd thoroughly kissed her, of course. "I need a smoke."

"No, Teddy, listen," Charlotte began, but he already knew what she was going to say.

"I know," he muttered. "You're just like Ellie. You don't like the smell. I'm heading outside."

With that, he was up and out the back door onto the deck before they could stop him. The sea was as dark and fierce today as his emotions.

Lighting a cigarette, he sucked in the smoke at the same time as white-hot anger coursed through him, both at Ellie for her headstrong ways and at Stoddard for his delaying tactics. Mostly, he realized, he was angry at himself, for thinking he would come back to find her all domesticated and waiting for him.

Damn! He'd told her to stay put. And what had she done? The very opposite.

Just then, the door opened and Charlotte stepped out, casting him a grim glance before standing beside him at the railing, staring out at the ocean.

"What is wrong with that woman?" Thaddeus asked her. "I come clear across the country to tell her—"

"She's expecting," Charlotte blurted out, wrapping her arms around her own developing stomach.

"Expecting what?" he snapped. But then his sister's words seemed to reverberate inside his brain, like an echo in his copper mine. He heard the last one over and over. *Expecting. Expecting.* His child!

Well, hell! He hadn't seen that coming. Dropping the cigarette, he ground it out with his boot while his heart slammed around against his chest wall. No wonder Reed had hit him.

"And she doesn't want me to know?" he surmised.

"I don't know what she's thinking," Charlotte admitted. "Obviously, she has feelings for you. And you for her?"

He nodded, feeling desperate now to talk to Ellie.

Charlotte looked at him, apparently seeing the anguish he felt, because she reached up her delicate hand and placed it on his cheek.

"I'm sorry, Teddy. You were wrong by the way. She did thank us. She left a note."

His gaze darted to hers. "What did she say? Did she leave a message for me?"

Charlotte's expression told it all. Ellie hadn't mentioned him.

"All she said was thank you, expressed it with heartfelt gratitude, and that she'd be in touch."

He gripped the railing. After all they'd been through, she'd left without a word for him.

"Eliza may be experiencing a myriad of feelings," his sister explained. "She might be ashamed or she could be angry."

Ashamed of having relations with him? That made the most sense. But he could also imagine her furious at the way he'd left her. But he'd had to go. He'd had to set up his future so he didn't need to depend on gambling ever again. Hadn't he told her he'd be back? Evidently, she hadn't believed him.

"Women don't always think reasonably when they're in my condition," Charlotte offered. "I can attest to that. Besides, Eliza might not know how you feel about her."

He heard the harder edge to her tone, condemning him.

"Teddy, we'd heard nothing from you, and you've been gone a long time."

Over four months, closer to five, and he'd thought of Ellie every day. He ought to have done more than that. He should have sent her a telegram the minute he'd got to the station in Butte and before he got on the train to Boston. Would that have made a difference? Or would she have fled even sooner?

Right now, he needed more answers from Reed, and he had to decide which direction he would looking for Ellie. No doubt in his mind he would track her down. As he turned to go inside, his sister's hand on his arm stopped him. One glance at her face and he realized Charlotte was getting her hackles up.

"What *are* you going to do regarding Eliza having your child?"

Thaddeus wanted to growl at his sister. His woman was out in the world somewhere, probably annoying people, making enemies. And now she carried his baby along.

He felt helpless, and he hated that, hated the way his breathing came in spurts when he thought of her in danger, the way his stomach sank at the idea of not being there to help her. But he saw the concern on Charlotte's lovely face, and he calmed himself.

"I intend to marry Eliza Prentice and raise my child."

She paused, judging his sincerity with narrowed eyes.

"What about your incessant wandering?"

"I came back, didn't I?" he ground out. So much for staying calm.

Charlotte made a disparaging sound, which he knew meant "too little, too late." Then she sighed.

"But how will you keep her and provide for her?"

A few months ago, that question would have made him stammer with uncertainty. Now, it wasn't even an issue.

"I have money, dear sister. Plenty of it and an income. More than enough to keep a wife and son or daughter. But all I have right now is a missing woman who thinks she's still married to another man."

He grasped her hand and dragged her back into the parlor.

Patiently waiting for their sibling discussion to come to an end, Reed stood up.

"Ready to go?"

It seemed he understood Thaddeus's near-frantic desire to head out immediately.

"Yup." He reached for his bag when he noticed silent tears slipping down Charlotte's cheeks. Even before Reed could reach for her, Thaddeus drew her into his arms.

"Charlie, it's going to be all right," he promised, although all he could do was hope he was telling the truth. "I'm going to find her and hogtie her if need be. You wouldn't mind Ellie being your sister-in-law, would you? I mean, I know she's not your favorite person in the world."

Charlotte managed to stop crying and wiped her face with a handkerchief she pulled from her sleeve.

"Of course I wouldn't mind, Teddy. Don't be ridiculous. I've come to quite like her, actually. She's awfully smart and was good company. But she has a melancholy about her that goes bone deep. So, if you're marrying her solely because of the baby . . ." She let her words trail off, looking as if her tears were about to start flowing again.

He wanted to comfort her, but the last thing Thaddeus intended to do was discuss his conflicting feelings for Ellie with his sister and his brother-in-law.

Reed cleared his throat. "It's her condition," he offered. "My sweetly emotional wife cries over everything. Frankly, I'm surprised it's taken twenty minutes for the tears to start."

"Stop teasing me," Charlotte said, shooting her husband a watery smile. Then she looked up into Thaddeus's face. "Do you want to take some of her things with you?"

He frowned. "Didn't she take them?"

Charlotte shook her head. "Eliza left most of her new clothes. She took only her carpetbag."

Glancing uncertainly at Reed, she added, "We thought she was coming back at first because she had so little with her."

Thaddeus shrugged. "That woman can travel light, I tell you. I'm sure she has everything she needs in that bag. But don't you worry. We'll send for her clothes as soon as I find her and get her settled."

Please God, let him find her safe. "I've got to go, Charlie."

"I'll take you to the station," Reed said.

Thaddeus sat mutely in the clarence beside Reed. He felt exhausted and energized at the same time. *Which way to go first?* Reed was talking, but Thaddeus couldn't concentrate on his words.

He'd scarcely had time to digest the incredible news—Ellie was carrying his child. A small smile crossed his lips, and he shook his head in wonder. His child. *Good Lord!* He had damn well better convince her he could do the job of husband and father. He couldn't remember ever wanting anything more than to claim Ellie as his wife and to raise their baby.

Yet she'd run away from the one place she knew he could find her, and a nagging fear kept telling him she didn't want him, not in either of those capacities. To her, he would always be aimless, a drifter, slightly on the wrong side of legal.

A thief, she'd called him. Is that how she truly saw him? Not worthy of her or their child.

"Miss Prentice is completely out of debt," Reed said, bringing Thaddeus's attention back to the specifics of Ellie's case. "I stipulated Mr. Stoddard dismiss her so-called debt of five thousand dollars. After all, she claims he cheated."

"That left only the ring," Reed continued, "and John had it with him when he and two marshals went to Hamilton. We decided that seeing it would make Stoddard sign in accordance with the judge's ruling if nothing else would. It worked, too."

Shit! Thaddeus broke out in a cold sweat. "Does Ellie know Stoddard has his ring back?"

"No." Reed frowned. "She'd become increasingly removed the past two weeks and didn't even want to discuss her annulment. She wanted to know when it was complete, and that was all. When she left so abruptly, I never had a chance to tell her what my partner was doing."

Wild thoughts raced through Thaddeus's brain. What if Ellie had decided to take matters into her own hands? If she got anywhere near Stoddard and tried to use possession of his precious ring as protection, she'd be defenseless. But why would she go near the vicious gambler? True, she was pregnant and might be having some crazy notions, but he had no reason to believe she'd do anything rash.

Except try to force Stoddard into giving her an annulment!

Obviously, she'd grown tired of waiting, both for Stoddard to agree to set her free and for Thaddeus to return.

His stomach roiled with uncertainty. It felt like he'd swallowed a bag of rocks.

Into the silence, Reed said, "I'm sorry I let her get away, especially in her condition."

"It wasn't your fault. Hell, she can be as slippery as an eel and has escaped before, even without my help. And she's run away from me, too. She can do just about anything she sets her mind to."

As he said it, Thaddeus realized it was true and how much he truly admired her for the incredible woman she'd become. If only he could tell her to her face.

"You should have articulated to Miss Prentice how you felt," Reed admonished, saying his first condemning words over the whole unsavory situation. "And you shouldn't have promised her you'd return when we both know you weren't certain of doing so."

Reed shot him a sideways look as they reached the train station.

Thaddeus met his gaze for a moment, then dropped it. How did the man know how conflicted he'd been when he'd left Boston? In his usual impulsive manner, he'd told Ellie what he knew she'd wanted to hear, and in his heart, he'd meant it, wanting to be with her, the same as he'd always wanted to. However, in his head, he'd been planning a new life.

If he'd liked it enough, he might still be in Montana. That is, if he was the kind of man he'd previously believed himself to be, one who could live for making money, live without family, and live without the woman he loved.

And make no mistake, he realized as swiftly and surprisingly as Reed's punch to his jaw, he loved Ellie with all his heart. And nothing else in his life was worth more than that, not the copper mine, the poker games, and not even his cherished freedom.

CHAPTER TWENTY

Eliza couldn't stop crying, and it made her madder than a stuck pig. Head bowed, she leaned against the window in the corner of her train seat. Train travel without Thaddeus was like trying to eat without a fork or spoon. Just plain wrong, but it was better than staying put, abandoned by him, and wondering if she'd ever see him again.

During the first month at Charlotte's, Eliza had still hoped he'd return. A month seemed like long enough to finish whatever business he had. Daily, she'd looked out for the mail, hoping Thaddeus had at least sent her some missive concerning his situation.

Once she'd realized she was pregnant, she'd spent her days trying to hide it, hoping he would come whisk her away before his family realized the extent of her shamefulness. When the second month had passed, she'd begun to feel resentful. While she felt her body changing in subtle ways, Thaddeus was off somewhere freely living his life. Without her.

She doubted if he thought about her at all. Their association had been brief and troublesome, and he'd never offered her any clue or hope about his intentions. Neither Charlotte nor Reed had heard from him, either, and as Reed said in passing one day, a man could easily lose himself in the West.

By the third month, when her stomach was given to heaving even while empty, she'd grown angry. *Damn him! And damn her for a fool!*

When Charlotte approached her in private one afternoon to confirm she was with child, it had been the single most humiliating experience of her life, worse than when Stoddard had made her strip naked looking for his ring.

To her credit, Charlotte had not offered her pity regarding her condition, nor futile hope Thaddeus would come back. Instead, she provided sympathetic understanding, as well as Jeanine's special tea for soothing the stomach.

Reed was doing what he'd promised, getting her an annulment—methodically, legally, and it seemed, excruciatingly slowly. Eliza had stopped asking why it was taking so long, after he'd mentioned Stoddard's refusal to sign. Perhaps the blasted gambler would never sign and she'd be stuck on a wharf in Boston forever.

Except she would still be waiting for Thaddeus, pathetically mooning over a man who'd had no trouble abandoning her. Truthfully, she was plain tired of herself. Her father was probably turning over in his grave and his feisty daughter's meekness.

Then, one evening, she realized she didn't have to stay. She could simply leave. No one was forcing her to remain. And she could only imagine the relief the Malloys would feel after her departure. She decided at the beginning of her fourth month, if Thaddeus still hadn't shown up in a week, she would leave.

After that, she kept more to herself, not wanting to burden her hosts with her constant presence in their dining room and their parlor. She longed for her own home and started to dream of setting up her old bedroom as a nursery. Yes, she would get her life back, free and clear. She would start behaving as a Prentice should, not this helpless, dependent woman she didn't recognize.

Stop sniveling, she ordered herself as the train rumbled through another town, and she did stop. In little less than an hour, she would be at the Oquawka Junction where she would spend the night before changing railway lines to Hamilton.

Besides the frisson of fear at confronting Jack, Eliza felt immensely satisfied in arriving back at Stoddard's boat of her own accord, not because he'd dragged her. She pictured herself marching right up to him and telling him she'd had enough of this nonsense. Finished! She was through running and way past done being scared.

By the time she reached Jack, she might already be a free woman, but if she wasn't, she was determined to beat him at his own game—all or nothing.

Thaddeus discovered Ellie had boarded an east-bound train. Unfortunately, he hadn't found out until he'd wasted hours at Boston's main terminal, asking everyone if they'd seen her. Finally, he met a conductor changing trains who recalled the stunning blond lady traveling alone.

After Thaddeus determined her route, even though she could be heading to Spring City, he knew with sick certainty she was, indeed, returning to Stoddard's riverboat.

For God's sake, why? He tossed his bag onto the rack above him and took a seat on the train. As he stared out the window, thinking of the rumpled bed in the boat's stateroom where he'd found Ellie in the bathtub, he entertained the briefest of notions the baby she carried was Stoddard's. But he banished the appalling idea as violently as he hurled his last pack of cigarettes out the train window.

If he got her back, he vowed he would never smoke again.

Summoning memories of their lovemaking, he knew Ellie had never been with any other man but him. What a humbling gift she'd given him. Try as he might to pretend she'd casually chosen him, she was beautiful enough to have any man she crooked her finger at. Yet for some reason, she'd picked him.

And he'd treated that remarkable occurrence as if it were ordinary.

He smacked his head against the headrest and closed his eyes. He should have been down on his knees, begging her to wait for him to return from Montana territory and promising his undying devotion. Instead, he'd left her with hardly a backward glance.

Thaddeus knew why, if he was honest with himself. He'd been scared, plain and simple. What if he'd ask her to wait for him and she'd up and left anyway, crushing his pride again the way someone squashed an unwelcome bug?

Truth be told, four months ago, he'd been even more afraid she *would* have waited for him, depending on him to open the mine, make a steady income, and become the man she needed.

Either way, his feelings for her frightened the bejesus out of him.

He fidgeted in his seat. She was days ahead of him, and the train seemed to be moving like molasses in December. Chilling thoughts tormented him, of Stoddard playing the ultimate trump card and keeping Ellie, taking their baby and raising it as his own, out of pure spite. Stoddard had already played for high stakes—for life and death and for a woman's hand in marriage. Wouldn't playing for the life of an unborn child be the next most exciting prize imaginable?

Thaddeus ruminated for hours. That she would leave the safety of his sister's home, especially while carrying a child, seemed so pig-headedly irresponsible. However, he could understand her wanting to end the long threat. After all, she'd always been a headstrong, independent woman. If her dander was up, she would think nothing of waltzing back onto Stoddard's boat, making threats, issuing demands.

But she didn't know Stoddard had his ring back.

Thaddeus hit his fist against the armrest, imagining her believing she held that particular ace up her sleeve, only to have Stoddard flash the gem at some devastatingly inopportune time. She was walking into an ambush.

He was tempted to buy another horse and get to Hamilton faster. So tempted, that's what he did. No more stopping at stations and waiting for endless passengers to board and disembark.

Jumping off the train in Pittsburgh, he bought a horse and began a long, more direct trek across Ohio and Indiana, and finally into Illinois, heading back to the goddamned Mississippi River. He couldn't beat Ellie to the riverboat, but he could try to reach her in time.

"Take your hands off me," Eliza said to Blackheart Bart, who had an iron-clad hold on her upper arm. "I am here to see Jack."

The man grinned, showing his yellow teeth. "Oh, you'll see him all right."

He shoved her ahead of him up the inside staircase into the main cabin. Jack was seated at his personal table with no other gamblers anywhere in sight. It was Sunday, she realized, so the boat was closed up, nearly deserted, at least until nightfall.

He didn't appear surprised to see her. After she'd been spotted walking along the road toward the boat, Bart had picked her up in Jack's signature black and red carriage. She'd appreciated the ride, but not the way she was being treated.

Jack rose to his feet. He was not a tall man, and standing, he was eye-to-eye with her. He had on his familiar bowler and a pinstripe suit, a cigar in his right hand and his other hand casually in his pocket.

He smiled at her, but it didn't encourage her. His smile usually came on the heels of a big win, or in this case, as a prelude to what he must see as her abject defeat. She had returned, and she was unaided and unaccompanied.

"No one runs out on Jack Stoddard," he said, taking a puff at his cigar. "I was sure you'd be back."

She almost laughed. "So sure you sent your men," she gestured toward Bart and another who lounged on a chair, "chasing me clear across the country months ago. Not to mention your Indian tracker. So sure that you had to kidnap me twice already. Yet still, I slipped away." The second time, with Thaddeus's help. *But now, she was all alone.*

Without being invited, she took a seat at his table. "I've had my lawyer working on an annulment," she added.

"Yes, I know. His partner was here recently."

Eliza felt a prickle of fear. Why was Jack smiling then? And where *was* Reed's partner?

"Is he still here?"

"No, I sent him on his way."

Bart laughed, and Eliza hoped Reed's associate had been smart enough to come with a sheriff or a marshal. She fervently hoped he wasn't now lying at the bottom of the Mississippi because of her.

"What did he say?" she asked.

Jack took another puff of his cigar. "Don't you know? He works with *your* lawyer."

She ignored the cat and mouse game.

"I assume you signed the annulment papers."

He cocked his head. "And if I didn't?"

"Then I will instruct Mr. Malloy to sell your ring."

He clucked and shook his head. "That wouldn't be very nice of you, Eliza. And what will you do if I have signed?"

"If you were anyone other than who you are, I'd say, thank you, kindly." She tossed her head and then returned his level gaze. "In your case, however, I would simply be on my way without another word."

"And my ring?" He stuck the cigar back in his mouth and crossed his arms.

At that point, she saw it plain as day. The diamond ring sat firmly on the small finger of his left hand.

She gasped, realization dawning at once.

"We're not married anymore," she surmised, her voice becoming a whisper. Reed would never have let Jack have the ring back, not unless he'd signed the annulment papers.

A sense of sweet relief washed over her after all these months. The huge debt had evaporated, and her Spring City property was her own again. It was as if she'd never stupidly entered into Jack Stoddard's private train car and played poker with him.

She looked around herself. Instead, she'd even more stupidly returned to his riverboat. On a Sunday of all days, with no witnesses and no help of any kind.

"I reckon you're right," Jack agreed. "You are no longer my 'beloved'." He laughed, and Blackheart Bart joined in.

Suddenly, she felt like a hen in the rooster's clutches. Trying to recall the speeches she'd rehearsed on the train, full of bravado and nerve, Eliza took a deep breath.

"Then we have nothing more to discuss," she said, keeping her voice calm. *Don't show him you're scared,* she told herself. She would simply stand up and walk out.

"How about a little game?" he asked, sitting down across from her. "For old time's sake."

She felt sweat break out in the middle of her back. He was not going to let her go easily. She didn't answer, so he continued.

"If *I* win, I keep your daddy's holdings."

She chuckled, trying to sound at ease. *Why would I do that?* she nearly asked, but because she had a feeling she wasn't going to be given a choice, she asked instead, "Why would you want anything in Spring City?"

"I fancy owning a town. Maybe I'll be the mayor." He looked at his men, lounging at tables nearby. "Right boys?"

"Sure, Mr. Stoddard. I mean, *Mayor* Stoddard," one said with a snigger.

Bart merely stared.

Eliza could imagine the disgust on the faces of the people she'd known all her life. She couldn't let Jack get his claws into Spring City. Why, he would make her father's domination of Spring look like a little girl's tea party. Ada's saloon would become an all-out bordello. Fuller's would be turned into a gambling house.

No! It didn't matter how good she knew she was, she wouldn't play with him, not for such important stakes. He was a cheater, after all.

"Spring City doesn't have a mayor," she said, standing up. "And I prefer not to play."

"Well, that won't do at all." He shook his round head before puffing on his cigar. "You have to give me a chance. Besides I beat you before, and now I'm left with nothing. No wife and no property."

For someone who professed to have nothing, he was sitting pretty. And he'd never "beat" her before. Not fairly. She still wanted to call him a cheat to his face, but she'd heard it was a certain path to a quick demise.

"And if I win?" she asked, deciding not to pussyfoot around.

"I let you live." He slapped his hands on the table making her jump.

Involuntarily, she clasped her hands over her stomach. Then she watched while his horrid smile evaporated as rapidly as water in the desert. His eyes narrowed, but he said nothing more.

She'd been foolish to react as she had. Slowly, she dropped her arms to her sides, relaxing her posture. She prayed he hadn't detected her condition, not with the pregnancy corset she wore, all laced up nice and tight.

"I'll need some kind of assurance you won't renege," she said, knowing she actually had no leverage at all.

"Renege?" He stood up, all bluster. "Are you calling me a cheat?"

She arched an eyebrow at him and said nothing. She was not going to give him a reason to kill her outright.

After a moment, he took his seat again and rubbed his hand over his chin.

"Okay, little lady. Bart here will give you his gun."

"Boss?" Blackheart Bart ground out the word.

Eliza flashed her gaze up to his ugly face. Uncertainty and even defiance settled onto his features.

"Give it to her," Stoddard ordered. "Set it on the table. That should be assurance enough."

Then he pulled out his own gun, a small but deadly derringer with intricate silver scrollwork on the cylinder, laying it on his side of the table.

"A little assurance for both of us," he added.

Watching distastefully as Bart laid a heavy-looking, long-barreled Colt revolver on the table, Eliza met the man's gaze briefly. He fixed her with a cold stare, making a point to rest his hand on his other firearm, still seated in its holster at his waist.

Her hopes dashed that the brute had been disarmed, Eliza swallowed with a mouth dry as dust. How she wanted to be on her porch in Spring! *Goshdarnit!* Maybe she could still get there.

"I choose the game," she insisted, taking a seat once more.

He paused, then nodded. "Ladies first," he agreed.

"Five-card stud," she said, picking her best game. She'd be able to see some of his cards, and some was better than none. Less luck, more skill. And she never considered luck to have been her closest companion anyway. "Twenty points over to win, or we can do two out of three."

Jack eyed her with more appreciation. "Good choice. Let's play. Twenty points over."

He pulled toward him a deck that was already on the table.

She laughed. "I wasn't born yesterday and I *was* your wife, no matter how briefly. Don't take me for a fool."

Standing, she went to a cupboard behind the bar where she knew he kept the cards. Pulling out a new pack, she brought it over and broke the seal in front of him. Perhaps she could have palmed an ace, perhaps not, but she didn't want to be shot before they even started, so she restrained herself from trying.

She slammed the deck down between them.

"Now we can play."

And they did. The twenty-point spread meant an indefinite number of games. Closely matched, they'd each won one hand and were on the third, bringing her five points up over him.

"I need a beverage and something to eat," she said. This was going to take a while and she might as well be comfortable.

Stoddard whistled loudly and a lady appeared as if out of nowhere wearing the same style gown Thaddeus had stolen from the other dancing girl. Eliza smiled ruefully. It seemed a lifetime ago. And here she was, back in the same pickle. The girl went off with orders for meat pies and sarsaparilla.

Eliza lost the next hand. It was becoming insufferably hot in the boat's main saloon with the late afternoon sun beating down, and she was tired. Still, she won the next round and surged ahead ten points.

The food came and they ate. Briefly, she considered asking him if they could stop and resume the next day. She'd been counting cards for too long and her weary mind was bound to become sloppy. Of course, if she ever got off Jack's boat again, she was never returning, game or no game.

Stoddard laughed at her suggestion to break. "We keep going. If we sleep, who guards the deck? No, we play on until I win."

"Then I need coffee," she said, and he sent his man to get coffee. Another half hour and despite Stoddard's smug grin, she was up by thirteen points. Then she heard *his* voice, the same one that occupied her memories and her dreams.

"Stoddard!" Thaddeus called out. "Where the hell is she?"

Eliza's heart skipped a beat then began pounding, even as she felt a sweet wave of relief. She wasn't alone anymore. Thaddeus had come. How he'd found her, she had no idea, and she wasn't sure exactly how he could help matters. Perhaps if she lost, Stoddard wouldn't kill her in cold blood, not with Thaddeus as a witness. There was that.

But she wasn't going to lose. Not this time.

She stood up, and Stoddard grabbed for his gun.

"Keep your shirt on," she snapped. "I'm merely going to show Mr. Sanborn I'm all right." In truth, she was dying to lay eyes on him.

Walking out of the gaming room, she strolled over to the railing.

"Ellie," he called out when he saw her.

"Thaddeus." She feasted her eyes on him, love of her life, on a tired-looking horse, his gun drawn. "How on earth did you find me?"

"Never mind that. What are you doing here?"

"Playing cards," she said, as if it were the most natural thing in the world. "Playing for my freedom."

"You don't need to do that. Reed got you your annulment."

"I discovered that, albeit a bit late. Now, I'm playing to keep Spring City." No need to mention the threat to her life.

"Christ! Ellie. That's—"

A shot rang out, and the dirt next to Thaddeus exploded into the air.

"Thaddeus," she screamed as his horse bolted for the trees while he struggled to get it under control. Next to her, Bart grinned and kept his weapon raised.

"Boss says he wants you to finish the game." She eyed him but had little choice. After glancing back to where Thaddeus remained out of range of any more gunfire, she went back inside and stopped dead. She'd left the cards on the table. Not her own hand of cards, which she clutched tightly, but the rest of the deck.

The cards remained right where she'd left them, or did they?

She'd broken one of Kelly's first rules: Never let the hot deck out of your sight. She had bungled, perhaps fatally.

"Let's continue," Stoddard said, grinning and gesturing to her chair.

"I want a new deck," she stated flatly.

He shook his head. "Nothing in the rules says you can ask for one. It wasn't me who left the table."

He had her there.

"Tell you what I'll do," Stoddard said, smiling even more broadly as she sat down, and her heart sank. "I'll let Sanborn live, too, if you win."

Showing up right when he had, Thaddeus might very well have gotten them both killed.

CHAPTER TWENTY-ONE

Without a crowd and without Jo to dazzle the men who worked for Stoddard, Thaddeus saw no way to get on the boat without being seen. An armed man stood at the rail on the starboard side, and he'd seen one go to the port side, preventing him from trying to climb aboard somehow from the river.

When darkness fell, he would have a chance, but he didn't want to wait that long. Nor could he try to pick them off one at a time, as he would have done if Ellie hadn't been inside. Carrying his baby. With that profound circumstance, everything had changed.

The world had narrowed down to her safety and that of the life she carried. And he'd never felt more inadequate. He could not afford to make a mistake. No doubt Stoddard would come out with a gun held to Ellie's head when he heard the first shot.

But what if there was nothing for him to hear?

Thaddeus wasn't as accurate an aim with a blade as he was with a gun, but he was better than most. Of the two knives on him, one for hunting and a smaller one for skinning, both could kill. He merely had to get close enough, which turned out not to be so hard after all. Stoddard hadn't picked an unadorned bank for his steamboat's dock. It was at the end of a parade of trees, lining either side of the walkway to the gangplank.

Thaddeus took to the trees and worked his way closer to the boat, until he crouched in a branch within feet, not yards, of the upper deck. Waiting until the man on the leeward side ventured close enough, Thaddeus hurled his best knife. A moment later, it stuck out of the man's chest, right above his heart.

Mouth agape, but with nary a sound, the goon slumped slowly to the railing before tumbling over the side onto the dock below. Thaddeus scrambled down to the ground and approached him.

Silent. Dead. Perfect!

Retrieving his knife, Thaddeus wiped it on the grass and slipped it back in its scabbard. With no one in sight, he had no idea how many others were on board. The man on the port side, hopefully mesmerized by the water, posed no immediate threat. Then there was Blackheart Bart, probably standing guard inside.

Stepping soundlessly over the gangplank and onto the boat, he made his way to the upper deck.

A few feet away stood the double-door entrance to the main saloon, standing wide open. Crouching below the line of windows, he could hear Ellie and Stoddard inside, arguing.

"You cheated," she said loudly.

Thaddeus gritted his teeth at her tone and held his breath. *Would she never learn?*

"That's the wrong thing to say, little lady. Here, on *my* boat at *my* table. I won."

"Fair and square?" she challenged.

"I won," Stoddard repeated. "I own Spring City." Then he laughed. "And I own your life and Sanborn's, too."

Thaddeus heard a loud noise, perhaps a chair being shoved back and falling over. He could picture her doing that, maybe standing up in a huff. And then Stoddard's voice filtered out the open windows and doors.

"Put it down."

"No. You gave it to me. Did you think I wouldn't use it?" *What had Stoddard given her?*

"Stop where you are," Stoddard commanded, and Thaddeus heard another chair push away from the table.

Apparently, Ellie declined to follow any of Stoddard's orders. Thaddeus heard her voice again.

"Why? Are you going to shoot me in the back?"

A chill raced through him. *Hell!* Why would she taunt the gambler that way? Shooting her in the back was exactly something that man would do!

He held his weapon ready, but before he could take a step closer, Ellie appeared on deck, clutching a large revolver that she waved around as if it were a handkerchief or a lady's fan. Stoddard hounded her heels.

Unfortunately, she blocked Thaddeus from getting a clear shot at him, and Stoddard was too short even to be seen over her head.

Hurrying toward the stairs and straight toward him, Ellie drew up short and stopped stock still, visibly astonished to see Thaddeus blocking her path.

At that point, everything happened so fast, Thaddeus wasn't sure he'd ever recall it correctly. With his roundish belly, Stoddard bumped into the back of her, pushing her forward before bouncing back a step. At the same time, Thaddeus moved to the side for a clean shot.

Distracted by Ellie's movement for the briefest instant, Thaddeus focused again on Stoddard only to see the gambler had already raised the fancy silver derringer he favored and was aiming it right at him.

Thaddeus heard a popping sound—once—and he felt a shard of fire slicing into his side—then twice—this time, a sting to his chest. Ellie screamed.

Move, he told his feet, and incredibly, they did. He lunged sideways, grabbing for the railing, determined not to fall over the side to his death next to Stoddard's man.

Crack! He heard a louder gun shot, but this time, he felt nothing. Clutching a hand to the burning sensation searing his side, he tried to find Ellie through the odd darkness that closed in on him. He could feel his own blood, sliding over his fingers.

Damn it! Where was she? Someone moved into his narrowing line of vision—Blackheart Bart, pointing a gun to Thaddeus's left. At Ellie?

With his last measure of awareness, Thaddeus raised his gun, which seemed to be growing heavier by the moment. He aimed and fired. The bullet struck Bart squarely in the chest, but the man stayed on his feet, swaying slightly, as his head swiveled toward Thaddeus, his mouth pulling into a sneer.

Firing again, Thaddeus watched Bart drop, mirroring his own descent, as the deck rose up suddenly to greet him, knocking him senseless.

Eliza's hands shook, perhaps from the weapon's reverberation, but that didn't explain why the rest of her was shaking so hard. Even her teeth were chattering. Around her, she was the sole person still standing. Jack lay where she'd shot him, blood pouring out of his chest and covering his fancy suit. Thaddeus had brought down Blackheart Bart before they'd both crumpled to the deck.

Thaddeus! She dropped the ugly revolver she'd snatched from the gaming table and rushed toward him. She could already see the blood seeping out from under his torso.

Struggling to turn him over, she was relieved to feel the warmth of his body and to see his chest lightly lifting and falling. He was alive. *Thank you, Lord.*

But how to keep him that way? She had next to no experience with wounds or injuries. If only Riley were there. Still, she knew enough to understand she had to slow down the bleeding if she could figure out how.

"I'm just going to take a look, Thaddeus. All right?" she said, even though his eyes were firmly closed, and she didn't think he could hear her.

Gingerly, she opened his jacket and saw that he bled from his side, next to his ribs, but nowhere else. In the moments of confusion, she'd been certain Stoddard had shot Thaddeus twice. Could both bullets be in the same wound? Or better yet, had they gone clean through him?

She realized she could hardly see because of her own tears, and she brushed her face on her sleeve. Thaddeus was bleeding to death. She had to do something!

Running back inside the boat, she grabbed a tablecloth off the nearest table. But as she crouched beside him again, she heard footfalls on the stairs. Another one of Stoddard's men was coming up from the lower deck.

Almost without thinking, she snatched up Thaddeus's gun from where it lay beside him, and with as steady a hand as she could manage, she pointed it toward the steps. By the time the man saw her, with his own gun raised hip high, she was aiming right at his heart.

He seemed to take quick stock of the situation, particularly Stoddard's prone position, then Bart's body.

"Lower your weapon," she demanded, wishing her voice wasn't quivering.

He hesitated, but he didn't argue. Then he lowered his gun.

That was promising, she thought. He didn't wear the malicious expression she'd seen on Bart's face, nor did he seem simple-minded as some of Stoddard's men.

Still, if this man began shooting, he would undoubtedly be a better shot than she was. Perhaps there was another way out of this.

"Jack Stoddard's dead, and I killed him," she admitted, refusing to surrender to the nausea that was pushing bile into her throat. "I'm free now and you're free, too. This is all yours." She gestured around her with the tip of Thaddeus's gun.

"Take this infernal boat and . . . ," Eliza paused, then on her hands and knees, still dragging the gun although it was no longer pointed at anyone, she crawled over to Jack. Lifting his pudgy, cold hand, she pulled off his diamond ring. "Take his blasted ring, too."

She tossed it toward the man, who caught it, snatching it out of the air and enclosing it in a tight fist.

Feeling the tears slipping down her cheeks and her throat closing with sorrow, she sank down next to Thaddeus again.

"But let me live and help me get my friend into Stoddard's carriage. Then I'll ride away from here and you can have everything."

He'd said nothing, this stranger with the dark hair and even darker eyes. He opened his hand and looked at the jeweled ring resting on his palm.

She wondered what he was thinking—perhaps that two more bodies meant nothing to him.

Or perhaps he thought the killing could stop now.

Frustrated, she struggled to get the tablecloth under Thaddeus, so she could tie it tightly around his middle and over the bleeding wound. He might not be dead, but his body was completely inert and so heavy, she couldn't imagine how she would get him off the boat.

Looking back over her shoulder at Stoddard's last man, she pushed her hair out of her face and pleaded with him.

"For the love of God, I'm carrying this man's baby. Help me. Please."

Finally, he made a decision. She watched him shove the diamond ring in his pocket, and in two shakes of a horse's tail, he was beside her, helping to bind Thaddeus's wounds.

"Wait here," he said after he staunched the flow of blood, disappearing inside the main saloon. He was gone so long, she thought he wasn't going to bother coming back. When he reappeared, he had a leather pouch tucked in his pocket. Wordlessly, he bent down and picked up Thaddeus, cradling him like a child.

"Let's go," he said, the veins bulging in his neck from the strain of holding an unconscious man.

Following him, she stopped only to retrieve her bag from the base of a tree where she'd left it so many hours earlier. It seemed a lifetime ago.

When they reached Stoddard's carriage, the stranger laid Thaddeus down gently on one of the plush seats. Climbing up onto the driver's perch, Eliza thanked him, but he shook his head at her words.

"I never held with Stoddard's way of doing things," he said. "Lotsa people didn't." He pulled the pouch from where it dangled half out of his pocket and set it on her lap.

"For you and your baby," he said, and then he gave the horse a slap to get her on her way.

Eliza kept a white-knuckled hold of the reins, hearing Thaddeus groan behind her with every bump in the road. It was many minutes later when she relaxed enough to hold the reins in one hand and open the pouch with the other.

Money, and lots of it. More paper money than she'd ever seen in one place.

"Sweet Jesus!" she muttered aloud, realizing for the first time precisely how lucrative a gambling operation could be. No wonder men killed for and died over cards. She had the sinking suspicion, however, the stranger had been so generous because he didn't think Thaddeus was going to survive.

Eliza knew only one place to direct the horse, and a short while later, she pulled up outside The Pork and Swallow. Jumping down off the carriage seat, she ran through the open door, feeling fortunate to see Josephine leaning against the bar.

Immediately, the woman stood up straight, her face wavering between a smirk and concern.

"Please, Miss Holland," Eliza implored, ignoring the men who slumped at various tables. Walking right up to her, she grabbed her arm but choked on any further words, a ball of terror and tears stuck in her throat.

Josephine looked her up and down, starting to yank her arm away, but then she noticed the blood on Eliza's gown.

"Honey, what is it?" Josephine asked, a frown on her otherwise unmarred face.

Feeling desperation whip through her, Eliza managed to utter, "It's Thaddeus. He's been shot." She gestured behind her, indicating he was outside.

Josephine's lovely face went ashen.

"Pete," she called to the bartender, alarm lacing her voice. "Can you assist my friend here? Quickly."

Within minutes, they had transferred Thaddeus from the carriage to Josephine's bed and stripped him to the waist. Eliza noticed his skin had become colder and his face, pale. Although she felt certain the tablecloth tied around him had helped, he was bleeding freely again, no doubt from being bounced around on the short journey over the bridge from Hamilton to Keokuk and then being carried up the stairs.

Having already sent one of the boys who worked at the saloon to fetch the doctor, Josephine, herself, efficiently set to cleaning Thaddeus's wound, and then pressed a bleached towel against it until the bleeding stopped again.

"You're good at that," Eliza admitted, with no grudge. She didn't care who helped him, as long as he survived.

"I have three brothers, and one or the other was always getting shot up," she said, as if she was talking about a splinter and not a mortal wound. But Eliza saw Josephine's hand was trembling, too.

"Look at that," Eliza said, pointing to a red mark on the skin below his left nipple, close to his heart.

Jo touched one finger to the sore-looking spot that was coming out in a bruise.

"Looks like something stopped a bullet from taking Teddy straight to the Pearly Gates."

Eliza grabbed up his discarded duster. Sure enough, from the coat pocket over his heart, she retrieved a few coins, not regular ones like she would hand over for a loaf of bread or a pound of chops, but gold ones, an inch in diameter at least and thick as a slice of cheese. Only four of them. But that had been enough. And wonder of wonders, she spied the spent bullet. Clutching them all in her hand, she said a prayer of thanks under her breath.

Josephine moved the basin of bloody water from her lap to the floor, keeping her hand on the towel against Thaddeus's side. He neither moved, nor even moaned.

Eliza felt the tears well up in her eyes, looking at his handsome face, so vulnerable, his dark lashes feathering his shadowed cheeks. Her heart was heavy in her chest. She had to stop herself from saying to Josephine something awful—if you can save him, you can have him. But she couldn't. She wanted him, both as her man and as the father of her baby.

A few minutes later, a skillful young doctor arrived, reminding her of Riley. He removed the derringer's bullet and administered disinfecting powders before sewing up the wound and bandaging Thaddeus.

When eventually she stretched out on a lumpy bed in another room, Eliza had never been more tired in her whole life. Josephine had claimed the place beside Thaddeus. After all, it was her bedroom in which he lay prone, hopefully recovering.

Thus, for the time being, Eliza hadn't argued, too grateful Thaddeus's life had been spared. Ignoring her hunger pains, she gave in and let sleep claim her.

The first thing Eliza saw when she opened her eyes was Josephine, who'd apparently tossed the door open and awakened her. Before she could ask after Thaddeus's health, Eliza's stomach heaved. She jumped up, looking wildly around.

A washstand yielded a large bowl, and she retched into it, even though nothing came up but bile. When the heaving stopped, Eliza looked at Josephine, who was staring, eyes narrowed, hands on her hips.

"Is it Thaddeus's child?" she asked.

Eliza nodded, using a towel to wipe her face.

"Does he know?" Josephine's voice was low, not her usual brassy bold tone.

Eliza shrugged. "I don't know. I didn't tell him."

The other woman paused, considering. "You want to tell me how he got shot?"

Her question made Eliza come over all weepy again, but she took a deep, raggedy breath.

"It was my fault. He was saving me."

"Again?" Josephine said, tossing up her hands. "Honey, you're more dangerous to that man's health than any bullet."

Was that true? She hadn't asked Thaddeus to save her. "How is he?"

"Sleeping but no fever. Just regular slumber from exhaustion and loss of blood. He'll probably be hungry when he wakes up."

She turned to leave but then looked back, raising a perfectly plucked eyebrow.

"What about you? Can you keep something down?"

Eliza didn't know. She was starving and nauseated at the same time.

"I'd like some tea and toast. Please," she added, thinking of Charlotte. She ought to send her a telegram immediately and let her know what had happened.

Without another word, Josephine left her alone. Now that she was on her feet, Eliza wanted desperately to see Thaddeus. She didn't bother to look at herself in the mirror, or use the brush and comb on the washstand. She was past caring whether she looked appealing or like something a mountain lion had dragged into its den.

Tiptoeing across the hall, Eliza found the door ajar and everything quiet. Thaddeus was lying in the same spot as she'd seen him the night before, but now his skin was infused with color and the pinch of pain around his mouth had vanished.

He looked so good despite everything, as if he were simply resting, like Josephine had said. But Eliza couldn't help recalling the terrifying moment when Stoddard had fired his gun, and she'd been certain she would never see Thaddeus Sanborn take another breath.

Yet here he was. His broad shoulders, strong arms, and sculpted chest were bare, although the rest of his torso was bandaged in clean, bleached-white strips. Someone, maybe Jo, had folded the blanket neatly above his waist.

Eliza sat down beside him on the mattress's edge, careful not to let the bed dip and move him. Ever so lightly, she swept the hair off his forehead and then touched his firm lips with her fingertips. He didn't stir. He didn't miraculously awaken and grab her to him. He had no strength to capture her and kiss her and make love to her.

Emotion, strong and fierce, caught her by surprise. A sob tore out of her before she could tamp it down. And then another. She couldn't stop. She'd loved him for so long and then nearly lost him. Having him ride off and not look back was one thing. That was painful. But to have his life flow out of him at her feet, that was excruciating.

Trying to stem the tide of tears, she failed.

"Good Lord, woman. Get ahold of yourself."

Josephine stood in the doorway, an expression of disdain on her attractive face.

"If he awakens to that caterwauling, he's gonna think he's dying for sure. Why don't you go downstairs and eat? Your food is on the table. No one else is in the bar right now." Her voice was firm but not unkind, and she held out a handkerchief.

Eliza got up and took the proffered square of cloth, wiping her cheeks and dabbing her eyes, ignoring the heavy scent of perfume making her want to retch again. Instead, she hiccupped.

"Thank you," she murmured and went downstairs.

CHAPTER TWENTY-TWO

Thaddeus came to in a haze of confusion. His first thought was he couldn't believe he was waking up at all. In swift succession, he remembered seeing Ellie and Stoddard and then being shot. He was dead, wasn't he? But the bed was soft and smelled good. In fact, it smelled familiar. Maybe he *was* in heaven.

Turning his head, he took in his surroundings. He was in Jo's room. Heavenly things had occurred there, that was for sure, but he definitely wasn't dead.

"You're awake." Jo's voice. A pang of disappointment pricked him. She was not Ellie. He *wanted* Ellie. *Where the hell was she?*

In short order, he felt the panic begin to rise. Had she been injured?

"Where's Ellie?" he asked, getting the words past his dry tongue with difficulty.

Jo didn't answer. Instead, she handed him a glass of water. When it was obvious he wasn't going to be able to drink it while lying on his back, she lifted his head with one hand and brought the glass to his lips, her hand wrapped over his to help him.

That was how Eliza found them as she stood, frozen in the doorway. They looked like a couple who cared for each other. Intellectually, she knew Josephine was a saloon girl who let men buy her favors, but her heart ached knowing Thaddeus had been one of those men, more than once.

Why, that was practically a relationship, and more than she'd ever had with him!

She stepped back soundlessly, so neither would know she'd ever been there. She was Eliza Prentice, *dagnabbit*, and she would not go join his whore to help tend to him, not in that room where he'd been intimate with the other woman.

This romanticizing of Thaddeus Sanborn, wasting her life by keeping her heart for him alone, was going to end right there, right then. She'd spent enough years wanting something that could never be. Not with the likes of him.

Taking another quiet step backward, she convinced herself she was making the right decision.

He might be off to Canada tomorrow in search of the next big gold strike. Or jump on a ship to Europe. She simply had no idea. But he was not husband and father material. That fact had finally sunk in.

Creeping down the stairs, her heart breaking with each step, she found solace in the fact she wouldn't be alone anymore. She carried Thaddeus's baby, and instead of worrying about her own feelings, she would turn her attention to someone other than herself.

She was determined to bring this child such joy, its happiness would overflow and sweep her along with it. And she was going to do that in her own beloved home.

As it turned out, slipping away without another word to either Thaddeus or Josephine proved the easiest thing in the world. Asking one of the saloon's boys to find her horse and hitch it to her late ex-husband's luxurious carriage, she rode swiftly and comfortably out of town, beginning her journey back to Spring City.

Taking the first road that headed due west, she knew Thaddeus would have a conniption fit if he could see her all by her lonesome. But she wasn't completely witless. She'd picked up his revolver, rather unthinkingly, while Stoddard's man carried Thaddeus off the riverboat. She'd placed it on the carriage floor with her bag, and now it was hers. Having used a gun successfully—twice, now, to protect herself and the man she loved—she wouldn't hesitate to use one again to protect her unborn baby.

By late in the day, she arrived at a town so distant from the Mississippi River it made her head spin to think how far she'd come. The next day she did it again. And the next, traveling under a bright sun, unimpeded by weather or terrain, with no more worries Stoddard or his men followed her.

By the fourth day, however, when the roads got too rough, she realized it would take her a month of Sundays to get home in the impractical conveyance that was more suited to town and city driving. Selling it for a tidy sum, she boarded a train once more for the last, long stretch to Colorado.

When Eliza arrived at Spring City's small station, just planks of wood and a small ticket booth, her tears battled with a genuine smile. Lord, it was good to see her hometown after all this time!

Right away, she encountered half a dozen people she knew as she descended the platform, only her carpetbag in hand with Thaddeus's revolver tucked inside and enough money to last a very long time. Each person raised a hand in greeting.

"Hey, Eliza."

"Hi, Miss Prentice."

Some stared at her curiously, perhaps realizing by the fit of her gown and the futility of the maternity corset that she carried a baby. It didn't matter.

Returning each greeting with a smile and a wave, she felt a lightness of spirit. She wasn't the same unhappy woman who'd broken her engagement and run away, with a heavy heart and a bleak outlook on her future.

Oh, she knew she had some fences to mend, but she was looking forward to doing so. Mending fences, hopefully making friends, building a life with her child the way Charlotte had built one with her new family.

Mostly, she refused to dwell on what, or rather, *who*, was missing from that ideal life. She merely felt grateful for having made it home alive.

When Eliza reached her house, staring up at its welcoming facade, a trembling started deep inside her. A part of her imagined her father would be in the house waiting. While traveling, she'd comforted herself by picturing him in his favorite chair. But now, she shook off that fantasy. If things had happened differently, she would have returned as the last Prentice.

But she hadn't.

Smiling slightly, she spared a glance toward the Sanborn homestead. She couldn't actually see it except in her mind's eye—down the street, around the corner and past a copse of pines. She knew it stood empty, abandoned.

Taking hold of the railing, Eliza climbed the steps, five of them, and then she was on her own front porch. How many times had she thought she would never see it again?

Even devoid of any furniture, which had all been put away so it wouldn't rot, her porch was still the most comforting sight she'd ever seen. By nightfall, she intended to have her swing out and be sitting on it, watching the sun go down behind the mountains. She'd sat there many times, alone or with her father or even with her one-time fiancé, Riley, but she didn't think she had ever enjoyed it as much as she would that night.

Taking a key from under the mat, she had her hand on the doorknob when the door was wrenched open from inside.

"Eliza! I heard footsteps. I can't believe it's you."

Mrs. Longwood had looked after the house while she was away and, before that, had taken care of her father for as long as

Eliza could remember. And she didn't think she'd ever truly thanked the woman.

Throwing her arms around the familiar figure, she hugged her.

"I'm so glad to see you, Mrs. Longwood."

She felt the woman stiffen, apparently shocked. They hadn't touched much in all the years. The only hugs Eliza had wanted were impossible to have, from her dead mother or from Thaddeus. So, she'd taken none and given none, except rarely to her father and even more rarely to Riley. In friendship, of course.

Gradually, her housekeeper relaxed and hugged her back, squeezing her hard. Then the woman pulled back and looked at Eliza. Did her glance pause on Eliza's middle?

"Welcome home, child. Welcome home."

And she did feel welcome. Why had she never let Mrs. Longwood close to her before? Or let anyone for that matter? *What a martyr she'd been!* And it had been so easy to use her loneliness as a weapon and make everyone else around her suffer, too.

She peered around her. Everything looked just as she'd left it, except the sofas were covered.

"You've taken such good care of our home," Eliza said, realizing it was just as much Mrs. Longwood's as hers.

"If you'd sent a telegram ahead," the housekeeper scolded, "it would have been even better. I would have removed all the covers from the good furniture and made some fresh bread."

Even without fresh bread and with her front parlor draped in white, her home seemed like the best place she'd ever seen.

"We'll do it together," Eliza said. "Have you eaten? I haven't. I'm starved. I could eat a whole hog, I swear."

Mrs. Longwood gave her a long look. "Are you sure you're Eliza Prentice?"

Eliza laughed. "Yes, I am."

She was so relieved not to be Eliza Stoddard she could just burst. And she might as well let the housekeeper in on the news that would certainly come to everyone's attention when she walked through town.

"I'm eating for two, by the way."

Would Mrs. Longwood be shocked? Maybe refuse to live with her anymore? Eliza held her breath. She didn't want to see condemnation in the eyes of the woman who'd been with her all her life.

The housekeeper's gaze traveled up and down Eliza's tiny form before she stopped herself. She cleared her throat.

"I noticed." Instead of condemnation, however, she smiled. "Well, then child, we'd better get you fed and right quick. I may not have fresh bread today, but I have roast beef and at least half a huckleberry pie left."

To Eliza's surprise, Mrs. Longwood put her arm around her waist and walked with her to the kitchen. Yes, Eliza would tell her everything in due course.

As it turned out, they did not get the swing put up. Between a delicious home-cooked meal for supper and walking into town midmorning the next day to ask Dan for help with that very task, Eliza learned a lot about what had happened while she'd been away.

She'd already found out from Charlotte how Doc had retired, but to discover the Cuthins gone, even temporarily, was a surprise. Doc and Sarah were traveling the world, seeing the famous sites of Europe, and they even had plans to go to India. Such a huge change made the whole town seem different.

Eliza was eager to meet the new doctor, whom she quickly learned was a woman. *Gracious!* Everyone had always believed it would be Riley's position, but he was in San Francisco with bigger fish to fry and starting a family of his own with Sophie.

She paused at the entrance to Doc's surgery. His old sign was gone. A new plaque was hanging in its place: C. Bell, M.D.

Pushing the door open, she peered inside. Everything looked the same and smelled the same, except instead of Sarah sitting behind the desk, a middle-aged black woman was in her place. She shot Eliza a welcoming smile.

"A stranger in Spring City," remarked the woman. "My, oh, my."

Eliza chuckled. "I'm not the stranger here. You are." Then she clamped her hand to her mouth, realizing how rude that sounded. "I apologize."

"That's all right, honey. If you're not a stranger, how come I've never seen you before?"

"I've been away, ma'am. But I was born and raised here. I'm Eliza Prentice."

"Oh," the lady said, narrowing her eyes, her friendly expression dimming a little.

Eliza sighed. "Apparently, you've heard of me."

The woman nodded and frowned and took her measure of Eliza, from head to toe.

"Funny, you don't look like you're going to send poisonous curses my way."

Stifling a gasp, Eliza shrugged. "Not today, anyway."

Lordy! What had people been saying about her? *Clearly, the truth.* It gave her a strange desire to laugh.

The lady cocked her head, and then she gave Eliza another smile.

"I'm Marie Taylor, nurse to Dr. Bell."

Just then, the door to the examining room opened and out came another unfamiliar face.

"You must be the new doctor," Eliza said, appraising the woman who would help to bring her son or daughter into the world since they didn't have a midwife. Of medium height that put her a few inches taller than Eliza, the woman had very fair skin, dark red hair, and intelligent eyes.

Eliza made the first move and took a few steps toward the doctor, holding out her out her hand.

"Good day. I'm Eliza Prentice."

For a moment, she wished she could give a different name and not be judged by the hearsay that had come before her. However, the grey-green eyes staring back at her weren't condemning.

"Miss Prentice, it's good to finally meet you. I'm Dr. Bell. Cassandra Bell. I owe you my gratitude for the stipend that pays for this position and the upkeep of my practice."

Eliza had forgotten about that. "You're most welcome, I'm sure." Then she fell silent, not knowing how to broach the topic she wanted to discuss.

"I assume that's why you're here. To check on how things are going since Dr. Cuthins' retirement?"

"Oh, no," Eliza said. "What do I know of such things? I'm sure if he hired you to replace him, then you're an excellent doctor."

Dr. Bell and the nurse exchanged a glance. Obviously, her reasonable words were not expected. The doctor took a step closer.

"Is there something else you wish to discuss with me?"

Eliza looked at the floor, then back at the doctor.

"If you're not too busy, yes."

"I'm not, as it happens. Come on into the back."

Eliza followed. How strange to go into the surgery and not see Doc and Riley. Both gone. It seemed unthinkable. She'd been so sure Riley would always be there, her good, good friend, the only one she could turn to even when she really wanted Thaddeus.

"Is something wrong?" Dr. Bell asked, seeing the unsettled look skitter across Eliza's face.

"Ghosts of the past," she confessed, then she took a seat. "However, I'm not here concerning the past. It's the future I want to discuss, mine and . . . my baby's." There, she'd said it out loud to a stranger.

She'd told Mrs. Longwood that she'd fallen in love, but the baby's father wasn't the settling kind. Would the doctor ask her painful, prying questions?

But Dr. Bell didn't stare at her in judgment or disgust.

"I see," she said matter-of-factly with a little nodding motion. "How far along do you think you are?" Then she conducted a brief examination and listened to Eliza's heart, but she made no mention of the father.

"You seem in perfect health," Dr. Bell said. "But you're a small woman. Let's hope your hips spread a bit in the next few months."

Eliza's eyes widened. *Her hips would spread?*

"Yes, let's hope so," she agreed, feeling this was yet another area in which she would have benefited from the advice of a mother.

At least she had Dr. Bell and Mrs. Longwood, although to the best of Eliza's knowledge, her housekeeper had never had any children.

As they stood up, Dr. Bell added, "Eat heartily, but don't overindulge. And stay away from strong spirits."

Eliza nodded.

"And Miss Prentice, if you ever need to discuss anything, baby-related or otherwise, I'm a good listener." The doctor's face seemed even kinder with the encouraging smile she offered.

A lump filled the back of Eliza's throat at the doctor's compassion.

"I'll remember that." Then she added, "Thank you."

CHAPTER TWENTY-THREE

Riding into Spring City, Thaddeus had never been happier to see his homestead. But he didn't even stop at it. He went straight to Ellie's house.

Weeks earlier, following a hunch, he'd sent a telegram from Boston to Dan at the feedstore and found out she was back.

Without his agreement, Thaddeus had been carted back to the house on India Wharf so his sister could tend to him. It had taken him ages to heal from the gunshot wound, which weakened him, angered him, and frustrated the hell out of him. And he'd been a bear of a patient, uncivil and ungrateful, until Charlotte had finally released him.

In the two months since he'd awakened at The Pork and Swallow to discover Ellie had left without even a goodbye, he'd thought of nothing but her. And she was all he wanted—to talk to her, to tell her how he felt, to hold her, and God willing, to overcome her stubbornness and convince her he could settle down.

He rapped his knuckles on the door, waiting impatiently for an answer. When Mrs. Longwood pulled it open, the same as she'd done his whole life, he couldn't help smiling.

"Why, Thaddeus Sanborn, as I live and breathe."

That seemed friendly enough, but then she narrowed her eyes and pursed her lips, and he felt as if he were twelve years old again, caught stealing berries from Elijah Prentice's garden.

Yanking his hat off, he knew he had a dirty sweat stain on his forehead from riding hard the last few miles, determined to shave off even a few minutes from the time until he could lay eyes on Ellie.

"Is Eli—" He stopped short at the look of disapproval that crossed Mrs. Longwood's face. "I mean, is Miss Prentice at home?" he asked.

She crossed her arms in front of her, and he wondered if she was going to give him an answer. He shot her his most winning smile, a smile that had served him well over the years, and after another second, he saw her start to thaw.

With a raised eyebrow, she stepped aside to let him into the front hall. At the same time, Ellie came from the kitchen at the back of the house. He saw her a second before she caught sight of him—all golden-haired, a sweet expression on her face, blue eyes shining. His heart skipped a beat.

"Mrs. Longwood, who's at—?" Ellie began.

Yup, he knew the very instant she saw him, for she stopped dead in her tracks and actually blanched paler than her usual fair skin.

"Thaddeus!" Her hand drifted up to her throat as if she were choking, and her other hand went immediately to her stomach, which was where his gaze traveled next. He'd only caught the merest glimpse of her on the deck of Stoddard's boat, but he could see her stomach had blossomed in the many weeks since.

Instead of her standard trim-fitting shirtwaist that tapered at her waist, she had on a blouse gathered only inches below her breasts before it fell away from her stomach and hips. In her favorite shade of blue, with flounces on both sides, ample buttons, and a hint of lace at her décolletage, the whole impression made him want to scoop her into his arms and feel her roundness where his baby was growing.

But not in front of Mrs. Longwood.

"You look good. Very . . . healthy." He wanted to say she looked so desirable his head, as well as other parts of him, could explode, but he didn't.

He ached to touch her, and without even hesitating to consider the propriety of his actions, he approached her and took her hand right off her stomach, holding it in his own.

"Mr. Sanborn!" Mrs. Longwood exclaimed when Ellie stayed mute, staring at him as though she couldn't believe her eyes.

Then Ellie came to life, pulling her hand from his.

"No, it's fine. He's fine," she told her housekeeper.

Triumphantly but not gloatingly, he shot another friendly grin at Mrs. Longwood. He'd made it past the dragon at the gates, but he still had to convince Ellie he was ready for all the responsibility that came with being a husband and father.

Her lovely eyes suddenly widened.

"*Are* you fine? I sent a telegram to Charlotte asking after you, and she assured me you were recovering. It seems she was correct."

Charlotte hadn't mentioned a telegram, probably knowing he would have jumped out of bed too soon if he'd known Ellie was worrying over him.

"It took longer than I liked, but I'm doing well. I need to speak with you, though."

"All right," she agreed, sounding neither welcoming, nor off-putting.

She turned and led the way down the hall to the back door. Mrs. Longwood's steps trailed behind them. At the doorway, Ellie paused.

"Would you please bring us some sarsaparilla out back? My friend here looks as though he's thirsty."

Thaddeus had never heard her speak so kindly, particularly not to her help. Impending motherhood was gentling her in more ways than one.

He held his tongue until they reached the back veranda with its swing and table. He smiled, remembering Elijah. Prentice boasting at the feedstore one day that he had the only house in town with a swing at the front and the back.

Minding all his manners, he waited until she took a seat before sitting down beside her.

Thank you, God. He was next to her again.

"It's a lovely view, isn't it?" she asked, her gaze wandering over her large, perfectly tended yard.

However, he had eyes for her alone, watching her lips curve in a contented smile. *Would she mind if he kissed those lips that very instant?*

"See, Thaddeus," she directed when she realized he wasn't enjoying the sight. "Mrs. Longwood told me Dan kept it up so it wouldn't be all running wild. Wasn't that sweet of him?"

Thaddeus tore his gaze from her face and glanced at the garden with its white-painted arbor and its colorful flowers. Where the cultivated area left off, the natural beauty of Colorado took over and stretched away into the distance. However, at that moment, he didn't give a fig for what was out there, only what was right beside him.

"It's beautiful," he agreed. "I don't think I ever saw it before from this angle, not during the daylight, anyway."

He was teasing her. If he'd ever been on her back porch, it had been at night, trying to get her to come to her window or, that fateful time, to sneak a kiss and take her back to his barn.

She didn't seem to hear him. "When I got back here, after such a long time and all those adventures, I was happy as a clam at high water."

He noticed she rubbed her hand over her curved stomach. Apparently, she held no resentment over being pregnant. That thought had worried him from the moment Charlotte blurted out Ellie's condition, wondering if she was plain pissed off at carrying his child. Yet, she didn't seem mad at all.

"It's odd, though," she continued, "that everything wasn't quite as I left it. I mean, Doc is gone and Riley," she added, her voice low. "All the small changes seem huge. Everyone looks a little different, and they treat me differently, too."

Mrs. Longwood came out with a pitcher, ice clinking in the pale liquid, two glasses, and a plate of finger sandwiches on a pale green tin tray.

"Oh, my," Ellie said. "That looks heavy. You should have had Thaddeus carry it. Just set it down. Do you want to join us? You've made enough for an army."

Thaddeus met the housekeeper's gaze over Ellie's head. With a small look they exchanged, he knew Mrs. Longwood had noticed the astonishing alteration in her employer's behavior, noticed it and by the crinkling of her eyes, liked it.

"Now, dear," Mrs. Longwood said, "you know the doctor told you to eat well. So have two sandwiches, and I'm going right back to my kitchen to put my feet up. Let me know if you need anything else." She shot Thaddeus another glance, neither a particularly friendly one, nor a hostile one, either.

Ellie shook her head as the older lady left.

"Everyone is so sweet. Is it because of my condition? Or did I never see before what a nice group of folks we have living in Spring?"

He nearly laughed at her strange perception. She didn't seem to get how her own shift in attitude was the real change. He assumed everyone she interacted with in town noticed it, too, and were responding in kind. But at least she'd mentioned "her condition" for the first time, as if it was an old topic between them.

What's more, Mrs. Longwood had mentioned a doctor. That one word had snagged his attention, spiking a surge of anxiety.

"Why did you need to see a doctor?"

She froze, keeping her gaze far afield.

"Ellie?"

She turned her head and looked right at him, yet he couldn't begin to decipher the swirl of emotions he saw in her eyes.

"I thought you knew." Her cheeks suffused with pink.

"About the baby?"

She nodded.

"Of course, I do." Did she think she wasn't showing? Or that he was such an oaf he wouldn't notice? "Charlie told me. Even if she hadn't, don't you think I might have noticed something a little different about you?"

He smiled wryly, but she still looked serious, so he asked her again, "Why did you need the doctor?"

"I simply wanted to see who was going to deliver my baby. And I like her. Dr. Bell is her name. She is very no-nonsense but kind, too."

He breathed a sigh of relief. Nothing was wrong with mother or baby. Now, he could finally ask her the question that had haunted him while he healed.

"Why did you run away? And for God's sake, woman, why back to Stoddard?"

Ellie bowed her head and looked at her lap. Then she reached for a sandwich, which she didn't eat.

"He's dead, you know." Her voice was barely above a whisper. "*I* did it. *I* killed him, myself."

Thaddeus clenched his jaw and felt as though he'd been punched. This petite woman beside him, carrying a baby, had taken out Jack Stoddard.

"I knew he was dead," he said. "You told Jo and she told me, right after she let me know you'd left The Pork. Ellie, darlin', I'm sorry you had to shoot him. That was my job."

"You sort of mucked it up for me," she said, not harshly but with a regretful laugh. "I had the winning hand. I just know it. I was ready to beat him fair and square, but then I heard your voice. I took my hand but left the rest of the deck on the table. Alone. With him."

Thaddeus whistled. "Even if you'd turned over a winning hand, you're crazy, if you think he would've let you walk away."

She shrugged. "I was playing for three lives at that point," she murmured. "I had to continue. He thought so little of me, he gave me a gun for insurance, and it was loaded! Can you believe it? That's what surprised me when the time came."

When the time came to shoot Stoddard.

He wanted to take her in his arms, but he wasn't sure she'd welcome it. She seemed distant as the puffy white clouds hovering over the mountains on the horizon.

"You saved my life," he told her. "Twice."

Ellie glanced at him. "You shot just about everyone else, both on the train and on the riverboat, so you saved mine, too. More than once."

"You wouldn't have needed saving again if you hadn't run away from Charlie's house. Why did you do it?" he asked for a second time.

She took a sip of her sarsaparilla and a bite of her sandwich. He could wait her out. Grabbing a sandwich off the china plate, he took a small taste and then recalled with the first delectable swallow of baked ham and fresh bread that Mrs. Longwood was known as a great cook.

Wolfing the rest of it down, he reached for another. He could sit with the woman he loved in companionable silence and eat a sandwich, but he would get his answers from her, make no mistake.

Finally, she leaned her head back on the swing.

"Do you recall when we stopped at that hotel near Burlington?"

What a silly question! That was when they'd made love for the first time. Well, the first time he could actually remember, the first time when he was sober and in control. He'd treasured every moment in that hotel bed, not to mention every other night and every day he'd ever spent in her company.

"Of course," was all he said.

"You went down the street to the saloon on the corner, after we argued."

He nodded and strands of his conversation with the old cowboy drifted back to him.

"I followed you," she added.

He choked on his sarsaparilla, spraying some onto the porch floor.

"You did?" he asked when he could speak again.

She nodded and handed him a napkin from the tray.

"I was upset," she said. "We'd had a quarrel."

He remembered it distinctly despite how they'd argued over nothing important. He recalled how his skin had felt too tight and the hotel room had become too small. It had been the first time in his life he'd loved the person he'd been to bed with, although it had taken months for him to realize that's what the prickly emotion was. Love. Stunned by the sheer terror at feeling so connected to her, he'd bolted for the door.

"I was behaving childishly," he admitted. *Why was it so easy to say that now?* "But you knew I'd come back, didn't you?"

"I trusted you wouldn't leave me stranded, but I was confused, too," she admitted. "I thought you might have gone out looking for . . . that is . . . to find some female company."

He shook his head. She had no idea how gone he was for her. He'd not wanted another woman, hardly looked at one, since he'd found her in the boxcar.

"We had just been intimate. Why in heaven's name would I look elsewhere?"

She twisted her own napkin in her hands. "How was I to know if I'd done it right?"

Well, damn! Could she really not tell she'd rocked his foundations, shaken him to the core?

"Ellie, I only wanted a drink and a cigarette."

"I found that out, but I was eavesdropping."

"Oh." What had he been spouting off about that night? The old cowboy was full of advice concerning women, none of which made sense or sounded right. But Thaddeus had been happy to agree and drink with the man anyway.

"What did you hear?"

She glanced at him, then away. "That the last thing on God's green earth you'd ever want was to tie yourself down to the likes of the hellcat, meaning me, who was waiting for you in your hotel room."

She bent her head as if to sip her drink, but he heard her sniffle.

Hell's bells! "Ellie, I—"

"That you'd always been free like a mustang, and you liked your life that way and wanted to stay that way until the end of your days. Unless something better came along. But not that bitch who—"

She stopped and tried to take another sip, but her hand was trembling, and he knew she was starting to cry.

"Ellie, sweetheart." His heart broke into little pieces at the sight of her tears. He took her glass from her and put it down with a clunk. Then he took both her hands in his.

"I'm sorry. I was . . ." *Christ!* He didn't want to tell her he was scared. "First of all, I never called you a bitch. You're misremembering for sure. Second, I was angry. You were angry, too, that night."

"Yes, I was, but *I* didn't walk away from you and go complain to a stranger."

Her lower lip quivered, and she dropped her gaze to their clasped hands.

"In answer to your question, I left your sister's house because no one could make me stay if I didn't want to," she said solemnly. "It took me months to realize I could simply leave, just the way you had. Months of waiting for you, I might add."

He tightened his grip on her slender hands. Before he could apologize again, however, she continued.

"I was through letting other people handle the mess I'd made. The only way to fix it was to go see Stoddard, or so I believed." She wiped at her face once more, crumpled up the napkin, and tossed it on the table.

"And you know something, Thaddeus, unlike you and that ol' cowboy, I would have gladly 'tied myself down,' if you'd asked."

His heart thumped painfully. *Here goes everything,* he thought.

"Well, I'm asking now." He wished his voice had sounded firmer instead of hoarse and gravelly.

Her gaze, which had remained on their entwined hands, flew up to his. She looked shocked and doubtful. Definitely not the trusting, loving expression he'd imagined.

He swallowed past the nervous lump in his throat.

"I would like us to be married." He'd planned a speech about how much he loved her and always had done, and how they'd been destined since childhood. But as he looked into her blue, jewel-bright eyes, it all fell by the wayside, and his brain felt swept clean of any useful or coherent thoughts.

She stared at him, maybe waiting for the rest of that fancy speech.

Come on, Thaddeus, think.

"We're good together, like rye and whiskey," he added. "When you're with me, darlin', everything comes out aces high."

She tried to pull her hands out of his. He tensed. He had to do more.

"And there's our baby. I'm not going to beat the devil around the stump. I'm willing to acknowledge it's mine and do right by you and it, I mean, him or her."

She frowned and, at last, managed to pull free. Standing, she looked down at him, not with the old imperious expression of late but with simple weariness.

He stood up, too, wanting to take her into his arms, but she shook her head, her eyes tearing up again.

"I'm sorry. I seem to cry over everything, even a cracked eggshell. Mrs. Longwood tells me it's because of my condition. It doesn't mean anything." Then her hands fluttered in front of her, warding him off.

"I'm tired. I bet you are, too, after your long journey. Why don't you go home?"

By God, she was dismissing him and his half-assed marriage proposal.

"I hope you still have some furniture and whatnot. At least a bed." She stopped abruptly and blushed.

He had never intended to be confrontational, but suddenly, he stood facing her, feet planted, arms crossed, feeling his jaw tense before he asked her the question that would change his life.

"Are you saying you won't marry me?"

She pursed her lips, her sweet pink lips that he ached to kiss.

"I'm saying I appreciate your kind offer to *acknowledge* your child."

He winced. It sounded even worse when she said it.

"But with or without your acknowledgment, I'm having it," she said flatly. "And right now, the baby is making me tired. I'm going to lie down."

"Ellie—" *Shit!* What should he do? He'd expected to leave there as an engaged man.

She took a step away from him before swinging her glance back, staring him right in the eye with all traces of tears vanished.

"Your proposal doesn't interest me the way it once would have. *That's* what I'm saying. If it were still only me, I might try my hand at taming the wild *mestengo*, but I'm going to have my hands full soon enough."

Mrs. Longwood appeared as if on cue.

Ellie smiled at her, a genuine loving smile, the one Thaddeus wanted for himself.

"Would you please show our guest to the door?"

Well, hell! How dare she talk about him like a guest, as if they were a couple of old ladies who'd had tea together. He snatched up his hat.

"I know the way. I can show my own damn self out." And right when he wanted to be the most grown up of men, someone she could count on as a husband, he stomped off like an angry child.

CHAPTER TWENTY-FOUR

Thaddeus walked through his empty house, recalling the past but trying to see the future. He poked his head into the study where his father's desk had always been. Charlotte had that now, along with anything that had been of any quality or value.

Years ago, he'd made it clear to his sister he wasn't ever coming back there to live, and she'd taken him at his word. The study appeared strange, nearly painful to look at, without the books on the shelves, without Charlotte seated at her typewriter.

Down the hall in the sitting room, he smiled to see both his mother's uncomfortable sofa, with its hard, straight back, as well as her old upright piano. Sophie and Riley had fallen in love over that piano. At least, that was the story at their wedding. Thaddeus touched a few keys and listened to the notes die out in the stillness.

The only other things left in the house were a table and chairs on the ground floor and a bed upstairs. But a mattress and pillows, remained, too, so he counted himself lucky.

He sat down on the bed, feeling defeated. Yes, he was so surefire lucky! *What an idiot!* You didn't go asking a woman like Eliza Prentice to marry you without your speech ready and a shiny ring.

Riley would've known that. After all, he'd persuaded two beautiful women to agree to marry him.

Thaddeus cleaned himself up and went to Ada's saloon for a chicken dinner and some good beer. After dinner, he accepted free drinks from every man-jack who was glad to see him home again, but he didn't accept the invitation from Ada for "dessert" in her room. He'd known her since he was a young lad, when she was already a woman of middle age. She was one saloon "girl" who'd never tempted him, not with her dyed black hair, thickly rouged cheeks, and painted lips.

No way, no how! Not enough whiskey in the world. He and Riley had a pact, in fact, that Ada was one woman with whom they'd never entertain themselves, not after Riley learned about certain ailments and explained to his friend how one contracted them.

"Where's Dan?" he asked, changing the subject from her insistence on taking him upstairs. He missed seeing his old friends at the saloon. He knew Riley was in San Francisco. And his other friend, Ely, had a wife and, as Thaddeus had just learned, a young boy, too. He certainly wouldn't be showing up at the saloon.

But Dan? Where would he be on a Friday night?

"He's home with his missus," the bartender offered.

Thaddeus choked on the liquid going down his throat.

"What did you just say?"

"He's been married about four months." The bartender turned to Ada. "Four months for Dan, right?"

She leaned closer to Thaddeus. "That's right. Now, with Dan, I can understand him turning me down. After all, he's got relatively new flesh at home. But you, Sanborn, why aren't you up for a quick jaunt? From what I've heard over the years, you're quite the studly skirt-chaser."

She squeezed her bosom up under his nose. "It's not often you can find me available without a prior appointment." She giggled as if the idea of men making reservations for her services quite tickled her funny bone.

Studly skirt-chaser! No wonder Ellie had turned him down if that was his reputation. But he smiled at Ada. He didn't want to insult her. Not twice in one night anyhow. After all, he liked her chicken dinners.

"Miss Ada, I was riding all day. Everything down there," he lowered his gaze to his lap and back up again, "is right sore. Another time, maybe." *When hell freezes over.* "But sit down a spell and talk to me, and I'll buy you a drink."

Ada laughed heartily, not bothered that her nipples appeared and disappeared as she did. "You don't need to buy me a drink in my own saloon." But she slapped the bar anyway and soon a glass of whiskey was sliding her way along the polished oak.

"I'll tell you about Dan. First, we all thought he was sweet on Anna at the mercantile, but then she got engaged. Then, when that Malloy girl came to town, she went out with Dan once, but it turned out she was in love with Riley." She shrugged. "But he was taken."

Ada paused to adjust her corset, which only served to expose more of her bosom.

"Of course, you already know that. Eliza Prentice and Riley were engaged a long time, the whole time you were away. Next thing you know, Miss hoity-toity Prentice gave him the boot."

Thaddeus winced at both the term and the topic, feeling disloyal and wishing Ada would finish telling him about Dan.

Ada downed her drink and let the bartender pour her another one.

"I think Eliza caught wind of Riley liking that Malloy girl. He brought her in here once. Pretty thing with dark hair."

Thaddeus didn't want to talk about Ellie's past. "I'm aware of all that, Miss Ada. I went to Riley and Sophie's wedding."

"*I* didn't get an invitation," she complained.

Thaddeus thought fast. "Who would have minded the saloon if you'd gone to San Fran?"

"True enough." She drank almost the whole second shot of whiskey in one swallow and turned dreamy eyes his way. "You're sore, huh?"

"So . . . uh . . . Dan?" Thaddeus asked, trying to steer the conversation once again.

She was staring at his crotch. "Right, right. Well, then the new doctor came to town. She's a woman, mind you," she added in case Thaddeus didn't know. "You haven't met her yet, have you?"

"Nope. So, Dan married the doctor?"

She shook her head and drained her glass a second time.

"No, that's what we were all thinking might happen, because they went out a few times, just to Fuller's. Not here, mind you. Maybe she don't like chicken."

Ada laughed to herself. "And then all of a sudden, Dan got himself engaged to Jessie's niece."

Thaddeus furrowed his brow. *Why couldn't he picture the girl?*

"You know Jessie?" Ada asked, seeing his expression.

"Of course, I know Jessie," he said. She'd been working at Fuller's for roughly fifteen years. "But I can't picture her kin."

"Belinda," Ada said, as if that should clear things up.

"Belinda?" He shook his head, drawing a blank. "Is she my age?"

"Roundabout. Jessie's sister moved away when Belinda was around two years old."

No wonder he didn't remember her.

"Five or six months ago, she came back to Spring. Presto, she's Mrs. Dan Freeman," Ada said. With that, she got up and walked away. Apparently, the conversation was over when her glass was empty.

Dan had moved lightning fast to make Belinda his wife. Thaddeus decided to pay a call the next day and offer his congratulations. Maybe he'd even get some tips on how to push Ellie in the direction of looking kindly on his proposal.

Hell, if Dan could do it, he could! He tipped back his drink and felt better than he had in hours.

"You sent that young man packing pretty quick," Mrs. Longwood declared as she brushed out Eliza's hair at bedtime.

They'd fallen into a routine that was as close to friends as Eliza could recall. And something about Mrs. Longwood tending to her reminded her of her mother—or at least, having a mother.

"You didn't work for us before my mother died, did you?"

"Why, yes I did. I knew your parents because your mama's mother and *my* mother were friends."

"You grew up with my mother?"

"We did. And then after your mama had you, I offered to help out. She never had much strength after that, but I loved being here in this house. Everything was so nice and genteel, and your parents were such good people, although your father was all business." She laughed. "Yes, indeed. He always paid me to the penny, even when I said I'd stay here for free."

Eliza wanted to ask Mrs. Longwood questions regarding her life without sounding rude or nosey, such as whether she was a missus and not a miss and where was her husband?

"Even when you were a little thing," the housekeeper continued, "I used to sit in the room here while your mama brushed your blond curls. And if she needed to lie down, she'd do it right on your bed and let me take over."

"That's why this seems so familiar, then," Eliza said. "Why did you . . . I mean, why did we stop?"

"Stop brushing your hair?" Mrs. Longwood laughed.

"Not only that. I mean, at some point, you and I stopped being close. Didn't we?"

"I've always loved you, Eliza. As if you were my own."

Eliza's breath caught in her throat. She hadn't expected that open declaration. Why hadn't she ever realized before that this woman was so much more than the cook and cleaning lady?

Mrs. Longwood continued to run the brush through Eliza's blond locks.

"I loved you before your mama died, and I promised her on her deathbed I would continue to do so. It hasn't always been easy."

Eliza considered what a difficult girl she'd been, and of course, her temper had often flared.

"Because of my behavior." She bowed her head.

"Oh, no, I didn't mean that, child. I meant because I didn't know what to do with such a headstrong young lady. And your father insisted on doing things his way when I believed you might need more of a gentle touch. It wasn't easy for me to see you make mistakes and then . . . this."

Mrs. Longwood put the brush down and their eyes met in the mirror. Eliza could see the woman was trembling.

"I've failed you and your mama. I should have stopped you leaving after your father died."

Eliza stood up and took the woman's hands in her own. She pulled her to the bed so they could sit together.

"You couldn't have stopped me. I was so unhappy and so lonely." Oddly, she didn't feel either of those things anymore. "And I'm not sorry I'm carrying this baby. He or she is most definitely *not* a mistake. Nor was going away and realizing how much of my life I was squandering feeling sorry for myself and how I truly value what I have right here."

Everything she'd been through over the past year, from her extensive travels to making up with Charlotte and, of course, to finally experiencing a perfectly blissful union with Thaddeus Sanborn—more than once—yes, it had all been worth it.

"I'm going to be a better person because of my child. You'll see."

"You've already changed. I noticed it from the moment you returned. I guess you finally grew up."

Was that what she'd done? Maybe so. Well, a grown-up lady would know how to deepen their friendship.

"May I please ask you something without your taking offense?"

The older lady shrugged. "I don't know until you ask."

"How are you a *Mrs.* Longwood? What happened to your husband?"

"Why would I take offense at that? I'm a missus because the most handsome man in these United States, Patrick Percy

Longwood, fell in love with me and asked me to be his wife. I didn't hesitate. I didn't scarcely breathe before I was saying yes, yes, yes."

Eliza smiled because Mrs. Longwood's entire face lit up as she talked.

"Did my parents know him?"

"They did. He worked for your father at the mine, and your mother liked him. She said he was perfect for me, and she was right. But he was from New York and determined to fight in the war. He rode off one day and he never came back. The Union Army sent me his things eventually."

Eliza didn't know what to say. Not so many women in the West were war widows, but she'd met numerous in her travels the farther eastward she'd gone. She reached her arms around Mrs. Longwood and hugged her.

"I got his name, but I sure wish he'd given me a child. That was one reason I was so happy to help raise you."

"Now, you can help me raise my baby."

"Yes, I will indeed, but I hoped I'd be looking after a whole family. You and a handsome husband. I thought you'd found your special someone when you got engaged to Mr. Dalcourt, even though I never saw any sparks between you two."

Eliza shook her head. "No, we never had any sparks. A whole lot of affection, though, and respect."

"He seemed like a nice enough fellow, but if there weren't any sparks," Mrs. Longwood said with a shrug before glancing at her from under her eyelashes, "not like you have with Mr. Sanborn."

Eliza gasped, but Mrs. Longwood patted her hand.

"It wasn't hard to see, child, nor to realize he's the baby's father, just by the way he looks at you."

Eliza dropped her gaze to her lap and couldn't contain a large sigh.

"You always had a soft spot for that boy. Well, not a boy, anymore," Mrs. Longwood added. "Did he come back to claim you?"

Claim her? That was a funny way of putting it. As though she were a piece of land he wanted to stake.

"I suppose so. He offered to marry me and take care of us." She indicated her stomach.

"Why aren't you over the moon, then? Your face brightened like the dawn when you laid eyes on him."

Eliza put her hands to her cheeks. Had it really? How could she explain her reluctance to let Thaddeus back into her life when she hardly understood it herself?

Most women, many, in fact, would be perfectly delighted to accept his offer of marriage, even if for the sole purpose of erasing the stigma of unwedded motherhood. Why, she knew many people of her parents' generation who'd accepted marriages of convenience in order to run a business and raise a family, or to have enough hands on a ranch or a farm.

Who was she to scoff at a potential husband?

She was Eliza Winnifred Malcolm Prentice. That's who!

Ultimately, any answer to Mrs. Longwood would have to wait until she could put into words what she was feeling. Instead, Eliza asked a question.

"Didn't you ever find another man you wanted to marry?"

Mrs. Longwood shook her head of gray-streaked hair.

"I never bothered looking. I knew everyone in Spring City, and there wasn't anyone like my Patrick. He was just perfect for me, like your mama said."

She eyed Eliza thoughtfully. "Besides, I always felt as if I'd given Patrick my heart and didn't have it in me to give to another man."

Standing up, Mrs. Longwood stretched and offered Eliza an encouraging smile.

"Maybe if I'd gone out in the world like you, I would have found someone else. But I wasn't that brave. Besides, I liked tending you and your father. It was the least I could do for your mama. Now, it's time for prayers and bed."

Eliza was tired, too, but she found it difficult to sleep. She kept thinking of her long-departed mother brushing her hair and of Mrs. Longwood being a young woman in love. So many things she had never even considered. And her own baby was coming. *She* would be the mama this time.

Gratitude, pure and simple, coursed through her.

And Thaddeus wasn't dead or missing, not ripped from her life like her housekeeper's beloved Patrick. No doubt, if Mrs. Longwood knew how long Eliza had loved Thaddeus, and how deeply, she would think her a fool not to grab him with both hands and hope for the best.

Why couldn't she open her heart and her arms to him as she'd done before? He already owned her heart. He always had. Like Mrs. Longwood said, Eliza simply didn't have it to give to any other man. Then why had she actually refused him?

Giving her pillow a sound punching, she turned on her side, staring into the darkness beyond her window.

Of course, she knew the answer: When she was younger, she'd believed she didn't deserve any better than for him to use her in his barn and then ignore her. The belle of Spring City, whom no one liked and who liked no one—that was her! Except Thaddeus had been the exception. She'd loved him blindly, unconditionally, even after he'd taken her so summarily in his barn and then passed out in the hay.

She recalled leaning over him, staring down at his handsome face after he'd disengaged from her quivering young body and closed his eyes. She'd kissed him but, getting no response, she'd fixed her skirts and crept home, fully expecting him to be on her doorstep the next morning, declaring his love.

Even when he hadn't, she'd tried to tell herself it was all right. After all, his had been the only affection she'd received from any man, except her father. And as unsatisfying as it had been, she'd taken the experience and locked it deep inside of her, a strange and brittle treasure.

She'd cherished the memory, holding onto it so tightly that she hadn't realized when it had slipped from her fingers and shattered, like one of those beautiful glass ornaments on a Christmas tree, all too easily ending up in shards on the floor.

A little older, a little wiser, she wasn't willing to settle for Thaddeus offering to look after a wife and child whom he didn't really want. She was quite able to take care of her family all by herself. Mrs. Longwood was correct. She *was* brave, and whatever was coming next didn't scare her.

No, what *scared* her was the tepid Thaddeus, the one who'd entered her home that day, all hat-in-hand, with his talk of "liking them" to be married in the same way as someone liked a good slice of pie. What's more, he'd spoken of their baby as if it was a burdensome responsibility he would grudgingly own up to.

Where was the Thaddeus who'd hungered for her so badly he'd grabbed her off her front porch when they were eighteen? She'd seen glimpses of him while they were traveling, and truth be told, she yearned for him still.

As if thinking about the past stirred it up and called it forth, she heard something hard strike her window—a pebble, perhaps—and knew at once who'd come calling.

CHAPTER TWENTY-FIVE

"Ellie," Thaddeus called up to her faintly. He most certainly didn't want Mrs. Longwood to answer and come at him with a broom.

He tossed another small rock at her window, hitting the sill. "Ellie."

Something in the back of his mind told him this was not a good idea. But he couldn't help himself.

"Ellie."

And there she was, at the window, the moonlight making her white nightdress seem to glow and causing her golden hair streaming over her shoulder to gleam radiantly. He grew hard and protective all at the same time. But the damn earth was rolling under his feet, and he had a feeling it might hit him in the face if he wasn't careful.

"Thaddeus, what are you doing?" she asked.

"Trying to get your attention, darlin'."

"Well, you have it. Now what?"

"I dunno. I didn't think that far."

"I doubt you're thinking at all." She rested her elbows on the windowsill and her head on her hands. "You're swaying."

"Am not."

"You are, too. Go home and sleep." Her voice sounded a tad annoyed. That wasn't how he wanted her to feel.

"Why don't I come up and get in your bed? Just like when we were on the road together. Don't you miss my arms around you?"

"You shouldn't be saying stuff like that so loudly," she admonished him.

The devil take it! "I'm coming up."

"No, you're not."

He ignored her words and grabbed onto the railing first and then the trellis, and he began to climb. If only the blasted house wasn't moving so much. He had to cling firmly to the lattice and the climbing roses, thorns and all. *Damn it, they hurt!*

He halted, hanging there, a couple feet from the ground.

"Thaddeus, stop it."

She was right. He'd never reach her at this rate. He let go and fell with a thud, lying on his back in the night-damp grass, looking up at her. She was the most beautiful creature in the world. She had his whole heart and soul. But she didn't want him. She never had.

"Are you all right?" she called down to him.

She did care! He was elated.

"Yes," he managed, although the wind had been knocked out of him.

"Then go home. I mean it. Right now."

She didn't care! He was crushed. He watched her pull her head inside and slam the window. Rolling over, he got to his hands and knees, and then he heaved, once, twice.

Man alive! Mrs. Longwood was not going to appreciate finding that in the grass the next morning. He had to do something.

Wandering over to Drake's barn, he helped himself to two buckets, filled them with water from the pump and forgot momentarily why. After a minute, he felt like throwing up again and did so, this time behind the barn. He felt enormously better and remembered why he was getting buckets of water.

Returning to Ellie's house, he threw the water on the mess he'd made and hoped that made it better, despite how it seemed to spread it around some.

He sighed and returned the buckets to Drake's so they wouldn't suspect a nighttime thief. He had nothing left to do but stroll home.

Home was empty, cold, and lifeless. None of which should have bothered him. Never would have before. Yet now he longed for Ellie's warmth in his bed, her laughter, and her wry wit, even her scathing comments no matter if they were directed at him.

Normally, he would have another drink and call it a night. But he had no liquor in the house and no stomach for it either, apparently.

He patted his pockets. Surprisingly, he had some cigarettes, but remembering how they made her hold her nose and not want to kiss him, he left the packet on the kitchen table and climbed the stairs for bed.

Was he whipped?

Hell, no! But he *was* weary.

He'd been on the move so long, it seemed strange not to be rummaging around in his bag for something to lay his head on. Not bothering to look for sheets, he stretched out on the bare mattress, and then he felt around for the pillow, tucking it under his head.

He'd made his fortune, secured his future, and he'd grown up, but he still had very little to offer a woman. Except his love. He drifted off to sleep dreaming he was jumping from train to train and from riverboat to riverboat, searching for Ellie.

Thaddeus climbed the stairs attached to the side of the feedstore. Above it, Dan lived with his new bride, exactly as the man's parents had lived there when Dan's father ran the store. His friend looked the same as ever, except maybe a little rounder in the middle. If Belinda was any bit as good a cook as her Aunt Jessie who ran Fuller's restaurant, that explained why.

Thaddeus kept his mouth shut about his friend's slightly thickening middle as Dan grabbed him firmly by the hand and shook it. Dan, however, wasn't so tactful.

"You look like shit," he said.

"What?" Thaddeus was surprised. He'd put on a clean shirt and pants.

"Your eyes are bloodshot, you haven't shaved, and your hair looks as if you've been dragged through sagebrush. I guess you didn't want to show me up in front of my missus."

Thaddeus laughed but tried to smooth his hair down. "Where is the unlucky lady?"

Dan chortled. "You're right. *I'm* the lucky one. Follow me."

A moment later, after they strode through to the small kitchen at the back and Thaddeus had met Belinda, he couldn't help but think Dan was right. He was damn lucky, for sure.

Belinda was pretty and sweet, soft-spoken and, as he found out, a blessed good cook. She offered him a plate containing slices of vanilla cake, lavender cookies, and toffee squares, and the robust aroma of fresh coffee teased his nostrils.

Thaddeus pretended to look behind him for the rest of the guests. Then he laughed.

"I can see why Dan is filling out so nicely."

Belinda blushed and lowered her gaze. "He does love my cooking. I think that's why he married me."

"Heck, no," Dan said, grabbing her around the waist and hugging her. "At least, it wasn't *only* her cooking. Her coffee is over the moon, too."

Thaddeus saw how they looked at each other.

"I imagine it was her good nature and lovely face that caught you."

"Damn straight," Dan agreed. "Sorry for my language, Bel."

They settled in for some of her delicious coffee, and Thaddeus found her as easy to talk to as Dan ever was.

"Where did you grow up?" Thaddeus asked, cramming another piece of cake into his mouth and brushing the crumbs onto his plate.

"Denver."

He hoped he wasn't picking at a scab by asking questions. "Why'd your parents leave Spring?"

"Pa needed to go to Denver for a job, despite how my mother didn't want to leave. She still misses Spring City."

"What made you come back after all this time?"

Belinda laughed. "Same reason my dad made us leave. For a job. Aunt Jessie needed help at Fuller's. I love it. Everyone is so nice, in particular the owner."

Thaddeus knew whose name she'd bring up next.

"Miss Prentice," Belinda continued, "though she insists I call her Eliza. What a sweet lady."

Dan spluttered his coffee onto the table. And Thaddeus swallowed his too quickly, scalding the back of his throat.

"Danny!" Belinda scolded and jumped up to get a dishtowel.

Thaddeus locked eyes with his friend, who returned the look with an exaggerated eye roll.

"I didn't believe Bel either until I went in for pie and had a heaping helping of Eliza's kindness."

Belinda mopped up the mess, making tut-tut noises.

"Why are you so determined to paint Miss Prentice as a spoiled, temper-tantrum throwing brat?"

"Because she always was," Dan said. "Only person who could ignore it was Riley."

Thaddeus sat up straighter and stiffer. He should have been there to protect her, befriend her, and take the brunt of her temper. Especially when, for how he'd treated her that night in his barn, he was the one she ought to have been angry at her entire adult life.

"Her temper never bothered me," he said, feeling better for speaking up for her.

"Cripes!" Dan exclaimed. "I thought she was one of the reasons you left. To get away from the Prentice irritation."

Thaddeus shrugged. "No. Truthfully, I missed her more than anyone."

Now, why had he confessed that? Probably because Dan was being so hard on Ellie and because Belinda was leaning her head on Dan's shoulder, looking so tender and loving. Thaddeus wanted that for himself. He'd experienced something like it more than once during the time he'd traveled with Ellie. She was the one woman he could imagine spending his life with, and he was going to proclaim it right there, right then.

"I'll tell you something more, Dan. I love her. The real reason I left Spring was *because* she got engaged to Riley, and I couldn't stand the sight of them together."

"Well, I'll be." Then Dan's face went slack, and he swallowed hard. He and Belinda exchanged a furtive glance, after which Belinda squeezed Dan's arm and nodded encouragingly at him. Dan stared hard into Thaddeus's eyes and looked for all the world as if he was about to be hanged.

"Eliza has changed her personality some, that's for sure. But I have to tell you something. Something important. Not that I've noticed or I'm looking or anything."

His cheeks turned bright red. "Rumor has it—but it's not really just a rumor because, you know, anyone can see with his own eyes, if you were looking, as I said, not that I am—she's with child." He whispered the last words as if saying them too loudly could cause a mine explosion.

Thaddeus nodded, unable to stop the cheerful smile from spreading over his face.

"I know. It's mine."

Belinda and Dan both exclaimed aloud. Then she recovered first.

"But that's wonderful! You're back in Spring City, and Miss Prentice is here. Neither of you are attached."

"Are you?" Dan interjected.

Thaddeus grunted and shook his head. "Not since I laid eyes on Ellie a few months back." No need to mention he'd never been attached to anyone else before her either.

Dan leaned forward. "Then stop beatin' the devil around the stump and ask that girl to marry you."

Belinda clapped her hands and added more gently, "Yes, go tell her how you feel." Then, in a voice scarcely audible, she added, "We're trying to have a baby, too."

Dan blushed from his neck up to his hairline.

Thaddeus ignored her last remark because he could see quite clearly Dan didn't want to discuss his marital relations. Considering Belinda Freeman, however, he decided she would be his ally if he needed one.

"I asked Ellie to marry me yesterday, and she showed me the door. I think she still sees me as the shiftless drifter who ran out of Spring and never looked back." Not to mention a skirt-chaser, if he recalled Ada's comment correctly.

"Is she right?" Belinda asked, fixing him with a perceptive stare.

"No, ma'am. I've changed, but I don't know how to make her see that."

"Where would you live if you married her?" she asked.

He shrugged. That had been on his mind that very morning. "My house, I guess."

Dan slapped him on the shoulder playfully. "If you're going to ask a woman to share your life and your home, you better have a place to keep her."

He gestured around him at the set of rooms they lived in above the store, as if it were a palace. And by the way Belinda glowed, Thaddeus could see it made no matter to her where they lived, but Ellie was different.

Dan caught his eye and added, "If you don't mind my saying so, your old house is a bit run down. Maybe you could work on it a bit and then ask her again."

Dan might be right about that. He remembered Ellie's harsh words for Riley's house and how she'd never intended to live in it.

"I'll do that," he said, making up his mind to start immediately. At least it would give him something to put his mind to besides fretting over his pregnant woman. The security of knowing he had a large payment coming in from his copper mine had left him at loose ends with too much free time and too little to do.

"You both know Miss Prentice better than I do," Belinda said, bending her napkin around and around her fingers. "Do you think she'd mind if I called on her? Not as her employee, but as a female friend?"

Dan shook his head, while Thaddeus smiled.

"I think she'd like that."

Dan gaped. "But she never had no friends, female or otherwise, that I can recall."

"About time then," Belinda said, not being put off one bit. "Besides, despite having my Danny here, I'm a bit lonely for the friends I left behind in Denver. Miss Prentice and I are roughly the same age." She looked at Thaddeus hopefully.

"You have nothing in common," Dan grumbled.

"I think she'd enjoy your company," Thaddeus said. "*Danny* can't keep you all to himself."

In fact, the more Thaddeus considered it, the better he liked the idea of Dan's Belinda becoming Ellie's friend and showing her how delightful marriage could be.

He started at once on his house. It wasn't a home, and he sure as shootin' didn't know how to make it into one, fit for Ellie and their child, but he aimed to try.

First, he swept from top to bottom and from inside out. Then he sat for a while and wondered what to do next. He considered sending a telegram to Charlotte, asking her advice. But then he realized he'd never seen his sister do much cleaning or caretaking, either. Maybe it simply wasn't in their blood.

He went to Fuller's Hotel, looking at Ellie's vacant front porch as he passed. Jessie's restaurant, inside the hotel, was always spick and span. She'd know what to do to clean a house and get it ready for a lady.

He wasn't expecting her to put her hands on her hips and laugh at him.

"Really? Thaddeus Sanborn wants to nest?" she mocked.

"Shush, please, Jessie. Don't be so darn loud about it."

"It wouldn't be because you've fallen for a certain birdy who already has an egg to lay?" She laughed again.

He felt himself go red in the face and nearly turned on his heel to leave, but he needed her help.

"Just give me some pointers, Jessie. I can handle the carpentry." Or could he? He could swing a hammer and just about hit a nail squarely, although he'd never measured and sawed wood, but how hard could it be? "I need to know what to do to clean and pretty up a place. After sweeping, that is."

He must have looked desperate because she took pity on him and got serious.

"All right, come with me. We'll go to the mercantile, and I'll show you what kind of soaps and oils to use to get that place in apple pie order. You'll need paint, too, right?"

"Ur, right." *Paint?* He hadn't even noticed what color the house was, inside or out.

"What condition are the rugs in?"

"Rugs?" *Did it have rugs?*

She stared at him. "*Hm*, let's start with the cleaning. Then you can worry about the rest of it later, I suppose."

Eliza woke up the next morning feeling antsy. Thaddeus's appearance at her window the night before had reminded her of their younger years, and all her feelings for the wild young man he used to be rushed back, blending with her desire for the man he'd become.

With difficulty, she'd shut the window on him and turned her back. Lying awake, she'd imagined how it would be if he'd succeeded in climbing the trellis and slipping into her bedroom. More than anything, she wanted to kiss him and run her fingers through his thick chestnut-colored hair.

She longed for his touch on her skin, torturing herself with memories of the last time they'd lain together. At Charlotte's house, *she'd* ridden *him*, although he'd guided her hips, and then he'd rolled her under his taut body and filled her. And given her a child.

It would be easy to give in and say yes. But if she put her faith in Thaddeus and he ended up spending his days smoking cigarettes and playing cards, and his evenings in Ada's saloon drinking whiskey, she'd want to shoot him. And what about the baby?

Groaning at the early morning light and her own tortured musings, she got up and dressed. Going downstairs, through her beloved house toward the kitchen, she could hear Mrs. Longwood already making breakfast. She paused in the sitting room, picturing Thaddeus on the sofa, feet up on the table, drinking coffee, reading, with her beside him doing the same.

When they were traveling together, spending endless hours on Lucky, they'd surprised each other with their similarities. He'd even pulled out an identical tattered copy of Mr. Twain's *Tramp Abroad* from his bag that she had in her own.

She frowned. Jack Stoddard must have stolen hers, she realized, when he'd stripped her on the boat and taken her things. As easily as she'd lost her book, her dream dissolved before her eyes, and doubt trickled down her spine.

What if Thaddeus got bored with her? That had never been a problem before, but that might have been because they were always running for their lives or jumping off a riverboat. She wouldn't be doing any of those things in her present condition or after, for that matter. Not with a baby in tow.

Of course, they could play a friendly game of cards. She loved beating him at faro or poker. She loved talking to him. She loved . . . *him.*

It would destroy her if one morning, he got the urge to hop a boxcar and decided he couldn't take a wife and child with him.

Eliza might have spent the entire day driving herself crazy, despite Mrs. Longwood's best attempts at distraction, except Belinda Freeman showed up midmorning. She offered a smile and some rich chewy molasses cookies and professed a need to chat. Bemused, Eliza invited her in, sat her down, and listened.

For some reason, even though Belinda was a married woman and around the same age, Eliza had thought of her as a girl. Most likely, it was due to seeing her working at the restaurant, all bright-eyed and smiling, seeming as happy to mop floors as to serve food.

In her home, at her table, Eliza realized Belinda was also clever and innately cheerful, and for some reason, she'd sought out *her* company. The specter of Charlotte infiltrated Eliza's thoughts as she poured their tea. What had Charlotte said: *It was nice to have a friend to go shopping with.* She'd been quite right.

Here in Spring, it would be nice to have a friend other than Mrs. Longwood. An hour later, Belinda rose to leave.

"I'm so glad you stopped by," Eliza couldn't help saying, and she meant it.

"Me, too." And Belinda took her hands in her own. "If you need anything, you let me know. I know your housekeeper is an excellent cook, but I love to bake, so holler if you have a sweet-tooth emergency."

Eliza smiled. "I'll do that. And if you need anything—" *Good gracious!* What could she offer? She paused uncertainly.

Belinda nodded. "Getting to know you and being welcomed into your home means the world to me. Next time, you can answer some questions I have about the people in town."

Then an impish smile spread over her pretty face. "You've known Danny all your life. Maybe next time we visit, we can have a little chat regarding the menfolk."

Another quick squeeze of the hands and she was gone.

Eliza hummed to herself, pleased Belinda had indicated they would have another get-together. Then Eliza shook her head. *Danny!*

Never had she thought of solid Dan Freeman as Danny. And what did Belinda mean by "menfolk"? Did Belinda know of her history with Thaddeus?

With a warm flush of embarrassment, she considered Thaddeus and Dan's close friendship. Would Thaddeus have told Dan anything? Did people already know who the father of her baby was? Because for certain, everyone seemed to already know she was expecting, if the way they stared at her stomach first, then smiled at her face second was any indication.

That was all right, though. She wasn't ashamed at having a baby despite knowing she ought to be. In the earliest days, fretting at Charlotte's, Eliza had feared she'd be an outcast. The townsfolk could so easily have humiliated her and pointed out how far she'd fallen, having a bastard. They hadn't. So rather than shame, she felt excitement and anticipation. For the first time in her life, she was doing something worthwhile.

Nevertheless, the next time she saw Belinda, she would ask her which people already knew and what they were saying. Meanwhile, she decided to pay a visit to the doctor. Her questions were piling up mighty quick. Were her breasts supposed to become tender as they were, and why was she suddenly desperate for Jessie's lemon cake when she'd always despised citrus?

Eliza took a leisurely stroll down Main Street to Dr. Bell's. No one was in the outer office, no friendly Miss Taylor to greet her. That wasn't surprising, given it was noon, and she'd already found out Marie liked Jessie's turkey pie at midday.

Just as she turned to leave, Eliza heard a noise in the back room and noticed the door was ajar.

Probably Dr. Bell was cleaning instruments as Riley always used to do. Pushing it open, she gasped at the sight.

Thaddeus stood, unclothed to the waist, with Dr. Bell seated in front of him, clasping one of his hands, while her other hand rested on his naked torso. Her head was bent over the hand she held, and he was looking down at her.

At Eliza's entrance, he'd ceased to move although his fingers were outstretched as if he was about to run them over the doctor's glossy red hair.

Even as his surprised gaze swung her way and before the doctor lifted her head to see who had barged in, Eliza backed out with a mumbled apology.

She fled the practice, unsure what she'd seen, thinking she heard Thaddeus call out her name. But deep inside, fear coiled like a vicious snake, fear that Thaddeus was already smitten with the beautiful new lady doctor.

After all, it had taken only a single encounter for Riley to fall for Sophie Malloy. True, he'd fought his attraction for Eliza's sake because he was the most honorable man she'd ever met. In the end, however, even *he* had succumbed to his desires. And one terrible day, her then-fiancé had sat in public with Sophie, sharing a meal at Fuller's restaurant, embarrassing Eliza beyond words.

Obviously, no one in town knew of her brief association with Thaddeus, except for Mrs. Longwood, so it wasn't embarrassment she felt at present. No, it was nasty, painful jealousy mingling with the doubt she could ever be enough for Thaddeus Sanborn.

Unthinkingly, she found herself ducking into the feedstore, catching sight of Dan who was standing behind the counter with a stack of papers. He gave her a puzzled smile. When was the last time she'd set foot in his store?

Nodding in greeting, she pretended to examine the various types of grain he kept in large burlap bags. Inside of her, utter turmoil reigned, making it hard to catch her breath.

"Can I help you with something, Miss Eliza?" She looked up to see Dan's bemused expression as he wandered over, and she let the handful of seeds filter through her fingers back into the bag.

"Actually, I came in to thank you for tending my gardens. Mrs. Longwood told me you did, and I would like to compensate you for your troubles."

"Oh, no," he said, a bashful smile crossing his attractive face. "No need for that. I did it for the love of the land, Miss Eliza, plus you can see your backyard from the deck out behind the store. It's just the way the land angles away. I hated to stand here day after day and watch it all go to hell . . . uh, I mean, heck."

He paused. "Do you want to see your yard from the deck?"

"Um." No, she didn't particularly want to, but then a shadow fell across the window. Thaddeus, with his shirt back on, walked along the sidewalk, craning his neck and scanning the street. Was he looking for her?

She did not want to meet him in the middle of town and have another heartfelt discussion. Wouldn't everyone see as easily as Mrs. Longwood had how much she cared for him?

"Yes, Dan, I would." She grabbed a hold of his arm and half-dragged him to the back of the store.

They looked at her well-kept garden. "You really did a splendid job," Eliza said. "By the way, I had a lovely visit from your wife today. It still seems so strange that you're married," she added.

"Don't I know it," he agreed, and his eyes sparkled at the mere mention of Belinda. "And it's strange, too, that you're going to have—"

Eliza's lips formed a perfect "O" at the same time as he cut himself off, his own mouth gaping open in horror at what he'd started to say. They stared at each other in mutual mortification until the bell on the door rang, indicating another customer. She could only pray it wasn't Thaddeus.

"I . . . uh . . . I'm sorry," Dan whispered.

Just walk away, she prayed.

"My mouth has a mind of its own," he continued, backing away from her. "Or maybe it needs one. One of us does, me or my mouth." He turned and bolted.

She sagged against the railing. Hearing voices from inside the shop, she knew it wasn't Thaddeus who'd entered, so after a moment, she ventured in. While Dan's back was turned, helping a rancher with feed choices, she slipped out the front door, cringing at the sound of the bell that seemed to be tolling the tumult of her life.

CHAPTER TWENTY-SIX

Thaddeus hadn't come by in four days, not since she'd seen him at Dr. Bell's. Misery kept Eliza company, and anger befriended her but good. If he took up with the doctor, while she carried his baby, she vowed she'd retrieve Thaddeus's own revolver from the lockbox under her bed and let him experience her displeasure.

Everyone knew he was working like a fiend on his house, but surely, he had a moment to come woo her, seeing as how he'd said he wanted to marry her.

"I hate him," she said aloud, sitting on her front porch, waiting to catch a glimpse if he went by in his wagon or on his horse.

She understood at last why he'd left Spring City in such an all-fired hurry. The torture she felt even imagining seeing him walk down the street with Dr. Bell on his arm had to pale in comparison to how he'd felt when she'd run up to him flaunting her engagement ring.

Thaddeus had been smitten with her then, but years had passed since.

Twice, she'd got rid of him, after his half-hearted proposal and when he'd acted like a naughty rogue trying to climb her trellis with a very different type of proposal altogether.

Would he come back a third time?

Why not go see him? All she needed was a halfway plausible reason. After all, they were still friends—although ever since he'd used the word to describe their relationship, she'd started to hate it. Then she remembered what she had in the drawer of her bedside table, and she smiled.

Fifteen minutes later, she knocked at the front door of Thaddeus's house, thinking the sound of her knuckles on the freshly painted wood was no louder than her pounding heart. No answer. She could still walk away with him none the wiser.

She straightened. No, she wasn't going to act like a hog-nose snake and play dead. She had a strong backbone, by God, and she aimed to keep it. Picking her way carefully through the weeds and overgrown grass, she tried again at the back door.

Still, no answer. It was unlocked, but propriety restrained her from letting herself in. She looked around the yard. His absence was curious since his wagon was unhitched in the drive, and she could hear his horse nickering softly.

Exploring a little farther, she strolled to the small paddock and called to Thaddeus's new horse, who came sauntering over. Letting her stroke from its white blaze down to its velvet muzzle, it whinnied appreciatively.

"You're a sweet thing," she murmured, thinking of Lucky and hoping their old horse was being treated kindly.

"Shit! Shit! Goddamnit all to hell!"

She opened her eyes wide at his blistering curse. That didn't sound good. Startled by the ferocity of Thaddeus's words, Eliza patted the horse one more time before pushing away from the fence and heading toward the barn to investigate.

The double-wide doors were open, and she walked through them before stopping to let her eyes adjust to the comparative dimness of the interior.

It didn't look any different from most barns, except messier. And of course, Thaddeus was there, making it different from any other barn in the world.

He stood in the far corner, scrabbling at something on the old wooden workbench. Shirtless, wearing denims. She faltered, feeling that familiar twist in her stomach, definitely something more substantial than butterflies.

If only he hadn't been shirtless!

He was muttering and banging at something metal on the table. Taking a deep breath, she walked over to him. She even said his name, perhaps too quietly. When she got within arm's reach, he still hadn't acknowledged her, even though she was close enough to watch the sweat-sheened muscles play across his back as he hammered.

Reaching out, she touched his shoulder ever so lightly.

"No!" he yelled, dropping everything, spinning around and grabbing both her upper arms as if ready for a fight. There was nothing tender in the grip that bit into her flesh. His face was a mask of hostility for a split second until recognition dawned.

"Ellie!" He didn't immediately release her as his eyes widened in surprise.

Mutely, she stood unmoving, stunned by the violent expression he'd worn a second earlier and by the certainty that if it hadn't been her, he wouldn't have hesitated to strike out. She looked to where his hands gripped her shoulders, one of them trailing a soiled white bandage from his finger, then back at him. He released her at once.

"I'm sorry," he said, running his hand through this hair. "Didn't I tell you before never to do that?"

"You mean not to sneak up on an armed man?" she asked, then felt her face go hot as she recalled the last time she'd snuck up on him in Charlotte's house. His "weapon" had been sensual torment. She blushed to the roots of her hair at the memory, her heart racing while standing so close to him.

Perhaps he was remembering the same encounter because his gaze dropped to her lips, and his hands reached out for her again. Hurriedly, she stepped back.

"I'm sorry I startled you," she said.

"You're lucky my guns are in the house," he teased. "I have to admit that when attacked from behind, I usually shoot first and ask questions later."

She could imagine that technique had kept him alive. Thinking of which, she noticed on his left side, where his chest tapered to his ribs, that he carried a scar, raised and still pink. If Stoddard had been a better shot, Thaddeus wouldn't be standing in front of her.

She fisted her hand to stop from reaching out to touch the scar. In her mind, she saw Josephine Holland tending him. Josephine, who'd been intimate with him over the years.

"You were busy," she said, dragging her gaze to his face. "I guess you didn't hear me. But speaking of guns, I have your revolver, back at my house. I forgot to return it."

His brow furrowed. "How did you . . . ?"

"I picked it up after you were shot. I don't know why."

"I'm glad you did." He grinned, as though being shot were inconsequential. "It's a damn accurate weapon."

He paused, cocking his head as if expecting her to explain her presence, but she didn't know what else to say. She wasn't really sure what she'd hoped to accomplish by seeking him out.

She winced as the silence grew, never having felt awkward with him before.

"Can I come by later and get it?" he asked, seemingly unperturbed by her uneasiness.

Was that what she'd wanted? To entice him into coming back a third time, using his gun as bait? She was pathetic.

"What were you doing?" she asked instead of answering his question.

Grimacing, he swiveled back to the workbench. "I'm repairing a few things in the house, but I bent my saw."

He held up the rusty tool by its splintered wooden handle, and she could see a definite wave to the metal-toothed blade. She looked past it to the hammer he'd been wielding.

"You were *hammering* your saw blade back into shape?"

Giving her a sheepish smile, he shrugged before dropping it back onto the workbench with a clatter.

"I already broke the only other saw I could find." He gestured with his head. She looked to see a mangled blade in two pieces on the floor by the ladder, the ladder to the same loft where she'd rather carelessly lost her virginity and her heart.

Unable to stop herself, she lifted her gaze to the platform overhead, then shot a glance back at him.

He looked stricken. Was that regret she saw on his face?

"I'd better be going," she said. It had been a mistake going there in the first place.

"Wait, darlin'. Why'd you come? Do you need something?"

Did she need something? *Yes. My old childhood friend, Thaddeus Sanborn.*

She glanced at the ladder again. Why was she standing there, gawking at his chest and recalling that long-ago night? Somehow, he'd climbed that ladder, drunk as he was. She bit her lip, thinking how he'd sent her up ahead of him. He must have had a fairly good idea of the prize awaiting at the top, more so than she had understood.

She stuck her hands in the pockets of her skirt. Then she remembered her errand.

"Oh, silly me." Was it her pregnancy causing her mind to leap from one thought to another and then forget others completely?

"I brought you something. Hold out your hand."

He did, never taking his eyes off hers, until she pulled her precious treasure out of her pocket and dropped the contents onto his outstretched palm. She made sure not to let her hand linger too long against his calloused skin despite how she wanted to.

He stared a moment and then frowned. "My coins and . . ." His gaze flew to hers.

"That's the bullet that would've killed you," she explained, reaching out, touching the area over his heart where she'd seen the bruising mark, long since healed. Then she snatched her hand away.

Barely able to meet his green gaze, she added, "I'm sorry you got shot because of me, Thaddeus."

Embarrassingly, her throat closed up, thick and tight, and she knew a bucketful of tears wasn't far behind.

"I have to go," she practically squeaked, turning and sprinting for the open doors.

She should've known he wouldn't let her get away so easily. Thaddeus caught up to her in three steps, his big warm hand shackling her wrist and holding her in place.

"Don't run away. Please." He turned her to face him, and then he slipped the coins and bullet into the front pocket of his denims. With two free hands, he took hold of hers.

She felt his thumbs caress the backs of her hands, then start to lightly drift over her knuckles. She closed her eyes. How else to keep the tears from falling?

He groaned. "Why do I always end up making you cry?" he asked, his voice sounding anguished. "When all I want to do is love you."

"Love me?" she repeated, her eyes snapping open. *Where had that come from?*

This week, she hadn't believed he even liked her, let alone loved her. He'd kept his distance, seeming to be easily distracted by whatever he was doing there at his house.

Shouldn't he be coming to her house every day, begging to be allowed to rub her feet and her back, which had begun to ache something awful? Shouldn't he be holding her hand as they walked down Main Street showing everyone she belonged to him?

"I don't think you know what love is," she accused, ignoring her own irrational thought of how he would, indeed, have been holding her hand in public if she hadn't turned down his marriage proposal, lackluster as it was.

His jaw clenched, and his face darkened like a thundercloud across the sun.

"Is that so?" He reeled her in by her hands, which he still clasped, until her body was pressed up against his, or at least the rounder parts of her body. Then he released them so he could spread his fingers at her waist and anchor her there.

Like the large bell that Ely, the town barber, rang if ever there was a fire or some other emergency, her body jangled its own alarm. Putting her palms on his bare chest, whether to keep him away or to merely to touch him, she relished the feel of his warm skin under the pads of her fingertips.

She'd all but baited him, just to get a reaction like this one, proving he had genuine feelings for her.

Raising her head, she peered up at him, wishing, not for the first time, she'd gained a little more in height. But the look he gave her, down the end of his nose, was an angry one.

"Words are not getting through to you, Ellie, as if you simply don't want to hear. Or you think I'm lying." He gave her the smallest of squeezes, showing his frustration.

She wanted to believe him, but a flicker of doubt must have shown in her eyes because he growled his frustration.

"Well, damn!" Lightning fast, he moved his hands to cradle her head. His fingers wove into her hair and held her still while he claimed her lips, not punishingly, although she could feel the tension in his body where they touched.

He moved his mouth against hers, then changed direction, slanting his head the other way and fitting his lips to hers again.

Delightfully sizzling shards of pleasure glided through her from head to toe. As her lips softened under his, he relaxed into her, never releasing her from the kiss, but somehow enveloping her with his broad chest and shoulders and arms.

Her hands skimmed up his naked skin to lock behind his neck.

She sighed, and he took her open lips as an invitation, widening the stance of his legs to hold her even closer before sweeping his tongue into her mouth. Heat swirled low in her body, and she could feel her own pulse in her throat. Daringly, she touched his tongue with the tip of her own, and he groaned.

His tongue circled hers, then retreated as, at last, he lifted his mouth from hers. Slipping his hands from her hair, he roamed them over her body, encountering the hard cotton-encased steel of her corset stays.

"What the hell is this?" he asked, not loudly, but sounding irritated, perhaps because it impeded his ability to feel her body and her breasts.

"A corset," she said when she caught her breath. Of course, he must know what a corset was. "A maternity corset."

"A maternity what?"

Without another word, he proceeded to yank her blouse up so he could look underneath.

"Thaddeus, stop!" she protested, taking note of the fact they were in his barn in broad daylight. She batted at his hands to no avail.

"That looks uncomfortable."

"It's not too bad."

"You never wore a corset before," he pointed out.

She blushed, but he continued, "Well, did you?"

"No, I never did, until Boston."

"Does it help?"

She looked at him, puzzled by his strange question.

"Help what?"

"I mean, does it offer you some support for your stomach?"

She laughed, feeling shaky from their kiss and a bit nervous at this Thaddeus who behaved so unpredictably. Squirming from his hands, she turned her back to him trying to tug her shirt into place, but now he was holding it up from behind.

"No, you dolt," she said, yanking at the fabric and trying to escape. "It's not for support. It's supposed to make my figure look like it did before. It's *hiding* my condition for as long as possible."

"That's ridiculous," he scoffed. "You can't hide your condition. And you could be . . . I don't know," he stopped, and she looked over her shoulder to see him running his hand through his unruly hair, frowning, as he stared at the back of the offending undergarment. "You could be squishing the baby."

"Poppycock," she muttered. "It said on the advertisement that it is 'universally endorsed by eminent physicians.' See, I can let it out with these laces."

She ran her hands over her sides where sturdy laces went from her hips to under her arms. "Besides they wouldn't sell them if—"

"Nope," he interrupted, reaching his hands around her and turning her gently to face him again. "I don't like it, not one bit. Charlie wasn't wearing one. She blossomed when I was taken back there to heal from the gunshot wound, and she looked perfectly acceptable. Downright pretty, even." He shook his head.

"There's nothing wrong with having a baby, and everyone knows about it anyway," he added, "so no more silly corset."

With that, he began undoing the hook and eye fastenings over the front of her stomach.

"Stop it," she hissed, grabbing at his wrists. But he continued, until it was wholly undone and her small rounded belly popped out, along with her burgeoning breasts—and all of it clad in a shift. He chucked the offending garment from him onto the dirty barn floor.

Open-mouthed, she gawked. "That cost me $1.50!"

However, as he placed his hand on her stomach, still holding her shirt up with his other hand, she sucked in her breath and fell silent, the heat of his touch searing her through the thin, soft cotton.

In truth, with the corset off, she wanted to scratch the tingling skin over her stomach, but this seemed neither the time nor the place for such an unladylike performance. Especially not while his face held an expression of pure reverence.

"Look at you," he said, his voice thick, as he stroked around her navel and over her hips. His gaze moved higher to her full breasts, outlined against the shift, which seemed to grow tighter every day.

She tingled under his scrutiny. And then his hand followed his glance, brushing the under-curve and round the side of her right breast with his knuckles.

Finally, as if waking from a trance, she yanked her blouse from his grasp and tugged it down to fall below her low-waisted skirt. His actions were beyond the pale.

Stooping, she picked up her corset and shook it, but it was covered in dirt and hay remnants.

He stared at her, his eyes like two hard emeralds.

"Don't put that on again," he warned.

"That's absurd. You can't tell me what to do."

He held up his hand, pointing a finger at her middle. "I'll be checking regularly. And it won't matter to me where we are, if I find it on you, I'll remove it."

She knew he meant it. "Fine!"

"Fine," he repeated, his tone firm. Then he sighed. "Look, Ellie, the only baby I ever saw being born was one of Riley's colts, and that thing needed room to move."

She knew her eyes must have grown to the size of organ stops. *What an idiot!*

"Babies are not like colts," she reminded him.

"Maybe not, but I want to treat you and our baby as good as any horse. What about Lucky? You'd want Lucky to be comfortable, right, if she was foaling?"

Eliza felt a wave of nostalgia at the mention of their loyal steed, picturing Thaddeus holding her so securely for so many days upon its back. A lump formed in the back of her throat, which became a hot ball of tears.

Goshdarnit! She was welling up again.

"I loved that horse," she wailed to Thaddeus, backing toward the barn's double doors. "And you just left her behind." With that, she ran from him, swiping at her tears, which were already falling like a hard rain.

"Ellie?" he called after her, running as far as his front yard, but she figured even he wouldn't run down the middle of the street without his shirt on.

Her chest heaving by the time she reached her own front steps, she sat down in a huff. *Blast it all!* She hadn't even asked him what he was doing at the doctor's, although the bandage flapping on his finger gave her an inkling. Obviously, the man was not as good with tools as he was with guns.

He'd said he wanted to love her. He didn't say, *I love you with all my heart, and I'll never hurt you again.* No, he most certainly didn't.

"I want to love you" was his fancy way of saying he wanted to bed her again.

She wasn't totally naive on intimate matters anymore. Truthfully, thinking of his incredible kiss, she wanted to go to bed with him again, too.

With his saw blade nearly straightened, Thaddeus marched back into his house, feeling irritable and frustrated. Wasn't that just perfect? Wasn't that just Ellie?

"Corset," he mumbled to himself, setting his warped saw to the lumber he'd cut three inches too long the first time and stupidly had nailed into place without checking. No woman with a figure like hers should ever wear a corset, except a lacey one to hold up some pretty stockings, inviting a man to remove the whole damn thing as soon as possible.

He braced the wood with one hand and started to saw. *And a corset could be useful for thrusting her breasts up, just so,* he amended his mental image of her in black satin. He considered her fuller figure from what he'd shockingly done a few minutes before. Her breasts appeared plumper than ever, and her nipples had been darker.

His mouth actually watered.

The saw slipped, cutting into the side of his hand where he held the wooden stair tread he was attempting to fix.

"Goddamnit!" He dropped the saw and grabbed up an old cloth he had for this very purpose, to staunch the blood. It was already spotted with dark dried stains.

He would never get through this house restoration until she agreed to be his. He knew by the look in her eyes and by the way she returned his kiss she wasn't opposed to him. He simply hadn't convinced her properly.

Charging up the stairs, he grabbed a shirt. Why, he would go over to her house right then and . . .

He paused. He ought to do it properly this time. He had plenty of money, but Spring City didn't have a real jeweler, only a small assortment of trinkets at Webster's store. He'd have to go to Denver for the best selection of rings.

And then there was the other delicate issue of Lucky. Incredibly, Ellie had cried over that wretched horse. Even Riley, who loved horses, had never cried over one. At least, not that Thaddeus had seen.

Still, he hated to know that thinking of Lucky made her sad. When he thought of Lucky, he often smiled, remembering holding Ellie close for hours and talking to her about everything under the sun. Worse, still, she blamed him. What was he supposed to have done? Bought the blasted horse a seat on the train and taken it to Boston?

Christ Almighty! Save him from weepy women!

Without thinking, he was shoving items into his leather bag—a pair of denims, a shirt, unmentionables, a razor. All that remained to do before he left was to go talk to Dan and Ely.

CHAPTER TWENTY-SEVEN

Thaddeus nudged Lucky into a faster gallop as they neared Spring City, his own horse ponying along beside, keeping pace. His trip had robbed him of more days of his life than he'd intended, and he was chomping at the bit, so to speak, almost as hard as Lucky. He couldn't wait to be back within touching distance of Ellie.

First, he stopped at his house. In the week and a half he'd been away, Ely and Dan had performed miracles. Someone had cut down the hayfield in the front and back, and made it look like a civilized lawn again. The shutters were hanging straight and had been freshly painted. Even a few missing shingles had been replaced on the roof.

He rode past the wagons parked behind his house and turned the two tired horses into the paddock where Dan and Ely's horses already grazed.

Heading into the barn to hang up his saddle and bridle, Thaddeus stopped at the entrance and whistled.

"Jesus, would you look at that?" he exclaimed, taking a few steps inside and looking around.

His barn was swept, tidied, and hung with tools he didn't even own. Or maybe he did own them now. He seemed to recall asking for the other men's help so enthusiastically, he'd said something along the lines of "Buy whatever you need."

He smiled to himself. Even when his father was alive, it had never looked like this, but then, John Sanborn had spent more time reading and writing in his study than doing anything at all in the barn. And Thaddeus had inherited his father's lack of carpentry know-how.

Entering his back door, the smell of varnish and new paint assaulted his nostrils.

Sure enough, when he followed the sounds of voices to the parlor, he found Dan, Belinda, Ely, and Ely's young son, Jack, all talking at once, standing in the middle of the freshly painted room.

"Hey," Thaddeus said, grinning from ear to ear at the changes in his house.

The once boarded-up broken window in the sitting room had been replaced, and the ceiling plaster, which had been falling in flakes, looked pristine. The musty dark curtains were gone, and although the old sofa and piano were in the center of the room covered in sheets, everything else looked welcoming and ready for a new bride.

Dan came forward to grab him by the hand and slap his shoulder in greeting.

"You've been busy," Thaddeus said, rubbing his shoulder as Dan always did pack a hell of a wallop.

"Like bees in the hive," Ely said. "All the woodwork and repairs are done. And then we had some recruits to help with the painting and such."

Belinda smiled shyly at him. "I hope you don't mind that we went ahead and painted, but all the rooms were so drab."

"All the rooms?" Thaddeus repeated. "You mean you painted the whole house?"

She nodded. "Jessie came by to help, too. We chose colors we liked, so you can blame us if Eliza isn't happy."

The mention of her name reminded Thaddeus why they were doing all this.

"How is she?" he asked, knowing the others had kept an eye on her, like he'd asked.

Dan snorted. "She don't do much."

"Danny," Belinda scolded. "She's making a baby."

Ely covered his son's ears, and they all laughed.

"It's hard work," Belinda said. "My cousin could hardly get out of bed toward the end. But Eliza's not like that," she reassured Thaddeus, after his smile died with a pang of worry.

"She's only being contemplative," Dan's wife continued. "I see her sitting on her front swing, thinking, reading, talking with her housekeeper. But when I went to visit two days ago, she was chatty as you please and friendly and beaming with health. She was also full of questions," she added, looking pointedly at Thaddeus.

He shrugged. "I know. I should've talked to her before I left, but she would've got it all out of me. Probably would've wanted to come with me, too."

Belinda crossed her arms. "Well, don't make her wait any longer."

Thaddeus grinned. "I'm heading over there now."

"No, you're not," Dan protested. "Not like that. You're covered in trail dust. What did I tell you about asking a lady to marry you?"

"That I needed a better house," Thaddeus quipped. "And you've taken care of that. All of you have."

Dan scowled. "I meant you needed to fix yourself up, too."

"We'll all get out of your way in a jiffy," Belinda offered, "but first, let's show you what we've done. We'll start in the kitchen."

By the time they sat in their wagons, ready to leave, Thaddeus felt infused with the warmth of their friendship, thoroughly astounded by their generosity.

"You must have spent more time here than at your own homes and businesses," he said.

Ely shrugged. "Gave the boy some good experience on repairs and swinging a hammer. Something you should try sometime." With that, he gave his horse a "hiyah," and the animal pulled Ely and Jack out of the driveway.

"I think I've just been insulted," Thaddeus said, addressing Dan and Belinda, but he couldn't remove the grateful smile from his face. "If you two need anything I can do, let me know."

"We'll do that," Dan said. "And we're not done yet, by the way."

"That's right," Belinda said, snuggling up close to Dan on the bench seat. "I'm sewing some darling curtains for the kitchen, blue and white checks. And Dan's stripping the kitchen table to refinish it. It's back at the store, on the deck."

Thaddeus hadn't even noticed it was missing. "What can I say except thank you?"

He watched them drive away, all wrapped around each other, and his heart seemed to tighten in his chest.

"Please, Lord, let me have Ellie. I haven't asked for a lot, have I, in all my years? But this woman is mine, Lord, like you made her perfectly for me. And I'm starting to believe I'm the man for her. I *know* I am. I need her. I love her."

He focused in on what he was holding and his mouth twisted. He'd been having a sincere moment, praying to God, with a dirty paintbrush in his hand. He hoped that didn't negate his prayers.

Puffing hard, Eliza sat down on the rocky outcropping, halfway up the aptly named Lookout Hill. She loved this walk and the view from the rocks, but it was the first time she'd ventured up the trail since she had returned from her adventures.

The mild climb was a tad more arduous than she recalled, particularly in what she figured was her seventh month of pregnancy, but it was worth the effort. From her vantage point, she could see all of Spring City, its tiny station and train tracks going east and west, disappearing off in the distance just as she had done a year and a half earlier.

All she felt now was bone-deep gladness she wasn't starting her journey that day. No, sirree. For today, she was satisfied, knowing Mrs. Longwood would draw her a hot bath later and then prepare her a scrumptious meal. Those small comforts were bliss.

The only blight in her happiness was Thaddeus's disappearance, without even a goodbye. The *only* blight! She frowned. That was like saying the Pacific Ocean was only a drop of water.

He'd up and left without so much as a farewell, fond or otherwise. For the first two days, she'd been utterly shocked by his disappearance, feeling his absence like an actual pain in her body. Her brain puzzled at how she had transformed from a lost and bitter woman to a hopeful, expectant one, whereas he seemed not to have changed at all. Would he bother to return by the time his child arrived?

Over the next two days she stewed with anger, wishing she could punch him in the nose for his selfishness. Didn't he know she would worry about him endlessly, now that they had such a strong connection?

Then she grew sad, wallowing in a melancholy that felt achingly familiar, letting herself suffer for three days, all the while longing to see his tempting grin and intense green eyes.

At which point, she ceased her ridiculousness, offering Mrs. Longwood her first genuine smile all week that very morning.

If the man never came back, would she let his absence poison her like snake venom? No, she would not. She'd be a happy mother to their baby, showering it in love and laughter, and he could go to the devil.

She would get over wanting Thaddeus Sanborn if it was the last thing she ever did.

Leaning her head back, she closed her eyes, wishing she'd had the forethought to bring something comfy to rest on. Next time, she would. But even with only a sun-warmed rock for a pillow, the droning of the bees combined with the late-afternoon sun and her general tiredness over the past few weeks caused her to drift into a dozy sleep.

"Ellie," she heard Thaddeus's seductive voice sometime later, and she smiled. She'd been dreaming of him again, about making love in a boxcar.

Slitting open her eyes, she reached up to wrap her arms around the neck of the robust, handsome man who leaned over her, knocking his hat off in the process.

"You're here," she said. "Am I still dreaming?"

He knelt beside her and gathered her against him.

"I'm as real as can be, darlin'." And he claimed her lips in the tenderest of kisses. He smelled like soap, and he felt and tasted like Thaddeus!

All at once, she realized where she was, and she started to squirm, pulling away to look at him.

"Thaddeus?" *Was he real?* She still wasn't positive, with her head in such a faraway fog.

"I hope you weren't dreaming of another man. Yes, it's me."

"What are you doing here? How'd you find me?"

"I got back to town a little while ago. Mrs. Longwood took pity on me and told me where to find you."

As he spoke, he stripped off his duster and bundled it into a ball before placing it behind her head. She settled back on it with a sigh. When he was near, he looked after her as if she were made of glass. But when he wasn't around . . .

"Where'd you go?" The pent-up emotion made her voice catch.

"I'm getting to that. Are you all right?" He had her chin between his thumb and fingers, holding her still and taking a long look into her eyes. "It's a long way to walk up here."

"I'm good," she said. "I feel better for walking around than sitting still. But the climb did me in, I'll admit. I don't suppose you're carrying any water on your horse?" She'd heard it whinnying behind him and knew he hadn't walked.

Looking past him, she saw Lucky pawing the ground. *Lucky!* She sat bolt upright, feeling a surge of surprise and delight.

"Lucky! That *is* her, isn't it?"

"Yup." He looked just as delighted as she felt. "She's all yours."

"Thaddeus!" She couldn't say any more, but held her hands over her mouth. Was she going to cry again? No, she felt too happy for tears. *That dear horse.*

He laughed and jumped up to grab the supplies, then sat down on the rock beside her. He handed her his waterskin and watched her drink thirstily.

"After Mrs. Longwood said where you'd gone, she also packed some cake. She said it's your favorite." He unwrapped the wax paper and handed her the tart and sweet confection.

Grabbing the thick square he offered her, Eliza stuffed it into her mouth in big chunks, not caring how she looked. She hadn't realized how hungry she was until she'd seen the cake.

"I can't believe you like Jessie's lemon cake," he said, his eyes fixed on her hungry mouth "after all these years."

It was perfect. She washed it down with more water and then felt wide awake.

"The baby likes it, not me," she protested, wiping her lips in an unladylike manner on the back of her hand. "Aren't you having any?"

He shook his head. "Watching you eat like that was better than eating it myself. It sort of gave me the horn."

"Really!" She felt her cheeks turn red. Was he jesting or was he truly aroused watching her eat?

Leaning over, he kissed her again, licking his tongue over the corner of her mouth before he pulled away.

"*Mm*," he murmured. "Lemons."

His kiss had certainly given her the horn, too, but she wasn't going to state it out loud.

She slapped at his hand as he went to take the water, but she'd already forgiven him his week-long disappearance. After all, he was back and he'd brought their horse. She took another sip before handing him back the waterskin.

"You rode all the way back to Burlington to bring Lucky to me?"

"I did. I couldn't stand thinking of you feeling sad about her. Plus, I missed her, too. One of the best horses I've ever owned."

They both looked over to where Lucky stood, with her funny swayed back and broad, scarred rump, fidgeting her front feet.

Eliza giggled, and then he joined in with a hearty laugh.

"I didn't say she was the most attractive horse!" he added.

"Thank you, Thaddeus. It was a considerate thing to do," she said and meant it.

"Don't go making a saint out of me yet, darlin'. I had other places to go besides Burlington and other reasons for my trip besides that horse."

And quick as a summer storm, the sunny spot in her heart hid behind a black cloud of mistrust. He'd had to venture right past Keokuk to get to Burlington. Of course, he would stay at The Pork and Swallow, where a certain dark-haired beauty would be persuasively enticing.

"I have to go home now," she said, but he grabbed her arm and held firm.

"You're not going anywhere, sweetheart. I've ridden all over the Mississippi Valley and then to not one but three big, dirty, crowded cities in search of—"

"What a hardship! Traveling along the Mississippi!" she scoffed.

"What in the hell!"

She cut him off again. "Visit any good saloons?" she asked, struggling to free herself from his grip.

He sighed. Then taking hold of her other arm, he gently but firmly dragged her onto his lap, seating her sideways and anchoring her with his arm around her burgeoning stomach. When she was securely imprisoned, he leaned back against the rocks, pulled her against his broad chest, and rested his chin on her head.

"Miss Prentice, you are the only woman I care for. I mean, I *care* for my sister, but not in the same way, of course. And just so we're absolutely clear, I have no interest in Dr. Bell, either, except in knowing she'll help bring our baby into the world."

She felt his chest rise and fall under her cheek as he took a breath. "There's no one else for me but you, and God's honest truth, there never has been. So stop worrying about that. And no, I didn't go see Jo. Never crossed my mind."

She let his words wash over her and sink in like late-summer rain into the parched earth.

"Thaddeus, I—"

He placed a finger against her lips.

"*Sh.* I'm not done. I should have done a lot more talking to you years ago, and while we were on the road and at Charlie's, but I'm learning. Now, I know you worry over women I've been intimate with, but, harsh as it is to say, they meant nothing. Even Jo, although I feel gratitude for her help. But when I had relations with these women—no, don't turn away, hear me out. When I was with them, it wasn't making love like you and I did. It was . . ." He sighed, sounded exasperated, then he tried again.

"You know how when you're hungry and you want to eat, you eat? Just because you have to fill your belly, and it doesn't matter if the food is very good. You eat. But to me, you're a fine-cooked supper. I want to devour you, but I also want to take my time."

He released his hold and, instead, took her face between his hands, gently tilting it. She gazed into his familiar, beloved eyes.

"I want to taste every part of your body, darlin', then I want to touch you all over. I guess I want to . . . to play with my food!"

Eliza smiled. That was the single weirdest, most wonderful speech she'd ever heard.

"Well?" he prompted.

Well, what? "If you're asking do I want you to make love to me, the answer is yes. I've never denied you my body." She gestured to her obvious condition as proof. "And having you 'devour' me sounds divine." So why did she still feel anxious?

He jiggled his legs impatiently so she bounced up and down.

"No, that's not it," he said, sounding peeved. "That's not what I'm asking. Ellie, will you marry me?"

If he'd expected a different reaction from the first time he asked her, he was sorely disappointed. She still didn't appear joyful, smile at him, and say yes.

"I don't think I told you this," she said, dipping her head and hiding her face from him, "but ever since I started noticing boys, even after I got engaged to Riley, it was *always* you."

Her voice was subdued and a little sad, and her melancholy sent panic racing through him. Ellie didn't sound as though she intended to accept his proposal.

"But now, it's *not* me?" he suggested, scarcely able to breathe. Had she actually been sweet on him all her life, only to stop now?

"There's a little one to consider," she whispered. "And I can't spend my life selfishly pining for a man who doesn't want to commit to the kind of stable life a child needs."

His heart twisted at the idea of her spending one single moment pining after him. *Him!* She deserved the world. She deserved much better than he could offer her, except he was dead certain his love would be stronger than any other man's ever could be.

"How about taking a chance on a man who loves you with everything he is?"

She teared up, her eyes filled to the brim.

Before she could speak, he grabbed one of her hands, bringing it up to his mouth and caressing her knuckles with his lips back and forth, breathing in the scent of her skin. Then he kissed her other hand. If he let her go, he feared she might vanish just as in all his dreams.

"You're the sole person in this whole wide world who makes me want to not be a screw-up. You *know* me. And you know who I'm most certainly not, a perfect man with a clear idea of what I'm supposed to be doing. I've never known that. The only thing I've ever been sure of is that you're the one for me."

He ran his free hand through his carefully combed hair, feeling himself making a mess of it and sighed.

"I don't know why I believed I could run wild, drinking and such, and still somehow deserve you." He shook his head in disbelief at the stupidity of his younger self.

"But when you chose Riley," he paused, still having trouble saying those words without wanting to lash out in anger, "it was like the one truth I'd counted on—that you were going to be mine—turned out to be a lie. Like the sky was really green instead of blue. But I never stopped loving you, even when I thought it didn't matter anymore."

She was gazing at him with those big blue eyes, blinking to keep her tears from spilling over, and he could see she wanted to believe in him.

"Damnit, Ellie. I *want* to be your husband, the best one ever. I'll be steady as this rock." He slapped it with his open palm. "And I'll do whatever I have to do to be a good father to our child. I won't mess this up, I promise. There isn't anything else for me. There is nothing out there," he spread his hand over the horizon, "that I want more than what I've got right here on my lap. Gamble one more time on me, darlin'. Please."

Thaddeus gathered her close and wrapped his arms more firmly around her.

"I love you, woman. Always have. Always will. Will you be my wife, Eliza Prentice?" He almost didn't expect to hear an answer.

"I will," she said without hesitation. "Yes, I will."

She would? She would! *God Almighty!* Then he remembered how he was supposed to be doing this proposal. *Shit!* The ring!

"Wait, wait." He sat up straight and reached for his balled-up duster, nearly tipping her off his lap. "Damn," he swore, trying to find the right pocket, fumbling around until he pulled out a box, prettily tied in silver ribbon.

"Ok, let me start over." He took a deep breath and sent her what he hoped was a winning smile.

She smiled back, while wiping tears off her cheeks at the same time.

"One of us has got to buy some handkerchiefs," she said.

"I will, I promise." Meanwhile, he used the edge of her dress to wipe her face. "Now, here," he said, "take this and open it."

With visibly trembling fingers, she tugged at the ribbon and lifted the box cover.

"Oh!" she exclaimed.

Did she like it? Was that a good "oh"? He couldn't tell. Uncertainty tore through him. He wanted to grab the box from her and hurl it down the slope.

"Ellie?"

"It's the most beautiful ring I've ever seen."

Thank God. "As soon as I saw it, I knew it was the one. Well, I hoped anyway. I went to ten stores before I found it."

She lifted out the gold ring with twin settings of circular-cut diamonds and held it up to catch the sun's rays. Branching off from the two prominent stones were silver swirls embedded with single-cut diamond accents. In between the larger stones, a smaller single diamond sat suspended.

"See, that's you," he said, pointing to one of the larger diamonds, "and I'm the other one. And the little stone between us is right here." He placed his hand on her stomach. How he wanted to strip her down and run his fingers over all of her, but that would probably ruin the romantic moment, which seemed to be taking a turn for the better.

Then something amazing happened.

"I felt it," he said, keeping his voice low so as not to startle the baby. "He moved."

"He *or she* does that quite often now," Ellie told him, her face beaming. "And you don't have to whisper."

Thaddeus stayed that way for a few more moments, shaking his head in wonder at what was going on under his fingertips. *Lord have mercy!* She was making a baby! It hit him like a ton of boulders.

"Thank you." What else could he say?

She held out the ring. "Thank *you*." She wiggled her bare fingers.

Grinning, he took the ring from her and slipped it on her finger. Then he took her face in his hands again.

"May I kiss you?"

"You never have to ask," she said.

"I'll hold you to that," and he lowered his head. After a long kiss, he leaned back against the rock and briefly closed his eyes.

"Man, this is uncomfortable, but I don't care if we ever leave this spot. This is perfect."

"I think your legs are probably going numb right about now," she teased. "I have put on a little weight."

He slanted a look at her. "Just a little, but in some mighty pleasing places."

She giggled.

"Honestly, though, get up," he begged. "I need to stand."

On his feet, he began hopping around. "It feels like pins are being shoved into my legs. But that's all right."

He faced away from her, cupped his hands to his mouth, and shouted across the valley, "Eliza Prentice has agreed to marry me! Yee-haw!"

She laughed so hard, she nearly choked. When she stopped, he decided it was time to get her home. *Home!*

"You know I've been working like a dog to fix up my house." He grinned. "Well, Dan and Ely have, anyway. Will you move in with me right away?"

She paused with one foot on Lucky's stirrup and his hands under her rear end.

"No, I won't."

He felt his smile die. "You won't move into my house before the wedding?"

"No, I mean I won't ever move into your house."

He frowned, still holding her buttocks in his hands. "But you *will* marry me, right?"

"Yes."

"OK, just making sure I got that right."

She laughed again and let him help her onto Lucky, which certainly wasn't as easy anymore. He got up behind her, wrapped his arms around her waist, and took the reins from her. Perfect!

"When we get married, I want to live in *my* house. I love my house," she reminded him. "I don't mind where we travel in this world, but I'd like to always come back to my own bed in my own house." She paused, then she asked, "Is that all right with you?"

He grinned against the back of her head, breathing deeply to take in the familiar floral scent of her hair.

"Sounds like it has to be," he pretended to grumble.

She elbowed him in the ribs, and he laughed.

"Honestly, I don't care where we live. It's all the same to me, as long as I have you. You understand that?"

He felt her nod. They traveled on a few minutes in silence, with Ellie holding up her hand to admire the ring as Lucky picked her way over the rocky soil to the grassy flatland below.

Then out of the blue, she said, "I love you, Thaddeus Sanborn." Her words stopped his breath and sent shivers up his spine.

What a gift to have her say it to him again, and this time he knew it was true. *She loved him!* What a miracle! He kissed the shell of her ear and found it to be as delectable as the rest of her.

"Darlin', do I have to wait until we're married to make love to you again?"

She laughed and pressed her warm self against him, igniting a fire of anticipation. He was nearly desperate to see her pregnant body unclothed. He cupped her breast with one hand. Yes, definitely plumper.

He heard her breath hitch and felt her body grow taut at his bold touch.

"No, you don't," she said, her voice husky. "But you do have to wait until we're off this horse."

"Agreed," he said, pushing her hair aside and nuzzling her neck.

She sighed. "I'm right where I'm supposed to be this time. Right fiancé. And soon, the right husband."

He growled a purely animal sound of possession and felt her body tremble in response.

EPILOGUE

❧

"Hurry up, Ellie. We're gonna be late," Thaddeus called up the stairs.

"Your wife's coming," Mrs. Longwood said, appearing at the top of the stairs, clutching Ellie's wrap. "So is that baby. Won't be long now."

He blanched, excited but half-terrified at the same time.

Mrs. Longwood laughed at his expression, as she descended and handed him the soft blue shawl. "Don't worry, son. I don't think it'll happen tonight over dinner."

"Good God, I hope not," he muttered, then looked up at the sound of his wife's footsteps. He whistled when he saw her. She was growing lovelier by the day, if that were possible, and his heart filled up like a hot-air balloon.

He took her hand when she reached the bottom step and held her still so he could simply admire her.

"You are beyond gorgeous, Mrs. Sanborn." He had yet to tire of calling her that, reminding her she was entirely his own.

Her cheeks blushed pink. "How's that possible? I'm round as a sow in springtime." But she smoothed her blue dress over her bursting stomach and flashed him a smile.

"Have you looked in the mirror, darlin'?"

Her skin glowed with a peaches-and-cream radiance, her eyes sparkled like moonlit water, and her hair seemed even thicker and shinier. *What was that baby doing to her?*

"It's not merely that dress, although the color suits you to perfection. It's all of you." He gazed at her, and she gazed back. He sighed and smiled. She did the same.

Perfect!

"Would the two of you get a move on?" Mrs. Longwood urged. "If you stand here any longer, there'll be a third Sanborn in the room. Besides, my own supper is getting cold."

"Yes, ma'am," Thaddeus said, draping Ellie's shawl around her shoulders and giving her his arm to hold. "Let's take the wagon."

"But we're only going to Dan and Belinda's," she protested.

"You're too far along to walk, even that distance," he said. "Dr. Bell told us so. End of discussion."

After getting Ellie seated comfortably in the wagon, Thaddeus directed Lucky at an easy pace toward his old house. While helping him, Dan and Belinda had fixed it up exactly as they wanted it, so selling the Sanborn homestead to them had been an obvious and easy choice.

Far more spacious than their rooms above the feedstore, Dan told Thaddeus he would now get to "baby-making" in earnest. After all, Belinda wanted five children.

Thaddeus would be eternally grateful when his wife was safely delivered of *one* child, and it lay squalling loudly in its crib. They'd been discussing baby names since before the wedding two months earlier, neither telling the other what gender they were hoping for.

"You have something big you said you wanted to discuss with Dan tonight," Ellie said, leaning in close, putting her head against his shoulder. "Is it a secret?"

He smiled into the twilight. "I think I've decided what I'm going to do next. I can't have my son or daughter thinking I'm a shiftless slacker."

"A wealthy, copper-mine owning shiftless slacker," she amended.

"True, but when the other kids ask my child, 'what's your pa do?' he or she has to have an answer."

"What are you thinking, then?" she asked, absently stroking his arm while she spoke.

"I can't think anything at all when you do that."

"Sorry," she said, giggling delightfully. He loved the way the tears that marked her early pregnancy had been replaced by her constant merriment in the final weeks.

"We'll pick that up again later," he promised and dropped a kiss on her lips. "Where was I? Oh, right, I've been reading about beer."

"Beer?" He felt her stiffen beside him. "Oh, Thaddeus, you're not going to open a saloon, are you?"

He nearly said yes, just to tease her, but he didn't like to agitate her in her advanced condition.

"No, I wouldn't do that and risk angering Ada. You know how much I like her chicken."

"Who doesn't?" Ellie agreed. "What then?"

"I'm gonna ask Dan if he wants to open a brewery with me. He's got the grain, or could get the right stuff for cheap, and we've got the best spring water in Colorado. It's perfect."

She was quiet.

"What do you think?" He wanted her to like the idea. *Hell,* he needed her to like it.

"I think you'll make an excellent brewer," she offered.

He exhaled the breath he hadn't realized he was holding as she reached up and touched his face.

"I believe in you, Mr. Sanborn. Whatever you put your mind to, you'll succeed at."

How he loved this woman! They'd arrived at Dan's new home, letting Lucky pull the wagon around back. Instead of jumping down off the seat, however, Thaddeus gathered her to him and kissed her thoroughly, lingering at the corner of her lips, nibbling her gently.

"Let's turn right around and go home to bed," he murmured against her ripe mouth before sucking on her lower lip. They'd been quite successful at finding conjugal positions that were both comfortable and immensely satisfying. He was game to try another.

She didn't answer at first, content to let him kiss her, but as his hands roamed across her body, she pulled back with a reluctant sigh.

"You have business to discuss with Dan."

"Who?"

She giggled again, and he couldn't resist hearing that sound. Slipping his hand under her, he pinched her bottom, and she shrieked with delight before starting to laugh in earnest.

The back door swung open.

"You two all right out there?" came Dan's booming voice.

Thaddeus sighed. "Now you've done it. We'll *have* to go in."

He scrambled from the wagon, grabbed a step-stool from the back, and placed it on the ground next to the seat. Then raising his hands, he took both of hers in his to steady her as she climbed down.

"Maybe we can even take a tour of Europe and sample some foreign beers," she mused, her thoughts apparently returning to his business idea.

"You're going to let me go into bars? In Europe?" He wiggled his eyebrows suggestively.

"Oh, Thaddeus, when you enter with your wife beside you and a child in your arms, I don't think I'm going to have to worry about those saloon girls."

"Darlin'," he looked into her eyes, brushing a finger across her sweet and pouty lips, "you never did have to worry."

Presenting him with her signature Eliza Prentice Sanborn smile, smug and satisfied, she grabbed his hand in hers, and without another word, they strode into the house.

Some eighteen hours later, after a long night and another half a day of labor, Trey Prentice Sanborn came into the world, a healthy bundle of willpower and strong lungs.

As Thaddeus took the wrapped bundle from a smiling Dr. Bell and placed his son into the crook of Ellie's waiting arms, he reckoned himself the luckiest man on earth. And for once, it had nothing to do with cards.

Finis

AN INCONCEIVABLE DECEPTION
BOOK 4

and the rest of the Defiant Hearts series
including

AN INTRIGUING PROPOSITION
PREQUEL

AN IMPROPER SITUATION
BOOK 1

AN IRRESISTIBLE TEMPTATION
BOOK 2

AN INESCAPABLE ATTRACTION
BOOK 3

AN IMPASSIONED REDEMPTION
NOVELLA

are available in print and ebook.

ABOUT THE AUTHOR

USA Today bestselling author Sydney Jane Baily writes historical romance set in Victorian England, late 19th-century America, the Middle Ages, the Georgian era, and the Regency period. She believes in happily-ever-after stories with engaging characters and attention to period detail.

Born and raised in California, she has traveled the world, spending a lot of exceedingly happy time in the U.K. where her extended family resides, eating fish and chips, drinking shandies, and snacking on Maltesers and Cadbury bars. Sydney currently lives in New England with her family—human, canine, and feline.

You can learn more about her books, read her blog, sign up for her newsletter (and get a free book), and contact her via her website at SydneyJaneBaily.com. She loves to hear from her readers.

www.ingramcontent.com/pod-product-compliance
Lightning Source LLC
Chambersburg PA
CBHW060858190726

48286CB00002B/290